More Praise for Jill Amy Rosenblatt

"*Project Jennifer* combines funny and bittersweet in equal doses. *Project Jennifer* was a hoot to read, and kudos to Ms. Rosenblatt for a great first novel."
—The Good, The Bad, The Unread (goodbadandunread.com)

"*Project Jennifer* is an excellent read, a fascinating story that will keep readers turning the pages. Don't miss this one!"
—Romance Reviews Today (romrevtoday.com)

"I found *Project Jennifer* delightful. Once I started turning the pages, it was hard to put down."
—Coffee Time Romance (coffeetimeromance.com)

"The author takes a common relationship dilemma and manages to keep her readers laughing throughout the book. Even with this approach, Ms. Rosenblatt delivers a poignant message about the fallacies of real-life relationships."
—The Romance Readers Connection
(theromancereadersconnection.com)

For Better or Worse

JILL AMY ROSENBLATT

KENSINGTON BOOKS
www.kensingtonbooks.com

KENSINGTON BOOKS are published by

Kensington Publishing Corp.
119 West 40th Street
New York, NY 10018

ISBN-13: 978-0-7582-2371-5
ISBN-10: 0-7582-2371-4

First Kensington Trade Paperback Printing: August 2009
10 9 8 7 6 5 4 3 2

For Mrs. Danvers

Acknowledgments

I am so grateful for the assistance of so many wonderful people. As always, my thanks to my agent, Agnes Birnbaum, for her continued friendship and support. Thank you so much for all you do on my behalf. Thank you to my wonderful editor, Danielle Chiotti, who is so amazing to work with, and the terrific team at Kensington, Maureen Cuddy and Colleen Martin.

There were a number of people who generously gave of their time to read the manuscript and grant interviews. I am incredibly grateful to:

My friend Philippe Lacarriere, for providing French translation.

Jennifer, for your comments and insight.

Laura Sue Phillips, for sharing your vast knowledge of art and the artist's life.

Dr. Gary Gray, for speaking with me about the hedge fund industry.

Lisa Timmel, for walking me through the process of developing a play for production.

Blair Voltz Clarke, for information about the art market and the process of artist representation.

Rob Povlitz, for providing comments and corrections.

And always, thank you to my mom for her support, encouragement, understanding, and willingness to read endless drafts and always offer honest commentary.

For Better or Worse

SUMMER

Chapter 1

Ian MacKay took a deep drag on his cigarette, exhaling a long spiral of smoke. Standing outside the gothic-style church in Midtown, he watched the parade of limousines as the stone saints on either side of the doors watched him. New York City was baking under another day of unexpected heat and he held his jacket draped over his arm. As the limos discharged their cargo, a rainbow of couture hurried past him, as if afraid of melting under the onslaught of the sun. The beautiful people cast cool glances at his jacketless form and open-collared shirt.

"I told Emily, June is best," he heard a woman say. "There is nothing more romantic than a summer wedding in New York."

He squinted through the smoke at the men in their finely tailored suits; no doubt financial wizards, like the groom. He wondered if Michele had chosen a man like one of these to take his place, to be her next husband. Feeling his blood pressure rise at the thought of his ex-wife, he threw his cigarette down, grinding it into the concrete with the tip of his polished shoe. That was the first and last time he'd be walking down the aisle. Turning, he entered the church.

Inside the narthex, he inhaled the welcome blast of frigid air and shrugged into his jacket. A bridesmaid emerged from a side door. His eyes traveled the length of her, lingering on the rose-colored slip of a dress hugging her slim form. Her blond hair was swept into a neat French twist and she fidgeted with the small bouquet of orchids in her hand. Wondering what scent she wore, he was instantly sorry he wasn't closer. She caught him in his scrutiny, her delicate features furrowing into a frown.

"Which side?" she asked.

Ian couldn't decide whether she was annoyed or bored. "Sorry?"

Her hazel eyes moved over him. "The bride or the groom's side?"

"Neither," Ian said, amused to find himself the subject of her examination.

She pointed to a large book lying open on a stand. "Would you care to write a wish to the happy couple?"

"I don't think it will help."

She gave a short, clipped laugh before catching herself. "Your accent—England, no, Scotland."

"Very good."

"You've come a long way to witness a wedding when you have no faith in marriage."

"I didn't say that. It's not for everyone though, is it?"

"Let me guess, it's not for you."

"Not for me, no."

She chuckled, this time without the smile. "Still finding yourself?"

"I'm not lost."

"You need your space."

"My flat is quite roomy." He smiled, enjoying her look of irritation.

She straightened. "A man who knows his own mind, how refreshing." She waved the bouquet toward the chapel. "Sit anywhere you like." Turning on her heel, she disappeared back into the room she had come from.

Entering the sanctuary, Ian spotted Robert maneuvering his sturdy six-foot frame through the clusters of guests chatting and laughing in the aisle. He approached his friend and received Robert's firm handshake.

"Eighty grand on flowers," Robert lamented. "There isn't a pink rose left in Manhattan. What a waste."

"It's not a waste. They'll use them for the divorce party."

Robert gave a laugh.

"How do you know what the flowers cost?"

Robert leaned in. "Because the groom hasn't shut up about it since we got here."

Ian glanced over his shoulder toward the narthex. "Did you notice the girl I was talking to?"

Robert nodded. "That's Karen's friend, Elizabeth, a money manager. Did you notice she's not your type?"

"You don't know what my type is," Ian shot back.

"Oh, I beg to differ. As your oldest friend, I have seen your taste across five countries and two continents. She's not your type."

Ian gave Robert a sharp look.

"But I don't interfere anymore."

They stood in awkward silence.

"If you're that interested, I can put in a good word. If I tell Karen about your many chivalrous exploits, I'm sure it will get back to Liz. Rescuing damsels in distress stranded by no-good boyfriends—"

"It was hardly a rescue."

"Providing room and board to countless weary travelers, including myself."

Ian smirked. "All right, are you done amusing yourself? How much *have* you told Karen about me?"

Robert shrugged. "Nothing. You told me not to say anything. You haven't even told me what you've been doing for the past two years. Why all the secrecy?"

Ian shrugged, glancing back at the narthex. He thought he caught sight of Elizabeth again. "It's not secrecy. It's a new country, a new life." He turned back to Robert. "Best to leave the past where it is, don't you think?"

"Whatever you want." He gave Ian the once-over. "You're not wearing a tie."

"I was hoping they'd ask me to leave."

"Not a chance. The bride loves you and your no-tie, who-gives-a-shit artist attitude."

"If she truly loved me and my attitude, she would've bought three of my paintings, not one." Ian put his hand on Robert's shoulder. "Now, let's have it. What's your prediction?"

"One year. Then they flame out."

"And you're never wrong."

"Almost never."

Among their friends, Robert's keen understanding of human nature had rendered him a seer. His uncanny aptitude for foretelling the future was an urban legend, with one exception—the happily-ever-after he had predicted for Ian's marriage.

Elizabeth and Karen watched Robert and Ian from the narthex.

"So who's the operator talking to your betrothed?" Elizabeth said, taking in his slicked-back blond hair curling over his open-collared shirt and the short, trimmed beard. She lingered over his slim, wiry frame. *I am enjoying this way too much.*

"Robert's best friend, Ian MacKay, from Scotland."

But he hasn't been there in a while, Elizabeth thought. The accent was watered down, the thick brogue long gone.

"I don't know that he's an operator, he seems like a good guy. Robert didn't say much about him."

"He wears the most delicious cologne," came a voice from behind them. They turned in unison, finding Emily glowing in her Badgley Mischka gown. It was perfect for her, the scoop neckline revealing the right amount of cleavage, the dropped waist making her five-foot-nine-inch frame seem even taller, more regal. A descendant of a founding father and subsequent captains of industry, Emily's money was as old as her lineage and it showed; she didn't walk, she flowed, her elegance a hallmark of her birthright.

"And, his beard is like velvet," she added.

Elizabeth feigned a look at her watch. "You still have twenty minutes. Would you like to switch grooms?"

Emily rolled her eyes. "I kissed his cheek."

Elizabeth folded her arms.

"Okay, both cheeks, it's the European way." Emily laughed, coloring. "I invited him for tea a few times, strictly business. He's going to paint my portrait."

"And why is this the first I'm hearing about Ian MacKay of Scotland and his beard of velvet?" Elizabeth said, turning an enquiring eye on Karen.

"He just got here," Karen said. "You haven't come up for air since your promotion. I hardly see you anymore."

"Uh-hunh," Elizabeth said, giving Karen a sharp look. "Painting Emily's portrait?"

Karen sighed. "Yes, he's an artist."

Elizabeth gave a disgusted laugh, and headed back to the dressing room.

"Liz, you can't judge all artists by Josh and certainly not by William," Emily said, trailing after her, Karen close behind.

"I do not judge all artists. I simply have an intimate understanding of their basic nature."

"Which you use to judge them," Emily persisted as they entered the dressing room.

"Whatever."

Emily held out her hands to draw them into a circle. "Now, my dearest friends, this is it. This is Act Two of our lives." She held up Karen's hand, with its glittering diamond ring. "We've all found our soul mates."

Karen's eyes darkened with concern.

"Now, don't fret, your wedding will be perfect," Emily said. "Lots of people have crazy parents. Who is that philosopher you study?"

"Lao-tzu. Taoism teaches stillness, and giving up fear, anxiety, and control so all things flow naturally to the right ending," Karen said.

"Oh, I love that," Emily squeaked. She turned to Elizabeth. "After Karen and Robert are married, you and Nick will be next. You two are my crowning triumph, a perfect match—and Nick knows it."

"It's only been six months."

"He told Parker you were the one after the first date."

Elizabeth smiled. *He knows it, and I know it too.* She glanced at Karen and caught her friend's look of doubt.

The wedding planner, flanked by her team, blew into the room. They whisked Emily away, all the while clucking at Elizabeth and Karen to take their places.

"How are you, really?" Elizabeth whispered to Karen as they fell into line for the processional.

Karen sighed. "Did you see Page Six? My parents are at it again. Divorced for ten years and they don't see that as a reason to stop fighting. The Tao says troubles are like rocks in the middle of a stream. The rocks try to interrupt the water's calm flow, but they can't. My parents aren't rocks, they're boulders."

"You haven't told them you're engaged, have you?"

"I couldn't. She's in Europe, on a book tour, but still found time to give a satellite-radio interview. The subject? My father's plagiarism. She quoted chapter and verse from his solo works, claiming it was stuff she wrote when they were married. She can't prove it. She can never prove it. You know when they created audioconferencing, I don't think this is what they had in mind." She sighed. "Twenty years of marriage, twelve books together, and this is how it ends. Actually it doesn't end, it just keeps going."

"What about your father? Did you tell him you were getting married?"

"He's been too busy."

"Is he finishing a new book?"

"No, his fifth marriage."

"Oh."

"I need to remain calm, be still, and it will all work out. The Tao says be flexible and learn to let go of the most important issues. Then they work out by themselves."

If only it were that easy, Elizabeth thought.

The first bars of music began; there was a palpable rustle as the crowd turned in unison toward the door.

* * *

Elizabeth counted silently to five before taking her first step. Making her way down the aisle, feeling the eyes of the crowd on her, brought back a flood of memories; the steps she had taken to the altar. Up ahead she saw Parker, the groom-to-be, whispering something to the minister. For a second he became Josh, her Josh, pulling her aside and whispering that he couldn't go through with it. He was sorry; he didn't mean to hurt her.

It seemed a lifetime ago and yet still fresh as yesterday. She gave herself a mental shake and focused straight ahead. That was almost fifteen years ago. *I'm almost thirty-five years old. I'm a grown woman. Why think about the past?*

She caught a glimpse of Ian MacKay as she passed by; those deep, blue eyes, the hint of baby-smooth skin peeking out from the corners of his beard. Her eyes rested on him a second too long; she shook off any thought of him, scanning the crowd until she found Nick.

Chapter 2

Ian turned away from the Rainbow Room's windows and the majestic view of the kingdom that was New York City. Champagne corks popped, glasses clinked, the orchestra played. Like the *Titanic*, the band playing as the ship was sinking, he thought, as this marriage will sink. Wandering back into the crowd, he caught sight of a woman looking him over. She gave him a smile of invitation. He imagined her a nice girl with a pretty face and a busy life. They would fall into something easy and convenient. She would come and go until realizing he would give nothing more. After a time she would drift away on her own. If it even lasted that long. He lingered a moment, then turned away from her.

He scanned the room, settling on a woman in an expensive sequined gown. He could tell by the way she held herself she was maintained, but not a pedigree. She was on the arm of a debonair man, with unruly long hair tucked behind his ears, a long angular face; a European. The money was his, not hers. This was the kind of man Michele had left him for, someone able to give her everything she wanted: money, travel, ease. *All of the things that weren't coming fast enough being married to me,* Ian thought. The art shows weren't big enough, he wasn't the rising star she expected, the enfant terrible she hoped for.

Ian's attention returned to studying the woman. She couldn't compare to Michele. Michele was exquisite, skin like porcelain and azure eyes that cut through you. One look at her and there was no going back. She could have any man she wanted. And there had been several, he found out. Michele had tried them out first, in secret, to see if they had enough to please her before finally making her choice.

Ian could feel his anger rising when a hand settled on his shoulder.

"Let's get a drink," Robert said.

Ian nodded. It was the least they could do to salvage the evening. When they passed Parker, the groom had a glass in one hand, its contents splashing over the side as he waved his arm, describing his real estate empire.

"Thirty thousand square feet," he was saying. "The front entrance will be all marble. Italian. And that's just the main house. I'm putting in a one-thousand-square-foot pool house."

The men clicked glasses and drank to the pool house.

"You know, one of my guys quit last month. I had him on debt acquisition. I buy fifty million in debt from some shithole country—whose name I can't pronounce—for pennies on the dollar. When they default, I send Nick to court, he sues, we win, and that shithole country has to pay me the whole fifty, maybe more."

One of the men spoke up. "In what century will you collect?"

"Any dollar comes into that country, I get first. This guy's whining to me about our moral obligation, aren't we victimizing impoverished nations. I told him, if I wanted to, I could make a few currency bets and change that country's economy in a heartbeat."

He took another swallow of his drink, then laughed, talking almost to himself. "He says we should be safeguarding the economy. I *am* the economy, asshole. I'm moving the value of currency. He couldn't take the pressure, dickless wonder. You know where he is now? Putting in eighty hours a week at some plain-vanilla mutual fund for a shit bonus check. Good luck with your fiscal responsibility, shithead. I'll be at my compound in Greenwich, stepping out the door to the helipad to bring me to Manhattan."

"To Parker Davis," they said, raising their glasses.

Shaking his head, Ian hunkered down next to Robert at the bar, watching the bartender set up glasses and pour. Taking a long drink, Ian let out a sigh of relief until a heavy slap on his back made him jump and slosh his drink onto the bar.

"Hey, I hope you're enjoying my wedding," Parker said. "You're looking at one and a half million."

Elizabeth was only half-listening to Karen as they lounged at a table by themselves. Her eyes were fixed on Ian MacKay.

"I still don't understand the change in attitude. Not six months ago you said having Emily as a matchmaker is like asking an arsonist to house-sit. She's broken more engagements than her nails. Are you listening to me?"

"At least she had the right idea. She left them." *She should have left one more. Why did a woman who made her society debut at Le Bal Crillon marry a low-life like Parker Davis?*

"Liz, how is it really going with Nick?"

"Fine." Elizabeth continued to stare out into the crowd. "He's kind and attentive. He takes me to dinner and sends me flowers. We discuss matters of business because we share common interests. Is there something wrong with a serious, focused man? He's a grown-up."

Karen was silent for a moment. When she spoke her voice sounded hurt. "Robert's a grown-up. You don't have to be in business to be a grown-up."

Elizabeth turned to Karen. "Of course not. I didn't mean it that way. Robert is a brilliant writer and so are you. I'm sorry I've been so busy with the job and these dinners with Emily and Parker. That doesn't change us or our friendship. But this relationship with Nick is what I want now."

"Sometimes I think I made a mistake convincing you to come to New York. You had a life in California."

Elizabeth turned to give her friend a sharp look. "What life?"

"A life as a painter."

"I was a painter. I'm not anymore. Are we going to go through this again?"

"Liz, you can't keep punishing yourself for what your mother did. She hurt herself. You didn't hurt her."

"Really? Didn't I?"

Karen leaned forward, her voice low. "I was there, remember? She knew exactly what William was doing."

Elizabeth made a face. "What William was doing—what I was doing. There were two of us."

"She did everything she could to destroy you, Liz. I just feel like you keep moving further away from who you are."

"Ancient history," Elizabeth snapped. "Nick isn't the past. He's the present and the future. My future. I'm with him because he's the right one for me."

Elizabeth returned to watching the bar, her signal that the subject was closed. Guests moved in and out of her line of vision and then a pocket would open, revealing a glimpse of Ian MacKay.

Ian sucked in a deep breath, trying for patience, his empty stomach complaining bitterly while Parker's rambling gnawed on his last nerve.

"Let me tell you, gents, I walk into a room with this woman and every man wants what I have. Beautiful, built." He elbowed Ian. "And the family fortune doesn't hurt either. Now I've got the money and the girl, and it's all legal. I can't believe how happy I am," he said with a hearty laugh, giving Ian another robust slap on the back.

Ian raised his hand, attempting to signal the bartender. He reminded himself that artists of small reputation could not afford to tell their client's husband to piss off and lose any referrals that might come their way. He kept his mouth shut and smiled.

Parker gripped his shoulder. "You need to get married, my friend."

Wanker. What I need is a scotch and a smoke.

"Now I realize how empty my life has been," Parker continued.

"That's not what I heard."

At the sound of the soft, even voice, the men turned to see Elizabeth sliding onto the empty stool next to Ian.

"I heard your *business* lunches at the Plaza Hotel were quite full and satisfying," she said.

Chuckling, Parker wrapped his arms around her, squeezing her to him. "Listen, cookie, I'm a changed man! You're just jealous because you passed on your opportunity."

"I yielded to the better woman," she said.

Parker cackled. "You don't know what you missed, babe, on so many levels."

The lights threw colorful shadows across the planes of Elizabeth's face. Ian felt a rush of blood surge within him and had a fleeting thought of Hemingway's Lady Brett Ashley draped on a bar stool in a café in Spain, waiting for her bullfighter to return. *She could be Lady Ashley, she looks unhappy enough.*

A passing guest caught Parker's attention. Stepping away from the group, he pointed at Ian. "You should see this guy's stuff, Liz, it's not half-bad. The resale value sucks but maybe he has something for your office."

"My office is decorated."

"Something for your flat?" Ian said.

"My apartment has everything in it I need."

"Pity," Ian said. He glanced over to Robert; he had retreated to a stool, a silent observer.

"Are you enjoying the wedding?"

"Brilliant party," he said. "You don't seem pleased. Don't you fancy weddings, Lizzie?"

"Elizabeth," she corrected. "Weddings are fine but they have nothing to do with marriage."

He edged closer. *There it is,* he thought, catching her scent, a warm, drowsy duet of delicate flowers with a hint of vanilla. "Don't they? I believe you need one to have the other."

"You do, but all of this"—she waved her hand—"is not included."

"But you're not married, Lizzie. How do you know this?"

"Elizabeth. Because the principle of any successful endeavor is work." She leaned back, revealing a little self-satisfied smile. "Marriage is not a four-tiered vanilla cake and a garter."

"It's not?" Robert interjected. "Karen has some explaining to do."

Ian smirked in spite of Elizabeth's sour look. "Perhaps you're right. Why marry at all? Two people can simply enjoy each other's company without complications."

Elizabeth laughed. "In the colonies, we call that a one-night stand."

Ian smiled. "You Americans, always in a hurry."

"You Europeans and your lovers, always chasing after romance."

"Very well then, I concede. Marriage is not romance. What is it then, Lizzie?" Ian asked. "Portfolios and property, profit and loss?"

Elizabeth slid off the stool. "Not just that. Respect, understanding, and yes, hard work, to build a solid financial future."

Ian laughed but the sound came out hollow. "Everything but your heart. Isn't that right, love?"

Elizabeth paled and Ian looked away, tossing back the rest of his drink. *Brilliant, you stupid git.* He scrambled for something soothing to say as a tall, clean-cut man approached. His dark hair was salted with gray; his stride, easy and confident. Ian judged him to be in his late forties.

"Am I interrupting?" he said.

"Not at all," Elizabeth said, her eyes still locked on Ian. "We're finished."

Nick slid his arm around her. "Gentlemen, excuse us," he said to no one in particular as he led her away.

Elizabeth's soft laugh floated back to Ian and he felt a knot forming in his stomach as he watched Nick and Elizabeth disappear from sight, lost in the crowd.

Ian cursed under his breath.

Robert gave his shoulder a friendly pat. "So much for tales of chivalry."

"Shut it," he said, raising his hand and signaling the barman.

At dinner, the bride and groom worked the room, pausing at each table.

"I've finally found my path," Emily was saying as she stood by Elizabeth's table. "I've designed clothes, bags, perfume, but nothing can make a connection with people like the culinary arts. I intend to create the ultimate experience for my clients, allowing them to see new cultures through foods of the world. I'll be like Anthony Bourdain—only without the travel. I wanted to study with Iron Chef Batali—but he's always booked. So I'm studying on my own. A lot of the great chefs were self-taught. I'll be the next Julia Child—without the hump, of course."

Elizabeth caught Nick's smirk. She knew that smirk all too well.

"I always thought Parker would be smart enough to pick brains over eye candy," Nick whispered.

"Emily is not stupid," Elizabeth said. *Except for marrying Parker,* she finished silently. Parker's brains were on a perpetual elevator between his head and his pants. She thought about all of his come-ons and propositions to her when they first met. She marveled that it took him so long to figure out there was no way it would happen.

She came back to the present, smiling as she felt Nick nuzzling her neck. "Would you like a wedding like this?"

Liz pulled back to gaze into his handsome, sturdy features and ran a light touch across his cheek. "Maybe."

"You're going to keep me guessing. Okay. I like a woman of mystery."

And I intend to remain that way, she thought, dropping her gaze. *You must never know about California, about my mother.*

Suddenly Karen's words about her past came to mind. *She did everything she could to destroy you, Liz.*

I should never have gone to my mother's after Josh left me, she thought. *If I hadn't gone home, everything would've been different.* She chided herself again for being so stupid about William. Listening to him when he said he just wanted to comfort her, be a support for her. *Why did I keep letting him get closer? I should have told her . . . apologized . . . done something.*

"Hey, are you still with me?"

Elizabeth found Nick viewing her quizzically.

"Yes, I'm here."

Even as she forced a smile, Elizabeth stole a glance at the next table. Ian looked her way, giving her a bemused smile. She ignored him, turning back to Nick.

The reception was over. A steady stream of limousines pulled up, picked up, and pulled away. The stifling heat had given way to still, humid air, clinging to everyone like a damp blanket. Ian said good night to Robert and Karen, raising a hand in farewell as they disappeared into a limo and it pulled away.

Later that night, lying in bed, Ian smoked a final cigarette, letting his thoughts wander. After Michele left, everything had gone wrong. He couldn't paint anymore. It was as if he had never picked up a brush in his life. Now, he felt his ability returning. He could concentrate here and start over. He took a last drag and thought of Elizabeth, her silky dress clinging to her soft curves, her serious, stern eyes locking with his. Robert was right, of course. Uptight, cool, calculating money managers weren't his type. But he sensed there was more to her than that. He was intrigued enough to pursue her. He stubbed out the cigarette in the ashtray on his nightstand, switched off the light and began to formulate a plan. A tea and a chat with Karen would be his first step. She seemed a decent sort and he detected a guileless openness, even a subtle sense of helplessness. If that didn't work, he would have to resort to doing Emily's portrait. He frowned at the thought. Robert would keep his word and not say anything about his past. He was glad he hadn't told Robert about the last two years. What was there to say about tramping about Europe, producing nothing but quick tourist portraits for a few euros to barely live on, and a parade of girls with pretty faces and busy lives in and out of his bed?

But the past was the past. He was making a fresh start, leaving it all behind, and he hoped to make the ever-intriguing Elizabeth a part of it.

Chapter 3

Two weeks later, on a Monday morning, the blaring of the alarm pulled Elizabeth from a fitful sleep. She yawned, scrunching further beneath the sheet, drifting in and out of impure drowsings. Feeling a spike of heat within her, she jolted awake, realizing thoughts of sturdy, solid Nick had morphed into lean, cool, blue-eyed Ian.

Feeling disloyal, she shook her head to clear her thoughts and refocus on Nick. His dark, predatory features should have conveyed warmth, and yet the thought of Ian caused her temperature to rise. *It's nothing,* she told herself, *nothing at all, a stupid daydream. A sexual fantasy,* she corrected, *and a steamy one at that.* "And that's all it's ever going to be," she muttered, throwing off the sheet. Nick was strong and in control, orchestrating their evenings of waiting limousines, intimate dinners uptown, parties with his friends. Exactly the life she wanted. She forced herself out of bed and decided a morning run was in order.

When Karen had provided refuge at her mother's Park Avenue penthouse, Elizabeth looked down from the window every morning to watch the runners, mere specks, intent on beating their bodies into submission, and laughed at them, rats on a wheel.

Call me Ben, she thought.

When she returned an hour later, she checked e-mails and

messages, showered and dressed, padding barefoot in and out of the rooms of her L-shaped apartment. By seven-thirty, she stepped outside again in a sleek Escada sleeveless dress and jacket. Walking to the corner, she raised her arm for a taxi.

She gazed out of the window of the cab at the black, white, and gray of the city. It was a far cry from the Laguna art colony and a landscape made for gentle watercolor washes, cerulean blue, raw sienna, even a splash of alizarin crimson, flowing together, wet into wet, blending seamlessly. That was fifteen years ago, she thought, still hearing the voice of the celebrated watercolorist Lillian Montgomery ringing through the studio, her arm waving, her ever-present drink in hand. *You've taken my talent, why don't you just take everything else? Do I even need to be here? Why don't I just end it all so you can take everything?*

She couldn't tolerate her daughter in her midst, surpassing her, creating paintings she could no longer produce. Elizabeth blinked at the remembrance of her own work, years of work, torn into pieces, destroyed: Lillian Montgomery's final statement on her love for her daughter. The taxi pulled up to the curb, but she didn't move. *I was a painter, I'm not anymore.*

"Ten seventy-five," the driver said.

She looked up and nodded.

She handed over some bills and, grasping her attaché case, she exited the cab. She stood at the curb for a long moment, the sun warm on her back. Taking a deep breath, she forced herself to relax and then headed into the building.

Elizabeth stepped off the elevator on the twentieth floor. Sometimes she still marveled at how far and fast the last decade had taken her. Chartered financial analyst, private wealth adviser, Director of Private Banking. She had built a reputation for handling some of the wealthiest and most difficult of men, billionaire Stanton Perry being the feather in her cap.

At first, her male clients greeted her with skepticism, throwing their questions at her like rapid gunfire. She answered them all, never giving an inch. Eventually, they regarded her with surprise and then amused acceptance.

As she came into the office, her team of advisers greeted her as she passed their desks. Some were bright-eyed, others were still trying to erase the hangover of yet another Hamptons weekend.

Elizabeth stopped at the desk of her assistant, Debbie, an inheritance from the last director. A small, thin dynamo in her thirties, Debbie had a flawless memory, a quicksilver mind, and a unique talent for surviving every company shake-up that left her with a new boss.

"Good morning," Elizabeth said.

"Good morning," Debbie said. "Your personal decorator is here."

Decorator?

Glancing beyond Debbie, she saw Ian MacKay leaning against her desk; at his feet, a small package wrapped in brown paper. He was smartly dressed, a crisp white shirt open at the collar, black slacks, black shoes.

She sucked in a breath, her annoyance rising.

"I only have a few minutes," she said as she entered her office, retreating behind her desk. "I'm not purchasing any art."

"I'm not selling any."

Elizabeth felt her eyebrows quirk.

Lifting the package, he placed it on the desk. "This is for you. If you fancy it, of course."

He undid the tape with care, revealing a small watercolor beach scene. She pored over the waves rolling toward the sand, a sky resembling a morning in Laguna, the sun glistening on the water. She held it up, catching herself in her admiration.

He had chosen a simple palette, a cerulean blue, a yellow ochre for the rocks and the sand. Exactly as she would've painted it. Exactly as she had painted it, innumerable times.

"Nice," she said, suppressing her enthusiasm.

"I thought it might be your style," he said.

"It isn't."

"What is your style?"

"Something else." He was standing too close, giving off a heat both warm and sweet, a mix of cinnamon and coffee. Her thoughts flashed back to her morning dreams of long kisses and gentle caresses. She glanced down at the quarterly analysis report on staffing trends to break her thought pattern. *Enough nonsense.* She wanted him, his canvas, and his scent out of her office. She had made her choice. Ian was nothing more than the past, and the countless mistakes she had made. *Keep that door closed.*

"I hope you have better luck reaching out to other potential clients."

"Reaching out," he repeated.

"It's just a business expression." She enunciated slowly to contain her annoyance. "I'll try to refer you."

"Why? You don't like my work."

"I didn't say I didn't like it," she snapped. "I'll have to revisit it."

"Revisit? Do you plan to like the picture later, Lizzie?"

"Elizabeth," she snapped. "I'm afraid I have no more time to chat."

She pulled in a long breath. In the heavy weight of silence, she felt a twinge of guilt; she knew the fragile psyche of the artist and she had hurt him. He had done a masterful job; he was good, better than good. But she snapped herself out of it. *It doesn't matter how good he is. Remember, he's Josh, he's William. I was a painter. I'm not anymore.*

He strolled behind the desk, moving closer. "Pity. You know, I was thinking about you and your dislike of weddings." His voice came out soft, intimate, a whisper in her ear.

Elizabeth stiffened. "I don't have one. The problem is that men dislike them. You dislike them."

"I have no desire to be married."

"As I said, you dislike them."

"Not at all. I simply prefer to watch others partake."

"Not all men feel as you do, thank goodness."

"Ah, your significant other, from the wedding. Of course. Lovely. He seems very—"

"Responsible?"

"Stiff."

"Pragmatic."

"Cold."

"The boardroom may not be as glamorous as emulating Monet and Renoir and spending your life in the café—"

"University."

She stared at him for a long moment. "You teach?"

"Yes. In London, now here. When were you in the café, Lizzie?"

"Everyone spends time in the café; most of us grow up."

"Indeed. Well, how soon to the happy day then?"

"Very soon," she said. She glanced past him, a smile on her face as she waved. "It's all a matter of timing."

Ian turned as Nick entered the office and came to Elizabeth's side.

Slipping his arm around Elizabeth's shoulder, he caught a glimpse of the painting and smirked, pulling her closer. "Making a sale?"

"Not today," Ian said.

Nick chuckled. "Well, in *our* world, the measure of an artist is the resale value. How's your appreciation?"

"Coming along. Enjoy the painting, Lizzie," Ian said, looking at Elizabeth. "Have a good day," he said to Nick.

"We will. Today and every day," Nick answered.

Nick closed the office door, cutting off Elizabeth's view of Ian strolling toward the elevator.

He turned to her and she accepted his kiss. They were comfortable with each other, partners enough to be compatible but without the emotion to make it volatile. It was one of the things that had originally appealed to her, made her feel safe. When they parted, Elizabeth studied his face, feeling that sense of coolness again. She found it odd she should notice it now. Suddenly it irked her; she shrugged off the feeling. She couldn't have it both ways.

He gazed down at her. "Artists obviously have no idea that Monday morning is actually for working."

Elizabeth pursed her lips. *You have no idea how hard artists work.* She caught the thought, forcing it out of her mind. Nick's attitude grated on her but she had no intention of getting into the habit of defending Ian MacKay.

"What are you up to today?" he asked.

"I have meetings all morning."

Nick straightened up. "Just remember to keep the pressure on. You've got to keep them off guard or on the run. Keep weeding out the dead wood. Be aggressive with the boss. Saunders expects you to give it to him straight. That's why he hired you."

"Thank you. You do know that I've been managing to take care of myself."

"I've been around directors a long time, kid, a lot longer than you've been on the job. This is still your first post and you haven't hit the two-year mark yet. You want there to be other posts, bigger and better. Do this right and you'll be able to have your pick of what you want."

"I know, Nick. Are you going to bill me for the advice?"

Nick ran his hands down her arms. "I give you advice, kid—" Elizabeth opened her mouth to protest, but Nick held up a slender finger. "And I say 'kid' with respect and affection, but I am still the older, wiser person in this dynamic."

She raised her eyebrows but said nothing.

"You're a rising star, Liz, you have what it takes and I know it. But you did just have one of your best advisers jump ship."

"It happens," she protested.

"It shouldn't happen. It leaves you vulnerable. Less than two years. You're still blood in the water."

Don't remind me, she thought, feeling her nerves spike.

"I thought you were headed downtown this morning," she said, changing the subject.

"I can't properly start my day if I don't have my evening planned. How about dinner at Demarchalier?"

"Dinner meeting," she answered.

"Stop letting your secretary book your appointments."

"Tomorrow."

"Put it on your calendar. There's a conversation we still need to finish."

Elizabeth pulled back. "Yes?"

Nick pulled her in. "Yes. The conversation we started at Parker's wedding, about weddings. Are you ready to continue the conversation?"

Elizabeth smiled but didn't answer.

"Or are you still gun-shy?"

Elizabeth stiffened. "Why would you think that?"

Nick ran his hand over her back. "I'm a lawyer. I've done my research. I have to if I'm going to make my case. And you haven't told me everything."

Elizabeth felt her breath catch.

"I know you've been down the aisle before, kid," he soothed. "That was a long time ago. He let you get away. I'm not going to make that mistake." He gave her a quick kiss. "So we'll talk over dinner."

She nodded.

She waited for him to step into the elevator, gave him a smile, and then shut her office door. She sat at her desk, compulsively tapping her pen. Letting out a muttered string of obscenities, she tossed the pen, watching it sail across the room. Emily had been spilling secrets.

Chapter 4

"Emily, what else did you tell Nick?" Elizabeth demanded. "And when?"

Pacing the airy second-floor loft boutique, Elizabeth fumed at having to run out of the office and take time to come down to Soho. Emily, perfectly tanned, champagne glass in one hand, pored over a collection of delicate, flowery dresses. Karen, in her usual Village grunge of T-shirt and ripped jeans, gave Elizabeth a sympathetic look. Elizabeth checked her watch. She was late for a meeting but this couldn't wait.

"Emily, I came into work this morning to find out my significant other knows intimate details of my past, something no significant other of mine needs to know. You just got back from your honeymoon. When did you find the time? What else did you tell Nick?" she repeated.

Emily gave Elizabeth a critical look, shaking her head. "How can he connect with you when you don't tell him anything? You could be a little more open, you know."

Without taking a breath, Emily took a sip of champagne and motioned for the hovering assistant to hold up two more dresses.

Elizabeth looked at her, mouth open.

Emily disappeared into a dressing room.

"For God's sake, Emily," she said finally. "This . . . after everything! I didn't confide in you so you could spill your guts."

"She meant well," Karen soothed.

"That's a great consolation." For Nick to know about Josh leaving her at the altar was bad enough. But William, what if she had mentioned William? *My God, what will Nick think of me if he discovers I had an affair with my mother's lover?* She closed her eyes at how that even sounded. It reminded her of her mother's favorite expression: life is drama, you can't have one without the other. But when Karen had spirited her away to New York, her misery wrapped around her like a wet blanket, she vowed to rebuild her life. She left the drama behind in California. Elizabeth shook her head, remembering how Karen introduced her to Emily and Emily had been open and accepting, sympathetic. *I talked too much.* Now Emily was someone who couldn't be trusted.

"Hey," Karen said softly. "It's going to be okay."

"No matter how many clients she sent me, my private life is off limits. She should know that. When I want Nick to know something, I'll tell him myself," Elizabeth whispered.

Emily emerged from the changing room. The V-neck sheath in creamy beige clung to her curves in all the right places. "I really need some new things. I don't want Parker to see me in the same old, same old."

"Did you tell Nick about William?"

Emily's expression turned to a pout. "Of course not. I would never do that. How could you think I would do that?" She pirouetted. "What about this one? Très chic?"

"Emily, knowledge is power," Elizabeth said, mentally grinding her teeth. "This is not the way I wanted this relationship to go."

Karen sat up, accepting a cup of tea from another assistant. "It doesn't matter that he knows about Josh. Why do you care?"

"Because he knows there was a weakness in my life, and now he has the upper hand," Elizabeth said, only she wasn't thinking about Josh. She was thinking of William and his attempts to comfort her after Josh, how he encouraged her to come home and live with her mother. *I'll be there, too. Lillian is so distant now, I could use the company. We can comfort each other.* All the time the bastard was playing her, exerting his power over her.

"I don't think it's healthy to equate power and relationships," Karen said. "The basic Taoist principle is to release everything and it all works out. The more you try to control something, the more it controls you."

"I agree," Emily chimed in. "Why do you do that?"

"Oh, I don't know," Elizabeth said dryly. "Could it be because I spend all day, every day, with power-hungry alpha males? Emily, what exactly does Nick know?"

"I mentioned Josh. I said that you almost married but he wasn't worthy of you."

"Emily," Elizabeth said when she trusted herself to speak, "I know you mean well, but please, do not discuss my past with anyone . . . ever."

Emily came to Elizabeth, wrapping her arms around her. "Don't be mad. You know I'm just trying to help. I want him to be madly in love with you and I want you to be happy. You deserve it. You're still coming to the housewarming, aren't you? It won't be the same if you're not there."

Elizabeth let out a sigh. "Yes, of course we're coming."

Emily bounced in excitement. "A new house and a new business. This catering venture is going to be like nothing you've seen. Parker's inviting his clients to help me spread the word. I want you both to come early."

Elizabeth pulled her purse strap onto her shoulder. "We'll be there."

Karen got up, grabbing her jacket.

Emily frowned. "You're leaving too? What about lunch?"

"I'm sorry, Ems, I can't. I have a Webcast to catch. It may be two o'clock here but it's eight o'clock in Brussels. My mother is giving an interview for her new book. I'm sure she'll manage to work in how my father's emotional, psychological, and sexual deficiencies nearly destroyed their careers."

Emily's eyes widened. "You know they probably shouldn't be in the same room—ever. What are you going to do about the wedding?"

"Yes, what *are* you going to do about the wedding?" Elizabeth asked. "Can you take out the part where the minister asks if anyone here knows of any reason why these two should not be joined . . . ?"

"I think that's the standard speech."

"Your parents still object at weddings?" Emily asked.

"No, they don't . . . no one invites them anymore."

They exchanged good-bye hugs and kisses.

"Every girl should have her special wedding day," Emily said. "Don't worry about your parents. They won't object at your wedding. It's different when it's family."

Chapter 5

On a Saturday, Elizabeth wandered the University Place street festival, a bottle of water sweating in her hand. The July sun was relentless in its attack; the people moved in slow motion, glistening in the noonday heat. Elizabeth held the bottle to her cheek; the chill was already off. She passed the booths; they were the same every year. She liked the one with the curtains, nothing more than strips of sheer fabric. They looked cool and inviting. She was about to walk over when the buzzing of her BlackBerry caught her attention.

"So, how goes it with the Nichols and May of Greenwich Village?" Elizabeth said into the phone.

"We're going to a first read-through," Karen answered. "Where are you?"

"I'm at University Place. At the festival."

"Which is a few short steps from Parsons. Are you taking the watercolor class?"

There was a beat of silence over the line.

"I prefer to think of it as briefly enjoying a former minor hobby."

"Also known as your former career, your original true path, that you lived, ate, and slept, and was your heart and soul."

"*Was* being the operative word. I'm perfectly happy as I am."

"Which is why you didn't throw out the school catalogue."

"Is there a reason you called?"

"My mother just e-mailed. She's coming back in two weeks. It would be nice if I told her I'm getting married."

"You should send a telegram, or a carrier pigeon. Anything but face-to-face."

"I can't. You'll come with me?"

"It's going into my BlackBerry as we speak."

They said good-bye and Elizabeth clicked off.

She scanned the crowd, stopping when she saw Ian, surrounded by a gaggle of adoring young women. Their eyes met and he broke away from them, strolling across the street toward her.

"Oh shit," Elizabeth muttered. He was in faded jeans, beat-up sneakers, and an old shirt covered with multicolored smudges of paint. A shiver of excitement ran through her in spite of the heat.

He stopped in front of her, considering her for a moment with a smile. "Nice to see you again, Lizzie."

She nodded toward his stained shirt.

"I teach . . . remember? At Parsons."

"Yes, of course, you mentioned it." She glanced around. There was no escape hatch. "I just came for the festival."

Ian reached out and fingered the dried color on the edge of her shirt, making her flinch. "Did you now?"

She could feel her hair plastering to the back of her neck in wet strands. He appeared relaxed, not at all uncomfortable. *Bastard.*

"I happen to appreciate art and culture," she snapped. "Yes, I'm taking a class."

She watched his eyebrows rise. "I'd like to see your work, Lizzie." He laid his hand on her wrist, his touch light as a feather. "Shall we have a go? You don't mind, do you?"

"I do mind. It's a work in progress," she said, her voice strong.

He gave a wide smile. "Not afraid of a little constructive criticism, are you?" He took a step closer. "I promise I'll be very gentle."

Suddenly lightheaded, Elizabeth sucked in a breath. "Sure. Why not?"

He followed her through the maze of private cubby workspaces, every step eliciting a symphony of creaks and groans from the old wooden floorboards. The smell of plaster, paint, and turpentine assaulted her nose and she shivered as the cold air hit her skin.

"You know your way around," he said. "Been here before?"

"I've never been directionally challenged," she said.

They entered the classroom studio and Elizabeth went straight to her things. He came up behind her and waited.

She put her bottle of water down and hoisted her portfolio onto the table, struggling with the zipper to open it. Without looking, she felt him near her, hovering, watching her, causing a flutter in her chest.

Elizabeth handed over a folder of quick compositions. He held up each paper, then compared them. She caught his look of confusion. A rush of fear went through her. Some of it was her old work, when she could still paint. He was trying to figure it out. Outside, a siren wailed in the distance.

"You've painted professionally?" he asked after a long moment.

"I dabbled . . . occasionally," she answered.

He scrutinized the paintings, finally gathering them and handing them to her. "Watercolor is a fluid medium, Lizzie. Some of your work lacks spontaneity, relaxation. You need to use more water and let the happy accidents happen, yeah? Do you remember what you were thinking about when you did these?"

She would never forget what she had been thinking. Her mother was gone and her own ability to paint was dying as well. In the midst of it all, she turned to William to find him pulling away, done with her as if she were a half-finished canvas not worth completing. She snapped back to the moment, feeling dizzy, whether from the heat, the memories, or the close proximity of Ian MacKay, she couldn't be sure. "No," she said.

Standing so close, he overshadowed her slim frame. She imagined herself shrinking, like Alice, through the looking glass. He brushed a stray tendril of hair away from her pale cheek. She heard her own breathing, shallow and ragged.

"Are you all right, Lizzie? Would you like a drink of water?"

"Yes, please," she said, and her speech sounded slurred in her ears.

He handed her the bottle and it shook in her hand. She took a long swallow.

"It's just the heat, love. Take a deep breath."

She looked up at him, but she didn't see him, only a bright kaleidoscope of colors. She felt herself weaving and then his arms were around her, pulling her close to him.

"Steady now," he murmured.

After a moment, the colors receded and he was there again, embracing her. She leaned in closer, breathing deeply. *I don't want this to end.* Stunned, she jerked away from him and stepped back into her chair, sending it sliding into the table, tipping over her water bowl, the tinted water pooling, then running off the table.

At that moment, students began filtering into the classroom.

"She was a bit overcome by the heat," Ian said to the instructor.

"I'm fine," she said in as strong a voice as she could muster, bending to blot at the water with a wad of paper towel.

"So you are," he said. "Well done with your paintings, Lizzie. You should continue."

She sank onto a chair, not trusting herself to speak, watching as he walked out of the classroom, taking the upper hand with him.

Chapter 6

By the middle of the second act, the reading had to be stopped. Robert expected a romantic experience, full of magic and kismet, working in the theater where he and Karen first met, seeing their first coauthored play produced. While he was prepared for the rough dialogue and the reworking of plot, he wasn't prepared for a reluctant director and the uncontrolled weeping of Larry Hammond, one of the most luckless actors in New York City.

To struggling New York actors Larry was a legend. From his humble beginnings, stepping off the Amtrak train fifteen years ago and getting mugged in the men's room, Larry's existence consisted of audition rejections and rathole apartments he vacated so that his girlfriends could move in with his roommates. The coup de grâce was losing out on the part of *Death of a Salesman*'s Biff Loman—twice. Larry was either the poster boy for suffering for his art or for just suffering. The only bright spot had been gigs as an extra on *Law & Order*.

Now Larry stood in the middle of the stage, waving a script at Karen. "I die?" he whined. "Since when am I dying? This is a reinvention of *The Iceman Cometh*, as a comedy. I'm not supposed to be dying. I gave up a commercial to do this!"

"For dog food," Karen said.

"It's still work!" Larry said, lunging forward. "I'm still communicating with an audience!"

Karen took a step backward.

"If this script stays like this, all our careers are going to die," Morris muttered. "I'm not directing a play, I'm directing a funeral. Junie!" he called.

Larry threw his arms out, reaching for a short, stocky woman with flaming red shoulder-length hair and bangs cut straight across her forehead. She wore bright plaid shorts and Keds without laces on her pink, swollen feet. She closed up the cell phone as Larry bore down on her.

"Junie," he whimpered.

"Larry, baby, take a deep breath. It's just a draft, baby, right? Just a draft."

She settled Larry in a chair, leaving him sniveling into his handkerchief, motioning for Vicki, a thin, pert blonde with ironed straight hair, to comfort him.

Junie, Morris, Robert, and Karen conferenced in the fourth-row center section.

"I thought everyone is supposed to act normal when a production first starts," Karen said.

"Maybe it's a full moon," Robert said.

"Okay, kids," Junie said, "everyone's a little nervous in the beginning. But it's all about protecting the actors, right?"

"And the director," Morris said.

Larry rushed back to center stage.

"Bobby, you said this was my part, my part! An homage to O'Neill like never before. This isn't straight O'Neill, this is satire O'Neill. I can't die in the second act. I have no face time! What am I going to tell my mother?"

Vicki patted Larry's shoulder. "Don't worry, Lar, *SVU* is having an open casting call next week."

Larry moaned in response, burying his face in her shoulder.

Karen felt her cheeks flush warm. "He's still working every night," she whispered to Robert.

"The part is one quarter of what it used to be."

"Is he afraid he won't get another job?"

"No, he's afraid he'll die in the rent-controlled closet he lives in."

"I thought he lived near Lincoln Center."

"He lives *behind* Lincoln Center, Karen. It's not the same thing."

"Look, kids," Junie interrupted, "I thought I was producing a comedy."

"I thought I was directing a comedy," Morris cut in.

Junie patted Morris's shoulder. "*This Guy Walks in to a Bar* is O'Neill on Prozac, that's what we said, right? Hickey's not a hopeless murderer. He's a reformed existentialist, a self-made Tony Robbins type, embracing the corporate culture. That's funny. Larry discovering Hickey's his father and offing himself in front of Hickey to highlight the existential theory that life is meaningless and absurd? Not funny, kids."

"Yes, not funny," Morris said, glaring at Karen.

Karen leaned over to Robert. "Why does he always look at me when he says that?"

"We're doing rewrites, Larry," Robert called out as Larry's sniveling grew louder.

Larry rushed off the stage to throw his arms around Robert. "Thank you, Bobby," he whined softly. "I can always count on you."

A ring tone of the Village People's "YMCA" sounded and Junie flipped open her phone.

Robert peeled Larry away from him, inspecting his shirt.

Morris looked squarely at Karen. "It is not funny."

Karen shrank back, huddling against Robert.

An hour later, Karen and Robert got off the subway near their apartment in Greenwich Village.

"Maybe you should do this by yourself."

Robert stopped short. "No! We work together. We're a team."

"Maybe I just can't write comedy now. I mean, look at my role models. How can I write about positive relationships when my mother had adulterer spray-painted on my father's cars?"

"All of them?"

She nodded. "Even the one idling while he was having lunch. He came out of the Four Seasons and had to ride through Midtown like that. It was on the eleven o'clock news."

Robert pulled her in for a squeeze. "Didn't you tell me that Taoism sees the irony, the whimsy of life, and that you should approach your work with a sense of play?"

"I'm not feeling very whimsical lately. I'm feeling realistic."

"Comedy and reality don't mix, babe. Comedy takes reality and shows it for what it is: ridiculous. And you've seen plenty of the ridiculous over the years. Trust me, you have an endless well of material. You just don't realize it. That's why Larry can't drop dead before the second act." Robert brought her to a stop and turned her to face him. "Did you tell your parents we're getting married?"

Karen stared at the ground. Robert ducked his head in an attempt to meet her eyes. "Not yet," she said.

He pulled her into an embrace. "Remember when we met? I was with a friend at the playhouse and he introduced you. *Oh hey, this is Karen,* he said, like he hadn't just changed my whole life. I see this beautiful girl with raven hair and almond eyes and she's warm and gentle and gives off such a peace—"

"That's very good."

"Thank you. I'm a writer. Don't interrupt, I'm on a roll. And I thought, I am going to marry this girl. Now, let's see some of that peacefulness. No parent thinks any man is good enough for their daughter. And your parents' insanity isn't a part of our life. Now, you're brilliant, you're beautiful, and I predict we will write a hilarious comedy."

Arms around each other, they walked home.

Chapter 7

The gloom of the conference room was interrupted by an LCD unit casting a blinding white light, projecting a pie chart onto the screen. Parker stood next to the screen. Seated next to him, his protégé and fund manager, Darryl, a tall, lanky young man with a clean cut, Ivy League face, a shock of blond hair falling forward onto his forehead, watched Parker's every move.

Across the table sat Stanton Perry. In his late fifties, Stanton was thick but trim, with a handsome, rugged face. His elbows rested on the arms of the Italian leather chair, fingers interlaced, in an attitude of prayer, staring at the screen with half-closed eyes.

Two small, wiry, cheerless men sat behind Perry, briefcases at their feet. Parker knew the suits were the research wizards, pocket-protector boys, little MBAs who would spend their middle age boring the shit out of the next generation of MBA students at Harvard. He had his own drone on the payroll to make it look good. They sat around with their mathematical formulas but they didn't know shit about money or how to use it; Ivy League pricks. They didn't understand a thing.

"Stanton, you asked for this meeting," Parker began, barely concealing his annoyance. "I hope you don't mind my being blunt."

"Not at all," Stanton replied.

"I'm not really in the market to take on new clients now. I've got four-and-a-half billion in capital, one hundred and seventy-five billion in assets. I've got futures contracts worth three hundred billion alone. And all you're bringing to the table is one hundred fifty million." Parker gave an exaggerated sigh and a bored glance around the room. "That doesn't show a lot of faith. I mean, I'm personally invested. My family's in the fund."

Stanton smiled. "Really? I heard the mean average income in South Amboy was sixty thousand a year, before taxes. That doesn't leave much to invest."

Parker forced a tight smile. "My wife's family, my wife, and myself. We both know I'm not some asshole taking people's money, and if the wind blows south you draw dick while I'm lying on an island with my two percent and last year's twenty percent profit."

Stanton smiled but said nothing.

"Would you mind if I asked everyone else to step out for a moment?"

Stanton nodded to the MBAs and Darryl followed them out.

Parker sat down across from Perry, leaning back in his chair. He didn't see Stanton Perry. He only saw that all he ever wanted was to be Stanton Perry. And now he was bigger than Stanton Perry. Parker blew out a mouthful of air. "I just don't know if I want to take on anyone else. Now, if you would consider moving your entire portfolio to me," Parker smiled, "I'm sure Liz would understand."

"I'm sure she wouldn't. That's not an option. She doesn't handle all my interests, she never expected to. I believe in the diversified portfolio. Liz understands that. And you understand creating twenty-five percent returns."

Parker leaned forward. "Well, it's true. There's nothing like eating what you kill. I don't just go out and run your money to make you a twenty-five percent return. No one can touch me on currency bets. No one. I'm not chasing returns, I'm creating them. Momentum investing, value investing, quantitative methods, market neutral. Who gives a shit? Do it all and if a company looks good, fuck it, buy a controlling share and take over. I wouldn't give you shit for most of the CEOs in this country. People want to call me a vulture? Fine. But if I own it, it's making money. No one posts returns that can touch mine."

Parker sat silent for a moment, staring into space. "Liz put in a good word for me?"

"This is my decision. Elizabeth didn't venture an opinion."

Bitch, Parker thought. After a moment, he shrugged. "One hundred fifty million?" He shook his head.

Stanton Perry lapsed into silence, eyes closed. Parker forced himself to remain quiet. He wanted Perry's money, he could almost feel it itching between his fingers.

"Two hundred fifty million to start," Stanton said, opening his eyes and giving Parker a cool, assessing look. "With another three hundred to follow if all goes well."

Parker smiled.

Parker stood in the middle of the conference room like a god surveying his kingdom, a stream of profanity running through his head. Two hundred and fifty fucking million. He didn't get out of bed for two hundred million. He shook his head. What the fuck. He was eating into Liz's territory. *Shit, for that I would've done it for nothing.*

Stanton's crack about Jersey griped his ass. Growing up in that shitty town, watching his old man slumped over in his chair at night, sucking down beer after beer, staring at the TV; his old man was a has-been before he ever got started. What a life, driving a desk for a shit salary and a crappy bonus and a fucking watch after twenty years. *But I finally made it across the river.* Now everywhere he hung his hat had to have a view of his new domain, Park Avenue, Central Park—Jersey forever behind him and New York in front of him. The only thing out of whack was that damn downtown townhouse, a concession to Emily; the rooftop terrace had a clear view across the Hudson.

Parker looked down. His tailor had sent a new seamstress. The attractive blonde stretched a measuring tape up his inseam. The top two buttons of her white blouse were open, her plaid skirt resting slightly above her mid-thigh. He gave her a sly, satisfied smile. She had her blond hair pinned up; he bet she had great hair. Emily had great hair, flowing over her shoulders, sparkling like spun gold in the sunlight. Walking her into an event, he enjoyed watching every man's head turn. He knew they'd love to get her on her back. She was the perfect addition to his portfolio; five nine, blue eyes, a perfect ass, and a name that meant money. They weren't on the map, they *were* the map.

He opened his cell phone again and hit the speed dial. His call went straight to voice mail. Fuck, he thought. Marianna wasn't home. He didn't pay for an Upper East Side apartment, new clothes, and a car and driver for her not to be home when he wanted her. He snapped the cell phone shut as the blonde stood up and slung the tape measure over her shoulder. Her strappy sandals made a soft, slapping sound against the bottoms of her feet as she moved around him, occasionally brushing against him.

"I'm finished," she said. "Will there be anything else?"

"Just one thing," he said with a smile.

An hour later he had the blonde naked on her back in the corporate suite at the Plaza Hotel. Afterward, she said maybe they could see each other again. He swatted her backside and said "sure." Dressed, he stood by the window, staring down while redoing his tie; the blonde saw herself out. He checked his watch. He should stop by Liz's office to say hello on his way back, he thought. Drop the news about Perry to see her reaction. Maybe he'd just let her read about it. *She has it all*, he thought, *the brains to go with the beauty*. He curled his lip at the thought of how he'd chased her two years ago, making her offers, not just to work for him, but the whole nine yards. He would've married her. He burned thinking how she never gave him an inch, turning him down every time, no hesitation. Ice queen bitch. He'd been waiting to find a way to say thank you. This could be the break he was waiting for. He'd like to see her on the downside; he'd like to see her begging.

He called Emily from the car on his way back to the office, half listening as she chattered on about the menu for the party.

He reminded her to make sure the mock-up of the Greenwich estate would be on display for the party, then whispered about what he had planned for her for the after party, lacing his descriptions with expletives. She giggled as he gave her details.

The limo pulled up to the building on Park Avenue and Parker got out, taking a moment to linger. *This is my kingdom now; I belong here. I've finally arrived. And I'll be damned if I'm ever going back across the Hudson River again.*

Chapter 8

At the sound of Parker's booming voice, Elizabeth and Nick moved with the guests en masse into the great room on the first floor. Parker and Emily's downtown Art Deco townhouse had ceiling-to-floor windows and glass skylights, a feeling of openness, allowing the city to flow inside. Done in stark white, the only colors were oversized, red Chinese porcelain pots holding bamboo plants, and the occasional painting with explosions of splattered color. The upper floors were made of frosted glass, creating a moving mosaic of footprints over the heads of the guests. Servers moved between rooms and floors, disappearing back into the kitchen for refills.

A red silk cloth covered a large, bulky mass on a table in the center of the great room.

Karen leaned over to Elizabeth. "Is that the mock-up of the new kingdom?"

"Either that or a bloody horse's head."

Karen stifled a laugh.

Parker stood next to the table, the ringmaster of his circus. "Ladies and gentlemen, you've seen Mar-a-Lago. Now see the next evolution, Davis Manor." With a flourish, he flipped off the cloth, revealing a scale model of the palace that was to be the Greenwich compound. "Thirty thousand square feet, my friends."

A faint buzzing sound grew louder; all eyes followed a

miniature helicopter flying above their heads, watching it settle down onto the tiny helipad.

Scanning the guests, Elizabeth spied Stanton Perry, his trophy wife Deirdre at his side. Deirdre had everything Stanton or any other man could want: long, luxurious, flowing platinum blond hair, skin glowing with youth and vitality, a Victoria's Secret body, and legs that never quit. They approached Elizabeth, and Stanton offered his hand as he kissed her cheek.

"Hello, young lady," he said. "What do you hear?"

Elizabeth smiled into his perfectly tanned angular face, silver strands gleaming in the slicked-back dark hair. He had a sly smile that made him look a little dangerous. Elizabeth knew he was more than a little dangerous.

"It's all good, Mister Perry, all good," she said smoothly. "And yourself?"

"Excellent, as you know. You've put me in good hands. Your young Adam is doing a fine job advising me. And even though you're a big shot now, I expect you to visit us at Georgica Pond this summer," he said with a wink as he moved on.

As she watched him move away, she caught sight of a small painting hanging in the corner of the room. She strolled over for a closer look. It was a pastoral scene in the Impressionist style, thick brush strokes placing dabs of separate color next to one another, providing an optical feast to the viewer as the colors mixed before the eye. The work reminded her of Monet's purple lilies and she smiled. She looked for the artist's signature even though she knew it was Ian. A rush of excitement ran through her at the thought of seeing him again.

She felt Nick's arms encircle her. "How's my girl? Thirsty?"

"Yes, thank you," she said and watched him head to the bar.

She noticed Parker in deep conversation with Stanton, Deirdre close at Stanton's side. She wore the vague air of boredom that comes of having too much money and leisure time. Parker leaned toward Deirdre, always the attentive host. Close, too close, Elizabeth thought.

Elizabeth felt a tug at her arm and turned to find Karen.

"What's happening?"

"Take a look," Elizabeth said with a discreet nod toward Parker.

"No," Karen said. "He isn't. He wouldn't."

"He will," Elizabeth said. "He's never been as smart as he thinks he is. He's got two heads and he's always thinking with the wrong one."

A server passed them with a tray of unidentifiable white-and-gray matter, some of it wrapped in green leaves.

"Don't eat anything," Karen whispered.

Elizabeth looked longingly at the passing tray. "Why not?" she said as Emily floated past them, chattering with guests.

"I can't believe how easy this has been. Most of the foods aren't meant to be cooked anyway and raw bars are back in style," Emily said.

"Great," Elizabeth said. "I haven't eaten since lunch."

"Let's head up to the roof," Karen said.

Elizabeth caught Nick's eye across the room; he was engaged in conversation. She pointed her finger upward and he nodded in acknowledgment but made no move to break away. She thought wistfully of their first outings when they stayed close to each other, always touching. We're used to each other now, comfortable, Elizabeth told herself, as it should be.

Hearing Parker's angry voice, Karen and Elizabeth stopped short of cutting through the den.

"Why didn't the electrician install the spotlights over the replica?" Parker demanded. "Why the fuck didn't you call him?"

Emily hesitated a moment. "I did. He couldn't come back."

"Why not?" he persisted.

"I—I—" she stumbled.

"Never mind," Parker snapped. "You don't know. You never know. Next time, I'll take care of it." Stalking away, he left perfectly manicured, perfumed, and coutured Emily standing there, her mouth turned down in a quivering pout.

Karen moved in Emily's direction but Elizabeth held her back. "Don't, you'll embarrass her."

They backed away and found Robert disengaging himself

from a tall, slender, earnest professor sporting an outrageous handlebar mustache; part and parcel of Emily's attempt to create a modern day salon.

"Your idea is wrong, young man. I advise you to reconsider," the professor said, his mustache dancing with every word. "O'Neill's work can never be comedy. Comedy is only for those who overcome. O'Neill's final words were 'born in a hotel room and, goddammit, died in a hotel room.' What does that tell you?"

"He had poor planning skills," Karen said, taking Robert's hand to lead him away. "But that doesn't mean it can't be funny."

"Thanks for rescuing me," Robert said as he kissed Karen's ear. "What have I missed?"

"Parker and Emily had an argument, just as you predicted."

Robert checked his watch as they made their way up the stairs to the roof. "Right on schedule. It won't be long now. One way or another, this party's going to be over in an hour. Trust me."

The intimate roof space boasted a tall, red brick façade housing a compact fireplace where a healthy blaze crackled; candles and tiki torches flickered in the dusk. A luxurious blood-red silk carpet glinted in the firelight.

Elizabeth, Karen, and Robert enjoyed the peace and quiet until Parker, guests in tow, burst up the stairs and onto the roof. "This is one of only a handful of rooftop living spaces in Manhattan," he was saying. "It was a bitch bringing everything up by crane."

"You must love spending time up here," someone said. "You can see clear across the Hudson."

"Did you see Perry?" he asked as he passed Elizabeth.

"Yes, I saw him."

"Thanks for putting in a good word for me," he said, flashing one of his infamous predatory smiles.

"Here's a word for you," she said with a dismissive tone.

"Several, actually." She nodded toward Deirdre Perry disappearing down the stairs. "Keep your hands out of that cookie jar, or they won't be the only things to get chopped off."

He cackled, giving her a playful pat on the back and headed for the stairs.

Jerk-off.

A server paused and without thinking she took an hors d'oeuvre off the tray. *Maybe I'll just eat the cracker.* As she brought the food to her mouth, a hand encircled her wrist, making her jump.

"You don't want to do that, love," Ian whispered.

Her pulse racing, she opened her hand, allowing the mystery tidbit to drop into his palm.

She steeled herself and faced him.

"It's lovely to see you looking well," he said. "Are you sorted out now?"

"I'm fine."

"I do hope I wasn't the cause of anything."

"Not a chance."

"Excellent. You were quite overcome. What's the term for that?"

"Heat stroke."

Ian smirked. "Yes, of course. Is the Prince here with you?"

"Downstairs, feeding and watering his white horse."

"Ah," he said with a chuckle. "Rather foolish of him to leave you alone, don't you think?"

"Why? There's no danger here."

Ian nodded. "That's a great relief." He smiled, pulling out a pack of cigarettes from his pocket.

"We'll probably be married by next summer."

"Why wait? Dear Lizzie, if you really wanted to be married, I would think you would have done it by now."

"Not all Americans are in a hurry. Some of us like to make sure we do everything right. The right man, at the right time."

Ian smiled. "Of course."

A moan cut through the hum of conversation. Ian and Elizabeth looked at each other and then across the terrace to see a man, hand over his mouth, sink onto a chair. Almost immediately, the man's companion gasped and doubled over, clutching her stomach.

Robert and Ian rushed to their aid, Karen and Elizabeth on their heels.

"We need to get them downstairs," Robert said.

As they all moved down the steps, they were greeted by more strange, guttural noises.

"I'm pretty sure the party is over," Robert said as they reached the landing.

Peering into the great room, they found guests prostrate on couches, some bent over, moaning; others, holding their stomachs, lay supine on the floor. A woman in a silk chiffon Galliano dress wretched into an ice bucket.

"Don't you ever get tired of being right?" Elizabeth said to Robert.

When they made it to the first floor, they found Parker, his face the color of chalk, hovering helplessly at Stanton Perry's side. Stanton gripped his stomach with one hand while holding on to Deirdre with the other as she clung to the table in the great room. With a whimper, she vomited on the mock-up of the Greenwich compound.

"So much for the kingdom," Elizabeth whispered to Ian.

He nodded, suppressing a smile.

Stanton turned to Parker, his eyes blazing.

"Emily!" Parker bellowed. "We have an issue!"

Twenty minutes later, the townhouse resembled a mini infirmary, with EMTs triaging the sick.

Elizabeth and Karen flanked Emily, her eyes saucers of panic, holding a handkerchief to stifle her sobs. "I don't understand this. How did this happen?"

"I don't fucking believe this," Parker said with a grimace, hand on his stomach.

"Parker, lay off, this isn't the time," Elizabeth said.

EMTs passed them, some carrying Ziploc bags bulging with food, others wheeling gurneys bearing groaning guests.

"This is the perfect time," he said, color draining from his face. "What the hell is wrong with this picture? In my world, my housewarming party doesn't turn into a damn MASH unit!"

"Neither of you got sick?" Emily said to Karen and Elizabeth. "What did you eat?"

They didn't answer, watching a couple being wheeled past them and out the door.

"You'll hear from my attorney, Davis," the husband groaned.

"Nick!" Parker bellowed.

An EMT strolled over. "Which one of you is Julia Child? I need a complete list of what you served."

Parker turned to Emily. "Your job is to help me win new clients," he said, clutching his stomach. "Not poison them!" Leaning against a bamboo plant, he let out a guttural moan and threw up on his shoes. "Oh shit," he whimpered. "Not the Ferragamos."

Two EMT workers heaved him onto a gurney as Emily hurried to his side.

Nick appeared at the top of the stairs, helping a woman down from the second floor.

"Nick . . . Nick," Parker gasped.

Nick handed the woman off to an EMT and came to Parker's side.

"Take care of this, Nick," he sputtered. "Take care of this shit."

Nick patted his shoulder. "I've got it under control. Don't worry about it."

Elizabeth and Nick stood apart, taking a moment out of the madness.

"Are you all right?" she asked.

"I'm fine. I need to go to the hospital to babysit Parker. This is going to cost him money—some of which I will be collecting."

"I'll come with you."

"Nick!" Parker ordered. "Get the hell over here!"

"I'll be fine," he said. "It'll be chaos. You don't need to be involved. Head on home with Karen."

"I think I should—"

"I'll call you tomorrow," he said, his tone firm.

Elizabeth accompanied Stanton outside to a waiting ambulance. Dierdre's moans floated out from its interior.

"Thanks," Stanton said, his face glistening with perspiration.

"I'll check on you tomorrow," she said.

Robert and Karen joined her and they watched the ambulances pull away from the curb, sirens wailing. A small crowd loitered, watching the spectacle. It was only eight o'clock but it felt like the evening had been going on for hours. The air was still and humid, clammy against their air-conditioned skin.

"Well, that was a killer party," Robert said.

"Do you want to come back to the apartment?" Karen asked.

Elizabeth shook her head.

They said their good-nights; Elizabeth lingered, finally realizing she was hungry.

She was thinking of a muffin and a latte at the Starbucks near her apartment when she heard the click of a lighter behind her. She turned to find Ian taking a deep pull on his cigarette.

He came forward, offering his hand. "Come along now."

"And where are we going?"

"Just a wee drink."

"A wee drink? You know, it's a distinct possibility you're not as cute as you think you are."

Ian considered this statement. "No, I'm very cute." And then he grinned.

What a smile, Elizabeth thought, watching his features

soften. Her insides began to flutter and she forced herself to stay stern.

His hand was out, open, palm up, inviting, waiting. "I did save your life tonight, didn't I?"

"So you did," she said, ignoring his hand but falling into step with him. "One drink, that's all."

Chapter 9

Elizabeth lounged comfortably across from Ian at a sidewalk table. He had taken her to a quiet spot on Bleecker, barely noticeable and refreshingly empty in comparison to its tourist-packed neighbors. Ian leaned back in his chair, smoking, shifting the cigarette under the table when the waiter brought out plates of appetizers and set down two drinks.

She took a long sip, enjoying the liquid going down smooth and cold.

"You may want to slow down a bit. It's rather strong."

"I can handle my liquor. And I don't get drunk."

"Of course you don't," he agreed with a smile.

"So why aren't you in Florida? Art Basel is in six months. That's where all the rich and beautiful go to see the brilliant enfants terribles of art."

"I'm closing the deal on representation."

She raised an eyebrow. "A dealer? I'm impressed." Elizabeth raised her glass. "I hope you will be his Monet and he will be your Durand-Ruel."

They clinked glasses, regarding each other as they sipped.

"Is your father proud and your brothers jealous?"

"My mother is proud and my sisters are not jealous."

Elizabeth laughed. "Surrounded by females. A life of adoration and pampering."

"A life of learning sensitivity and understanding. So you see, Lizzie, you're quite safe with me."

He signaled to the waiter for two more drinks.

"I'll keep my guard up, just in case."

An hour later, the waiter cleared away another set of empty glasses with the picked-over appetizer plates. He reappeared briefly to bring yet another round of drinks.

Elizabeth smiled. She felt warm and relaxed. She noticed Ian's chair had inched around the table, edging closer to her. When they leaned back in their chairs, their knees brushed lightly against each other.

"So," Elizabeth began, "you don't ever want to be married?"

Ian raised his eyebrows and laughed. "That's a very direct statement, Lizzie. No. I don't."

"But you don't want, as we Americans say, a one-night stand, either."

"No indeed."

She shifted and her knee brushed his again. "That begs the question, what do you want?"

Ian smiled. "An arrangement."

Elizabeth laughed. "Uh-hunh. Meaning sex on a regular basis without any emotional involvement."

His eyes cooled. "Two people enjoying each other's company without misunderstandings."

She took in the frosty stare and sat back a little, watching as he caught himself and his features became benign once again.

"You do realize your proposal is just semantics. You can't possibly think two people will just agree to go on for as long as one or the other likes, without complications."

Leaning forward, he touched her hand. "For as long as *you* like, Lizzie."

Elizabeth stopped in mid-swallow. Her pulse jumped as her heart thumped in her chest; but she allowed his hand to remain resting on hers.

"I realize you're not interested, of course. But if you were, and if we did, and if you then decided that you'd had enough of me, then you would simply tell me—how do you Americans say it—when you want to get back in the game. It would be entirely up to you."

Elizabeth swallowed, straining to process the information. The perfect arrangement. To have control of everything and give away nothing. The upper hand. *But what about Nick? Nick is not a fleeting arrangement. He's the future, my future. There should be nothing to think about. So why am I thinking?* She glanced over at Ian. There was something about him, something in him, pulling her.

Her glance drifted to Ian's now soft blue eyes, the hair curling over his collar; she had a sudden desire to slip her hands under the cool fabric of his white shirt and feel his skin warm beneath her fingers. An involuntary sigh escaped her lips just as she realized her face was beginning to feel hot and strange. Leaning forward to take another sip of her drink, Elizabeth noticed the street seemed to be slanting, and something like a damp, heavy blanket was beginning to settle over her brain. Her head started to pound with a heartbeat of its own. She brought her hands to her cheeks. "My face is numb. I've lost all feeling in my face."

"Oh dear," he said. "I think you've had a wee too much."

"You think?" she slurred.

She followed his movements; they were slow and exaggerated. He laid some bills on the table, then he was at her side, his arms circling her waist. Her nose was assaulted by a barrage of scents, her mouth full of tastes: cigarette smoke, chicken, mozzarella, whiskey, and lemon juice. She leaned into him as he helped her to her feet, her head against his chest, breathing in his warm scent along with the humid air as they began to take slow, steady steps.

Stumbling into the loft, Elizabeth felt as if she were floating in the darkness and she tightened her grip on his shirt. Ian groped for a light switch; a soft glow spilled around them. His

eyes were soft and sympathetic. She glanced over at the canvases in progress, dabs of paint in muted, soft colors.

"Your paintings are beautiful," she breathed.

"Thank you."

She gazed over at him. "I would paint you."

"Would you now?" she heard him say, but his voice was
drowned out by the words in her head tumbling out onto her
lips. "I would paint you at rest, sitting in a chair, dressed in
black. After it dried, I would scrape away pieces and add blue,
a cobalt blue, so it would catch the color of your eyes," she
said, weaving unsteadily toward the canvases. His hands gripped
her waist, holding her steady. She ran her fingers lightly over
his face, his beard, his lips. "Everyone would see you as I do . . .
beautiful."

She let her fingers rest on his lips and he kissed them. Sliding forward, she caught his lips with hers. "Dear Lizzie," he
whispered, shifting her from him and kissing her forehead. "I
think we've done all we need to do tonight."

Elizabeth drifted in and out of awareness. She was lying
down, in her clothes, her shoes off. Her head was on Ian's chest.
She mumbled something. She heard his voice; it sounded far
away: "Not to worry, love, not to worry."

At seven a.m. Elizabeth was slouched over a cup of coffee at
the breakfast bar when Ian came out of the bathroom. He
looked handsome and rumpled, last night's shirt and pants
deeply creased.

"Well, now you know how I look in the morning," she said,
the thumping in her head having receded to a steady ache at
her temples.

He sat down next to her. "Have you found your face?"

"I have and it's still attached," she said, glancing around at
the airy, open loft. She caught him regarding her with an
amused smile. "Do you want to tell me what happened, or
should I guess?"

"Nothing happened. I told you, Lizzie, you're quite safe
with me."

"Uh-hunh. Did I say anything I'm going to regret?"

Ian smiled pleasantly. "Not that I can recall. What shall we do for our next outing?"

Elizabeth nearly dribbled her coffee in surprise. "There won't be one. Every time I'm around you, I end up broken."

"Only a little, and you're very pretty when you are."

She could feel the heat in her cheeks. She sipped her coffee in silence. At least she hadn't done anything foolish, although watching Ian move about the loft kitchen, she wasn't as relieved as she thought she would be.

Chapter 10

Robert woke to the familiar sounds of deep melodious chanting coming from the CD player.

When he emerged from the bedroom, he was met with a haze of incense smoke. He went down the hall and found Karen sitting at the kitchen table, sipping her coffee. He kissed her forehead, breathing in the apple scent of her hair. She was dressed in her signature jeans and T-shirt; a Saks Fifth Avenue bag sat on the table.

"You're bringing gifts to a divorce hearing? For the attorneys?"

"No, for their secretaries. I see them so often, it would be rude not to." She stood up and gave him a kiss, slinging the overstuffed bag over her shoulder. "I'll be done by eleven."

Entering the conference room, Karen found a familiar sight, a trio of men huddled around the oak table, poring over reams of legal documents. She knew them all: Albert—short, balding, perpetually perspiring; Eugene—tall, wire-rimmed glasses hiding his watery blue eyes; Kevin—the middleweight, thick and combative. They gave her a glance and a collective "Hi, Karen" when she entered, then returned to the huddle.

Edward Townsend stood at the window, sipping his tea, and looking like he had nothing more on his mind than admiring the New York City skyline. Karen studied him for a moment.

The years hadn't altered his frame, he seemed as sturdy as in his pictures as a young man. His skin still had that ruddy, healthy tone, his thick dark mane only slightly disturbed by strands of silver. Whenever she thought of him, she pictured him in a tuxedo, a white scarf around his neck; the columnist, the novelist, the proverbial man about town. Karen thought he had even more of a presence now than at any other time in his life.

"Hi, Daddy," she said.

Turning, he held out his hand to her. She went to him and he folded her into an embrace. Looking down at her, his onyx eyes were soft. "Hello, princess. You're very sweet to come. You didn't need to."

"You shouldn't go through this alone."

They stood, holding hands in silence, her head resting on her father's chest. She looked up briefly. Karen always found her father kind and encouraging, whether on trips to Positano, Paris, or during surprise visits at college. In the past, he never allowed her to witness his anger at her mother. Karen could read about it in the gossip columns, watch it on television, or overhear talk about it on the subway, but her parents had never let her be a direct witness. Karen didn't try to follow the logic. Years of lawyers and lawsuits, accusations and retributions, private investigators, and changed locks. Her mind reeled thinking about the Benz her father lost in the settlement. When it came time to turn over the car or its resale value, he sold it for five dollars, framed the bill, and sent it to her mother by messenger.

Karen shook off her thoughts. "Daddy, this is your fifth divorce," she said with a heavy sigh.

"Including your mother?"

"Yes."

"Is that right? I thought it was six," he said with a sigh of his own. "I should keep better count."

Footsteps and voices approached the doors. Albert rushed to Karen and Edward, prodding them to the table. "Get out of the corner, Ed," Albert croaked, sweat forming on his upper lip. "It makes you look desperate."

The doors swung open. Flanked by clones of Edward's lawyers, the fifth Mrs. Edward Townsend swept in, every platinum blond hair in place, diamonds glittering in her ears and at her throat. While Karen hadn't spent much time with her, she did know Laurette had a pervasive and hideous attachment to fur, including varieties of small dogs resembling oversized, hirsute rats. She wore a white pantsuit with long, fuzzy fringe; specks of white littered the carpet in her wake. Karen had never seen a grown woman shed.

She squeezed Edward's hand as Albert recited her father's offer of settlement. A round of arguments ensued over the summer house, the New York apartment, the car and driver, and the monthly allowance for maintenance of the rat-like canines.

"I don't see why I shouldn't have all of the property," Laurette said.

As she chattered on, Edward let go of Karen's hand to scribble on a sheet of the firm's letterhead and push it over to Albert. Albert ground his teeth and his complexion deepened into an alarming shade of plum.

"After all, he's never there. He's too busy with his—"

"Laurette," Edward interrupted. "Consider this."

Albert slid the paper under Laurette's nose. She read it once, then again. Her attorneys leaned in from each side, whispering into Laurette's ears.

"That should be enough for the dogs," Edward said.

"We accept," Laurette's lawyers said in unison.

Laurette gave Karen a long look as Albert made the summation. "In exchange for receiving the Lexington Avenue property and the monthly allowance, no details related to this marriage, including the material reason or events leading to the dissolution of the marriage, may be divulged. If such information is found to have been divulged, this agreement will be null and void."

Albert mopped his brow with a handkerchief.

* * *

At one end of the table, Edward's legal eagles gathered their volumes of papers. At the other end Karen sat next to Edward, who leaned back comfortably, one leg crossed over the other.

"Your mother and I made our final settlement in this room," he said in what Karen thought might be a regretful tone. "What a woman." He chuckled. "She never appreciated my contributions to our partnership, personal or professional. And she stole all my best lines."

Although he was smiling, Karen could see his eyes turning inky-black.

"She stole the brownstone too, Ed," Albert said, heading for the door. "You never should have given her the brownstone."

"Albert's never forgiven me for losing the brownstone."

"Which side? It was divided down the middle with tape, remember? That was the summer Mommy took me to Paris."

"Oh yes. She cut the power on my side of the house. It took two weeks to get it repaired."

"And mother came back to find her entire wardrobe mysteriously gone."

He chuckled. "I hope the electrician's wife enjoyed her closetful of Prada."

"You can't keep fighting with Mommy and you can't keep getting married. Daddy, why do you do this? Maryanne, Jessica, Amber . . ."

Edward gave her a sheepish look. "I forgot about Amber. I admit that was awful, but you know they are all a psychological manifestation of your mother's refusal to recognize my worth."

Slipping her hand into his, she gave a strong squeeze. "Daddy, you and Mommy write fiction, not psychology."

"Sweetheart, it's the same thing. What would Buddha say about all this?"

"I'm not a Buddhist, but he would say desire is the root of all suffering."

Edward sat back, pondering her words. "Quite right. Well, life is about change, Karen."

They sat in silence and Karen knew she had to tell him and it had to be now. She took a deep breath.

"Daddy, I'm getting married."

Edward sat up. "Good Lord, Karen, you've always been so sensible."

"He wants—we—want a wedding."

"Ah," Edward said, stroking her hand. "Beware a romantic man. They're always trouble. I should know."

Karen leaned forward. "I want you and mother to be at the wedding."

Edward frowned at her. "You haven't told your mother, have you? She's going to be very unhappy about this, Karen. She guards your trust fund like Fort Knox."

"I won't receive it until I'm forty."

"And you are nowhere near jaded enough. It's all that spiritual training. We should never have allowed you to go to Malaysia. Or was it Tibet?"

"Both. Daddy, you must understand why I want this. *You* keep getting married."

"And shouldn't someone have stopped me?"

Karen didn't answer.

"As I said, life is about change." He kissed her forehead. "I'm so proud of you, telling me first. It shows you're beautiful *and* intelligent. Always start with the weakest link. But you need to tell her as soon as possible."

"Daddy, why do you always put a clause in your settlement documents that the reason for your divorce can never be revealed?"

Edward squeezed her hand. "To keep the information from being published, of course. You know I detest public displays."

Karen smiled and did a mental eye roll. Ask a question, get an absurd answer. *I won't allow fear or anxiety to get the better of me. I'll follow my instincts and tell mother. Everything will be fine.*

Chapter 11

Elizabeth sat across from Nick at a small secluded table; the lovers' table. Nick appeared tired, worn down from eighteen-hour days sequestered in a data room at his firm, working on Parker's latest hostile takeover. A late-night dinner was all the time they could steal before he returned to the office. Elizabeth found herself stifling the urge to yawn.

"C'mon," he said, holding up a forkful of her lobster ravioli. "I have to keep you fed. I'm responsible for you."

She opened her mouth. He waited, then leaned over to take a kiss, and she was instantly flooded with thoughts of Ian—the strength of his arms around her, his scent. A pang of guilt shot through her. Nothing happened, she reminded herself. Nothing. Strictly platonic.

They ate in silence for a few minutes, Elizabeth bracing herself for the customary quiz that made their relationship a natural extension of their work. Tonight she felt unusually impatient. She didn't want to talk about it.

"I heard that Adam is moving on. What's your next move?"

Elizabeth grimaced. She had succeeded in creating a leaner operation. But she hadn't banked on a second star consultant moving on to other opportunities. It was a blow she hadn't expected. "We're still on target with our quotas."

"But—"

Elizabeth nodded. "The revenue growth plan is going to be fine, Nick."

Nick laughed. "You just showed you're a novice, kid. Nothing is ever fine. What about Ken Mitkey?"

Elizabeth felt her temper flare. "Mitkey is just ducky. His blood pressure is normal and I think he had steak for dinner last night. I don't care what Kenneth Mitkey's doing."

"If you want to come out on top, you damn well need to care, Liz. Mitkey is your competition. Always has been, always will be. He was passed over for your job, and he wanted it. You need to have one eye on what you're doing and one eye on what he's doing, because you bet your ass that's what he's doing."

Elizabeth shook her head. "He's busy with the investment banking side."

Nick took her hand. "Liz, I worry about you. You're not one-on-one with clients anymore. You're the linebacker facing the front four, head on."

"I know. But it's very possible I may know how to do this. Mitkey is scrambling. There's talk of a restructuring; Saunders may have already started a work group to discuss it."

Nick laughed. "I stand corrected; if Saunders has done that, Mitkey's screwed. Those are nothing more than bitch sessions looking for ways to take a guy out. Listen, be specific when you talk to Saunders; never be vague with the boss. He needs to know where you're coming from. Remember, kid, he could invite you out to a nice dinner like this on a Tuesday and fire you on Wednesday. Way it goes, babe. It's a zero sum game, remember that."

Suddenly anxiety gripped her; a common occurrence these days. She knew Nick cared for her and this was his way of showing it, like a husband who says I love you to his wife by building her a new set of kitchen cabinets. He needed to feel he was helping her, solving her problems. But he wasn't, he was making her more nervous and she felt that no matter where she was, she never left the office.

"Now, isn't it time we get to the most important point—us. I'm sorry we haven't had any time lately. What have you been up to?"

She experienced another momentary guilty flashback about the night at Ian's loft but immediately pushed it away. "I have to admit my indiscretion," she said, avoiding his eyes. "I've been spending time with Kenneth Mitkey."

He laughed and leaned over, giving her a kiss. "I'm pushing to wrap up this takeover by Labor Day. I have something special planned for the holiday."

"I look forward to it," she heard herself say, knowing there was a kernel of truth in there. He was steady, dependable, solid. He was the man she'd been searching for her whole life. She focused all her attention on him, giving him a smile. *He is the right one.*

Chapter 12

The next morning Elizabeth slowed her run to a walk, making her customary stop at Dunkin' Donuts near Greeley Square. She picked up a bottle of water, lamenting it wasn't coffee. She came out and ran straight into Ian.

He looked slightly tousled, a blue tee over jeans. *Breathe*, she ordered herself, *you run the show*.

He held up a white bag. "Good morning, love. Can I interest you in breakfast?"

"I just exercised."

"Then you need to keep your strength up."

In spite of herself, she smiled.

They sat at a table near the back of the square that served as an oasis, the miniature forest of trees encroaching around them, a protective barrier against the building traffic outside. The pace of the morning was slowly rising. It would reach a crescendo in another hour. They spent a few moments in comfortable silence, quietly munching on croissants and sipping coffee.

"It's been a while since I experienced the European breakfast," she said, picking out slices of ham and cheese from the waxy paper wrapping.

"When were you there?" he asked.

"I went to Paris when I was seventeen." She concealed her

fondness for the memory: three girls sharing an apartment, suitors calling up from the street late at night, everyone's apartment windows open with shades up, revealing other young girls clad in their slips, readying for an evening out. It was an exquisite chaos of cafés and museums, and meals of bread, cheese, and wine that were more than enough; just as Hemingway described it. ,

"And did you find it as Hemingway said, a moveable feast?"

She started as Ian seemed to be reading her mind again, and sidestepped the question. "When did you first go to live in Paris?"

"In my late twenties."

She nodded. *What if we had been there at the same time? What if we had met then? We weren't, we didn't,* she thought, shrugging it away. "Did you see the *Mona Lisa?*"

"Of course. Do you know why she's smiling?"

"She's in Paris."

"Are you always out so early, in Greeley Square, near the Dunkin' Donuts, where you *didn't* buy all this food?" Elizabeth asked.

Ian smiled. "Early lesson."

Elizabeth smirked. "Ah . . . private lessons, how quaint. How early, last night?"

Ian laughed. "My student is seven."

Elizabeth grimaced. She felt foolish; now she looked foolish as well.

"Her parents are determined that she properly learn Impressionist painting techniques. She rather likes making a mess with paint."

Now it was Elizabeth's turn to laugh. She found his eyes on her, studying her intently, and she glanced away, feeling a rush of warmth flowing through her. She shifted the subject, hoping to quell the rising tide of her feelings. "Did you ever study other forms of painting?"

"There are no other forms of painting."

"I beg to differ. Modern, cubist . . ."

Ian shook his head. "Absolutely awful. I hope there are no

traditional artists in your family. They'll be upset by your betrayal."

Elizabeth thought of her mother, caught in her downward spiral, a cyclone of alcohol, pills, and lovers, unable to complete her work, crying to her daughter to finish it for her. How could she refuse to help her mother? When she was done, she expected her mother to be grateful, only to suffer abuse and accusations of how she enjoyed humiliating her. She almost winced at the memory of Lillian in the studio, entertaining her friends, downing her wine, saying she always knew her daughter would surpass her and how she would teach her daughter what it was to suffer for her art.

She thought of her tattered paintings on the floor of the studio; her eyes began to sting. *She betrayed me,* Elizabeth thought as William's face flashed in and out her mind. *I had nowhere else to turn.*

"Lizzie," she heard Ian say.

"You can't always please someone else at your own expense," she said shortly, tossing down the croissant. She had lost her appetite.

Her watch slipped down toward her wrist but even with the watch face turned away from her, she knew the hour was late. He encircled his fingers around it, gently sliding it back up her arm, his warm hand lingering against her skin.

"I have to go," she said.

"Do you now?" he said, brushing a stray strand of hair back from her cheek and tucking it behind her ear, tracing his finger over the frame of her earlobe. He was leaning close to her. He smelled warm and she knew he would taste like coffee. *Just once.* She snapped herself back. *No.*

She got up, brushing stray crumbs away.

"Thank you for breakfast."

"Perhaps we'll meet again some time."

"Perhaps." She gave him a long look. There was a gate, a door to her past and a mounting weight on her to try to keep it closed. Somehow he was the key. If she got any closer to him, he would be able to open that door, revealing a ruined and bloody past of rolling California waves and her mother's bleeding wrists, men who came and went with the tides, and selfish artist lovers who said they loved you but never stayed to prove it. Her mother's nature was in her; her mother's weakness; she knew that. Gazing at him, the smooth skin, the careless blond hair, the blue eyes that changed without warning, running hot and cold, she knew she was in danger of him bringing that out in her. The way it had almost come out before.

"I'm sure in a city of eight million people we're bound to meet again, by accident of course."

He leaned in, kissing one cheek and then the other. "Until then," he said softly.

With a pounding heart, she walked away, steeling herself not to look back.

Chapter 13

On a bright, sunny Saturday morning Elizabeth and Karen got off the subway at Lexington and Eighty-sixth and strolled toward Park Avenue. They each had a Starbucks coffee cup and Elizabeth had an oversized double-chocolate cookie.

"Thanks for coming," Karen said. "I know she loves me, but I just can't face telling her alone."

"She'd do anything for you, Karen. I've never seen her refuse you."

"Only because I've never asked for anything she would consider unacceptable." They strolled in silence for a moment. "We've never been at odds. She may be my mother but she's also the woman who burned my father's priceless collection of first editions in place of logs in the solarium fireplace."

Elizabeth raised her eyebrows. "That was about your father, not you. By the way, how's Larry, the unfortunate thespian?"

"Back among the living," Karen said. "And we finally found our Hickey character. His name is Alfred. His last role was playing Jesus in *Godspell*. He's been a source of great comfort to Larry."

"Maybe he thinks if you kill him off again, Alfred will be able to raise him up," Elizabeth said.

Karen chuckled.

Elizabeth held out the cookie; Karen broke off a piece.

"S-o-o-o—anything new since you passed out in Ian's apartment?" Karen asked.

Elizabeth gave her a sharp look. Karen waited patiently.

"I've seen him. We keep meeting. Serendipitously, of course. I should just let Emily download my daily schedule from my BlackBerry and give it to him."

"And yet, you never turn him away," Karen said.

Elizabeth struggled for words. "He's just so . . . annoying," she finally blurted out.

"That's a good reason to continue to talk to someone."

"I always think I know myself, until I see him. He's always so calm, nothing bothers him. It's maddening."

"He's at peace, that's a basic Taoist principle. I'm impressed."

"His peacefulness is driving me crazy."

"That's because attraction, which is what you have, is not a Taoist principle."

Elizabeth gave her a sideways glance. "He thinks he has control. And he's wrong. I'm in complete control. He doesn't have the upper hand."

Karen gave a blank look in response.

"Oh, come on, Karen. You're the offspring of a thirty-year power struggle."

"That doesn't mean I want to live like that. Robert and I don't have a power structure."

"Trust me, you don't have a choice. There is one. Since you don't know about it, Robert has the edge. Ian thinks he has the upper hand. I can't let him win."

"We're talking about attraction and connection, not a pissing contest."

Elizabeth didn't answer.

"It could just be the accent."

Elizabeth shrugged. "Possibly. It is charming, and he's always a perfect gentleman."

Karen choked on the cookie. "Really . . . why?"

"It's a European thing. They're so formal. The next time

we 'meet,' I'll tell him I can't stay. Then he'll know that I have the upper hand and it'll be over."

"And you're sure you can do that?"

Elizabeth handed her the rest of the cookie. "Absolutely. I will not be outmaneuvered."

They reached Karen's mother's building; the doorman held the door and they squinted, adjusting to the gloom of the lobby. They stood in silence at the elevator until the chiming of the bell sounded and the doors opened.

"What would the Tao say about this meeting?" Elizabeth asked.

"The secret to the path is to be still. Then you'll know when to act and when to yield. Then the only true path will present itself. It's time to act. It's the right time to tell her."

Elizabeth nodded. "Well, here's a practical word of wisdom. Remember she'd do anything for you, even believe there really is one man in this world who is worthy of you. But if this flops and becomes a disaster, you'll have to guilt her."

Karen smiled as the elevator doors opened and they stepped inside.

When they stepped out, a dour looking woman in uniform was holding the door open.

"What happened to the last one?" Elizabeth whispered.

"She only lasted two months," Karen answered.

Suitcases littered the receiving room. They passed through the living room, Karen's favorite spot in the apartment. Each piece of Art Nouveau furniture was placed carefully, giving the room a calm, orderly feel. Passing the Gallé cabinet, Karen ran her fingers over it, tracing the carved floral design as she had when she was a child. Her mother's voice cut through her reverie.

"Mary, for God's sake, are you slaughtering the pig? Am I expected to starve?"

"It can be comforting to know in a world of change some things are constant," Elizabeth said, heading for the kitchen.

* * *

Karen inched open the bedroom door, peeking inside.

Sitting up in bed, Margaret wore Bulgari Lucea white-gold pendant earrings and an elegant, gray La Perla bed jacket and gown; her flawless complexion glowed, her auburn hair sculpted in thick waves.

"Mon petit cadeau," she gushed, thrusting her arms out toward Karen. She fingered Karen's shoulder-length hair, sweeping her hands across her forehead. "What are we to do about this peasant look? These bangs hide the devastating pools that are your eyes." She sighed. "Although, I must say, you do wear it beautifully."

"How was the tour, Mom?" Karen asked.

"The whirlwind never ceases. Louis continues to pester about the next novel. He simply does not understand, words do not appear out of thin air. Books are not composed by divine inspiration, but by work. For an editor, he can be such a child."

"Mom, Louis is forty."

"That's practically pubescent, my angel."

Margaret indicated the newspaper lying open on the bed, a picture of Parker and Emily on Page Six. "Miss Emily has learned a hard lesson about dabbling in the culinary arts. She'll feel much better after the divorce."

"Mom, she's not getting a divorce. She's redoing the town-house."

"That may work just as well."

Karen arranged herself on the bed, leaning on one elbow as Margaret picked through the pile of invitations and letters littering the pristine white silk coverlet.

"Now," Margaret began, "I have given some of your work to Henry. You haven't met him yet. He is a brilliant producer and you are a brilliant playwright. He's in love with you already."

"How does he know I'm his type?"

Margaret laughed. "Excellent, sharp as a tack. Good for you. Now—"

"Mom," Karen broke in.

Margaret swept out of bed without waiting for her to continue, disappearing behind a white satin changing screen. The jacket sailed up into the air, followed by her gown, both landing draped over the screen. "You are the next Simon, Williams, Stoppard of Broadway. Your work must be seen. I won't allow you to languish in summer stock with some . . . farmer."

"Robert's from Long Island."

"It's the same thing. With Henry you will not be putting on a show in the barn. Cows may provide a service to humanity but they cannot understand dramatic irony."

"I'm marrying the farmer, Mom."

Margaret emerged from behind the screen, wearing a dazzling white and cream Ralph Lauren ensemble, and a look of astonishment.

Karen sucked in a mouthful of air. "We're engaged. We've set a date. We're getting married next June."

Margaret stroked Karen's hair and grasped her hands in her own. "You know he will only disappoint you," she said, her eyes misting.

"I don't set expectations, Mom."

"Excellent, my darling. He can't meet them anyway. Oh, Karen, after everything . . ." She sighed. "Your father's been recycling material I wrote during our marriage and using it in his books. The lawsuit has already been filed. You are looking at your future. This, my darling, is what you will have to deal with. Wouldn't you prefer taking a nice trip instead? Someplace exotic. Everyone is going to Thailand these days."

"You've sent me there already."

"Have I?"

"Twice."

"Karen, I don't want you to experience your partner as a lesser man in almost every sense of the word. You cannot waste yourself. I cannot allow this."

"Mommy, I love him."

Sinking down on the bed next to her, Margaret brushed the hair out of her eyes. "Well," she said, "life is about change."

"That's what Daddy said."

"You've seen your father? Good. All daughters should spend time with their fathers, indulging them in the myth that man is invincible. That is a daughter's greatest gift." She paused, looking thoughtful. "He still owes me a Prada wardrobe."

"We discussed that. Mommy, what do you mean, you won't allow this?"

"Miss Elizabeth!" Margaret sang out, ignoring Karen's question. "I see you lingering there."

Elizabeth appeared in the doorway. "I was just visiting my old room."

"I provided room, board, nutritional and emotional sustenance during your time of crisis, and this is how I'm to be repaid? I leave my girl in your care and come back to find her affianced to a Clampett. What have you to say for yourself, young lady?"

"I missed a meeting?"

Margaret narrowed her eyes at Elizabeth. "And who have you been spending your time with?"

"An Impressionist-style painter who should be drinking absinthe in Montmartre," Karen piped up.

"Interesting choice, considering your history. Anyone else?"

"A lawyer."

Margaret stood up. "It's so refreshing when a profession explains the man."

"Mommy," Karen broke in, "what do you mean, you won't allow this?"

Margaret chucked Karen under her chin. "My buttercup, you know your father and I disagree on—everything, except marriage. You know we've made it our mission—our raison d'être, if you will—to do what we can, in our own humble way, to prevent these tragedies."

"Mommy, you can't object at my wedding."

Margaret raised her eyebrow at Karen. "I ask you, my nutmeg, what greater act of love can a parent bestow than to save their child from imminent destruction?"

Karen felt herself shrinking, her body curling into a fetal curve. "By objecting at my wedding?"

Margaret patted Karen's knee. "Muffin top, someone must stop the madness."

"But . . . but you won't need to object. You'll like Robert."

"Oh, that's irrelevant, darling."

Karen stared at Elizabeth. "My parents are going to object at my wedding."

"I heard."

Karen grabbed her mother's hand. "I want to get married."

Margaret sighed. "I know, my sweet. It's all that spiritual training. We should never have encouraged you." She swept to the bedroom door, stopping before Elizabeth. "By the way, do you love the painter, Miss Elizabeth?"

"Absolutely not," Elizabeth answered.

Margaret raised her eyebrow in response and kept walking.

"You didn't ask if I loved the lawyer," Elizabeth said.

Margaret laughed. "Of course not, dear, why would I?"

Karen lay back on the bed and Elizabeth flopped down next to her, listening to Margaret's booming voice fill the apartment.

"Mary, you wretched woman, you're getting your wish. We are going out to eat! Come along, my little buttercups! These are deep waters we are to traverse today!"

Karen lay staring up at the ceiling and sucked in a deep breath.

"So this is the part where you yield?"

"Did I have a choice?"

"What now? You just relax and do nothing and it all works out right, that's the Taoist way?"

Karen turned to stare at her. "Taoism never met my mother."

"True," Elizabeth said, "very true."

Chapter 14

Emily's chatter strained Ian's concentration down to the last synapse. It's just a bloody portrait, he told himself. I've done hundreds, thousands. Not that he wanted to do this one. But Karen had barely given name, rank, and serial number about Lizzie. Now he was stuck trying to paint and process Emily's babble in order to find an opening. He felt like he was trying to catch a runaway train.

"Try to sit up, love, and keep still."

Emily rearranged herself, fidgeting like a child bursting at the seams to get up. "Parker doesn't understand," she said, sounding like a petulant child whose toy was taken away. "I was trying to do something exotic and different."

"I know, darling," Ian mumbled.

"Now he wants to sell this place. I can't understand why he doesn't love this apartment. Don't you love it?"

Ian glanced around at the townhouse, now in disarray. Interior designers, workmen and painters had created an organized chaos with ladders, scaffolds and equipment. He noticed his canvas leaning up against the wall. *Shit*, he thought, spying the row of marble pillars lined up inside the great room. *The apartment is going from modern to Louis the Fourteenth. Leave it to Emily to bring Versailles to downtown Manhattan.*

It brought back memories of the Paris apartment where he met Michele; the balcony doors open to reveal a view of la

Tour Eiffel. Robert had talked his way round to an invite for them. There were two kinds of people at the party: the real aristocracy, like the owner—Michele's "friend," a collector; and people like Michele, friends of friends. They traveled to Monaco and Belize and other places where they ate, drank, and shopped, but never paid, and they certainly never worked. When he first saw Michele, her bright blue eyes sparkling under the fan of dark eyelashes, he couldn't speak. When she saw the look on his face, she laughed. *I was blind to what she was from the beginning,* he thought. At some point he should have seen, he should have known.

Ian snapped his attention back to Emily. It was time to find out what he wanted to know. *First let's find out how the Sun King is doing.*

"How is Parker finding life these days?"

"Did you see the latest interview?" Getting up, Emily snatched the *Wall Street Journal* from the table and held it out to Ian, ignoring his stern look.

"Parker has been elected to the board of another company. He compares the CEO to a leech, you know, sucking off the profits. That's how he does it, you know, targeted destruction. He's pushing to take over no later than Labor Day. He and Nick are at it from sunup to sundown, but he says they'll need to work through the holiday weekend to close the deal. My husband is a busy boy."

Parker has no time plus Nick has no time equals Elizabeth with time on her hands.

"It must be hard for you, love, to be away from him. Isn't Nick a friend of Lizzie's?"

"More than a friend. I think they'll be getting engaged soon."

Shit, Ian thought. "Then she must miss him, of course. Doesn't seem like her kind of chap, does he?"

Emily frowned, shifting in her seat. "Why do you say that? I introduced them. They're perfect for each other, although he is a little older, about ten years. But he needs a wife like Liz, young, beautiful, successful, someone he can dote on."

Ian fidgeted, trying to concentrate on the canvas. "Yes, of course, she's all of those things. How long has she been in New York?"

Emily glanced around, appearing bored. "About fifteen years. It took her a while to get used to the city. It was a huge change for her, leaving California, going to NYU, going into finance. Especially after she grew up in the studio—"

They were interrupted by the slamming of the front door and a deep male voice calling Emily's name.

Emily bolted for the door and Ian threw his brush down in disgust. *Damn. What studio?* After a moment she returned, wrapped in the embrace of a tall, thirty-something man with Mediterranean coloring and delicate, boyish features. His dark hair was long and wild, and the pout he wore gave him a spoiled, petulant air. Ian knew the type.

"Sebastian, this is Ian MacKay. He is a brilliant artist, and I discovered him."

Sebastian examined him from head to toe. "What do you paint?"

"Whatever takes my fancy."

"He's doing my portrait, finally, and he did that." She pointed out the canvas leaning against the wall.

Sebastian sniffed as a response and she patted his chest. "Sebastian used to design for one of the top houses. He has his own label now. I'm helping him get ready for Fashion Week. His collection is *très* fab. I've been his muse for years."

Sebastian sniffed at the comment and gave Ian a look of disdain. "Your work is not important. My work is not important. It is all superficial crap."

"Quite right," Ian agreed pleasantly.

"Come, Emily, we must go now." Sebastian broke away, moving toward the door.

"All right, I'm coming. I don't know what's gotten into him," Emily said to Ian. "He's become such an enfant terrible. Now he even insults people who adore his collection."

"Because it is all crap," Sebastian shouted.

"I'm afraid I do have to go. The muse must give inspiration." She giggled like a school girl.

"I suppose my crap won't be part of the redecorating," Ian said, nodding toward his painting.

Emily wrapped her arms around him, flooding his senses with her heady perfume and his body with her warmth. She kissed his cheek. "I'm sorry," she murmured. "I really want to do something exotic, something Josef Hoffman. You know, the antiques, mixed with modern pieces, all works of art together. Versailles meets the twenty-first century."

"Lovely," he said, his tongue feeling thick in his mouth, making the words difficult to come out.

"I'm going to put your painting into storage, for the future."

"Yes, of course."

"Did you know Hoffman designed interiors for Wittgenstein's sister, Margaret?"

"I didn't know that, no," Ian said.

As Emily chattered on about antiques, Josef Hoffman, and decorating for sisters of twentieth century Austrian philosophers, Ian worked out his own schedule. Now that Nick would be occupied as Parker's nanny until the takeover was done, Elizabeth would be free for the Labor Day weekend.

Chapter 15

Elizabeth came out of the Dunkin' Donuts near Greeley Square. Her eyes traveled to the square, smiling at the memory of her encounter with Ian. Her heart skipped when she spotted him by the gate. She hesitated a moment, then made her way across the street to where he waited for her, smiling.

"Any plans for the weekend?" he asked.

"I haven't decided yet. You?"

"Possibly. It all depends."

"On what?"

Ian smiled.

Elizabeth looked away for a moment, watching the traffic. "I may go out to the Hamptons with Emily or maybe to the Island with Karen and Robert."

"I would very much like to take you out for the evening."

Elizabeth began to protest but he cut her off. "Don't give an answer now. I'll be waiting by the entrance to Parsons at six o'clock tonight. I hope you'll be there."

He leaned over and gave her a light kiss on the cheek. "Lovely to see you, Lizzie, as always."

He walked away and she stood there, reminding herself to breathe.

At seven p.m. Elizabeth and Ian were strolling the cramped, crowded streets of Chinatown, passing sidewalk shops filled with cheap feather boas, knockoff purses, perfumes, and novelty toys.

She'd walked to Parsons thinking, *There won't be any arrangement. I will not sleep with him.* But as soon as he gave her a light kiss on her lips as a greeting she knew things were already different. He was different. How he looked at her, the way he placed a proprietary hand on her back as they made their way through the crowds. When she felt Ian's fingers reach for hers, her heart skipped but she wasn't surprised. She let his hand linger, lightly touching.

They passed a storefront with twine stretched across the top, holding plastic pigs with paper wings.

"Pigs are finally flying," she said, and he laughed, the hard edges in his face melting away.

Stopping at a jewelry stand, a cheap necklace of black and silver caught her eye; she hovered over it until he pulled a few bills from his pocket. He fastened it around her neck and slid his hands over her shoulders; they felt warm and strong. *I will not sleep with him.*

When they turned onto Mulberry Street, the chaos and clutter melted into the peace and tranquility of Little Italy. They decided on al fresco dining. They ate in an awkward silence, acutely aware of each other. She tried to diffuse the feeling by focusing on the waiters pacing up and down the sidewalk, menus in hand, always ready to entice a passerby to stop. But she could sense Ian leaning back in his chair, his eyes on her, considering her. When she trusted herself to glance at him, the heat in his eyes seemed to warm her skin.

As they got up and walked away from the restaurant Elizabeth stopped and turned to him. "Well, thank you for dinner."

He smiled, snaking his arms around her waist and gently pulling her against him. The embrace was easy, familiar; there was no space between them. "Don't you want dessert?"

An anxious laugh escaped her. "I try to stay away from things that are bad for me."

Grasping her hands, he took a few steps backward, tugging at her to follow. "Come along now," he urged softly.

They walked off their dinner and Ian led her to Ferrara's bakery for dessert, where they sat at one of the many tables neatly lined in a row. Ian leaned back in his chair, watching her eat a small sampler of confections.

Elizabeth could feel the heat even in the air conditioning. She had to cool things down, slow the pace before it got out of control, before she lost control. *I will not sleep with him.*

"I have to ask," Elizabeth began, "have you ever considered giving up painting?"

Ian looked away.

Bull's-eye, she thought.

"Oh, I suppose," he said. "At one point."

"Why?"

"Crisis of creativity; all very dramatic."

"Obviously you recovered."

"Well, I would have to, wouldn't I? It's who I am."

"No," she snapped. "It's what you do."

They fell silent. She took her napkin, dabbed her mouth and folded the cloth, laying it back in her lap.

"I suppose that's true as well, Lizzie."

Suddenly restless, Elizabeth shifted in her seat. He had a maddening way of diffusing her ability to engage him. *I will not sleep with him.*

"How did you meet Karen? It's unusual for a business woman and a writer to mix, isn't it? Did you meet at an art class?"

He's doing it again, keeping the spotlight off himself. I thought all men love to talk about themselves. Nick can go on for hours. She focused and prepared her answer.

"We met on a beach. They don't have separate beaches for business majors and writers."

He smiled. "Do you like your work, Lizzie? I'd be happy to hear more about it but you never mention it."

Elizabeth took a long drink of water and looked across the table. She couldn't give him her usual line of "effecting real change in peoples lives." She wouldn't risk seeing the look in his eyes, the one that said he thought it was just bull.

"You'd be bored."

"I'm not sure that's true, but I'll take you at your word. As long as you're happy."

"Yes," she said after a long moment, "I'm happy." The exchange did nothing to quell her feelings. *I will not sleep with him.*

Giving her a long look, Ian raised a hand to catch the waiter's attention.

They found their way to the entrance of the subway and faced each other, standing close. The serenity of Little Italy had seeped into Elizabeth's bones.

"This is the part where I tell you I had a good time and then I go home."

Ian brushed a strand of hair from her face. "Is it now?"

And then his fingers slid through her hair. She closed her eyes, listening to the low grumbling of the subway as it grew into a tumult, reverberating below them until she felt her heart racing with the train.

"Is that what you want, Lizzie?"

Elizabeth opened her eyes and found her hands grasping lightly at the fabric of his shirt. She stopped, resting her palms against his chest. He was so close. She breathed deeply. *No, this is what I want. I want you.*

Entering the loft, he pulled her in with a gentle force. His mouth was on hers and she felt her stomach somersault as their tongues touched. Adjusting her eyes to the gloom, his face looked soft, even tender. A surge of desire rushed through her.

"Ian," she murmured.

Without a word, he kissed her, pulling her into his embrace, his arms tightening around her. Coiling herself around him, she grasped him tightly, letting herself go. Gently, he slid his hands over her, peeling away her dress, leaving her exposed. She moved to cross her arms, to hide herself, but he caught her hands, bringing one to his mouth, kissing her open palm, sending a surge of heat through her. He moved his lips over her neck and shoulders, leaving a sensation of warmth along her skin. Disentangling her hands, she began undoing the buttons of his shirt, tugging him close, breathing in his scent. She didn't want to think.

Ian rolled over and opened his eyes. She was gone, her scent lingering on the warm sheets. It was five a.m. Shaking a cigarette from the pack, he lit up and lay back, watching the swirls of smoke curl into the air. Michele's game was to leave before dawn. Lizzie isn't Michele, he reminded himself. He took stock of everything he had told her, and hadn't told her, the lies and half-truths about his marriage and his work. All he cared about now was that she wouldn't know how miserably he had failed. If he did this right, he would win her and everything else could be explained away.

FALL

Chapter 16

The phone rang, jarring Karen out of sleep. Reaching over, she found the other side of the bed empty. With a moan, she pulled herself over to Robert's side and grabbed the receiver.

"Hello?" she grumbled.

"I slept with Ian last night."

Karen's eyes flew open.

Robert appeared in the doorway.

"You slept with Ian last night?"

Robert turned on his heel and left.

"Yes, yes I did. Several times."

"Where are you now?"

"I'm dressed in proper executive attire, with my briefcase, about to get out of a cab in front of my office building, where I'm going to behave like the rational, sensible adult that I am. It was nothing and I have this under complete control."

Karen propped up the pillows against the headboard. "It was the accent, wasn't it?"

"I . . . I guess."

"So he wasn't that good and you're over it."

"No . . . no . . . he was good. Better than good . . . really good . . . really, really, good."

"But selfish, right, so you're well out of it."

"No . . . he was attentive . . . really, really, really, attentive."

"Wow," Karen said. "That good?"

Elizabeth's voice came over the line in a low whisper. "You have no idea."

Elizabeth's voice grew muffled as she spoke to the cabbie, then grew stronger again, this time against a backdrop of street noise. "Look, I let him—it, the whole thing, the summer, the heat, get the better of me. I let my emotions get the better of me. It was wrong. I know it was wrong. I mean—Nick—"

"Liz, don't do this. It happened. If it's not right with Nick, better you should know it now."

"No, no. I can't say it just happened. It just happened with William, and that didn't make it right. I had an irresponsible affair with my mother's boyfriend right under her nose. I was a rotten human being. Like I'm a rotten human being now. Damn it, I'm acting the way she would."

Karen sat up in bed. "Liz, listen to me. You were twenty. William was forty. And twenty is no match for forty. He knew better. And your mother was only too happy to see you go down in flames because of him. We're not talking about the past. We're in the present. Maybe what happened with Ian is good. What do you want to do now?"

"I want to think clearly. I want to go into my office and do my job and not have any second thoughts or any drama. I want to behave like a grown-up. That's what I want."

Karen held her breath and her tongue.

"I just needed to tell somebody. Please don't mention this to Emily, okay?"

"Of course not, you know I won't."

Karen hung up the phone, settling her head into the depression in Robert's pillow. He came back in, rummaging on the desk for papers and books, grabbing items and filling his knapsack.

"Liz—"

"I heard. I wish I hadn't."

Grabbing a shirt from the teetering pile of clean clothes on a chair in the corner, he leaned over and she turned up her face for a kiss.

"Robert, Ian's a good guy, isn't he?"

"Ian's a gentleman. If there's a problem, it won't be from him."

Karen shuddered at the prediction. Robert had said it, and he was never wrong.

He stopped in the doorway to blow her a kiss. "I'm done teaching at two today and then we can go over your rewrites. Try not to kill anyone off, okay, baby?"

Chapter 17

Elizabeth dropped her BlackBerry back in her purse and took a deep breath before heading into the building.

"Good morning, love."

She whirled to see Ian, his expression benign, but a glint of anger in his eyes.

She stood there, feeling as if they were frozen in time while the world revolved around them, people hustling past carrying cups of coffee, briefcases, appearing to talk to themselves with space-age cell phone equipment tucked into their ears.

"I—I have an early meeting. I don't normally . . . leave like that. I don't normally do anything like that," she said. The silence hung between them and she felt her emotions rising. *Is he going to let me continue to babble?*

"Quite all right."

"Are you giving a lesson in the area?" She could feel her nerve ends jangling beneath her skin. She concentrated on the passing pedestrians, welcome distractions from the censure in his eyes. When she finally glanced back at him, she found his eyes had softened.

"I just thought to see how you are."

Elizabeth stifled the urge to show her relief and pleasure at his statement. "I'm fine . . . fine."

They stood in silence.

"Well, Lizzie, would you care to spend an evening this week?"

"Doing what?"

"Whatever you like."

"I don't think I'm interested in any arrangement."

Ian smiled. "I'm open to discussion. What do you have in mind?"

Liz felt her mind come to a screeching halt. What *did* she have in mind? What happened to the vow she made only moments earlier. It vanished once she saw him in front of her. *Tell him to forget it. I don't want to.*

"Lizzie, why don't we just have dinner together?"

"And whatever may come after?"

"If that's what you want, yes. Is that all right?"

Here it is. My choice. Everything is my choice. With no misunderstandings, no promises . . . no heartbreak. Just his warmth, his touch. She wanted him to touch her again.

She considered him for another moment. *He will be my lover. My lover.*

"Yes," she said finally.

"Good," he said in a gentle voice.

Elizabeth rushed into her office, dropping her briefcase on a chair, still breathless from her encounter with Ian. When she spotted the roses bursting from the vase on her desk, she broke into a huge grin. Then she read the card and her smile faded. "'Hail the conquering hero. I've missed you, kid. Nick.'" Oh shit. She sank into her chair.

"Liz?"

Her assistant's voice snapped her back to reality; she looked up to find Debbie standing in front of her desk.

"Mr. Reynolds's office called with a message. The limo will pick you up at seven for the dinner celebration with Mr. and Mrs. Davis."

Elizabeth's heart sank to her stomach, her mind swirling. *What should I do? Call Ian? Call Nick? Call it off? With whom?*

"Thank you," she heard herself say.

After Debbie left, she sat down. *I can't call Ian. I can't do any of it.*

Chapter 18

When she got to the restaurant, Elizabeth stepped into the bar and spotted Nick and Parker down at the end. She exchanged a light kiss with Nick, feeling a surge of guilt. She settled in with a drink and entered the tide of the conversation. Out of the corner of her eye, she spied Kenneth Mitkey and nodded acknowledgment. He left his group and approached. Mitkey was in his early forties, tall, and trim, but still had a frat-boy face and eyes that never stopped darting around. *He and Parker would get along well,* she thought; *he was second only to Parker in running his mouth.*

"Liz, I think we're in a position to blow the doors off our budget this year, I really do. I've got something that looks really good. This one's going to put me over the top."

Liz caught Parker's smirk as he ordered another round.

"But I hear your group is struggling. Didn't another one of your guys leave?"

"Whoa, two in six months," Parker interjected. "Tough break, Liz."

I'm sure you're crying a river. When is this going to be over? she thought. "Our new client initiatives are showing excellent results. My teams are exceeding expectations."

"How do you think you'll do this year?" Mitkey asked.

"The numbers are still fluid," she said smoothly. "We'll have a clearer picture at the end of the month." *Also known as*

English for get lost, asshole, I'm not telling you anything. I don't work for you.

"Good answer," Nick murmured as he kissed her cheek.

Parker chuckled and raised a glass. "Well, what shall we toast to? How about my acquisition of yet another component of the universe."

And your increasing humility, Elizabeth thought as they all clicked glasses.

Emily rushed into the bar, breathless. "I'm so sorry I'm late."

Elizabeth watched Parker swell with pride as the male patrons ogled his beautiful wife. *Schmuck.*

The host waited patiently as everyone got up from their seats at the bar. Nick and Parker shook hands in turn with Mitkey.

"Keep in touch," Parker said, giving Mitkey a wink and a slap on the back.

Elizabeth sat at the table, crossing and uncrossing her legs, fighting the urge to bolt and run. She had spent the day struggling through competition reports, analysis reports, and client demographics. Every time she buckled down to concentrate, the thought of Ian, his strong, lean body on hers, his gentle whisperings in her ear, the deep kisses as he rocked her in his embrace, made her face flush as her body temperature soared. Her concentration fled and she would have to begin all over again.

Stanton and Deirdre Perry stopped at the table. Deirdre, draped in a dramatic Badgley Mischka black lace sheath cocktail dress, her luxurious platinum blond hair cascading to the middle of her back, was her usual picture of perfection. Emily turned away as Parker jumped up to give Deirdre a kiss on the cheek.

The group made small talk and Emily gestured toward Elizabeth and Nick with pride. "When Liz came to New York I made it my mission to introduce her into proper society, and find her that special someone."

The comment grated like nails on a chalkboard. After all these years, Elizabeth had grown weary of Emily's subtle caste system, ensuring her place on the outside looking in.

". . . and I finally introduced her to the right person," Emily finished.

Nick draped his arm around Elizabeth's shoulder.

"Will you be at the tents for the shows?" Deirdre asked, ignoring Liz.

Emily smiled. *"Oui. Je suis la muse pour Sebastian Roderick.* He says he is the only designer who can dress me. He's working on a fabulous new collection—"

"My wife is very busy with her charity work right now," Parker cut in. "Handling the Davis Foundation is a full-time job."

Perry smiled. "Handling Davis himself is a large job as well, I imagine."

They all shared a polite chuckle. "Emily does a great job, as long as I keep her out of the kitchen," Parker said, fixing her with a warning look.

Emily's cheeks colored.

"Sorry about this circus," Nick whispered to Elizabeth, his concern only heightening her pangs of guilt about Ian. "I know you're tired." Avoiding his eyes, she gave a little shrug.

"The collection is showing in a few weeks at La Belle," Emily was saying to Deidre. "I'll have an invitation sent by messenger. This is my pet project—"

"I don't mind Emily's pet projects as long as I don't get sued because of food poisoning," Parker said. "I'm happy that she's concentrating on clothes. At least that's safe." He gave Emily a black look. "So Nick," he continued, "explain to our friend Stanton how to properly take over a company."

Nick laughed. "I don't think Stanton needs a primer."

As talk of the takeover began to dominate the table, Elizabeth caught Emily staring at Parker, a stunned look in her eyes, as if at that moment she had just seen him for the first time. *I'd like to be a fly on the wall when you two go home tonight.*

* * *

Two hours later, the group stood up to leave. Parker leaned over to Elizabeth. "Listen, cookie, I'm sorry to have taken Nick away from you these past weeks. I know he had big plans for the holiday." He flashed her an evil grin. "So . . . just between us, how are things at the office?"

Elizabeth met his Cheshire grin with a smooth smile. *Prick.* "Just fine."

"Great, great. That's something about Kenny's new project," Parker said.

"Fabulous," Elizabeth said.

Parker smiled. "He's hungry, you know?"

"Bully for him," Elizabeth snapped.

"All I'm saying is you don't want to get left behind, Liz. I hope your group is as revved up as you say. Look, if you need any advice, if there's anything I can do to help—"

"Right."

Chuckling, he squeezed her shoulder. "Still turning me down, hunh? Okay."

Liz blew off his comment, suddenly realizing she was tired. Tired of Parker's bullshit, tired of thinking, tired of the job. She had a sudden urge to walk out of the restaurant and leave it all behind. The thought scared her. What would she do? Paint? Even if she could, would she remember how? She refocused. *Get a grip. I was a painter. I'm not anymore.*

"I just don't understand why you had to bring it up," Emily said, trailing after Parker through the apartment.

"Babe, you did, in fact, make a lot of people sick, including myself."

"The fish was tainted, that was not my fault. I said I was sorry. Why did you have to bring it up?"

"Okay . . . okay," Parker said, rolling his eyes. "I will never again mention that you nearly killed off half of the New York financial sector."

"I should have kept that business going."

"Why? Do you want to bankrupt me? Do you know how much I had to pay to make that go away? No more cooking, or whatever the hell you were doing. From now on, just order off a menu, okay?"

Emily's lips puffed out in a pout.

"You are so sexy when you do that," Parker said, giving her a quick, hard kiss.

She forced herself to relax under Parker's kiss while stifling a sudden urge to cry. Lately, she always felt like crying when she talked to him. Actually, what she really wanted to do was raise her voice, yell at him, sometimes even scream. She felt uncertain and angry and she didn't know where it was coming from; pushing it down, she swallowed the feeling. Nothing had ever gone wrong before she married. All of her projects had been a huge success. She had been lauded as a brilliant entrepreneur, and now a fashion show was sending her into hysteria. She found herself dogged by a pervading sense of dread as the same question swirled in her head. *What if something goes wrong?*

Chapter 19

Nick followed Elizabeth into her apartment. He came up behind her, wrapping his arms around her, reaching in for a kiss. She smiled but her body wouldn't cooperate and he let go.

"You're awfully quiet," he said. "You have been all night."

"Was I? I hadn't noticed. Just thinking."

He tried again; his hands slid over her upper arms and he nudged her gently to turn.

"Thank you for seeing me inside."

He answered her statement with a kiss. "I can send the driver home for the night. Have him come back in the morning."

Elizabeth disengaged, avoiding his eyes.

"So, you've been thinking," he said. "Thinking can be good, depending on what you're thinking about."

She stepped away, retreating farther into the apartment.

"I know you've got a lot going on and I know we got off the track. I was hoping to get back on track. Now I'm thinking I missed a memo. Is it just business or is something else going on?"

She looked into his face, knowing she was staring at her possible future.

Nick moved closer. "Hey, I lost you again."

"It's nothing."

Nick gave her a tight smile. "So, what did you do over the holiday?"

"Spent time with friends."

She caught the expression on his face, the quick frown and small "mmm."

"You have nothing in common with Karen and her crowd now. You need new friends, kid, you know that."

"You're right. And you're right about work. I really need to concentrate on my work now. It's a critical time. I've lost some key people."

"I would never interfere with your work, kid. Would I interfere with something else?"

Elizabeth felt herself swallow; it hurt.

"Aren't you at least going to tell me who the competition is?"

Elizabeth watched as his gaze caught the watercolor beach scene hanging on the wall.

Nick gave a disgusted laugh. "You've got to be kidding. The painter?"

She opened her mouth to speak but nothing came out. Unable to defend herself, she watched Nick's face darken.

"Liz."

She shrugged. "He's just an acquaintance, barely a friend."

"Aren't we still friends—more than friends?" he asked.

She wanted to close her eyes, shut him out, shut everything out. *This is going as badly as I imagined.* "Yes, of course we are. I just don't want to hurt you."

Nick ran his hands through his hair, his jaw tensed. "Jesus Christ, Liz. What's going on? We want the same things. What line did he give you?"

"If I spend time with him, it's not right to spend time with you. It isn't fair to you."

Nick took her by the shoulders. "You're right. It's not. I think this new job is too much pressure for you, kid. Maybe you weren't ready. You're not thinking straight anymore. You know you're important to me and you have to let me counteroffer. I don't want to let you go without a fight."

Elizabeth didn't know what to say. She wasn't used to affairs of the heart being so cool, so civilized. Like an agreement one hammers down to the last detail, she thought. *Will I need to sign on the dotted line?*

He slipped his arm around her. "Have dinner with me tomorrow."

"I'm working on the revenue forecast."

"Make time. Friends do that."

"All right," she said, averting her eyes.

He gave her a quick kiss and left.

Elizabeth sank down on the couch and gazed up at the painting. Someone once said that not understanding the past means you will inevitably repeat it. *Am I repeating it? Or am I trying to finally get it right?*

Chapter 20

"Since when is the Hickey character a philanderer? Alfred won't like that. He's taken on his last role a little too seriously," Robert said as he and Karen entered the apartment and simultaneously dropped keys and scripts on the hall table.

Karen laughed. "Hardly. I found out Jesus Christ Superstar has already slept with two of the women in the cast. I was inspired."

Robert's eyes widened. "Who? Which women?"

Karen headed for the bedroom. "Tina and Kelly. And he went for coffee with Vicki."

Robert blew out a mouthful of air and followed. "Shit. It didn't take him long to zero in on the commandment to love your neighbor as yourself. But this isn't *The Producers*. I don't need Larry pulling a Leo Bloom in the middle of the production because Alfred is coveting his costar's girlfriend."

Karen began the nightly ritual of clearing away the various items they had left strewn across the bed that morning: hairdryer, hairbrush, Robert's damp towel. She winced in embarrassment as Robert fingered Albee's *Who's Afraid of Virginia Woolf* on her nightstand. She cast her eyes down as he came to her, wrapping his arms around her, nodding toward the book. "If you're that concerned about your parents, we can always have a cutlery-free reception with paper plates and finger foods."

She rested her head on his shoulder. "Not funny."

"I just hate to see you worry when it's all going to be fine. It's going to be a beautiful wedding with an intimate ceremony, a cloudless sky, and a gorgeous bride. I predict your parents will be charming, polite, perfectly behaved, and there will be nothing to print on Page Six."

"I know you're never wrong," she said, turning to look up at him. "But this could be a first. My mother said she's going to object at our wedding."

Robert chuckled and kissed her forehead. "Babe, I don't think so."

"How do you know?"

"Because she called this morning to talk to me. She wants to meet me. Finally."

Karen sank onto the bed. "You shouldn't do that."

Robert laughed again. "We'll be in a public place. She's not giving me a shave. I won't end up in a meat pie."

"Don't be too sure. She's never wanted to meet you before."

"We weren't getting married before."

"That's what I'm trying to tell you. We won't be getting married now."

"Yeah, and who's on first, what's on second, and I don't know's on third. Baby, calm down. It'll be a nice dinner with the four of us."

Karen gazed up at Robert, feeling the blood drain from her face. "Four of us?"

"Us and your parents."

Karen's mouth dropped open. "My mother and father cannot be in the same place. Bad things happen."

"It's amazing how civilized parents can be if it means their child's happiness. It'll be fine." He grabbed a copy of Neil Simon's *Barefoot in the Park* and held it out to her. "Read this. This is a happy story about a happy couple."

"They almost get divorced."

"They don't mean it. It's going to be a beautiful wedding." He held up menus. "Chinese or Italian?"

Karen rooted around for the phone. "Chinese. Speaking of happy couples, maybe we should have Ian and Liz over to dinner."

Robert planted a kiss on her forehead. "Not a good idea."

"My maid of honor and your best man are in a relationship . . . or whatever they call it. We should do something to acknowledge this."

"We should mind our own business and stay out of it. If they make it, fine. If they don't, that's their business. Manifest Destiny."

"Manifest Destiny was about US land expansion in the eighteen hundreds." Extracting the phone from under a pile of clean laundry, she handed it to him. "Don't forget the extra fortune cookies."

"Just regular destiny then," he said while punching in the numbers. "We're out of it."

Chapter 21

Enough nonsense, Elizabeth thought as she arrived at Ian's door, breathing deeply to steady her nerves and strengthen her resolve. *Tell him you can't go to dinner, and then get out.* She knew full well his powers of persuasion. She had to be ready. She had to face him, prove she was strong enough.

She knocked on the door and waited.

The door opened. Ian wore new jeans and his signature white shirt. His beard was freshly trimmed, his hair looking like he just ran his fingers through it. She felt a fluttering in her stomach.

He smiled, shifting aside for her to enter.

She took tentative steps inside and drew in a shaky breath.

Outside, the dusk was coming on; as the natural light slipped away, dancing flames from the candles dotting the loft threw shadows across the white space and the candlelight splashed against the half-finished canvases. A small table was set, two plates of food, steam rising, waiting.

Then he was behind her, sliding her coat from her shoulders.

"I . . . came to tell you I can't stay."

"But you're already here," he said simply.

"I didn't want to be rude. I didn't know you were going to go to all this trouble."

He took the news quietly.

He cupped her face in his hands. She closed her eyes as he caressed her cheek with a gentle stroke of his thumb. "Are you sure? I've cooked a lovely meal. Everything is ready."

She took a deep breath. "I'm not ready."

"Not ready for what, Lizzie?"

She stepped back. "Not ready for just dinner and whatever comes after."

He nodded his head. "You want to alter our arrangement? You're the expert at business, at making agreements. State your terms. What do you want, Lizzie?"

She had a moment's pause. This wasn't the answer she expected. She didn't want to play games.

"I—we can have dinner and whatever comes after. But you have it only with me."

He thought a moment. "All right, Lizzie. Will you stay now?"

"Yes."

She moved to the table.

"Lizzie," he said softly, behind her. "You haven't heard what I want."

She froze, waiting. He came to her, taking the clips out of her hair, running his fingers through the curls as they tumbled free.

"I want the same."

She let out a breath. She heard the words, knew what they meant. A fluster of excitement went through her, tempered by a twinge of anxiety. *Saying yes to Ian is saying no to Nick.*

"Agreed," she heard herself say.

He wrapped his arms around her, and kissed her.

"I have a little tip for you," she said when they parted. "Next time you tell a woman you've made her dinner, don't leave the takeout bag sticking up out of the trash."

Ian looked into the kitchen. "Oh dear," he said.

She laughed as he kissed her again.

At one in the morning, Elizabeth nestled in Ian's embrace; they watched the reflection of the candles send flickering shadows onto the wall.

"You have no paintings of Scotland," she said. "Why is that? It's your home."

"Painters don't have a home. The world is their home."

She made a mock expression of awe and he chuckled.

"Monet had Giverny," she said.

"And Venice, and London, and Paris. You can't capture everyday life if you don't travel and see life while it's happening."

"Van Gogh made paintings of his room."

"And look how well things turned out for him."

"Degas painted his ballet dancers and Cezanne painted the same countryside more than once."

"Travel is necessary. But I take your point. When you find the perfect place, you don't want to wander anymore," he said, suddenly getting out of bed and disappearing behind the room divider.

After a moment he reappeared, his arms full. He set down a small stand at the foot of the bed, and on it placed a vase with a single rose. He opened a small box and she saw it was a field paint box with solid tiles of color lined in neat rows. With the light hand of a surgeon he took out a pen-sized plastic water well and disappeared again. She heard the water running in the bathroom and then he was back, holding the well upright. He screwed a top on one end; the other end had a brown brush tip. He placed a book and a blank piece of watercolor paper on her lap, and held out the brush.

"No," she said forcefully.

"Why not?"

"I . . . can't."

"Is it because you never finished your class?"

She rearranged herself under the covers, pulling them up around her.

He held the book on her lap, and waited.

"I can't control the water."

"It's not meant to be controlled."

"I used to . . . it just doesn't work anymore . . . I can't . . ."

He held out the brush and waited. She took it, holding it as if it were a foreign object. "Just let it happen, Lizzie."

"It won't look right."

"Is that what you're worried about?"

He kissed her cheek and moved to whisper in her ear. "You can't create anything out of fear."

She looked up at him, feeling dangerously close to tears. She squeezed the well to draw water to the tip. Sweeping the brush across a tile of color, she put the brush to the paper. She zeroed in on the flower, trying to balance her eye and her hand. The tinted water ran in streaks down the page.

Ian closed his hand over hers lightly. "Loosen your grip, Lizzie, you're holding too tight," he said.

She tried again. And then she experienced that wonderful moment she hadn't had in years, when all conscious thought ceased and she was merely an extension of the water and the color; the petals of the flower became a tapestry of rivulets and gaps.

He kissed her forehead. "There, you see, a happy accident."

She nestled in close to him and handed him the brush. "I started, now you finish."

Chapter 22

Karen stood before the mirror in the dressing room, shrinking like Alice in Wonderland in a wedding dress bursting with tulle, as Elizabeth and Emily moved around her, fussing and primping. "Dinner—why would my parents want to have dinner?"

"Fresh kill?" Elizabeth offered.

"To paraphrase Morris the director, not funny," Karen answered. "Robert doesn't believe me. He thinks they want to get to know him. He thinks my mother sounds cute."

Elizabeth shook her head at she got on her knees to straighten the train of the dress. "Cute like a Rottweiler, just before it takes your hand off."

"That's what I'm afraid of. They'll probably ask little off-the-cuff questions like, Tell me, Robert, how are you planning to plunder my daughter's trust fund?"

"Poor bastard."

"Why were they so supportive of my spiritual journey if they were determined to destroy any shred of peace I might have? Do you think they'll spike his food?"

Emily placed a headpiece teeming with roses and pearls on Karen's head. "Of course not. Unless they hired a ringer for the kitchen."

Karen bit her fingernail. "I have a headache. I never get headaches."

Elizabeth stood up. "How did a year-long European tour, winter recesses in Gstaad, and trips to Positano qualify as a spiritual journey?"

"I went to Tibet, India, and Malaysia too, but everyone has their own religious experience. My mother's is skiing . . . and shopping. My father's is Italy. They wanted me to be well-rounded, well traveled, and well dressed. Is that wrong?"

"Of course not," Emily soothed, shooting Elizabeth a disapproving look.

Elizabeth stood up. "Look, you said there's a time to yield, right?"

"Right. Supposedly, while you conserve your strength, your enemy becomes exhausted and gives up."

"Right," Elizabeth said. "So let it go. Have the dinner. Bring a food taster for Robert. Then go off and elope."

"Robert won't do it and I don't blame him. Since his younger brother died, he is the sun in his parents' universe. They are over the moon about this wedding."

Elizabeth nodded.

"Robert is right," Emily said. "Your wedding day is just that, *your* day. You deserve to have it. Every woman wants to have her special day. Well . . ." She threw Elizabeth a quick glance. "Most women do."

"I assume that's meant for me, since you haven't said a word to me since we got here."

"I saw Nick at a benefit on Saturday night. He was alone," Emily retorted, hands on hips. "I thought you *wanted* to get married. How could you *not* tell me?"

Because I can't trust you anymore.

Emily shook her head. "After everything I've done for you."

"And you never let me forget it."

Emily's mouth dropped open.

"Guys, please," Karen said.

Emily and Elizabeth looked at her.

"I look like a show pony."

"You do not," Emily protested.

"Yes, you do," Elizabeth said.

They worked in unison to undo the rows of buttons on the back and sleeves of the gown.

"So how often do you see Ian?" Emily said.

"Whenever I want to," Elizabeth said shortly. "Can we please focus on Karen's dress?"

"He stays at your place?"

"No, I stay at his. I come and go as I please."

They finally extricated Karen from the folds of the dress.

An assistant came in, pulling a rolling rack of dresses behind her; she held them up one at a time. Karen sighed, finally choosing a strapless A-line gown, overflowing with organza.

Emily considered Elizabeth. "You know you're living like a man. You should be on *Oprah*. You're every woman's hero."

"According to the Tao, the goal is to live in harmonious connection with all living things," Karen said. "You need to make sure you're not living in harmony only because you have no real connection."

Elizabeth took her words quietly.

"And you'll never get the look," Karen said.

"I know," Elizabeth said.

"What look?" Emily asked.

Elizabeth and Karen stared at her. "The look," Karen said. "The one that tells you he's toast, he's finished, he's hopelessly in love with you."

"I know that look," Emily said. "Parker's eyes get all soft and mushy. Sometimes he even looks dangerous."

"Not the I-want-to-get-laid look," Elizabeth said. "The *real* look."

Karen took a deep breath. "It's the first time you see him with his eyes wide open and he's staring at you in wonder."

"It's a cross between totally defenseless and scared shitless," Elizabeth said.

"I love that look," Karen said.

"Who doesn't?"

Emily gave them a blank stare in response and then seemed to recover. "Oh . . . of course, the look."

Elizabeth mentally shrugged off the conversation. So she would never get the look. She hadn't gotten the look from Nick. It had never bothered her. He had been comfortable and safe and that was all she wanted. Wasn't it? She had learned that when the bond of intimacy was broken, it led to inevitable pain. *Who am I kidding? The bond is already there with Ian, at least on my end. I want the look from Ian.* She'd wanted it from the beginning. She watched Karen slip into the dress and stand before the mirror. Feeling her eyes begin to burn, she glanced away.

"I don't like this one either," Karen sighed. "Why am I looking for dresses? What's the point? It's like wasting my allowance."

"Your mother still gives you an allowance? Does she know you're shopping for the wedding?"

Karen nodded.

Elizabeth shook her head. "So in essence, she's paying you to purchase a product she's determined to keep you from using."

"You see why I have a headache."

"Listen, I have the perfect solution," Emily said. "Raise the stakes. Ask your mother to hire a designer to make a dress for you. She won't say no and you'll up her guilt. No woman is able to see her daughter in a wedding dress and not crack. You'll be blocking her checkmate."

Elizabeth couldn't believe the statement; it was clever, smart, and showed tactical planning. Emily continued to surprise her—in good and bad ways. "Emily's right," Elizabeth said. "You've got to get more Sun Tzu than Lao-tzu. You need *The Art of War*, not the *Tao Te Ching*, or you won't survive this."

Karen changed back into street clothes, and the three women exited the salon. They stood for a moment, basking in the sunshine on Madison Avenue.

"Emily, I'm sorry I didn't tell you," Elizabeth said.

"So how good is Ian, really?" Emily said.

Two pairs of expectant eyes fastened on Elizabeth's face.

Elizabeth took a deep breath. "Incredible."

Karen smiled. Emily did not.

Chapter 23

On a Sunday morning, Elizabeth sat propped up on the couch, her laptop resting on her thighs. She gave a cursory glance at the breakfast dishes littering the kitchen table, the sections of the *New York Times* scattered across the coffee table. She scrolled back and forth through pivot tables of information, digesting the statistics, referring to notes on meetings with her group. She had been given the goal of tripling her current annual revenue of eighty million in three years. Reviewing the client demographics, she began to see a window of opportunity. She stopped to run her hand through Ian's unruly blond hair, able to examine him uncensored as he dozed next to her, his arm draped across her stomach. The telephone jarred her from her thoughts. She picked up the receiver.

"Robert," she said to Ian.

He held out his hand, grunted hello, then listened.

"Dinner at seven?" he said to Elizabeth.

"Fine."

He mumbled "okay" and handed the receiver back. "Lovely Sunday in New York," he murmured, running his hand over her thigh.

Yes, it is. Dinners with Ian, Robert, and Karen felt right.

She felt soothed, calmer, knowing that she was where she was supposed to be, with her business plan and her personal life. She put the laptop on the coffee table and slid down next to him. He slid his hand under her shirt. She sighed.

Chapter 24

At five o'clock on a Friday, Parker and Nick lounged comfortably in the conference room. Papers and yellow legal pads from the meeting still lay scattered on the table. The conversation had petered out and they sat in contemplative silence, the LCD projector casting a blue light on the screen, the low humming of the fan filling the room. Parker hit a button on the remote and the machine shut off.

A secretary stood in the conference room doorway. "Mr. Davis, Darryl needs to talk to you."

"Fine, have him come in."

"Also, Mr. Mitkey left a message, asking for you to call him back."

Parker chuckled. "Leave his number on my desk. I'll get back to him." Parker smiled at Nick. "I've decided to move some assets through Kenny's group."

"I figured as much. You could've put them through Liz's group."

Parker chuckled. "I could have. You're not seeing her anymore, are you?"

Nick sat quietly, staring at his yellow legal pad. "No, I'm not."

Parker rapped his knuckles on the table. "Emily said you two were over. Good thing for you. You got out just in time. You don't want to be sailing on a sinking ship. Liz is about to lose out on forty to fifty million in profit. That's going to make a big difference to her bottom line. On top of losing two of her best advisers, it's not looking too good for her."

"Does she know about Mitkey?"

Parker chuckled. "She'll know soon enough."

Nick leaned back in his chair in silence.

Chapter 25

The restaurant buzzed with laughter, conversation, and the clinking of glasses. The company celebration had been going on for a little over an hour.

Elizabeth stood with Martin Saunders and his wife. Medium height, portly, with abundant silver hair, he had an air of joviality; unless you knew him. To outsiders, he resembled a kindly grandfather, ready to talk golf and grandchildren at a moment's notice. In reality, he had a reputation for throwing his division heads into the cage to see who would be left standing. Elizabeth could've tolerated the conversation except they were also joined by Kenneth Mitkey and his wife, a Barbie doll replica, and soon she found herself herself trapped in the conversation from hell.

"What's most important is a strong and diversified executive team," Saunders was saying, "versed in all the major areas and able to go to the next level in a seamless transition. I want my executives to not just know one area; our business is not comprised of just one area. It's not about lateral versus horizontal moves anymore."

The hell it isn't, Elizabeth thought.

"I couldn't agree more," Mitkey said. "I think it's a great idea."

Of course you do, moron.

"Liz, what do you think?" Saunders asked.

As she was about to answer, she felt a hand slide around her waist. Nick leaned in and kissed her cheek. "Sorry I'm late, darling."

Elizabeth stared at him in silence as he exchanged greetings.

At the end of the night, Nick and Elizabeth stood outside the restaurant.

"I see the flowers I sent didn't make my case, but we did get to dinner," he said.

She looked into his eyes; they were wary and cool.

"I told you I was not going to use you. Why did you come?"

"Did you notice anything while you were standing with your boss and your competition? They had their spouses with them. Before I arrived, you were alone. I didn't see Picasso with you. Is there a reason you left him at home, like he wouldn't fit in?"

She ignored his comment. "I'm sorry I hurt you, I am."

Nick shook his head, his lip curling in disgust. "I cannot understand why you insist on seeing that loser. He's only out for what he can get from you, you must know that. If you didn't, you'd still be in California. I thought you were smarter than this, Liz."

Elizabeth didn't answer.

"You're throwing away your future."

Elizabeth averted her eyes, knowing his anger was one part disappointment and three parts ego. He considered Ian beneath him.

"You're making a mistake, kid. A big fucking mistake. You need me. You have no idea how much."

Holding himself rigid, he strode to a waiting limo.

She stood quietly for a moment before stepping to the curb for a taxi. She slid into the backseat, took a deep breath, and gave the driver Ian's address.

Chapter 26

A week later, on Monday morning, Elizabeth stood in Jim Darrigan's office reviewing a report. An assistant flitted back and forth, engaged in the hopeless task of trying to locate memos and papers in the black hole that was Darrigan's pile of paperwork. Darrigan was a measured, soft-spoken man who rarely exhibited emotion. At first glance, he appeared to be in the wrong profession; insurance, rather than the risk of investment strategy, seemed more appropriate.

"This should be fine," Elizabeth said as they were finishing up. "I'll have the advisers incorporate these asset-allocation strategy options in their presentations."

She flipped through a few more pages and then caught sight of a memo on the desk. Minutes of a workgroup chaired by Kenneth Mitkey. Pretending to still read the report, she placed it on the desk next to the memo in order to sneak a quick scan.

She heard her heart thudding in her chest. The private banking division was "weak." "Going forward" they needed to "brainstorm" together to meet the "challenge" of making up the shortfall. This was a critical time and "pre-planning" was essential from the "get-go." They needed to increase new clients, go after the "low hanging fruit." *For God's sake*, Elizabeth thought, her teeth clenching, *did the bastard own a thesaurus of cheap shit business lingo?* She zeroed in like a laser on the last paragraph. "Davis Investments" was "on board" and "placing their assets" for a profit estimated at "over fifty million."

Looking up, she found Darrigan watching her. "Do you need something else?" he asked.

"No," she said, tapping the report with her finger. "I've got everything I need." Keeping her face carefully blank, she strode from the room.

A stranglehold of panic wound tight around Elizabeth but she forced herself to walk in a calm, easy pace back to her office. She closed her door and leaned against it, listening to her own shallow breathing, the beat of her heart in her ears, the queasy feeling of her stomach twisting into a knot. She stared at the corner of her desk. Until one month ago the space had always been filled with a vase of flowers from Nick. His words came back to her, a sickening self-fulfilling prophecy. *Watch out, kid, you're still blood in the water.*

Chapter 27

The canvases were lined up in a neat row. Ian stood a few feet away, smoking, leaning against the island in the kitchen, waiting. Paul Ferand stood, arms folded, a fingertip resting against his lips. His thin, tousled brown hair gave him a windblown look that made him appear unduly hurried, as if he were late for an appointment.

"They are not done," he said.

"Not yet. But the work is coming along brilliantly."

The canvas showed a mother letting go of her toddling child on a path in Central Park, as others looked on.

"Impressionist. Ian, my friend, when we met at the gallery, I thought, okay, perhaps you will be good, but I was wrong. You are superb."

Ian couldn't hold back his smile. *When we met.* He had pursued Ferand for weeks until managing an accidental meeting.

"And you are also late . . . one hundred and fifty years too late," Ferand said.

Ian felt the smile slip from his face. "I thought you still represented more traditionally minded artists."

"And how many of those do you think there are? You are a dying breed. The wants of the people dictate the market," Ferand said. "The people's taste is contemporary. Art isn't about beauty anymore, it's about—"

"How much you pay."

"Exactement."

"Pity," Ian said. Ferand lit a cigarette and came to stand next to him.

"So, my friend, do you teach?"

Ian took a deep drag, not meeting Ferand's eyes, and nodded. "Yes, my students are all quite bored with traditional study. They want to create contemporary masterpieces."

"Such is the life of the poor working artist. They will surpass you, of course, and you will sit at a sidewalk café, drinking your wine and becoming bitter. But you would not have it any other way. I am sorry I cannot be your Durand-Ruel, my friend, but I keep you in mind."

He gave Ian's shoulder a fatherly pat and let himself out.

Ian sat down in a chair, shoulders hunched. He had hoped Ferand would take a chance on him. His paintings were good—better than good—and yet . . . He needed the money and yes, the recognition. He wasn't sure he could hang on to Lizzie much longer without either one. A high powered, successful business woman and her genteel, poverty stricken artist-lover; he gave a dry laugh. He'd have to figure something out.

Chapter 28

As Debbie completed her recitation, Elizabeth listened with one ear, her mind split in two. For the past two days she had been thinking, planning, strategizing. She had two new advisers, promising leads for new clients and a new client strategy. *I can still pull this out. I have to.*

". . . and I returned all the calls and ran the profit reports."

"Good, thank you. What else?"

"I have all of your lunch meetings scheduled for the remainder of the week."

"I need to meet with Charlie and Steven. They need to be first and second."

"Already done."

"Thank you," Elizabeth said. If Debbie knew what was going on, she didn't show it. She was sure Debbie wouldn't shed a tear if she had to break in another director.

Charlie and Steven were young, pliable, and eager to make their marks. She was spending a lot of time mentoring them. They were working on landing three high-net-worth clients, and she was desperate for that hard work to pay off.

She heard Debbie say "Good morning, sir" and looked up.

Martin Saunders stood in the doorway. She stood as he entered her office.

"How's business?"

"Business is good," she said.

"That's what I like to hear," he said with a smile. "We haven't had a private dinner in a while, Liz. I'd like an opportunity to talk offline."

Elizabeth felt her whole body tighten into fight-or-flight mode. Dinner with the boss was usually a golden opportunity, a chance to get his ear, but in light of recent events, Nick's words buzzed in her head. It could mean the beginning of the end of her career. "I think that's a good idea," she said. "I'm putting together something that I think you'll be very interested in."

He knocked his hand on the desk lightly and he turned to leave. "Call my assistant, she'll set it up."

She stared after him, a slow, steady pounding beginning in her head.

Debbie came into the office a moment later carrying several cardboard boxes.

"What's this?" Elizabeth asked.

"They're empty," Debbie said, watching her carefully. "They came by messenger for you, no card, no name."

Parker, you little shit, Elizabeth thought. *It's not over yet. I didn't come all this way to pack up and lose everything. And I certainly won't lose it all by turning my head and playing games.*

"Get rid of them, and then I need you to make one more call."

Chapter 29

"**P**arker, that shit!" Elizabeth seethed to Karen. They were standing outside La Belle, the restaurant holding Emily's fashion show. Elizabeth stared down the street at the bustle on Broadway. "He's been orchestrating this the entire time. He and his new BFF, Kenny Mitkey. And don't tell me Princess Emily has been so busy with her fashion show that she didn't know this was coming. Muse, my ass."

"Liz, come on," Karen said, her voice soft. "You don't know that Emily is in on this. Don't take it out on her. Do you really think Parker tells her anything?"

Elizabeth clamped her eyes shut for a moment. "What was I thinking? I'm screwed, and it's my own fault."

"You don't know that," Karen said. "Forget Parker. Saunders hired you. Don't people have dinner to eat and talk?"

"In the Manhattan financial sector?" Elizabeth barely controlled an eye roll. "I've lost two of my best advisers. Parker just handed Mitkey another fifty million in profit. That's fifty million off my bottom line. All I need now is for one of my big accounts to go somewhere else and it'll be just like Nick said. I'll have dinner, Saunders will tell me I have all his support, and two days later I'm gone. And it will be my own fault. I've been screwing around, literally and figuratively."

"You're blaming Ian now?"

"If only it were that simple. No, I blame myself. This is my fault. I should've seen this coming, and I would have if I hadn't been busy with romance instead of finance."

"Then maybe finance is the wrong path for you."

Elizabeth sucked in a breath. "I have put fifteen years of my adult life into this. I built a career—"

"And you chose exactly this time to pull out your paints and look back at your old career, your real life."

Elizabeth didn't answer.

"Liz, what are you going to do about Ian?"

"I allowed my emotions to distract me. I should've remembered what happened the last time I did that. I lost everything and I won't let that happen again. I'm going to meet him in Greeley Square tomorrow morning. I'm going to tell him we're done."

"Oh Liz—"

Elizabeth sucked in a breath of air. "I have to do it. I have to. No more distractions."

"Okay," Karen soothed. "Just try to calm down. Maybe the show will be relaxing for you."

"I can't stay. I need to e-mail my advisers and mentor them on how to close with new clients. Then I have to prepare for a meeting I may never get to, and, oh, I have to go to a panel discussion tomorrow night as if I actually have a career."

The door to the restaurant opened and Emily rushed out, breathless. "You're here. Come inside. Hurry, we're about to start."

"I can't stay."

Emily bristled, her expression souring. "Meeting Ian?"

"Going back to work."

"On a Sunday? It can't wait?"

Elizabeth felt her temper rising. "No, Emily, it can't." Her eyes narrowed. "I shouldn't bother. Is that what you're saying? There's no point?"

Karen took hold of Elizabeth's arm. "She didn't mean it that way," she said quietly.

Emily looked puzzled. "I just thought it would be nice for you to support me . . . you know . . . the way I supported you. That's all."

"Good luck with the show," Elizabeth said through clenched teeth, and walked away.

"She has a lot going on right now," Karen said.

"I guess so." Emily's face soured momentarily, but her bubbly smile quickly returned. She ushered Karen inside. "I'm so excited that you're here!"

Chapter 30

Ian glanced around the living room at the piles of books, laundry baskets spilling over with clothes, boxes of reams of paper. The small student's desk before him was a rat's nest of computer cords and DVDs resting precariously on top of stacks of papers.

He shook his head. "How can you work like this?"

Robert was curled underneath the desk, struggling to get his ample frame around the computer's CPU box.

"We like it," he called out. "A cluttered desk means a productive mind. What we really need is a bigger apartment."

"So you can be even more productive. Right, I understand."

Robert shook the desk as he maneuvered, sending the listing pile of papers and DVDs sliding toward the edge.

Ian caught it and moved it to the floor, scowling his disapproval.

"Is it saying anything?" Robert asked.

"What should it be saying?"

"New hardware found."

"No."

"Shit." Robert extricated himself and fiddled with the mouse. "How's the play coming?"

Robert made a sound of disgust as he crawled back under the desk. "Our celebrated comedic genius of a director hasn't cracked a smile since he came on board. What's it doing now?"

"Nothing."

"Shit." Crawling out from under the desk, Robert sat on the floor, catching his breath. "Karen thinks he doesn't like her."

"Does he like her?"

"Who doesn't like Karen?" Robert said. "He'd like her better if she stopped killing off the characters."

"Shouldn't the storyline be set by now?"

"It is, it is. She's just tweaking."

A chiming sound came from the computer.

"Oh, there it goes. Karen's amazing. You should see the stuff she comes up with."

"But why did you need to be writing partners? I thought you were doing quite well on your own. Are you sure collaborating isn't more trouble than it's worth?"

"Some of the greatest love affairs were also the greatest collaborations. Hepburn and Tracy, Bogart and Bacall, Cronyn and Tandy—"

Ian laughed. "You're a hopeless romantic, you are."

"So were you."

Ian shrugged.

"Are you sure Liz isn't more trouble than she's worth?"

Ian smiled. "You don't know her."

"That's what Karen says. I can never see them as friends. Liz always seems cold; there's no warmth there."

"You're wrong. She's a lovely girl, is Miss Lizzie. And she's quite warm."

"I'll take your word for it. You know, you never told me what you think of Karen."

"She's brilliant," Ian said with an air of studied patience. "And she'll never do anything purposely to hurt you."

"See? I knew you liked her."

Ian handed Robert a TravelDrive and Robert plugged it into the computer. Ian leaned in, watching closely as Robert pulled up the JPEG of a canvas.

"Did you close yet with Ferand?"

"No. He won't take me on."

Robert gave Ian a slap on the shoulder. "It'll happen, don't worry. This is going to be great. Digitizing your work is going to be the best thing you've ever done. You'll get your own computer and be able to send your work to any dealer in the world."

Ian nodded.

"And in the meantime, look on the bright side. You can always paint Emily again while you wait."

Ian rolled his eyes.

Across town, Karen sat at a table next to the constructed catwalk, wishing she was back at the apartment, wondering how Robert and Ian were doing with Ian's project. Long, lithe women sashayed back and forth on the makeshift catwalk while waiters swarmed, fanning out through the maze of tables. She exchanged a smile with Deirdre Perry sitting four tables away. At the end of the show, Emily appeared on the catwalk one last time, glowing in a sheer, lacy, ice blue gown, strutting, pouting, putting on a show and obviously loving it.

Sebastian Roderick, dressed in ripped jeans and rumpled shirt, strolled out onto the catwalk, flanked by the models. He motioned for Emily to step out and take his hand.

Grasping his hand, Emily's face lit up, basking in the round of applause. The models lining each side of the catwalk waited, motionless.

Without warning, Sebastian seized Emily's dress, tearing it away, leaving her standing in a silky, pale blue chemise. A low murmur began in the audience but Emily's face remained serene, almost amused. The models followed suit, stripping off their ensembles and tossing them down onto the catwalk.

Holding Emily's dress in front of him, Sebastian pulled out a lighter, giving it a flick with his thumb. He touched the flame to the hem; it licked at the cloth. Sebastian dropped it onto the pile of clothing and clapped his hands.

"It is all superficial crap," he shouted, watching as a small flame shot up from the clothing, morphing into a hearty blaze. The wait staff came running in, shouting directions to the crowd, herding them to the exits. Chairs scraped against the wooden floor as people fled to the exits.

A waiter aimed a fire extinguisher, sending a blast of foam sailing into the air. Karen caught sight of Emily, her face frozen in shock as the foam found its first victim, Deirdre Perry. Overhead, a hissing noise sounded, making Karen look up. The sprinklers went off.

Robert and Ian heard the front door slam. They came out of the bedroom to find Karen, wet clothes clinging to her, hair plastered to her head.

"What the hell happened?" Robert said, rushing over to her.

"Turn on the news," she croaked.

They stood around the television, mesmerized by a video of smoke billowing out of the restaurant, filtering its way into the street.

"Sebastian's fashion statement *against* superficiality."

"That's an oxymoron, love," Ian said gently.

On the screen, police cars and fire trucks filled the background behind a reporter. They watched a stone-faced Parker escort a blanket-wrapped Emily out of the restaurant, his lips pressed into a thin line.

"Oh dear," Ian said.

"At the very least," Karen said.

Robert kissed her forehead, enveloping her in his arms. "I'm just glad you're all right."

"Was Lizzie with you?" Ian asked.

Karen shook her head. "She couldn't make it. She's been . . . busy."

Ian nodded his head.

Parker paced the floor of the living room, muttering under his breath, while Emily sat on the couch, staring up at him.

"I don't believe it," Parker said finally. "I don't fucking believe it."

"It wasn't meant to happen like that," she said. "It was supposed to be a teeny fire. He was making a statement. It's all part of his genius."

Parker stopped. "Who gives a shit about his statements?" he said, his voice rising as the veins stood out at his temple. "Starting a bonfire in a restaurant is not genius, it's fucking insanity. But you're the one I can't believe."

"What do you mean?" she asked, her blue eyes opening wide.

Parker stood over her, glaring down at her. "What do I mean? What the fuck do you think I mean? How the hell do you think this makes me look? I'm moving billions of dollars and I'm married to a brainless, irresponsible party girl who leaves a trail of destruction behind her. And why, *why*," he yelled, getting up in her face, "for fuck's sake, is Deirdre Perry always involved?"

Color rushed into Emily's face as she blinked back tears. "I'm very responsible."

"Responsible!" he thundered, watching her shrink back at the force in his voice. "We have a half-finished house in Connecticut you never pay attention to. Every time I ask you to do something to help me out, you create chaos. Do you give a shit about me, my reputation, this marriage?" He paced, running his hands through his hair.

She bolted from the couch, following after him, reaching out for him. "I care about you, I care about us!"

Parker waved away her attempts to embrace him, ignoring her sniffling. He stopped pacing and grasped her shoulders. "You need to grow up, understand? I can't carry you and take care of business at the same time. All I'm asking you to do is take care of the house and the charity fund. And that's it. Nothing else. Do you think you can manage that?"

Emily nodded. "I'm sorry."

Parker looked at his watch. "I'm late for a function. While I'm out you'd better do some thinking; you need to make some decisions. Are you going to commit to us, to me, or are you going to continue to tear us apart?"

Emily sat down on the couch, listening to the soft jingle of his keys and the slam of the front door. Then she was alone, her crying the only sound in the room.

Chapter 31

Elizabeth entered the Dunkin' Donuts near Greeley Square. As she paid for her coffee, she inhaled deeply. She had been mentally preparing all night. *Be quick and tough.* She repeated it like a mantra. If she let him talk, his soft voice would lull away her resolve; if she let him touch her with those warm hands, she'd never get through this.

She turned and saw him come through the door. He smiled and her breath caught in her throat. She made no move toward him, only nodding toward an empty table. Her heart squeezed as his smile slipped and his eyes clouded in confusion.

"I was concerned when your assistant called to reschedule," he said as they sat down. "Everything all right?"

He reached out to take her hand and she jerked away, nearly knocking over her coffee.

"I don't have much time."

His look became wary. For a moment they sat in silence. She glanced out at the ebb and flow of the traffic, avoiding his eyes.

"Something happen at work, Lizzie?"

She gave him a sharp look. "It's fine. Why wouldn't it be?"

He continued to stare at her, waiting.

She looked around, shifting in her seat. "It's the usual, reaching out to my advisers, studying trends in the marketplace, pulling the trigger on new client retention initiatives while working in tandem with my colleagues and associates to create win-win situations for everyone. Is that enough quaint business jargon for you, or would you like to hear more? Why do you care about any of this? Business holds no interest for you." *Get to the point. Get it over with.*

"Really, Lizzie?" he said slowly, his voice tight. "There's no business in art, then?"

"Have you closed with your dealer?"

"Not yet . . . why the concern? Suddenly my career seems to be upsetting to you."

"It's not upsetting to me. But if you can't close with a dealer, you won't get anywhere. You'll just drift without accomplishing anything and it will all be a waste of time. If you can't paint successfully, then you'll need to make the decision to force yourself to give up."

"Give up? I don't imagine I'll give up. I can't do that. My work is my life . . . whereas your work is just a part of your life."

"Don't you dare look down on my life."

"Lizzie, I'm not looking down—"

"I've made good choices." Realizing her voice was rising, she leaned forward, continuing in a strained whisper. "Realistic choices."

"Meaning choosing not to paint . . . and you never did tell me why—"

"Why I gave up painting is none of your business."

"Gave it up?"

She stared at her coffee. *This is not quick and tough. Do it.* "I'm not here to discuss art."

He shifted in his chair, posture stiffening, as if ready to protect himself. "Why are you here?"

She squeezed her eyes shut for a moment. "This—us—this isn't working for me."

"This is all rather sudden . . ."

She sighed. "Yes, well, I realized . . . I decided . . . I need to concentrate on my work. I allowed myself to be distracted—"

"I see. I'm nothing more than a distraction. Pity." His voice was clipped.

She looked up at him. His face had closed, his eyes shuttered. She knew what he was feeling, she'd been there. "Look, this was my fault. I was where I didn't belong. Life isn't a fairy tale. I need to get back on track." She picked up her briefcase.

"So I need to go back to never-never land while you attend to 'real' life. Is that it?"

"What else is there?" she said, getting up. "I don't have the luxury of being able to waste any more time."

Ian gave a sarcastic laugh and got to his feet, blocking her way. "This gets better and better. Anything else, Lizzie?"

"Don't tell me you don't know what I'm talking about. I'm sure you want to get back to your 'real' life."

"And what life would that be?"

"Trying to find the perfect model to inspire you, taking the model to dinner and before you know it, taking the model to bed. That's the life of an artist."

"That's not my life, Lizzie," he said. "I assure you."

She hesitated and then: "I can't have this—you—consuming me—consuming my time anymore."

Pushing past him, she shoved the door open and rushed to the curb to hail a cab. Afraid that he would be on her heels, she said a silent thanks as a yellow cab screeched to a sudden halt. She jumped in. "Fifty-third and Fifth," she ordered. "Go."

Chapter 32

Ian walked down to Thirteeth Street, then cut across the avenues, mulling over the disastrous breakfast. What had happened? Everything had been going well. The brisk Saturday afternoon walks in Central Park, Sundays at the loft reading the paper, croissants and coffee, quiet dinners in little out-of-the-way places. She always decided she preferred his order rather than her own, and halfway through the meal cajoled him into switching plates. Remembering, he smiled. For a brief time, he had liked his life again; New York had felt a bit like home because of her. What the hell happened?

He picked up the pace to get to Parsons for his class. Walking down the block he saw the limousine idling at the curb. Involuntarily, he stopped, his body stiffening. The limo door opened and a long leg stretched to the curb; and he knew. *Oh shit*, he thought. *Michele.* His heart stopped beating for a moment before it remembered and started again.

She eased out of the limo and came up to him to kiss his cheek. *"Bonjour, cheri,"* she said, her voice soft.

For a moment he could only stare, taking in the new golden color of her hair, the softness of her mouth. Her azure eyes looked directly into his, and, as always, his heart skipped. *How could I have forgotten how beautiful she is?* He remembered the night he met her, that party at the apartment in Paris. He couldn't wait to spirit her away to his flat, get her into his bed,

take her clothes off, take everything, all of her. The old familiar desire quickly turned to anger; he could feel his stomach
begin to churn.

Pedestrians gave them a cursory look, moving around them
to continue down the street.

"How did you find me?"

"This is not a nice greeting for your wife."

"Ex-wife."

She lay her hand on his cheek. *"Tu m'as manqué.* I have
missed you."

He jerked his head back. He didn't want to remember what
used to be, how she made him feel when it was new, how he'd
loved her; how he thought he knew her. How he'd been so
wrong.

"Your latest beau likes America, does he?" he said. *"Ce n'est
pas très chic."*

She smiled but her eyes remained cool. "I was at a charming little party uptown, for an exhibit. There was a woman, a
Mrs. Davis—Emily. She was talking about the brilliant painter
Ian MacKay. I made sure we had a nice chat about you. She
said you two are great friends. But, *cheri*, she did not seem to
know much about your life."

A rush of panic went through him as he realized his past—
the past he'd worked so carefully to conceal—was standing in
front of him. Had she told Emily about their relationship?
That would mean everyone would know. Liz would know.

Michele gave him a sly smile. "Don't worry. I told her I was
a friend, from home." She looked at him with narrowed eyes.
"Pourquoi te caches-tu?"

"I'm not hiding."

Michele gazed up at the building. "She told me you teach
now. You do not paint anymore?"

"You didn't destroy me completely. I'm still painting."

"Oh là! Time has made you cruel; I am sad to see it. I had to
go. I had to leave. *Tu ne peux pas savoir.*"

"I understand perfectly how you felt," he said, the heat of
his anger mingling with the lilac scent of her perfume. "You

married me. You said you loved me. You said you supported my career. You lied. I never made enough money for you. So you took lovers. When you found one with enough money, you left me. See? I understand perfectly. The only thing I haven't figured out is why you bothered to marry me in the first place."

"Because I did not lie. I loved you."

His laugh was bitter. "Right. By the way, taking off before I had finished the paintings for the gallery show was a lovely touch." He remembered those dark days, imagining her with someone else. It nearly drove him mad, made him unable to think of anything else, unable to finish his work, unable to exhibit in the show—the chance of a lifetime slipped away.

"This does not mean I do not love you."

Ian stepped back and shook his head. She was so fucking calm, it drove him mad.

"Peut-être je reviens pour rectifier tout ça," she said. "I want to make this right. I care about your work—about you."

Ian laughed. "Since when?"

"I have someone who wants Impressionist paintings. I did work in a gallery."

"No, darling, you slept with a wealthy collector who visited galleries. It's not the same thing."

Michele stroked his cheek. "I am willing to prove I still care for you, even though you hurt me. I can bring him to your workspace."

"No."

She touched his arm. *"Nous pourrions dîner ensemble."*

"Me, you, and your latest lover at dinner? How very Shakespearean. No."

"I thought New York is a civilized place where ex-husbands, ex-wives, ex-lovers still remain friends?"

"We were never friends, Michele."

She reached up and kissed his cheek. Ian closed his eyes and breathed her in as she whispered to him, *"Je vais rester pour un moment.* I will be here. We have a lot to talk about. Emily gave me your number. We talk soon. *Ciao, mon amour."*

Ian cursed softly under his breath as she disappeared into the limo.

Turning away, he lit up and stood there, trying to wrap his mind around this new complication. What the hell could Michele possibly want with him? He didn't buy the supportive, art patron act. Still, his lack of success was a deal breaker with Liz, and Michele's offer was a convenient chance to fix that. But at what price? Feeling hopelessly tangled, like an insect in a spider's web, all he could think was, *Why the hell is this happening? And what do I do now?*

Chapter 33

The restaurant buzzed with investment bankers, fund managers, and traders. Two hours of panel speakers discussing global market initiatives had come and gone. Elizabeth forced herself to make easy conversation during the meal. Who knew and who didn't? It was impossible to tell. Everyone always had their game face on. On the way back from the ladies' room, she stopped at the bar.

As she lifted her arm to signal the bartender, Parker was at her elbow. "So how are you, Liz?"

"Just ducky. How nice of you to inquire."

Parker leaned in. "I'm concerned about you."

"That's touching."

"I've spent a lot of time thinking about you."

"Not as much time as you spent thinking about Kenneth Mitkey."

"Yeah," Parker said with a heavy sigh. "I am sorry about that. But look at it from my point of view. Davis Enterprises is not a private account for you to manage."

She ordered her wine and turned to him.

"Where would you like the boxes sent? Your home or office?"

He chuckled.

"What's the problem, Parker? I wouldn't go to work for you? I wouldn't tell Perry he should run after you, begging you to take him as a client? That's a neat trick you've got. Act like you're not interested and everyone can't wait to give you their money."

Parker smiled. He pulled a card out of his pocket, fingering it as he spoke. "You know what your problem is, Liz? You focus too much on the tiny details; you miss the big picture. I don't want you to feel bad that you didn't see any of this coming . . . so . . ."

Parker held out the card. Elizabeth felt a sudden weight on her chest as she took it from him. Turning it over, she stared at the plain white card listing her name and cell phone number.

"I'm sure you'll have a rewarding career . . . doing something else. I'll send the rest to your office."

"Fuck you, Parker."

He leaned in, giving her a predatory smile. "You should have." He patted her shoulder and moved off into the crowd.

Elizabeth felt the air rush out of her lungs. She remembered to blink quickly to make sure no tears would escape.

Chapter 34

Alfonso, the maître d', took Karen's hand, giving it a small kiss. "*Buona sera, la signora bella*, and good evening to you, sir."

Robert nodded, handing off their coats to the woman in the check room. Karen fussed with his tie.

"Calm down," he said. "Stop overthinking this. Keep it simple. You can't control them, so let it go."

"You're right, you're always right," she said with a smile. "You're amazing."

He gave her a kiss. "I know."

Alfonso led them through the restaurant. "Your mother is at the table with her friend. Your father is at the bar with his friend."

Karen froze, causing Robert to stumble into her. "They . . . brought dates?" Her eyes flew to his face.

"Buffers, baby . . . they're just buffers."

Approaching the table, they found Margaret dressed in cool black, accented with a red silk, hand-rolled scarf; next to her, a twenty-something Ken doll with a perfectly coiffed head of blond hair and chiseled features.

"This is not a buffer," Karen muttered out of the side of her mouth. "This is a gauntlet and we're heading for a throw down." She gave Margaret a forced smile. "Hi, Mommy."

Robert blew out a mouthful of air.

Margaret held out her arms. "My buttercup," she said, returning Karen's embrace.

"Mother, this is Robert." And as a second thought she added, "My fiancé."

Margaret surveyed him with an arched eyebrow. "You would have to be, wouldn't you?"

"How do you do, Mrs. Wainwright," Robert said, taking her hand.

Margaret's eyes narrowed as he bent to kiss her hand. "I do very well, young man. What we must ascertain is how well *you* do."

"I look forward to the inquisition," Robert said.

Margaret gave him a measured look. "Marcus, say hello to my daughter."

Rising with both arms open, his smile revealing a perfect set of white teeth, Marcus reached for Karen.

"Just hello, Marcus," Margaret snapped.

Mumbling a greeting, Marcus sank back down, a sulky look on his face.

Robert held out a chair for Karen as Edward arrived at the table with a long, leggy brunette wearing a red dress with a rising hemline and a plunging neckline.

"Greetings and salutations," Edward said.

Robert offered his hand. "Robert Harris, sir."

"Of course, you'd have to be," Edward said, pumping his hand. "And this is Bambi."

"Good Lord," Karen muttered.

"Ah . . . she took out the pigtails for the evening," Margaret said. "How apropos."

"Hi," Marcus squeaked, his Adam's apple working as he gaped at Bambi and her daring décolleté as she fluttered her eyelashes at him.

"Good Lord, he speaks," Edward said. "That's a new one for you, isn't it, Peg?"

A moment of silence ensued.

"Well," Margaret announced, "shall we peruse the menu?"

Robert sat down and squeezed Karen's hand.

* * *

The table was an oasis of quiet in the midst of the low hum of conversation around them. Karen picked at the plate of baked clams she shared with Robert. Margaret cut through the silence.

"Now, have you two considered how you will handle life's petite emergencies?"

"We have a fire extinguisher and a carbon monoxide alarm," Robert said.

Edward gave a low chuckle.

"I was referring to your affairs."

Robert choked on a clam. "I don't plan on having any affairs."

"Trust me, dear boy, they're never planned," Edward said. "They just . . . happen."

"Spoken by an aficionado," Margaret said, lifting her glass and saluting Edward.

Bambi looked up from her plate. "Is there a show with dinner?" she asked.

"Isn't this it?" Robert whispered to Karen.

She poked him in the ribs.

"I understand your parents are still together?" Margaret asked. "That's rather unusual. How do you account for that?"

"They like each other," Robert said.

"How pedestrian," Margaret said.

Marcus leaned forward with enthusiasm. "My parents didn't like each other."

No one said anything.

"They didn't like me, either," he continued.

"Poor boy," Margaret purred. "Sit back now."

"Now I give myself to women who don't love me," Marcus persisted. "They buy me expensive trinkets to fill my emotional vacuum. Margaret has promised me a car."

Edward chuckled, reaching for his wineglass.

"How come you haven't promised me a car?" Bambi said, her full mouth puffing into a pout.

"His fifth wife has it," Margaret said.

Edward curled his lip and turned to Bambi. "If you want a car, I'll get you a car, my love," he said, kissing her bare shoulder.

As Margaret's expression turned feral, Karen dug her nails into Robert's hand. Squirming, he forced her fingers open and began massaging her hand.

Alfonso hovered around the periphery of the table, a white towel over one arm, wine bottle in hand. "For *la signora bella*," he whispered, refilling Karen's glass.

Robert leaned over. "Leave the bottle."

"Tell me, Robert," Margaret began, "once you've finished skewering O'Neill, do you plan to desecrate anyone else's work . . . Ibsen . . . Miller?"

"Miller?" Bambi said. "Oooh, what a great idea. I'd love a beer."

Alfonso rolled his eyes and walked away.

Karen glanced over at her mother to find her wearing a smug smile.

"She was referring to Arthur Miller," Karen said.

Bambi gave her a blank stare.

"Married to Marilyn Monroe," Robert said.

"Oh, right," Bambi squealed. "Was that the thin one?"

"Yes, dear," Margaret drawled, "the Pulitzer Prize–winning thin one." She turned to Edward. "I see you're getting your concubines from Mensa now."

"And where did you find him, gigolos dot com?"

"Would anyone like more wine?" Robert cut in. "When doesn't alcohol make everything better?"

"Do you normally drink, Robert?" Edward asked.

"No, but in a situation like this, it's mandatory," Robert said, casting a longing eye around for an escape route.

Edward chuckled.

"You should hit the bottle as soon as possible," Margaret offered. "All failed playwrights turn to alcohol. You'll be ahead of the game."

"Mother!" Karen said.

Margaret swung her scarf over her shoulder. "A little career planning never hurt anyone. Besides, if he's snockered, he won't have any time to steal your material."

"You won't have to worry about that with your little boy toy," Edward said with a sharp laugh. "He's barely old enough to read."

Robert fidgeted in his seat, glancing around the room.

"What are you looking for?" Karen asked in a hoarse whisper.

"I want to check out the restroom. Maybe it has a window."

"Don't even think about it."

Margaret sank back in her chair, fingering the scarf. "I'm not concerned about his cognitive prowess," she said with a small smile. "He has other exceptional skills."

"O-kay, something else I did not need to know," Karen murmured, taking another swallow from her glass.

Edward, his face darkening, made a low guttural grunt and shifted in his seat.

"That's all I'm good for," Marcus whined, looking at Robert. "You think it's easy being someone's stud muffin?"

Openmouthed, Robert shook his head.

"I mean, where's the love?" Marcus asked.

"In the Rolex on your wrist?"

"That's cold, man," Marcus mumbled.

"I'd like a watch," Bambi said. "How come you haven't given me a watch?"

"I have a watch for you," Edward said, his eyes never leaving Margaret's face. "Exquisite, set with fifty-two round-cut diamonds and a white gold bracelet."

Margaret's face flushed crimson. "That's my watch, you bastard," she said, her eyes narrowing dangerously. "I knew you had it."

"Possession is nine-tenths of the law."

"Not as far as my lawyer is concerned."

Robert leaned forward. "Okay, let's move on. Isn't the purpose of this dinner to grill me on my family background, college career, arrests and convictions, neuroses?"

Margaret waved away his comment. "Good Lord, whatever for?" she said. "We checked you out ages ago."

She leaned across the table, her scarf trailing precariously close to the butter dish, until she was nose to nose with Edward. "You were feckless and unreliable."

"You were needy and controlling," he hissed. "You always had to have your own way."

"If I had let you have your way, all our books would have been nothing but four hundred pages of heaving breasts and pulsing members. I made those books what they are . . . literature!"

"Literature, ha! If it weren't for those heaving breasts and pulsing members, our books would have been used instead of sleeping pills. Don't take an Ambien, read Townsend and Wainwright!"

Karen threw back the rest of her drink. "You're not supposed to be doing this in front of me." She turned to Robert. "They're not supposed to be doing this in front of me. I'm going to put a stop to this."

Robert refilled Karen's glass. "You can't stop a runaway train, baby. Just let them run out of steam." Lifting the bottle to his lips, he took a long swig.

"Are you making Barbie, here, wife number six?" Margaret asked, continuing to glare at Edward.

Bambi leaned forward. "It's not Barbie . . . it's Bambi."

"You're prettier than Barbie," Marcus said.

"Oh Marcus, you're so sweet," Bambi cooed.

"Perhaps," Edward said, his eyes burning. "What are you going to do with him?"

"I believe I'll marry him."

Edward made a rude noise.

"It's time I remarried, don't you think?" Margaret said, draping her arm around Marcus. "He'll fit right in at the penthouse. There's plenty of room in the four-poster bed." She stroked Marcus's cheek. "You'd like that, wouldn't you?"

Marcus shrugged.

Margaret turned, giving Edward a slow smile. "It was always your favorite place, wasn't it? You always said you found inspiration between those silk sheets." She gave him a cool smile. "Too bad you'll never see it again."

"You'd do that?" Edward breathed. "You would take another man into *our* bed?"

She sat back, rearranging the scarf. "Why not? I deserve a stallion instead of an old nag," she said.

With a snarl, Edward lunged across the table, gathering the ends of the scarf around his fists and dragging her to him.

Karen let out a shriek and everyone scrambled to their feet.

A look of shock crossed Margaret's face as Edward began twisting the scarf, tightening it around her neck.

"Oh my God," Karen cried.

"Holy shit," Robert muttered.

Gasps and cries from the tables around them filled the air.

Alfonso came running. "*Dio mio*, is he crazy? That scarf is hand-rolled silk!"

Robert and Marcus dove in, pulling Edward away, his hands still wrapped around the scarf. Edward stared at Margaret, a look of shock on his flushed face.

Karen rushed to Margaret's side. "Mommy—Mommy! Are you all right?"

Margaret's hand stole to her neck. She looked up at Edward, her mouth ajar.

Everyone stood still in the uncomfortable silence, until their breathing slowed to normal. Then Margaret stood up, smoothing her outfit.

She and Edward continued to hold each other's gaze.

"I want that watch back," she said finally, but without her usual bite.

"When hell freezes over," he said, his tone soft.

Bambi slipped the scarf from Edward's hand. "This is really pretty. If you don't want it, can I have it?"

Edward ignored her and turned to Robert. "Well, you've met the in-laws. Don't say you weren't warned." He held out his hand. "Good meeting you."

"Right," Robert said.

Edward gave Margaret a long look before taking Bambi by the wrist to lead her out of the restaurant. Bambi wrapped the scarf around her neck and used one end to wave good-bye.

Karen and Robert exited the cab in front of their apartment building.

Robert enveloped her in an embrace.

"My father tried to strangle my mother," she said.

"I know this may be hard to believe, but I don't think he meant it."

Karen stared up at him, wide-eyed. "What events of the evening would make you think that?"

"I think he still cares for your mother; and I think she cares for him. They still love each other, Karen."

"My father tried to strangle my mother."

"Love is complicated."

"Maybe their insanity is genetic."

"It's not genetic," he said softly. He looked down at her. "Hey—I love you."

"I love you, too."

Holding each other close, they went into the building.

Chapter 35

The next morning Karen pushed past the reporters camped out on her doorstep and hurried to the subway. She arrived at her mother's penthouse, finding it teeming with reporters, attorneys, and publicists. A bored-looking woman in a nurse's uniform sat with a cigarette in one hand and a coffee mug in the other.

"Is Mother okay?" Karen asked.

"As opposed to what?" the nurse asked.

In the kitchen, Karen locked eyes with Tom Willis. A tall, slender reporter, with sandy hair, an angular face, and inquisitive eyes, he had spent several years covering her parents' public antics. He smiled and they exchanged a hug and a light kiss.

"Hi, Willis."

"Hi, Wainwright. How are you doing?"

"I can't believe he did that."

Willis smiled. "I can't believe he didn't do it sooner."

Karen's mouth dropped open.

"Hey, I like your mother. I make a nice living because of her, but she's been baiting him for years."

She sighed. "It's just so upsetting." She studied him for a moment. "Speaking of making a living, I thought you were getting out of the newspaper business. What happened to writing the great American novel?"

"Still working on it." He put his arm around her and she allowed herself to linger for a moment. "You'd better go see her," he said. "She's been asking for you. I'll be here when you're done and we can talk some more."

Karen entered the bedroom as a reporter was leaving, to find Margaret propped up in bed in her La Perla bed jacket and gown, a new scarf dangling from her neck. Mary stood next to her, fluffing the pillows.

"Mommy," Karen said, crossing the carpet.

"Buttercup."

"Mommy, how are you? Are you in pain?"

"I'm still a little weak, but I shall soldier on." Margaret turned to Mary. "Unless you plan on plucking a goose to remedy the situation, stop doing that and find another pillow."

Mary rolled her eyes and walked out.

Karen sat down next to her mother, who gave a heavy sigh. "You should not have been witness to that ugly scene. Perhaps we should go away together. How about Cannes? I could get a personal companion—two—one for each of us."

"What about Marcus?"

Margaret gave a wave of her hand. "Marcus has decided to move on. He abhors violence. He's always afraid of damage to the face. It's how he makes his living, you know."

"I noticed." Karen sniffled as her eyes filled with tears.

"No, no, don't cry, my pearl. This is what I've been trying to tell you. This is marriage gone wrong, the inferior partner unable to reconcile to the loss." She sighed. "Is Willis still here?"

Karen sniffled. "He's outside."

"Good. I feel terrible that I can't offer him an exclusive. He's like family. You know it's all right if you confide in him. Completely off the record of course. Just to help you get the male perspective."

"I have Robert for that."

Margaret's eyes narrowed. "Yes, but I feel he's too close to the situation. You need someone more removed."

They sat quietly.

"Mommy, you know I'm going to talk to Daddy about all this. This has to stop."

Margaret stroked Karen's hair. "Of course, my little bon-bon. I expect you to." She grabbed an envelope and handed it to her. "Be sure to give him this."

"What is it?"

"The bill for the scarf."

Karen fingered the envelope in her hand and gave a heavy sigh.

Karen arrived at the attorney's office by noon.

Albert didn't look up when she entered the conference room. Edward greeted her stern look with a penitent smile.

Karen shook her head.

They sat down together at the conference table. When she slid a look at him, Edward's eyes were calm.

"Daddy, how could you? Why? What does it matter if Mommy marries? You marry all the time."

He patted her hand. "Yes, princess, but I'm supposed to. Your mother's always had better sense."

"And you had better anger management."

Edward gave a small, humorless chuckle. "It's just so damn hard to get that woman's attention. She won't see reason."

Karen glared at her father. "That's a drastic way to get someone to take notice, Daddy. How will you work everything out legally?"

"Oh, your mother isn't pressing charges. Did she mention anything about the scarf?"

Karen pulled the envelope from her pocket. "She sent a bill."

Albert raised his head. "You're not paying for the scarf, Ed. You're not admitting you touched that scarf."

"There were a dozen witnesses," Karen protested.

Albert was up and pacing now, his eyes feverish. "It was a darkened room! The scarf got caught on the chair; she fell!"

Karen turned to Edward. "Is he kidding?"

"She nearly strangled herself, that's right. That's what happened. My client saved her!"

Karen realized her mouth was hanging open. Edward patted her hand. "Albert's been up all night."

"Don't touch that bill, Ed. We're not accepting that."

"Daddy, what were you thinking?"

Edward kissed her forehead. "Don't fret over this. It's a minor disagreement. Let this be a lesson, Karen. Love is a complicated emotion."

"That's what Robert said."

"He's very wise. Did he tell you marriage only makes it worse?"

Karen sat back in the chair, exhausted.

Robert met Karen at the door when she came in.

"So, what happened?"

"My father's not going to jail. My mother is billing him for the scarf."

"That sounds about right. Are you okay?"

Karen stared at Robert for a long moment. "I'm not sure. I'm not sure about anything."

Robert stepped forward. "Do I want to know what that means?"

"I don't think we should get married."

Robert snaked his arms around Karen. "Baby, you're in shock, okay? This is not the time to talk about this."

"What if we end up like them?"

"Not a chance. You don't wear scarves."

Karen opened her mouth to protest but Robert interrupted. "Don't try to figure this out now. Or ever. You're not going to be able to understand their relationship. It's their problem, not ours."

Karen stood still for a moment and then tears began sliding down her cheeks. Robert cradled her in his arms, kissing her forehead, stroking her hair. "How about we go back to bed and hide under the covers together?"

Karen looked up at him. "Are you trying to take advantage of me while I'm emotionally vulnerable?"

Robert kissed her forehead again. "Absolutely."

Karen thought for a moment. She wiped a hand across her eyes. "Okay."

Chapter 36

Ian's face was a tight mask of control as he watched the two Frenchmen wandering through the loft, picking through his canvases, conversing in their own language. Michele slid onto the stool next to him, invading his safety zone, her scent filling his head. He took a long pull on his cigarette and shifted away from her.

"Tu pourrais être un peu plus aimable," she whispered.

"I am being nice but I didn't invite them. I didn't invite you, either."

"You need money," she said, laying a hand on his arm.

He shrugged away from her.

"You think I do not know all this is borrowed?" She waved her arm vaguely. "I am not the only one who accepts gifts."

"Michele," one of the men called, the one with the stern, petulant air. *"Que penses-tu de ça?"* He pointed to a scene of Montmartre. Michele crossed the loft; her easy, fluid step quickened slightly, imperceptible to anyone but Ian. *This is the lover, the money. And he needs to be kept happy.*

Ian listened as they conversed in French for a few moments. Michele spoke quickly, deferring to the lover's condescending tone. His voice was harsh and fractious and Michele attempted to soothe him. Ian winced mentally as Michele explained Ian's artistic virtues. The lover made a face, then shrugged. *"Bien,"* he said.

Bastard, Ian thought.

A half hour later, Michele ushered the men out to wait for her downstairs.

She moved about the workspace, her movements fluid, almost languid, her face composed. Ian clenched his teeth. *Unfuckingbelievable*, he thought, watching her float through the loft, running her hand absently over each painting, as if marking her territory, as if she hadn't given up the right to them—to him—long ago.

"*Où sont mes portraits?* Where are the paintings of me? You have put me away, *hein?* You no longer need inspiration?"

Inspiration, Ian thought. *Yes, you were that.* Maybe every painter has the one who inspires them, the one they can't get over. Manet obsessed over Berthe Morisot. He had to be close to her, paint her, again and again, trying to capture her, own her completely. *Manet was a fool*, he thought. *It can't be done.*

"*Bien*," she said, folding her arms and walking through the loft. "*Ta mère, ta mère va bien, oui?* She is all right, yes? The cancer does not come back?"

"My mother is fine now."

"It is hard for you to visit, being so far away. But maybe you prefer it. I know you are afraid. So close to losing her."

He didn't answer, hating that she knew him so well.

"Ian," she said, her voice gentle. "*Tu n'es pas retourné chez toi*, you have not gone home since she is well. Three years, Ian."

"I don't want to talk about my mother."

She raised her eyebrows but her smile came back. "My mother thought you could be the next Manet or Renoir."

"Your mother hated me."

"My mother hated your poverty. *C'est différent.*"

Something on the kitchen island caught her attention, and she strolled closer. She fingered the calculator and the pencils resting on a yellow legal pad. She scanned the writing on the pad. "Hum, *beaucoup de chiffres*," she murmured. "You are not one for business. This is not your writing." She gave him a sly look. "Who is she? Do you paint her?"

His lips tightened.

"*Alors,* you're seeing *une femme d'affaires,* a businesswoman. *Bien.* She requires a lot, no? Like me."

"She's nothing like you."

Michele picked up her purse, and before he could move she pressed herself against him, kissing him lightly on his lips. He jerked his head away.

A smile touched her lips. "Are you sure?" she said, moving toward the door. "It's good we found each other again. I can help you. He will buy your work. Think about a price. We keep in touch." Then she was gone, closing the door behind her.

Chapter 37

Elizabeth took a deep breath as she handed her coat to the checker. She had already spotted Saunders, sitting at the table, waiting for her. As the waiter led her to her table, she caught sight of Stanton Perry out of the corner of her eye. She asked the waiter to wait as she detoured to say hello.

"Hello, young lady," he said. "How are things?"

She hesitated. He knew, of course. Suddenly, the temptation to plead her case and solicit his help overwhelmed her. He was a kingmaker. If she got pushed out, he could help her make connections, help her find another job. A golden parachute. He was waiting.

"Something on your mind?" he asked finally.

"Not at all," she said. "Everything is fine, Mr. Perry. I always make sure of that."

He gave her an easy smile. "Glad to hear it. Enjoy your dinner with Mr. Saunders," he said, leaning in to kiss her cheek. "Make me proud," he whispered.

Elizabeth toyed with the spoon in her coffee cup. The meal was finished, the conversation pleasant, easygoing; it would have been better if there were buffers. If she had been with Nick, Saunders could've brought his wife. She should've been missing Nick; he was the obvious choice. Yet all she wanted was Ian, here, next to her. A sudden surge of longing for him washed over her, threatening to overwhelm her. She forced herself to focus.

"How are you responding to losing members of your team?"

"They've been replaced. Charlie and Steven are going to be tremendous assets to the group."

Saunders took a sip of his coffee and sat back. "I assume you've heard about Mitkey and Davis Enterprises. I would've thought that deal would've gone through you."

Into the cage, Elizabeth thought. Here we go. This is it. This is the moment. She took a deep breath, collecting her thoughts. "I heard about it. I'm more concerned about creating a long-term strategy. What I'm proposing will do just that. My research shows that the percentage of high-net-worth female clients has made a dramatic jump to just over ten percent. By the end of this decade, over twenty trillion dollars will be in the hands of women. This is something we haven't seen before. I've restructured my area so that each adviser has no more than sixty clients, to give them more time to build effective one-on-one relationships."

"Our clients aren't usually concerned with a one-on-one relationship," Saunders said.

"That's because most of our clients are men."

Saunders smiled.

"Women don't compartmentalize. And they prefer advisers that they feel are listening to them, looking at their entire financial situation, not just monitoring their accounts. This is a special niche market and we need to make adjustments. And it's not just a matter of high-net-worth female clients; it's the wives and daughters getting involved in the family finances. Charlie and Steven have made contact with two very high-profile clients, one of whom is Janice Pritchett. With her recent promotion to full partner in her father's real estate and hotel empire, her addition to our client base will attract other clients like her, and open a host of possibilities."

"Will she be our client?" Saunders asked.

"I believe so, yes," Elizabeth said, keeping her voice calm, measured. "Not everyone is taking advantage of this trend. This is our unique opportunity. I need to know. Do I have your support?"

Saunders stared straight ahead; Elizabeth knew that was his way of processing. "Liz, the most important thing in any company is having the right tools and the right people in place to use them. I brought you to this company. You have my total and complete support."

"Thank you," she said. "I appreciate that."

It wasn't until they'd said their good-byes and she was alone on the street that she realized she'd been holding her breath.

Chapter 38

Robert sat in the middle at the large conference table, the morning sun streaming through the blinds. Margaret sat at one end, Edward at the other. When they had summoned him, he expected a de facto meeting to mea culpa for freaking out their daughter, and to give their blessing—until they said the meeting would be in an attorney's office. Now they were sitting at opposite ends of the table, acting as if nothing had happened. Robert shook his head. Hedging their bets with a prenup, he thought. *It doesn't matter. Knock yourselves out. We won't need it.*

A small, nervous-looking man with an ill-advised comb-over came in, carrying two blue folders, and handed one to Margaret and one to Edward. Giving Robert a look of pity and contempt, he fled the room.

Margaret and Edward opened their folders in unison, read a moment, and then closed them in unison.

"I assume since you came to this meeting, Karen is still leaning toward the marital state," Margaret said.

Robert gave an internal sigh. At least they didn't know it had taken everything he had to keep Karen in a holding pattern. "Yes, but it was a nice try on your part."

Margaret ignored the comment. "All right then, young man. Let's get right to the point. One Broadway production and five thousand a month for six months."

"This isn't necessary, you know. You can draw up a prenup stating I get nothing. I'll sign it."

Margaret and Edward smiled tolerantly at him.

"We're not concerned with prenups, dear boy," Edward said. "This is an allowance . . . for you."

"I haven't had an allowance since I was twelve," Robert said. "Is there a list of chores I need to complete?"

"Only one," Margaret said.

Edward cleared his throat. "The allowance is compensation for *not* getting married."

As a writer, Robert found it ironic to be at a loss for words when he needed them most. Most parents of the bride wanted assurances of the groom's intention to stay by their daughter's side, to care for her, never leave her. These people were offering him an incentive package to take a hike.

"Now you're offering a cheap career boost and some cash for me to disappear?"

"Don't be melodramatic," Margaret said. "We're paying her the highest compliment. Do you have any idea how expensive a Broadway production is?"

"Don't take it personally, lad," Edward soothed. "It's not that we don't respect you. Think of us as patrons helping you create—without our daughter."

"There isn't enough money in the world for that."

Margaret rolled her eyes. "If I had a hundred dollar bill for every time I heard that."

Robert leaned forward. "You've done this before?" He didn't manage to keep the amazement out of his voice.

"A professorship here, a recording contract there. The other dalliances were nipped in the bud. You were quite clever, proposing so suddenly."

"That's what happens when you're in love," he said drily. "This is strange behavior, since you're planning to object at the ceremony. You know what I think? I think you don't have the nerve to come right out and ruin the happiness of your only beloved daughter, that's what I think."

"Two Broadway shows, a run on the London stage, and

double the money," Margaret said. "Last offer, take it or leave it."

Robert stood up. "I will not accept anything from you. If you want to run wild with your demented psycho-social-sexual issues, be my guest, but it won't change us."

"Well, I believe that changes things," Edward said from the other end of the table.

"It changes nothing," Margaret said, leaning forward.

"He loves her," Edward said, his voice rising.

"This is so typical of you," Margaret hissed. "Always the spineless one."

"And you always have to have control," Edward shot back. "Well, there are some things you can't control."

"Would you two like to be alone?" Robert asked.

"Young man, you are dismissed," Margaret said. "But this is by no means over."

Robert picked up his coat. "Fine, but if your next move is the bloody horse's head in the bed, I'd think twice. Karen just bought new sheets, black and white stripes, very retro European. She really likes them."

"You are not marrying my daughter," Margaret said.

"Yes, I am," Robert said, striding out and slamming the door behind him.

He stood outside the door for a moment, listening to the muffled shouting, and rolled his eyes.

The small, nervous man bustled up to Robert, hastily brushing all his hair to one side. "Who should I make the check out to?"

Pushing past him, Robert headed for the elevator.

Chapter 39

By eleven o'clock Elizabeth's migraine felt like a spike in her temple. The meeting had been in progress for two hours and was proceeding on schedule. Mitkey had been taking little digs throughout the morning. With little time left, he attempted to cut the legs out from under her.

"Tripling the total revenue in three years is a steep climb, Liz. Historically, this division has been the weakest link and it's not turning around on a dime. Face it, this is a stretch."

"Liz's group will be focusing on her new growth revenue strategy," Saunders said. "Liz?"

Elizabeth made her presentation, detailing the female wealth market and the long- and short-term strategies to appeal to women as prospective clients. The faces around the table became serious, attentive. Her voice remained calm, measured. "The addition of Janice Pritchett has brought new referrals."

"How much did she bring to the table?" Saunders asked.

"Four hundred million."

Elizabeth savored the sound of silence in the room.

"Thank you, Liz," Saunders said. "I look forward to the progress reports from your group."

Saunders had orchestrated the meeting perfectly, down to asking the exact questions he said he would. When Elizabeth looked across the room, Mitkey didn't make eye contact.

* * *

Elizabeth came off the elevator with all of her abdominal muscles constricted, her nerve ends jangling and so tightly wound she felt ready to snap. She forced her gait to an easy stride, returning to work as if nothing had occurred, just another routine day. Underneath her controlled exterior, her blood was dancing in her ears. The feeling of relief in the aftermath hadn't hit her yet.

At four o'clock a large bouquet of white roses was delivered to her office. The card read, "Congratulations, kid. Love, Nick." She ran her fingers over the petals, wishing the card, the flowers, were from Ian. Saunders appearing in the doorway of her office cut into her thoughts.

"Good presentation, Liz," he said.

"Thank you," she said, composing herself, giving him an easy smile.

"I always say I make good decisions. I have you to prove it." With a smile and a wink, he left the room.

Realizing that her legs were shaking, she sat down. *It's over. It's over and I'm still here.*

Chapter 40

Leaning back in his chair, feet resting on the desk, eyes glued to his computer screen, Parker listened to the talking heads on the plasma screen on the wall: *"Even hedge funds are expected to suffer this month. The losses could be as high as twelve percent."*

Darryl stuck his head into Parker's office, knocking on the open door.

"Hey, big guy," he said.

Parker snapped off the sound with the remote. "Assholes," he muttered as he waved Darryl in.

"Stanley said the fluctuations between the bonds and the underlying stocks are deeper than we thought. He's recommending we pull back. He said we can't borrow twenty dollars for every one dollar we have."

Parker took his feet off the desk. "Fuck him. The dollar will get weaker and the yen will go up. That'll make over a billion for us, I guarantee it. Just concentrate on getting the portfolio valuation going, juice it up a little. By the time we report in January, we'll be back on top."

"You're the boss," Darryl said, heading back out.

Parker turned up the sound as the announcer read, *"Janice Pritchett, newly crowned partner in her ailing father's umbrella corporation, Compton Holdings, made an important move today. Elizabeth Strait, the latest whiz-kid money manager on the street, boasted a huge coup today as the Pritchett family placed their future in her company's hands."*

"Fuck," Parker muttered, shutting off the television with a flick of the remote and tossing it on the desk. *The bitch managed to come out on top*, he thought. Shrugging the thought away, he looked around the office, an uneasiness beginning to gnaw at him. Stanley and his damn abacus. *So we're a little down this month*, he thought. Seven percent loss is nothing. Besides, he had just finished a buy for another shitload of defaulted debt that would be worth a few hundred million.

"Carol, I'm going out," he called, grabbing his coat. Marianna was history; the blonde he had met at the mixer should be on her way to the hotel by now. He made a halfhearted attempt to remember what company she worked for, and gave up. What the hell, it didn't matter. In forty minutes he'd have her bent over, moaning like a pussycat. She might turn out to be a decent replacement.

He settled into the backseat of the limo. "Downtown, Ernie, you know the place."

"Yes, sir," Ernie said, easing out into traffic.

Chapter 41

Elizabeth and Karen gazed up into the dome-shaped foyer of Davis Manor.

Elizabeth paced. "I'm not sure why *I* need to be here," she said, her voice an angry whisper. "Her husband just tried to screw me with my panties still on."

"Because she had nothing to do with that," Karen soothed. "And because—"

"Give me a Taoist principle, and I swear I'll scream."

Karen shrugged and let it go.

Elizabeth stopped at the foot of the winding stairway. "I feel like Cary Grant should be carrying Ingrid Bergman down any minute now."

"It is romantic," Karen mused. "Speaking of romance—"

"Forget it. Ian is out of the picture."

"I think he was good for you. You really liked him."

"To quote your mother, liking him is irrelevant. How is she? Is she pressing charges?"

Karen shuddered at the subject. "No. I've had some time to think about it. She never would. If my father went to jail, what would she do with herself? She'd cease to exist. Robert is right. They feed off each other." Karen stood silently for a moment. "I told Robert I think we should put the wedding on hold. It's not that I want to. I just . . . I don't know what to think."

"What did he say?"

"He keeps seducing me and talking me out of it. I used to love looking at my parents' wedding pictures," she said with a sigh. "They were so happy. But if this is how it ends—I can't imagine not feeling the love that I feel for Robert now. It scares the hell out of me."

Elizabeth ran her hand over Karen's back. "That is not going to happen to you and Robert."

"That's what he says. But how does he know? How does anyone know?"

"Karen, there's no guarantee. He can't give you a guarantee."

They dropped the subject at the sound of a door closing upstairs. Emily came flitting down to the landing, her face flushed, her hands fluttering as she talked. "So what do you think?" she said.

"The house is gorgeous. You're doing an amazing job," Karen said.

Karen shot Elizabeth a look.

"Very nice," Elizabeth said.

Emily heaved a sigh. "I'm so glad you like it. There's still so much to be done."

"What does Parker think?" Karen asked.

"Do you know he hasn't even been here? I just don't understand him. It was all he talked about, night and day, and he hasn't set foot here." She stood there between them, wringing her hands.

"Ems, are you okay?" Karen said. "What's happening with you?"

Two tears rolled down Emily's cheeks and Karen put her arm around her, shooting Elizabeth a look. Elizabeth's eyes narrowed but she took Emily's hand. They sat down on the marble bench.

"I just don't understand," Emily cried. "It wasn't supposed to work out this way. Nothing I do is right. He was so happy before we were married and now he yells all the time and rolls his eyes at me . . . and he's always working late."

Elizabeth looked away.

"I feel like I shouldn't try anything anymore because I won't succeed. It'll be a failure," Emily sniveled.

Karen gave her a hug. "Emily, you know that's not true. Everything you have ever done—before you were married—was perfect. You went to Brown University. You're an entrepreneur. The perfume, the jewelry. You were in the best off-Broadway revival of *Singin' in the Rain* in years. You were fantastic; you got the biggest round of applause. Remember what the reviews said?"

"Watson reinvents Lina Lamont," Emily said, dabbing at her eyes with a tissue. She gave Karen a thoughtful look. "You're right. I did very well . . . but since I've been married . . ." She glanced over at Elizabeth, a frown furrowing her forehead. "And you, you're always mad at me! What did I do to you?"

Elizabeth shook her head. "Nothing. You didn't do a thing. Did it ever occur to you that I have problems of my own?" she said, her voice harsh. She bit her tongue and started again. "Look, Emily, no relationship is perfect."

"Yours is," Emily said, "with Ian."

Elizabeth gave a dry laugh. "Was."

Emily gave her a sly look. "Was?"

Elizabeth disengaged and sat back. "Yes, was."

They sat for a moment in silence, each lost in their own thoughts.

"Thank you for coming to see the house," Emily said finally. "What do you have for the rest of the day?"

Karen stood up. "Back to Manhattan, I'm meeting Robert and Ian at B & H Video."

"What are they doing there?" Elizabeth asked.

"Robert's helping Ian buy a laptop."

"I just had a brilliant idea," Emily said, her eyes lighting up. "I could make a documentary about the construction and decoration of this house. Wouldn't that be super? I'll get all the equipment and have someone film it, and then I'll edit the film and voilà—a documentary! What do you think? Wouldn't that be the start of a wonderful career? Look at all the reality programs on television. They're still all the rage. Plus the print media. I could have a spread in *Town and Country.*"

Karen took Emily by the hand. "I think you can do anything you put your mind to."

Chapter 42

Ian and Robert wandered the aisles of B & H, checking out the laptops.

"Now she doesn't want to get married. She's thinking of studying Buddhism. She's concerned about our karma. I keep telling her they're not going to object, they won't do it," Robert said as Ian looked over a MacBook Pro notebook.

Ian didn't answer, his mind on thoughts of Lizzie: where she was, what she was doing. Then he thought of Michele and panic seized him.

"Hey, did you hear me?" Robert was saying.

"Sorry, mate. Her parent are nutters. Did you tell her they tried to buy you off with a career as a not-getting-married present?"

"I think that would blow her mind more than the objecting. She's spent her whole life believing the laws of the universe were guiding her path to the right husband and nothing could interfere."

Ian raised his eyebrows.

"I don't want to be the one to tell her that her parents feel this mystical process is subject to the power of their checkbook."

"So, technically, you're winning her by default."

"They're freaking her out. The apartment reeks of incense.

She's on yoga overload, and I think she's pulling away from me."

"Give her time," Ian said. "It's not every day you watch your parents attempt to commit bodily injury on each other. You have to make allowances."

Robert moved on down the aisle. "Hey, where have you been, anyway? I've been calling you all week and getting the machine."

"I'm painting at the workspace at the school."

Robert turned to examine him. "What for?"

"Michele's here. She brought a buyer to the loft . . . and I just wanted to be off by myself."

"In a building that she doesn't have ID to get into."

"Something like that. She says she wants to help me sell my work."

"She wants to push your buttons and move on. She never changes."

Ian nodded. "I know."

"Then tell her to get lost."

Ian didn't answer. He couldn't take that chance, not until he found out if Michele knew about Lizzie; and what she was really up to. Michele didn't want him, he knew that, but she could stoke the fire of Lizzie's suspicions and destroy any chance he might have of getting her back. He didn't want to think about it.

"What about Liz? What's happening with that?"

"Nothing. Doesn't Karen fill you in?"

"I don't ask."

Ian turned to find Karen and Emily coming down the aisle. They all said hello, and Emily pulled Ian into an embrace.

"No Lizzie?" Ian asked, gently putting space between himself and Emily.

"I think she had errands," Karen said quickly.

"No," Emily said, latching on to Ian's arm. "She went home."

Chapter 43

Elizabeth took a final swig of her coffee as she turned the corner onto Thirteenth Street and tossed the cup in the trash. She had no idea why coffee settled her nerves, but she'd been using it like Xanax for weeks; she even had a cup every night before she went to bed. *Good thing I'm not addicted to smoking,* she thought, *I'd have black lung by now.*

She skidded to a stop in front of her apartment building. Ian stood by the black gate that led to the steps.

"I never figured you for a downtown girl, Lizzie," he said without humor. "And so close to Parsons too. Convenient."

"What do you want?"

His eyes were cool, his features set.

"I wanted to let you know I secured representation and a showing."

"Why tell me?" she said.

"My career seemed to interest you."

"*My* career interests me."

Ian nodded. "Then we have something in common, don't we? I wasn't in the café, Lizzie, looking for a model. I was working. You were the only one I wanted to take to dinner and to bed."

"That's sounds touching and romantic, but it isn't that simple." She shook her head and took a breath, fighting the urge to cry. "What do you think this is? I can tell you what it isn't. It isn't Paris or Hemingway. It isn't a moveable feast or those fairy tales he wrote about how we eat, paint, read, go to bed, make love to the person we want to make love to. This is reality and it's hard and scary, and you can lose everything at any time—someone can take away everything you've worked for." Her voice inside her head sounded high pitched and far away. She realized that her cheeks were wet. "This isn't Paris. This isn't Hemingway."

"All right, love," he murmured, putting his arms around her. "Let me take you inside."

She allowed him to hold her close and they pushed through the gate and climbed the front steps.

He unlocked her door, ushering her in and handing her back the key. She sank onto the couch, allowing her misery to close around her. He sat next to her, stroking her hair, silent, watching her. "What set this off?" he said finally.

"Parker tried to screw me, working behind my back to get me thrown out," she said, drawing in a ragged breath. "He knew I was struggling. I lost some people. So he threw his business to another division. He planned the whole thing. Sending me empty cartons and business cards with no title. The son of a bitch."

Ian's eyes grew dark.

"He almost succeeded. I could've been out of a job. I would've lost everything." She began to cry.

"I would've taken you in," he soothed. "Why didn't you tell me?"

She shrugged and he reached behind him, grabbing a box of tissues. He held it out to her.

"You took care of him, did you?"

"I announced a new strategy; my boss supported me." She dabbed at her eyes and blew her nose. She shook her head in disbelief. "I'd like to kick Parker's ass all the way back to Jersey."

He laughed. "That's my girl."

She smiled a weak smile and wiped her cheeks with a wad of tissue.

"Lizzie," he said, forcing her to look at him. "He never would have won. You're smarter than he is. Don't you know that?" He pulled her close, kissing her forehead. "It's all over now."

"I said those things—"

He stroked her hair and kissed her temple. "It's all right."

"I wanted to drive you away—"

"I noticed."

"You distract me."

Ian kissed her cheek, nuzzling her ear. "Is that wrong?"

She pulled back from him. "Yes. I can't afford to be distracted."

He brushed his thumb under her eye and caught a tear. "Then you won't be. I told you, I'm here for whatever you want, when you want, for as long as you want. You won't get hurt, Lizzie. I promise, I won't hurt you."

She closed her eyes. *How can I be sure this will work out?* She sighed, thinking of the advice she gave Karen. *There are no guarantees.* She opened her eyes to find him watching her; her heart skipped a beat. She knew what she wanted. He opened his arms and she curled into his embrace.

At one a.m. Ian stirred, realizing he was cold and had only a scrap of the blanket covering him. He smiled at Elizabeth's signature move, rolling over and taking the covers with her. He listened to her slow, steady breathing for a moment, then slipped out of bed and stole out of the room. He put up a pot of coffee and lit a cigarette. He tried a few sketches on scraps of paper, giving up to wander between the living room and a small office cubby. Looking overhead, he spied a storage space. Seeing a drawing tablet, he searched further, bringing down a supply box and a watercolor behind it. He gave a cursory look through the brushes and paint tubes. He examined the picture, a lovely rendering of an ocean beach, somewhere on the West Coast, he imagined. It wasn't finished. He glanced down at the signature: Lillian Montgomery. He didn't recognize the name— perhaps one of the California Impressionists. He put everything back in its place and returned to the kitchen. Pouring himself a cup of coffee, he settled on the couch.

He was walking a tightrope, and the coils could still unravel under his feet. He had lied outright about his career, telling her what she wanted to hear. That was bad enough; if Lizzie ever found out about his past, about Michele and the dark period after her departure, she'd write him off as another no-good playboy artist. She'd wind up with that git lawyer, trapped in a marriage of convenience. He needed to find a way to work this out. His career was the first step—there was one more thing he could try.

Chapter 44

Ian stood with Paul Ferand in a Chelsea gallery over on Tenth Avenue. They examined an immense canvas: the short, thick brush strokes, applied with a heavy hand.

"It's Impressionist," Ian said. "As you can see."

"*Oui*," Ferand said. "And you show me this because . . ."

Ian forced himself to remain calm. "This man, Chocioux, has generated some interest. Impressionism still has some appeal. Not everyone wants contemporary. This could be the start of a revival."

"And you believe there is room for your work?"

"Possibly, yes."

"*Peut-être*, okay, maybe," Ferand said, giving Ian a sideways glance and then turning to him. "Okay, *mon ami*, we make a decision. I am arranging an exhibit. I have a space here, in Chelsea. You will not be the only one, but I have room for two pieces, in March. Do you accept this?"

Ian looked him in the eye. "Yes, I do, thank you," he said, holding out his hand.

Ferand gave his hand a firm shake and laid a strong hand on his shoulder. "*Bien, mon ami, très bien.*"

Ian felt the air rush out of his lungs in relief.

Chapter 45

Ian, Elizabeth, Robert, and Karen occupied a large oval table in the back of the restaurant. They were joined by a group of friends Ian had affectionately dubbed The Americans. Ian had met them in Paris years before—happy expats, wandering artists, writers, poets, dreamers—with Robert as their pied piper. The majority of them had since drifted back to Manhattan.

The Americans raised their glasses in hearty congratulations to Ian, and his friends followed suit. It was a quiet affair. If it had been years earlier, they would've been in a bar, assaulted by ear-splitting noise, liquor spilling over glasses, until they stumbled out into the street in the wee hours. They were older now, responsible adults a long way from the dive apartments and the dirty ateliers, glad that one of their own was getting a break.

Elizabeth smiled as Ian leaned in for a kiss.

"Congratulations," she whispered. "We should have our own celebration, later. What should we do?"

He wrapped his arms around her. "Surprise me," he breathed in her ear as he gave her a squeeze; she let out a small laugh.

Ian glanced toward the bar and felt his smile melt away. A woman with golden hair swirling around her bare shoulders was smiling into the face of the man next to her. Michele. As if sensing his scrutiny, her eyes shifted; she lifted her glass to him.

Shit.

Karen pulled her purse onto her shoulder and got up. Elizabeth whispered in his ear. "We'll be back." She followed Karen.

Ian watched as Michele's eyes followed Elizabeth.

Michele slipped off the stool, wending her way through the restaurant toward the restrooms. Ian cursed under his breath.

Elizabeth and Karen stood before the bathroom mirror. The door opened and a tall, beautiful woman came in. Elizabeth thought she could've been a classic California girl except for the style of her clothing and a smooth, polished air that outed her as a European. A perfect package, Elizabeth thought as she came to stand next to her and check her look in the mirror. Her sharp eyes flicked over Elizabeth and she gave a cool, deprecating smile. Elizabeth sensed a puzzling hostility.

"How are you enjoying the celebration for Monsieur MacKay?" she said to Elizabeth.

"You know Ian?"

Her eyebrows lifted imperceptively. "Oh, *oui.* The art world is very small."

It's not that small, Elizabeth thought, her antennae going up.

"I have not seen him for some time. But the exhibit, it is all very exciting. You know him well?"

"I'm his friend—his girlfriend," Elizabeth said, annoyed at sounding like a teenager.

"Does he still—how do you say—have moods?"

"Don't we all?"

Michele chuckled. "Oh là," she said, reapplying her lipstick, a cool, pale shade of pink. Dropping the tube into her tiny, square bag, she raised an eyebrow at Elizabeth, a small smile on her lips. "Enjoy the celebration."

"Aren't you stopping by the table?" Elizabeth asked.

"We will see each other," Michele said.

Elizabeth narrowed her eyes. *This Eurosnob is getting on my nerves.* "And how do you know Ian?"

Michele smiled. "I was—his friend."

And then she was out the door.

Karen and Elizabeth looked at each other for a long moment.

"All right?" Ian asked as Elizabeth sat down.

"Fine," she answered in a tight voice.

Damn you, Michele, he thought.

Ian pulled in a deep breath of the cool night air. He lit up, feeling his anger churning inside. He smoked and waited. In a few minutes Michele exited the restaurant and sauntered over to him.

"What the hell did you do?"

She stretched up to kiss him but he jerked back. She smiled. "I met your new belle du jour. Is that how you like them now? *Maigres.* Pale and skinny." She was smiling but he knew his ex-wife; she was seething.

Her eyes slid over his face. "Does she make you feel the way I did?" she whispered. "Without breath? Does she make you moan as I did? Such a satisfying sound."

He advanced on her. Shocked by the sudden urge to raise his hand against her, he stopped short. "Shut it. I don't want you talking about her and I sure as hell don't want you talking to her."

She smirked at him.

He glanced back at the entrance; Elizabeth could come out at any moment. "What did you say to her?"

Michele rolled her eyes and shrugged. "I said we were friends. If I make an innocent comment and she takes it wrong, what can I do?"

"I don't care what you do, just stay away from her, from us. I have an exhibit now. I won't sell to your lover."

"I know about your little show." Reaching out, she ran one

perfectly manicured nail up and down his chest. "But my friend will give you two thousand for two of your paintings. That will make you happy, no? More money to spend on the belle du jour." She looked up at him through her lashes. "You know, she and I can meet again. It can happen. An accident. We talk. If I tell her we are lovers now, do you think she will believe me?"

"Stay away from her, Michele," he warned.

"I can do that. All you have to do is sell the paintings. Meet me on Friday, at the park where they have the little skating pond and the shops, hmm? At noon." Turning on her heel, she walked away.

Walking around to the alley at the side of the building, he steeled himself, afraid he might be sick and lose his dinner, but the feeling passed. He should've known what was coming. He knew her methods. She enjoyed toying with people; once they revealed any emotion or weakness, she would strike, destroy, and move on.

He lit a fresh cigarette, letting out a stream of smoke, watching as the wind snatched it away. He wandered back to the entrance, and a few moments later Elizabeth emerged, huddling in her coat. She stood apart from him, not meeting his eyes.

They waited for Robert and Karen and The Americans to come out. The evening had started festive and boisterous; it ended standing in a semicircle of quiet and unease.

"Anyone want to come back to the apartment for a drink?" Robert said.

They looked around at one another and gave their excuses. With mumbled good-nights, the party broke up.

Ian and Elizabeth walked in silence for several blocks, fighting the brisk wind whipping up around them.

"I met your friend in the ladies' room," Elizabeth said.

"She's not my friend."

"One of your models?"

He didn't answer.

"Wow, right on the money. I'm so good it's scary. How long is she staying in New York?"

"How the fuck should I know?"

Elizabeth stopped short. "I'm getting a cab."

"Lizzie . . ."

"Go have fun with your friend or your model, or whoever the hell she is."

His heart lurched. "She's neither, dammit. For Christ's sake, Lizzie, this is bullshit."

"No, you saying you'd be here for me—just me—that was bullshit."

"Do you see me going home with *her*? No, I'm standing here. You're the one walking away, Lizzie."

She gave a short laugh. "You know what my problem is? I never learn." She walked away, shaking her head.

"Lizzie . . . Lizzie, stop!"

She halted, hugging her coat around her.

He walked over to her, his mind racing. *Tell her, tell her the truth, get it over with.* "I'm not with her now, am I? She's not with me. I'm here with you. What do you want from me?"

"Whatever it is, you can't give it to me."

She moved to leave.

"Do you want me to stay with you, at your apartment? Do you want me to paint in your kitchen, where you can watch me?"

She stopped and turned. "If I say no, I'll be lying."

"Then say yes."

"So I can feel like a jealous schoolgirl?"

"Yes. No. I don't care. Either way is fine with me. There's nowhere else I want to be."

"Are you going to see her again?"

"I haven't been seeing her."

She stiffened. "You didn't answer my question."

"No."

"Fine."

They started walking again. "You can paint in my kitchen anyway," she said finally.

Chapter 46

Elizabeth and Karen sat on the end of a long row of chairs in the Buddhist temple. Sitar music played; other worshippers sat with eyes closed. Elizabeth eyed the gigantic Buddha, a bowl of fruit on the table before him. The Buddha wore a mischievous smile. *Why is he so damn happy?*

"He agreed to stay at my apartment," she whispered. "Why is he so damn agreeable? He's sleeping with her, I know it."

Karen leaned over, whispering in turn. "You know, I'm convinced Robert and I are just acting out a karmic déjà vu. We're repeating my parents' path by working together. We are reliving their life, but in the same lifetime."

Elizabeth turned to stare at her. "Your mind is a scary place."

"I know, but it makes perfect sense."

"Why are we even here?" Elizabeth said. "You're not a Buddhist."

"I'll try anything. I'll practice the Noble Eightfold Path to reverse my parents' bad karma. I will speak in a loving, kind, non-injuring way and counteract my mother's open letter to my father—in every major newspaper—explaining why he's a pathetic hack as a writer."

"Good thinking," Elizabeth said.

They sat in silence for a moment.

"Do you think he's sleeping with her?" Elizabeth asked.

"No."

"So why do I think he is?"

"You're having a delayed reaction caused by job stress. Your emotions are fragile. That's what's causing this."

Elizabeth felt tears stinging her eyes, and cursed under her breath. "I'm in love with him. That's what's causing this."

"Shit," Karen said aloud.

Worshippers turned censuring eyes on them and they shrunk in their seats. Exchanging glances, they got up and left.

Once outside the temple, they walked, the scent of incense clinging to them. Karen regarded Elizabeth with open sympathy. "Do you think Ian is telling you the truth?"

"I don't know . . . I want to believe that he is. If you were me, what would you do?"

They stopped walking. Karen thought a moment before speaking. "All I know, is that Taoism promotes natural, unselfconscious flowing action. You don't have to think about what you do, you just do it, naturally. If you love him and you think he's telling the truth, take the risk. Let yourself go and let your feelings for Ian come out. Don't hold back anymore."

"Maybe I would even get the look."

"I hope so."

"Do you still get the look from Robert?"

Karen smiled. "Every day."

Chapter 47

Robert and Karen's apartment hummed with a mix of background music and conversation. People crowded the rooms, drinks in hand, chattering and laughing.

Robert and Ian were in the cube that passed for a kitchen, Ian watching as Robert mixed drinks.

"So what is all this supposed to accomplish?" Ian asked.

"It's a little something for the actors, so they can relax and bond."

Ian nodded his head. He looked out on the living room. "Which one is the unfortunate thespian?"

Robert pointed at Larry, standing in the midst of a circle as Alfred and the cast gathered around him, holding hands, everyone's eyes closed. Larry grasped Vicki's hand as Alfred's voice drifted through the apartment. "Let this, thy child live . . . for a character has a soul and a spirit and an artist bleeds for his creation . . . give wisdom and mercy to the playwright . . ."

Ian's eyes opened wide, taking in the satyr's beard and sandals. "And the chap giving the benediction would be Jesus Christ Superstar?"

"Also known as Alfred," Robert said, handing him a rye and ginger ale. "Every good actor takes a little of his part with him when he moves on."

"Uh huh. You could have saved money on refreshments by providing loaves and fishes and letting him do the rest. May I

ask why he's doing a laying on of hands on the arse of the
woman holding onto Larry?"

Robert's chuckle stuck in his throat as he took a closer look.
"Shit," he muttered.

"How are the wedding plans coming?" Ian asked.

"We're getting there."

"Did you buy a special gift for Karen?"

Robert looked at him. "Am I supposed to do that?"

"Of course. You buy a gift for her parents and a special gift
for her. Have you made arrangements for the rehearsal dinner? That's the groom's responsibility."

Robert nodded. "I took care of it. Since when do you know
so much about American weddings? Are you thinking of having one?"

Ian frowned at him.

"If you are, I hope you took care of the remnants of the last
marriage."

Ian didn't answer.

Robert looked up to see Karen greeting Tom Willis with a
warm embrace. They sat down on the loveseat in the corner of
the living room and began to talk.

Robert frowned.

"Who is that?" Ian asked, following his gaze.

"Reporter. Makes his living covering her parents' life under
the big top. It's nothing to be concerned about."

Ian kept watching. "She known him long?"

Robert nodded. "Yeah, why? What are you thinking?"

Ian turned back to focus on Robert. "I think you need to be
concerned, mate."

Robert's eyes narrowed. They looked over again as Willis
snaked his arm around Karen's shoulder.

"**I**'m so happy to see you," Karen said.

Alfred squeezed by with Vicki, chattering all the way.
"Yeah, being Jesus . . . I really grew as a person, you know what
I mean? Sometimes, when I go out, I still wear the robe."

"Awesome," Vicki said.

"Fifty bucks says no one notices," Willis whispered to Karen, causing her to stifle a laugh.

"That's how I look at each part, you know. Like being born again," Alfred continued, guiding Vicki toward the bedroom.

She nodded as Alfred ran a hand through her hair. "Really awesome."

The door closed behind them.

"Do you think she'll see God?" Willis whispered.

"Behave," Karen said with a laugh.

"So, how's the writing life?"

She hesitated. "I'm still having a little problem with the plot. Robert's been very understanding about it. I want you two to meet before you leave."

Willis nodded. "You know, you're having a problem writing about relationships and friendships because you haven't figured out the lives of the people in your own family."

Karen nodded.

"You can't move into the future until you take care of the past."

"I've been thinking about that a lot lately."

Willis moved closer, his eyes soft, his hand brushing hers. "I want to help you, Karen. We've known each other a long time. I'm very fond of you."

Karen smiled.

"I want to help you figure this out. Your writing problems are not going to stop until you do."

He pulled out a clipping from his jacket pocket and pressed it into her hand.

Karen opened the clipping and her mouth dropped open. "Not again."

"Look, I have to go, but why don't we have lunch next week? We can talk this out, try to come up with a game plan. Completely off the record. Would you like that?"

Karen nodded. Giving her a kiss on the cheek and a look she didn't want to decipher, Willis left.

Chapter 48

Karen caught Ian just before he left the party, pressing a note and a package in his hand. The note turned out to be instructions. The package held a book, *The Private Lives of the Impressionists*. The next afternoon he was smiling as he followed the instructions to Utrecht, where a package containing a small sketch pad and newly sharpened pencils waited for him along with another note. He followed the clues to the Magnolia Bakery. A woman behind the counter handed him a small box of cupcakes and another note.

A half hour later he arrived at the Metropolitan Museum of Art. He gazed up at the giant flag draped across the front of the building bearing Monet's painting, *Impression Sunrise*. He found Elizabeth sitting on a ledge at the top of the stairs with a Starbucks bag. He gave her an enthusiastic kiss, and she made a sound of appreciation.

"So," she began, "you have your book, a pad and pencil for quick sketching, your snack and"—she opened the bag and withdrew two cups—"your favorite coffee. I didn't want you to be hungry during the exhibit."

"You're a star, darling," he said. "You've taken care of everything brilliantly. You're spoiling me, you are."

They ate sitting at the top of the steps and then went inside. On the great staircase, he pulled her close and kissed her on her neck. "Thank you," he whispered.

They held hands, moving with the crowds through the rooms, following the history of the Impressionists through their paintings, from the early days in Paris to the end in Giverny. They admired the canvases in silence, Ian behind Elizabeth, his arms snaked around her. Afterward, they made their way to the cafeteria and settled with their trays in a back corner. After tasting her pasta, Elizabeth gave a longing look at his chicken francese. With a smile, he switched plates.

"Well, this is quite a feat you pulled off, Miss Lizzie. You should be proud."

She smiled. "I am." She thought a moment. "Until you see everything laid out in chronological order, you don't realize how many years they all struggled, how much time went by before at least some of them received recognition."

Ian nodded. "Under the circumstances, you'd think they'd give it up."

Elizabeth's face fell, and Ian grasped her hand, bringing it close for a kiss. "Just because a painter doesn't pick up a brush, for whatever reason, doesn't change who they are. You never stop being an artist."

"Do you ever think about twenty years down the road—for your art, for yourself?"

He gave it a moment's thought. "I do. Sometimes I think everything may be very different. I much prefer the daydream where everything will be the same." He looked into her eyes. "We'll be the same."

"Or maybe better," she said. "Are you sure you want to finish your pie?" she asked.

He put the fork down and passed the plate to her.

She shook her head. "I think you should leave room. There's more dessert at home."

Pushing the plate aside, he gave a low chuckle.

Chapter 49

"**I** can't believe they're back at it again." Karen was sitting up in bed, yoga style, the newspaper clipping in her lap. On the TV screen, Elizabeth Taylor continued to verbally demolish Richard Burton in *Who's Afraid of Virginia Woolf?* "She melted down my father's Plume Award and had it molded into a dagger. You see the symbolism, don't you? If this isn't Freudian, I don't know what is. We're moving toward full-on *la vida loca*. Strangulation, daggers. They're in their own little game of Clue. It was Edward in the reception tent with the scarf. No, it was Margaret, in the chapel, with the dagger. Baby, are you hearing me?"

"Yes, I heard you," Robert said from the bathroom. "Stop reading those articles. Maybe your mother is just going through a Hamlet phase."

"She had it gift-wrapped and delivered to him by special messenger during a book signing. The card said, and I quote, 'Stick it where the sun don't shine.' This from a *New York Times* bestselling author."

Robert came into the bedroom. "She could've gone for more originality, but economy of words is a crucial writing skill."

"It's official. My parents are the Energizer Bunnies of destruction."

He came to sit down on the bed, running his hand up and

down her arm. "Look, I think Willis is an okay guy. He has to be—you like him—but bringing you this article isn't helping."

"I remember when I was a kid. They were always affectionate with each other. The way they looked at each other; they couldn't be in the same room without touching each other." Her eyes grew misty. "Like us."

"Karen, remember one thing. Your parents have nothing to do with us," he said, taking her hand.

"Maybe it was because they had me. Maybe they never wanted a child? Or maybe they wanted a son and got me instead?"

"Now you think you're the reason for your parents' insanity? Not even close."

She was silent for a moment. "We're baiting karma by working together. Look how it turned out for them."

"Karen, your parents' marriage ended because of each other; work had nothing to do with it. It wasn't nurture, it was nature, with a fifth of Jim Beam thrown in."

"Buddha says all things are universally connected."

"If all things were universally connected, there would be no such thing as frequent flier miles." He kissed her forehead and got up.

She flopped back on the pillows, staring up at the ceiling. "Buddhism is the pursuit of enlightenment," she said after a while. "Liberation from delusion. All this time I've been deluding myself, searching for peace, thinking that was even possible."

"That's not delusion, baby, it's self-preservation. I think you've got a case of too much information, and too much contemplation." With one fluid motion, he popped out the video of Elizabeth Taylor and Richard Burton and popped in a tape of *Barefoot in the Park*. A young Robert Redford filled the screen, gasping as he struggled up flights of stairs, bursting into an apartment to fall into the arms of Jane Fonda. "You've traveled the world studying and learning how to be at peace. How about accepting this stuff as one of the Ten Thousand Things and moving on?"

"When one of the Ten Thousand Things is my father making a noose of my mother's scarf while she's in it, it's hard to accept."

"That's one of your parents' Ten Thousand Things, not yours."

"There's such a thing as common karma," she persisted. "Our whole family could share one karma. What my parents do may affect us. He tried to strangle her; she's fashioning weaponry to do who-knows-what to him." She looked up at him, her brow furrowing into a frown. "Do you know what that could mean for our karma in the next life?"

"You'll come back as an orphan?"

She made a sound of annoyance. "Why can't you be serious about this?"

"Okay, I'm sorry, not funny," he said, crawling into bed next to her. "I predict, we will not be George and Martha. Their life is not ours. We won't change, at least not for the worse."

She slid over and snuggled up to him.

"Buddha said there are three poisons: greed, anger and foolishness. They are the cause of all delusions and negativity in life. We have to extinguish the three poisons to reach nirvana."

"Buddha never said that. He said if you can't fix it, fuck it."

She looked at him, her almond eyes filled with apprehension. "That's easy for you to say; your parents are normal."

Robert couldn't argue with that.

"Why don't we elope," she whispered. "Take a weekend trip, get on a plane, go somewhere . . . anywhere."

Robert quieted her with kisses. "You know I can't do that. I'm all my parents have now. I can't take our wedding away from them. And I admit I have one of the three poisons. I'm greedy; I want to see you walking down the aisle to me." He pulled her closer. "I spoke to Mrs. Hendricks at the inn. We're having the rehearsal dinner there the night before the wedding. She's setting up the reception luncheon for fifty guests, and my parents are going to help. I still want to get married. Will you still marry me?"

Karen rested her forehead on his shoulder. "Yes, I'll still marry you."

They both were lost in their own thoughts for a few moments, watching as Robert Redford stomped around the apartment while Jane Fonda looked on.

"What about the wedding party?" Karen said finally. "Do you think Liz and Ian will stay together?"

"I have no idea."

"I think things are going well," she said.

"I think we need to stay out of it. We need to be totally neutral. We're Switzerland."

"Switzerland wasn't really neutral," Karen said.

"I know, baby."

Chapter 50

By midday, the skating rink at Bryant Park boasted a perfect Courier and Ives scene of adults and children moving in a continuous circle, their bright hats, scarves, and mittens creating a whirling blur of color as they skimmed the ice. Ian hunched against the biting cold, watching the skaters going round and round to the surround sound of Broadway music blaring from the stereo system.

Sensing someone standing near him, he glanced over; Michele gave him a slow smile. With a curt nod, he led the way, away from the crowd to the other side of the snow-white tents.

The park area was deserted; the round green tables dotting the landscape were empty. The wind whipped through the trees, whizzing past Ian's ears; the leaves crunched under their feet. They passed the pale green hut of the flower seller; she sat inside, arranging her wares for the wanderers that never came.

"All the little shops they have here, like our markets. *C'est Bruges, non?*"

Ian didn't answer, remembering Bruges. They had shopped for lace, eaten at a restaurant in the square—in the shadow of the Belfry, on the heated terrace—watching tourists take their carriage rides. Back then, he couldn't imagine life without her.

He gave himself a mental shake and stopped at the green

carousel, covered and closed now, the aged green ticket box dormant. She raised her hand to stroke his hair; he brushed her away.

"I came to tell you I won't sell, I won't change my mind, and don't come around again."

She smiled, her eyes calm and serene. "Two thousand dollars is a lot of money for a painter with no prominence. Most artists will get seven hundred, *peut-être* eight. *Mais je t'apporte deux mille.* Sell the paintings, Ian. Buy something nice for your belle du jour."

Ian shoved his hands into his pockets.

"Oh là là, *tu es amoureux d'elle.* You are in love with her."

Ian avoided her eyes.

"You cannot hide it. It's in the face, that look. Then you don't want me to have a talk with her. Do you think she's ready to meet your ex-wife?"

"Stay the hell away from her," he said.

The smooth smile slipped from her face. "Then you sell the paintings, Ian."

"Does your lover know you have an ex-husband? Does he know who his money is going to? Do you want me to tell him, assure him it's all over between us?"

"He will not care."

"Bullshit. I've met him. He's not that civilized. No one's that civilized."

Looking at her, Ian noticed the subtle change in her eyes. He saw the anxiety, maybe even fear. "We're done now."

"*Bien.* I think I talk to the belle du jour. I will have much to say, and she will listen. She will leave you. And you will be like before—unable to paint. What will you tell Monsieur Ferand, when you cannot deliver the paintings? Do you think he will give you another chance? You will lose everything."

He took a sudden step toward her.

"For God's sake, Ian, sell the paintings. I make this easy for you. I'll handle everything."

"You'll handle everything?" he repeated. "You want to help

me, but if I don't want your help, you'll ruin me, ruin my relationship with the only woman who ever cared about me—"

"The only one," she said with a harsh laugh. "I loved you until you forced me to leave."

"Forced you? I wanted you to stay. I begged you to stay."

"All you wanted was your little show."

"That little show would've given me national notice and a representative to sell my work. That little show would've helped me get the career I spent years working for. But it wouldn't be enough money for you. It was never enough money for you."

He closed the gap between them, grasping her arms. "Now I should sell for two thousand dollars. And what do you get? A commission? How much do you get for handling everything?"

"Enough," she said, looking away.

He let her go. "I don't believe it. I don't fucking believe it. You need my help? What do you need the money for?"

"A plane ticket back to Paris."

He stopped, considering her for a moment. "This one is so bad you need to run away from him?"

She shrugged. "I thought you would help me. After all, you always loved me more than I loved you."

"You never loved anyone, Michele. That's always been your problem."

She looked away, but not before Ian thought he saw her eyes glisten.

"You should help me. When we were married, I introduced you to the right people."

"Who didn't give a damn about my work."

Michele didn't argue. "Ian—"

"I'll have the paintings delivered. You handle everything."

Michele looked down at her shoes for a moment. "I take half, okay?"

"No. You take it all. It's better for me to have you across an ocean, as far away as possible." He stepped closer, standing over her. "Just make sure you get on that plane. If you stay here and have any problems with him, no one will help you. I won't help you. And I will tell him who I really am and who you really are."

Michele nodded her head.

Ian looked past her, taking a deep breath of the cold winter air; it burned his nose. Turning, he walked away, past the flower seller and down the steps surrounded by the black wrought-iron fence. He stopped to light a cigarette, cupping his hand around the lighter to protect the flame. Perhaps she had loved him; it didn't matter anymore. He would have to create new pieces for the exhibit, but he breathed a sigh of relief. He wasn't going to lose Lizzie. That's what mattered now.

Chapter 51

The ballroom sparkled with holiday decorations. Elizabeth moved on the periphery of a small group surrounding Parker and Emily.

"Parker, this is simply wonderful. Hedge funds giving back to the community, and so generously," a woman was saying.

"It's our pleasure. Emily was instrumental in putting this together and making it happen. It's not always about making money . . . well, yeah it is."

This was greeted with hearty chuckles all around.

"Emily, dear," a woman asked. "You've been so busy this past year. What have you set your sights on next?"

Emily slipped her arm through Parker's. "We are very excited about completing the house in Greenwich, and I'm making a documentary of the building process."

A chorus of oohs and aahs followed.

"My wife always does a fantastic job at everything she undertakes."

Murmurs of assent followed. Elizabeth glanced at Emily, to find her observing Parker with polite adoration as always, yet somehow it wasn't quite the same. Emily had bounced back from the sniveling pile of debilitating depression and zero self-esteem Parker had reduced her to. But to Elizabeth, she seemed more the competent actress, playing at the part of the adoring wife. Elizabeth suspected Emily's days of loving Parker were gone.

The group drifted away, leaving Elizabeth and Emily alone, watching Parker mixing with other couples, kissing the ladies' cheeks, pumping the men's hands.

"He certainly was singing your praises," Elizabeth said. "Obviously, he realizes how hard you work."

Emily didn't look at her. "Yes. Unfortunately he never says that when we're alone, only when there are people around."

Elizabeth avoided the swarming photographers looking for the perfect snap for Page Six or the Internet sites for New York's society doings. She found herself wishing that instead of a ballroom, she was sitting next to Ian among his and Robert's artist friends, sharing food and Christmas gifts.

She spotted Ian in an unlikely place, chatting with Stanton Perry. From a distance the conversation appeared relaxed. A flutter of anxiety rippled through her; she didn't know why she should care what Stanton Perry thought of Ian, but she did. Making her way through the crowd, she joined them.

"Elizabeth, your friend has definite ideas about art. For the sake of the value of my collection, I'm not sure I like them." He held out his hand to Ian. "I doubt very much I'll see you at the Whitney Biennial, but I am intrigued to see your work. We need to talk further."

"Any time," Ian said as they shook hands.

"If I may," Stanton said, pulling Elizabeth aside. "I heard your meetings went very well and you are celebrating new clients. Well done," he said. "Now, how are you? Really."

"Alive and kicking."

Perry was silent for a moment, regarding her. "I would've helped you if you'd asked."

"If I had asked, you wouldn't need me."

Stanton smiled, leaning in to kiss her cheek. "Well done, again. Happy holidays, young lady, and all the best for the new year." He glanced at Ian. "I always say everyone needs a vice. You've made a wise choice."

She watched him stroll away and put his arm around Deirdre.

An hour later, Robert and Ian were at the bar with Parker. They exchanged looks as Parker's diatribe went on.

"What do you Europeans do besides work a thirty-hour week and take eight vacations a year? Oh yeah, drink gallons of wine and go on strike. I am a controlling factor in the world economy, I understand that. I understand market movements and arbitrage," he said, and took a moment to drain his scotch. "You know what I don't understand? Marriage."

Ian and Robert nodded.

"It's just not what I thought it would be, you know? I thought it was, you know, easy . . . what's the big deal?" He rocked on his heels. Turning, he began to tap his glass on the bar; the bartender came over and poured him a refill. "I thought it was . . . I don't know. I didn't expect it to be so much—"

"Work," Ian said.

Parker held his glass out, pointing his index finger at Ian. "Right. It was supposed to be easy. I mean, she cries a lot."

"Perhaps it's your fault," Ian suggested.

Parker gave him a sharp look before bursting into laughter and slapping his arm. "Seriously, what is it with the crying?"

"Karen cries," Robert said.

"No shit?"

"All the time," Robert said.

Parker zeroed in on Ian. "I know Liz doesn't cry. She's a damned ice queen."

Ian raised his eyebrows.

"So what do you do when she cries?" Parker asked Robert.

"I hold her, say encouraging things, then we make love, and she feels better."

Parker's face screwed up in concentration as he processed this new information. "So . . . she cries and you get laid. Comfort sex."

"Yes."

"Fanfuckingtastic."

"Knock yourself out," Robert said.

As they were turning to leave, Ian turned to Robert. "You know what's even better? Celebration sex. And lately Lizzie has had quite a bit to celebrate. I wonder if you heard. She's been very clever, came up with a brand new program that's going to make her a bit of a star in the company. Her boss is quite pleased with her." He looked at Parker as he and Robert began to walk away. Parker was staring at him, his mouth open.

"Good luck with the world economy," Ian said. *Asshole.*

Elizabeth came away from the bar, and saw Nick moving in her direction. *Bring on the regret, bring on the guilt*, she thought as he caught sight of her. For a moment, she froze, unsure of what to do. *I can't run away, I'm not a child.* She had hurt him, at the very least disappointed him; she couldn't avoid him as if he didn't exist.

They edged toward one another until they met in the middle of the floor.

"Hey, kid," he said.

Elizabeth gave him a tight smile; she'd always hated the phrase.

She glanced beyond him to see a tall blond woman watching them. "What does she do?" Elizabeth asked.

"She's an attorney," he said.

"I'm glad you met someone. You deserve to be happy."

Nick gave a short, clipped laugh. "We've only been seeing each other a short time. I keep thinking you can't really be happy, so I keep waiting for you to come around. Did you get the flowers?"

"Yes, and they were beautiful. Nick—"

"I'm still a believer in guerilla marketing. Sometimes a message has to be presented several times to be effective." He raised his glass to his lips, emptying it with one long swallow. "Have you come to your senses yet?"

"Nick . . . let's not do this. I said I was sorry."

"I'm sorry too, Liz. I understand why commitment is so hard for you."

It took Elizabeth a moment to realize she was holding her breath.

"I had a long talk with Emily . . . I know about California—everything."

Elizabeth felt the heat of embarrassment and humiliation crowding in on her. She couldn't look Nick in the eye. She couldn't imagine what he thought of her. "That was a long time ago," she said shortly. She was sick of apologizing, sick of running away from that time in her life, trying to get further and further away from those years. *What would Ian think if he knew?*

"All that means to me," Nick was saying, "is that you're stronger than I realized. And it galls me that you're wasting yourself on the same kind of man. He's pulling your strings, kid, because that's what he does. I cannot understand how a smart woman with a brilliant mind can be so blind. Look at where you're standing now and remember you left it all behind, where it belongs."

When he took her hand, she couldn't meet his eyes. "I'll keep hoping . . . Merry Christmas, Liz," he said.

She nodded, unable to speak.

Parker spied Deirdre Perry in the foyer just outside the ballroom. His eyes slid from her ankles, up her mile-high legs, to the black satin dress glued to her slim form, to the deep décolleté, finally resting on the soft swell of her breasts. Her hair, long and straight, was pulled away from her face and held by a diamond-encrusted clip at the nape of her neck. She gave him a cool, assessing look as he sauntered over to her, a wicked smile on his face.

"Do you like my dress?" she purred. "Dolce and Gabbana."

"I approve of both Dolce and Gabbana," he said, his eyes moving from her face back to her plunging neckline.

She giggled.

Parker's eyes swept the hallway; the door leading in and out of the ballroom was still clear.

She leaned against the wall, her hands behind her, a little

smile on her lips as he hovered over her, an outstretched arm braced against the wall.

He ran his eyes over her again. "I have to tell you," he said, "I really want to fuck you."

Deirdre Perry smiled. "So who's stopping you?"

Chapter 52

The stillness of Christmas morning settled on New York City; no traffic din floating up to the loft, no blasting of horns from impatient motorists. The population of Manhattan was taking a collective breath after the frenzied season of spending and shopping. For those remaining in the city, the holiday was quiet and insular.

Ian rolled over, yawned, and stretched, smelling fresh coffee. He propped himself up in bed as Elizabeth came around the divider wearing a silky red satin nightgown.

"Oh dear," he murmured as she climbed into bed and curled up next to him. "Father Christmas sent me the pretty elf."

"An elf bearing gifts." She handed him an envelope. He pulled out a season pass to the Met. "Brilliant, darling, absolutely brilliant." He gave her a thorough kiss. "Now I have something for you."

She glanced over at the large canvas, a copy of Renoir's *La Dance à la Ville* that Ian had painted for her. The man, his face hidden, embraced the young woman, his hand on her waist, while the young woman's cheeks blushed with excitement, maybe even love.

"You already made me something wonderful," she said, kissing him. "You have dark circles under your eyes. You're working too hard."

"I have dark circles because you keep waking me up in the night to do unspeakable things to me."

"Poor baby," she purred. "I won't do that anymore."

"I didn't say I didn't like it," he said with a laugh.

Opening a drawer in his night table, he withdrew a small oblong box, wrapped in red foil and tied with a gold ribbon. She opened it slowly to find a slender gold chain strung with delicate amber teardrops. She smiled as he fastened it around her neck.

"I thought it might be your style," he said.

"It is," she whispered, brushing her lips across his and pulling him close.

"Lizzie," he said, his voice husky as desire for her surged through him. With one swift motion he slid her nightgown off, running his hands over her, gently at first and then with a forceful urgency. Her skin was soft and warm from the sudden heat rising in her body and he drew her close, moving his lips and tongue over her, tasting her. She moaned and he could feel her yielding to his touch. He crushed her lips in a kiss; he heard a sigh escape her and she murmured his name as she curved her body to his.

"Merry Christmas, my love," he whispered in her ear.

The necklace was cool against Ian's skin as Elizabeth nestled close to him.

He caressed her back and she sighed. She had changed, no longer wound so tight, with every emotion held in check. He could feel it every time they made love. Her inhibitions seemed to have vanished, and she met him with a force that left him exhausted and vulnerable. It was as if she had mentally done the exercise where you close your eyes and fall backward; he wanted to catch her. Maybe he wanted to fall backward too. The thought scared the hell out of him. He'd lost count of the moments when he had to fight to stifle the overpowering urge to blurt out his true feelings, even though this time was different. He knew Lizzie would never purposely hurt him—she didn't have it in her. But what if she changed her mind again? He couldn't get caught up again, letting his guard down. He had been fooling himself all along. Someone could get hurt.

Chapter 53

Something is wrong. Those were the words floating through the hills and valleys of Elizabeth's mind. It had started almost immediately after the holiday. Ian had become more capricious, prone to long silences and monosyllabic answers. The thought was nagging at her as she arrived at his apartment around seven. She looked over the paintings, noting their progress, and then tiptoed behind the bedroom divider. He was in a deep sleep, his breathing heavy and slow. His schedule of late was almost nonexistent; he slept and painted at odd hours. She had no doubt that only added to his mercurial moods. She woke him with gentle kisses, taking care not to startle him. As he came out of sleep, he returned her kiss and murmured her name.

After he showered and dressed, he sat by the window, leaving it slightly ajar to allow his cigarette smoke to be sucked away into the night air. When she finished changing, she came around the bedroom divider and found him lost in thought.

"Everything okay today?" she said.

He nodded. "Fine."

She tried to tell herself it was the pressure of getting the work done. There were moments of panic when she thought about the model in the restaurant; maybe she was back. Maybe she never left. She discounted the idea; he was always working and easy to find. None of the telltale signs were there; he never hid his movements; no phone call hang-ups when she an-swered. Yet she couldn't deny that his cool veneer, which had slipped away over time, had returned. She wouldn't hazard a guess as to what he was thinking.

She waited for him. He stubbed out his cigarette and came over to zip up the back of her dress, giving her a kiss on her neck. He was holding himself back—she could feel it.

After helping her with her coat, they left.

The dinner was sponsored by the Women in Finance Associ-ation. Ian moved through the room, watching Elizabeth work the crowd, looking relaxed, in her element. *These are her people*, he thought. *She's through with her past life, whatever that was. This is what she wants now. Where do I fit in? I don't. It's only a matter of time before she realizes that and moves on.*

He listened as Elizabeth stood at the podium, speaking for thirty minutes on the unique opportunities for women in today's financial sector, understanding how she had been able to achieve so much and hold her own in a male-dominated arena.

When they returned to the loft, the silence hung heavy and uncomfortable between them. They had run out of small talk. He watched her changing into his sweatshirt and sweatpants, enjoying her fluid movements, the light playing off her silky hair.

He sequestered himself in the kitchen, making fresh coffee, taking mugs out of the cabinet and placing them on the counter-top.

"The food was actually good," she said, pulling her hair up in a ponytail. "I never expect much at these functions."

"Yes, it was fine."

He poured two cups of coffee and lit a cigarette.

"I'm sorry you got stuck with Marcia Fox. She can kill a man with her tongue. I kid you not. Last year, at a fund-raiser, she was discussing cattle futures with Parker for forty-five minutes and the rest of us were taking bets on how long it would take Parker to die in self-defense."

"Lizzie," Ian said.

His tone was so sharp she stopped and looked at him.

"Yes?"

"I want to . . . tell you . . ." He looked over at her to find her waiting, her eyes wary. *I love you. I want to marry you.* He could feel his eyes widen, his heartbeat quickening at the sudden thoughts streaking through his mind. "It was a very informative speech, and you carried it off brilliantly."

"Thank you," she said. "I worked on it for weeks."

"Yes, I'm sure." He added milk to his coffee, stirring it slowly. "If all goes well with my work . . . if I sell my work, I may have to do some traveling . . . if all goes well," he said without looking at her.

"Oh," she said.

He shrugged. "Yes . . . I . . . should go back to Europe, spend some time there and see some dealers . . . exhibit . . . that sort of thing."

She didn't answer.

He stubbed out his cigarette and gave her a contemplative look. "It would be all right with you, yeah? You could come to visit . . . long weekends . . . if you like . . ."

"If I like?" she repeated.

His heart squeezed in his chest. He dropped his gaze, staring into his coffee cup.

"When are you planning on leaving?"

"I've no idea," he snapped. "It's a possibility. It may never be necessary."

"Travel is necessary, you said that."

"I'm sure I'm a bit premature. Let's forget about it, all right?" He came to her, giving her a quick kiss as he pulled at his tie. *Stupid git. Bloody brilliant.*

She nodded.

"You need to bring over more changes of clothes," he said. "Then I'll be able to wear my own now and again."

"Good idea," she said with a smile that never reached her eyes.

Chapter 54

Karen fetched another box of tissues and hurried back to the couch. Elizabeth plucked one, then two, then three tissues, covering the lower half of her face and blowing her nose. The tissues blew out like a flag in the wind.

"He's breaking up with me; he's laying the groundwork. It's coming, any day now, it's coming," Elizabeth cried. "First I get left at the altar, then I just get left and now I'm going to be left again."

Karen patted her shoulder. "But he wants you to visit him. He wants more of your stuff at the loft. You don't know that he wants to break up with you. He's been under a lot of pressure—"

"Oh please, it's the classic move: 'I have to go for the sake of my art.' Visit on weekends? Give me a break. It's the start of the kiss-off."

"You're jumping to conclusions. After all, he just gave you an expensive Christmas gift. Why would he do that if he was planning on leaving?"

"Guilty conscience," she sniveled, wiping her cheeks with a wad of tissues. "And I never got the look. Not once did I get the look."

"You need to wait and see," Karen persisted.

"Like I did last time? I don't think so." She inhaled a long breath. "You know what this means, don't you?"

Karen shook her head.

"I have to dump him."

"What?" Karen said, her voice rising. "Why? Why would you do that?"

"I have to beat him to the rejection. I must be the rejector, I cannot be the rejectee. Not this time . . . not again. If he's decided this is his station and he's getting off, I have to get off first. I knew something was wrong after Christmas. I just knew he wanted out." She looked at Karen, her eyes brimming with tears. "In the back of my mind . . . I knew."

She cried softly for a few minutes and finally lapsed into silence. She was beginning to feel the way she had when she lived in California—lost and uncertain, with an urge to cry that never went away. *I can't afford to lose control. I will not be my mother.*

She sucked in a long breath. "I know what I have to do," she said.

Chapter 55

Elizabeth gazed out of the window of the cab as it headed downtown. She didn't see the people, or the buildings, in the haze of heavy rain and fog shrouding the city. She was thinking back to the clear, calm night in Laguna when everything changed.

She stayed up watching William work. He was sullen and distant, as he had been for weeks, steadily drinking as he worked. She watched him; that was all she could do. Her ability to create had dried up like the sand on the beach. She knew something was wrong then too, that he was finished with her, but she ignored it, hanging on. When he was done painting, he took her to bed, taking her without feeling, without tenderness.

The next morning, his canvases were gone from the studio. He stood in the kitchen, drinking his coffee.

"I'm going now," he said, setting the cup on the counter.

She went to him, clinging to him, begging him to stay, telling him that she needed him. Disentangling himself from her grasp, he pushed her away.

"I love you, William," she whispered.

"But I don't love you. I thought you were different, but you're like your mother. Sucking the life from me."

Ignoring her protests, he strode to the door, slamming it behind him. She stared after him, feeling as if the walls were closing in on her, squeezing the solitary silence against her, making it difficult to breathe.

The cab stopped for a light and Elizabeth watched as people scudded across the flooded street, bowed under umbrellas and hooded coats. *This is what I've been doing these past months, isn't it*, she thought. *Playing the part of my mother; taking up with a feckless artist, refusing to see that it wasn't going to end well. He was the door I should've kept closed.*

Outside Ian's window, the rain continued to pour down in torrents. The knocking on the door shook him from his concentration. Muttering under his breath, he threw down his brush and went to open the door.

Elizabeth stood in the hallway, her coat drenched, her dripping hair matted to the sides of her face.

"What are you doing?" he said, taking her by the hand and pulling her inside. "Why did you come out in all of this? You know I would've come to you."

He moved to take her coat.

"No," she said, shrugging him off. "I came because I need to talk."

Ian swept the hair from her face and cupped his hands around her cheeks. "We'll chat as much as you like, but first you need a hot bath, tea with whiskey, and a lie-down under the covers, yeah?"

He took her by the hand but again she pulled away.

"You said you needed to travel—"

"Let's not talk about that, love. That will all keep. We must do something so you don't get pneumonia—"

"Ian . . . I need to—"

"Let it go, Lizzie," he said quickly. "Forget the travel, don't concern yourself. I'm not going any—"

"I want to get back in the game."

He stopped, staring at her for a long moment. Her face was wet from rain; if she had been crying it was impossible to tell.

"This is what we talked about. You said when I was ready, I would tell you and . . . remember?"

Ian went to the kitchen island, pulled a cigarette from a pack and lit up, his mind racing. *Get her to pull back. There must be a way.* He took a deep drag, his mind racing.

"Yes, I remember. Have you met someone?" he asked.

"No, no, but I need to be out there."

"So, there isn't anyone yet. We can still enjoy each other's company until the prince comes along. Everything will be as it is."

She shook her head. "No, it can't be. I need to get back to my life, my plans for my life. My career . . . marriage."

"Marriage. Oh . . . yes, I see." He stood, smoking, feeling as if he were navigating an intricately constructed maze and couldn't find a way out. "If this is what you want, Lizzie," he said finally.

"Yes, this is what I want."

They stood as awkward strangers, listening to the beating of the rain on the window panes.

"I have a taxi waiting for me," she said.

He nodded.

She lingered a moment; then, opening the door, she slipped out.

He stood looking at the door. *What the hell did I just do?* The phone rang and after a moment he picked up the receiver.

"It's Robert," he heard from the other end of the line. "Look, you know I don't get involved in your personal stuff anymore, but Karen told me something you need to know."

"She's already gone." He replaced the receiver on the hook.

Elizabeth ducked into the taxi and slammed the door shut. "Take me back, please," she said, and burst into tears.

WINTER

Chapter 56

In the darkness, grunts interspersed with moans, sheets rustled, a gasp, and then a cavernous moment of silence.

"What?" Emily squeaked.

The bedside light flipped on. Sitting up, Emily stared, openmouthed, at Parker, lying flat on his back, his eyes fixed on the ceiling, his breathing ragged.

"I can't believe you used that word," she sputtered.

"I just want us to experiment, okay? A little experimentation is good for a relationship."

"I know, but . . ."

Parker gritted his teeth. "Babe, I just need you to try a little harder, okay? I'm under a lot of pressure. I need to relax. You know I love you, right?"

Reaching for a tissue, Emily nodded her head as she blew her nose.

He reached for her and she stiffened. He let his arms fall away.

"You don't? Is that it? I married the only woman in the fifty states who can't do herself like a normal person?"

"I can," she protested, pushing away from him. "Just . . . not in front of you. I'm not a three-ring circus."

Plucking tissues two at a time from the box and dabbing at her eyes, she sat on the edge of the bed, stiff and unyielding. Reaching over, he began to stroke her back. "Of course not, baby, how can you say that, you know you're everything to me."

Easing her back down next to him, he pulled her close, kissing her cheek. He ran his hand over her stomach, sliding into her panties. Turning away, she curled into a fetal ball.

"No," she sniffled. "I can't. You've made me feel . . . cheap."

"Oh, for fuck's sake . . . cheap?" He threw up his hands and got out of bed. "Cut the crap, will you? What you mean is, you won't. You can't do a lot of things, Emily. You can't give me a decent blowjob, you can't give me children—"

"I said, I didn't know if I was ready for children," she said, sitting up and drawing the blanket around her. "I have the documentary project for the house, which I may launch into a business."

Parker laughed. "Another one? Be serious, will you? The only thing it will launch is another failure. Don't expect me to get excited about another one of your disasters. I should be grateful; at least you won't be able to kill anyone with a video."

"The catering business would have succeeded. It was just a glitch!" She glared at him. "I would have been able to straighten it out if you hadn't interfered and forced me into closing it down."

Parker stood over her. "Glitch? It was a clusterfucking disaster. Anytime your clients go to the hospital to get their stomachs pumped, you've failed—get it?" His eyes turned dark. "You could have ruined me. No wonder the old man won't let you get your hands on the trust fund. You'd blow it all on more of your brainless schemes. In case you haven't noticed, at this moment we have a house full of computer and video editing equipment that you bought, but don't know how to use."

"I'm learning how to use it. Making documentaries is going to be my new career—"

"You have a fucking career! Your career is being my wife! If you concentrated on that, you might succeed. In case you missed the fucking memo, my needs aren't being met!" he shouted, the veins bulging at his temples.

Suddenly Emily fell silent, no tears, no sniffling. "Then

don't you think we should talk about our sexual problems?" she asked, her voice cool.

His lip curled. "*Our* problems? Here's the four-one-one, princess: I don't have a problem," he said. "When my entire existence revolves around the front row at Fashion Week, then I'll have a problem. I'm a normal, healthy male. You think I'm the only man in the world who wants a little excitement?"

He ripped the blanket away from her. "You go ask your girlfriends about Ian and Robert. They want the floor show, they want the whole floor show. We're men and we're not ashamed. We want to watch, we like to watch, and we want it all on videotape so we can watch it over and over again! There's a demographic for you. If you learn to use the equipment, you should go into porn!"

Emily's mouth dropped open. "That's disgusting."

He leaned in, inches from her face. "You're ruining this marriage. Do you get that? You're pushing me away by not meeting my needs." His voice suddenly became low and even. "Think about it."

Tossing the blanket at her, he stormed out of the bedroom, slamming the door behind him.

She heard him rummaging in a closet, then the bathroom, and finally there was silence.

Emily sat on the edge of the bed, drawing the blanket up around her. *I'm not meeting his needs? Then who the hell is?*

Chapter 57

Ian peered at the canvas through red, irritated eyes. Empty liquor bottles from the past week were scattered like bowling pins throughout the loft, his neat, organized work table reduced to a hodgepodge of tubes of oil paints, paint-stained brushes and palette knives.

His tired eyes forced him to work slowly. His mouth felt hot and sour and a dull, painful ache had settled in his stomach, spiking when he gave way to his anger and frustration.

He fingered the tubes, tossing aside the grayed-out blues, the muted, soft colors in favor of something stronger.

With a steady hand, he laid in the figure of the woman, giving her eyes a faraway look as she stared into the distance, lost in her own thoughts.

He had to get the vision out of his mind and onto the canvas, and he pushed himself, working with increasing speed, driven from within. If he stopped, he might never begin again; he would surrender to the pull of sleep, of forgetting. With each stroke of the brush the woman emerged; she manifested before his eyes, all his love and anger flowing from the brush onto the canvas. His light touch in the midst of the bold color moved beyond Impressionism to Post-Impressionism. While the picture should be pleasing, the lines of the composition were well defined; the perspective meant to provoke the viewers, push them beyond their comfort zone. The painting wasn't meant to convey warmth or intimacy, but arouse heat and passion. It was the best work he'd ever done.

Chapter 58

Elizabeth and Karen got off the 6 train at Bleecker and Lafayette. They were early, and lingered outdoors since the sun had snatched some of the bite from the February cold. They strolled down the gray, dingy pavement toward Broadway, stopping to look in the window of a clothing shop. The garments were slim, sleek, and all black, conjuring images of a wild, dangerous New York night of love and lust. One outfit had a sparkling Buddha on the shirt, and Elizabeth decided she would come back and buy it for Karen as a surprise. Karen nudged her toward the diner as a limousine and a taxi simultaneously pulled up at the corner. Margaret and Emily had arrived.

At a back table, Margaret held court, a snow queen in a white Chanel ensemble, her hair in a twist, diamond tear drops in her ears. She ordered for the table.

Karen leaned over and covered Emily's hand with her own. "That's what he said?" she asked.

Emily nodded. "That's exactly what he said," she answered, her tone hushed. "He said all men want that, they want to watch their partner"—she lowered her voice to a whisper—"pleasure themselves."

"I thought Parker had offices uptown," Margaret said.

"That type of activity is for below Fifty-second Street. Does the man have no sense of topography?"

"So . . . umm," Emily murmured, "have you . . . ?"

They looked around the table at each other, then all eyes turned to Margaret. "Well, dumplings, who hasn't, but when a woman reaches a certain age . . ."

"Exactly," Emily agreed emphatically. "And to make such a request, as if I'm nothing more than a floor show."

Karen looked at Elizabeth. "Have you?"

Elizabeth flashed back to her former life, fun and games in a beach house with Josh so long ago. "I gave that up when I turned eighteen."

Margaret squeezed Elizabeth's hand. "And rightly so, my pet. After all, that's the purpose of man, is it not? It's a benefit of marriage—one of the few—someone's going to do that for you."

"I could've stayed single," Emily said, not bothering to hide her disgust.

Karen and Elizabeth exchanged looks, but said nothing.

Margaret sat back. "Don't distress yourself, my dear. He'll have an affair soon, if he hasn't already, and she'll handle all that unpleasantness."

Emily looked at Elizabeth. "I guess you know about that."

"And why would *I* know about that?"

"You see him more than I do at those business mixers. I'm sure you know exactly what he's been doing and who he's been doing it with."

Elizabeth pursed her lips. "I don't spread rumors."

Emily's mouth dropped open.

"Yes, there's always talk, but I'm not interfering in your marriage. If you're so concerned, hire someone."

Margaret rubbed Elizabeth's shoulder. "Excellent suggestion, Miss Elizabeth," she said, looking around the table. "Come now, my young ladies, let's not have any tiffies over men. We all know they're hardly worth it. Now I have gathered you all here for a reason. As friends of my daughter, I have been hearing about your 'situations' and it is my duty to inquire about your well-being. Now, Miss Elizabeth, as I have come to feel a sort of parental claim upon you, I want to know how you are weathering this storm."

Elizabeth stiffened, fiddling with her silverware. She swallowed the lump in her throat.

Margaret took Elizabeth's hand. "Good Lord, you're not going to cry, are you, dear?"

"No," Elizabeth said, taking a huge breath. "Absolutely not."

"I'm glad to hear it. That would be terrible for us both."

The waitress brought their food.

"I'm drowning myself in my work."

"Excellent, well done. You will excel now that the albatross has been loosed from your neck."

"Mom," Karen interjected. "She liked Ian."

Margaret's eyes narrowed. "This isn't the attorney?"

"The painter," Emily said.

Margaret picked up her spoon, giving Elizabeth a contemplative look. "The artist . . . you don't say."

Elizabeth took a deep breath. "He was going to break up with me."

"You don't know that," Karen said.

"He said he was thinking of going back to Europe, for his work," Elizabeth said, her voice tight.

"Ah, the old bon voyage," Margaret said, her lip curling.

"I had to break up with him. I had to beat him to the rejection."

"The preemptive strike," Margaret said, her rich voice ringing with gravitas and sympathy. "Excellent. Well done."

"So, I tell him it's over and he says 'if that's what you want.' "

"Mmm," Margaret said.

" 'If that's what you want' . . . that's it, that's all he said."

"You did the right thing. Although it is hard to let go of the artists," Margaret said with a sigh. "They have such a way of connecting with their souls, the very core of their nature. They feel everything so much more deeply."

Elizabeth stared at her bacon, lettuce, and tomato sand-wich, her eyes misting again.

"And of course," Margaret added, "the sex is stupendous."

"Is it wrong to say I miss that the most?" Elizabeth asked, a tear sliding down her cheek.

"Who can say what's right or wrong regarding a relation-ship. If it's one of his best attributes, you mustn't feel shallow. Was it really *that* good?"

"She never stopped raving about it," Emily said, a sour look on her face.

"It was the sex . . . and the accent . . . and the politeness."

"Oh, yes," Margaret agreed. "The Europeans have exquis-ite manners and . . ."

Her voice trailed off as she watched a party of two being seated near the front of the diner. The young woman, tall, bone thin, with a fresh face, had a fair complexion and dark hair. The man, medium height, with a receding hairline, had an energetic way about him. Everyone at the table turned to follow Margaret's gaze.

Karen's eyes grew wide. She turned to find her mother the picture of serenity, except for the tiny, crooked smile and the frigid look in her eyes.

"*This* is why we came downtown?" Karen said.

"Who is that woman?" Emily said. "I'm sure I've seen her. Didn't she just have a book published?"

"Penny Hargrave," Karen whispered. "My father's new . . . friend, with her agent."

Emily slid her eyes to Margaret. "You're not going to have her killed, are you?" she asked in a hoarse whisper, which rang more of curiosity than concern.

Margaret chuckled. "That would be de trop. If one is to make a point, one must do it in style."

Emily nodded obediently.

"I must say," Margaret continued, "she is perfectly anemic. How utterly charming." A small, pleased smile touched her lips. "Oh my, she's seen you, dear," she said to Karen. "Now, remember, be polite and say hello when we are on the way out."

Karen opened her mouth to answer but Margaret patted her hand. "It's important for you to acknowledge your father's parade of post-pubescent companions. It soothes his fragile ego."

"Daddy's ego is fragile?"

"It's not?"

Karen sighed as she glanced over at Penny; she was at least five years her junior.

Signaling the waitress, Margaret asked for the check.

"Now, my little lemon drops," Margaret said. "Here is what you must do." She took a business card out of her purse and handed it to Emily. "Contact this gentleman and explain your situation. He will take care of everything."

"Father has an attorney on standby for me."

"He's not a lawyer. He's a private investigator, and when he's finished, you will simply hand the dossier to your attorney and voilà, the Greenwich manse will be yours. It's all quite tidy."

She turned to Elizabeth. "Now listen to me, my girl. Get plenty of rest, a glass of wine every evening, and find a nice companion to sleep with, and then leave him. That's the way the men do it, you know. They may be on to something."

"Thank you, Margaret."

Karen and Margaret settled into the limousine, relaxing against the luxurious cushioned seats as the car inched out into traffic.

Karen swallowed hard. "Mommy, I want to talk about the wedding. You know how much I love you and Daddy. I want your support. I want you to accept my decision to marry. But no matter what you both do, even if you reject us both, I will marry Robert. I want to make that clear."

Margaret sat quietly, examining her daughter. After a moment, she gave a deep sigh and stroked Karen's hair. "As if there were anything under heaven or on earth that could stop us from loving you." She sighed. "*Mon petit chou,* for all your study of the Eastern religions, you still worry way too much." Her brows furrowed. "I should demand a refund," she muttered. "Your search for peace and transcendence wasn't cheap. You obviously didn't get my money's worth."

"Mommy," Karen began.

"Not to worry. Everything works itself out. And we will support your decision. Now, how goes the play?"

"I've completely lost touch with the motives of the characters. I feel like I don't know what's going on with my own work."

Margaret laid a gentle hand on Karen's arm. "Don't fret, my pearl, you have acquired an exquisite understanding of human nature. More than you know."

"But how is that possible?" Karen said. "I can't even understand you and Daddy."

Margaret stroked her daughter's cheek. "Children aren't meant to understand their parents, muffin. That is a burden no child should have to bear."

They rode in silence for the rest of the trip. When the limousine pulled up to the curb a uniformed doorman opened the door, took Margaret's hand, and helped her out.

She turned back to the car and Karen lowered the window. "By the way, watch over Miss Elizabeth. Miss Emily has moved on to the anger stage, but Elizabeth has yet to arrive. She will need you, and your excellent karma."

"How do you know my karma will be beneficial?"

"I know my Karen," she said.

Karen settled back against the soft leather seat with a little smile; her mother never failed to surprise her. As the car began to crawl out into the congested traffic, she twisted around to look out the back window. Margaret stood on the sidewalk, waiting. Another limo pulled up to the curb and her father got out. They disappeared into her mother's building. Why would her father . . . ? She felt her equilibrium tilt. Apprehension rushed through her. What were they doing together? *I should go back*. She scanned around her. The limo was hemmed in by a snarl of bumper-to-bumper traffic. She flopped back in her seat. What the hell was going on? She needed to know. Just letting things go was not enough. She needed to be enlightened.

Chapter 59

The Buddhist master sat on the floor, his spindles of legs crossed, his eyes closed in deep meditative thought, revealing deeply lined, crepey lids.

Karen and Robert sat on either side, facing each other, legs crossed. Sparsely furnished, the room had an earthy scent drifting around them from the incense burners.

"You have questions about marriage," the master said, opening his eyes.

"Yes," Karen said, leaning toward him. "My parents have destroyed their marriage. I've never really found out what happened between them. Recently, my father tried to strangle my mother."

"He didn't mean it," Robert interjected.

"I wonder, Master, with such a past, can we have a successful marriage?"

"I've told her," Robert cut in, "that we . . . are not her parents."

"Hui Meng said the meaning of life is to see," the master said. "You must learn to see."

Robert and Karen leaned forward.

The master fell silent.

"And?" Robert said.

Karen turned her whole body toward the master. "So, there is something I haven't seen. They're in me, aren't they? It's hopeless. Our marriage is doomed," she said, her shoulders sagging in defeat.

Robert reached out to her. "No, I'm sure he didn't mean that. We need to see how our marriage is going to be different."

"Ikkyu said I and other humans, no difference," the master said.

"Is that the koan?" Karen asked.

"What's a koan?" Robert asked, looking at her.

"It's the riddle I have to solve," she said.

Robert turned to the master. "Please explain that there is no riddle—well, her parents are a riddle, but one that no one needs to solve."

"I need to solve it," Karen protested. "He tried to strangle her a few months ago and I just saw them go into her apartment together. Why would they do that?"

The master held up his hands for silence. "You must look for the myo. The manifestation is the meaning. You have to see," the master said. "You must find your Original Face; your 'me' is the problem."

"No," Robert said, "it's the 'them' that's the problem."

"What is the myo, the manifestation, the meaning?" the master asked.

Robert smiled and leaned back. "It's our love for each other when we take our vows," he said.

"Even if my parents don't plan to object at the wedding, Master, should we get married?"

"Why are you asking him?" Robert said. "Haven't we already gone through this?"

"He's enlightened. He's walked the earth several times."

"As what?"

"Our actions determine our karma. The test of each successive rebirth is learning something and going on to achieve greater form. If we don't get this right, what will happen to us? What will happen to my parents?"

"Honey, trust me, your parents have flunked all their reincarnations. With the stunts they've pulled, next time they'll be coming back as algae." He reached out, taking her hands in his own. "Look, they're not going to object. Right? That's all we wanted. Let's go back to Taoism, okay? Let's be water, flowing around the wacky boulder that is your parents. Let's write our own vows, get married, and move on."

The Buddhist master sat peacefully, his eyes closed.

"Don't you think we should leave her parents as the unsolveable koan and just move on?"

The master held up one hand. "The Ten Thousand Things must come together, then you can go back to the Origins. You must both go back to the Origins."

"My origins don't have any problems!" Robert said. "My parents are normal. There are no attempted strangulations in my lineage. And what the hell are you talking about? What if the Ten Thousand Things don't come together?"

The master opened his eyes. "Then you are screwed," he said. "Why not elope?"

Chapter 60

Behind his mahogany desk, Parker scowled, mesmerized by the flickering of his computer screens.

Darryl came in, placing a thick report on Parker's desk. "The portfolio valuations are done," he said.

"I can see that." Parker flipped through the pages. "How did you make the adjustments?"

"I used some price positions from October to close the gap in biotech and oil. Total valuation of the fund puts you at a seventeen percent gain for the year."

"What was the actual?"

"Five percent loss."

Parker pushed the report away. "We'll make it up. No one will notice."

Parker returned to staring at the computer screens. The capital was plummeting; the tight-ass pocket protector prick, Stanley Werner, was in his office every day waving his statistical data in his face, screaming about the leverage. So he had made some bad bets. So the margins were piling up. He never missed on the currency bets. Never. The dollar would drop, the yen would rise and that would be one billion. More than enough to dig out. He wasn't going to be one of those schmucks whining about a "challenging" market. He gave another flip through the report. The auditors would rubber-stamp it like they did every year.

"It's all going to even out," Parker said. Turning back to Darryl, he gave the young man his signature Cheshire smile. When Darryl walked out, the smile slipped from Parker's face. *It had better fucking even out. And soon.*

Chapter 61

A biting wind assaulted Ian and Robert as they heaved boxes into the van. Robert slammed the teardrop-windowed doors shut.

"It's the wedding," Ian said as they trudged back into Robert and Karen's now empty apartment. His voice echoed against the bare walls, bouncing around them as they crouched down. Ian held a box closed as Robert ran tape across the top. "Because Karen is getting married soon, Lizzie thinks she should be doing the same. That's all this is."

"The wedding. Uh-hunh," Robert said.

"What?" Ian asked defensively.

They hoisted the last of the boxes and trundled them downstairs.

"Liz has been talking to Karen and Karen's been talking to me. Liz is really upset."

"She is, is she? Did I miss something? *She* ended it with me."

"You didn't say you were going to Europe?"

"I said I might be going to Europe."

"I think that bothered her a little more than the wedding. 'Cause it's hard to be together if the other party isn't in the same country."

They loaded the boxes into the van and Robert slammed the doors. "Did you really say 'if that's what you want' when she ended it?"

"Well, I wasn't prepared, was I? I realize I should've been a bit quicker, since this is the second fucking time this has happened to me." He stopped short. "Is Karen upset?"

Robert raised his eyebrows. "Her best friend has been sobbing on her shoulder. Yeah, Karen is upset."

"Shit. It will all get sorted out," Ian said. "The important thing is, Lizzie will be at the apartment. We'll talk, she'll cry, I'll comfort her, we'll go back to the loft and make love, and everything will be like it was."

Robert looked at him. "You're going to win her back by making her cry?"

"It's not as bad as it sounds."

"I'm pretty sure it is."

Robert double parked. With a one-two crack of the heavy doors slamming shut, they walked gingerly to the back of the van. As they opened the van doors, Karen came out of the building, a sweater her only protection from the cold.

"Go back inside," Robert ordered. "It's freezing."

"I came out to help," she said, her breath hanging in the frosty air.

Ian met Karen's frigid gaze. He searched for something to say; nothing came.

"We're fine, babe," Robert said, as he and Ian began to maneuver the dresser out of the van.

Ian took a step and slid on a patch of ice, his feet skating out from under him, sending him tumbling back against the van. He let out a string of obscenities. "Moving in winter was a brilliant idea, mate."

"Do you know how hard it is to find a nine-hundred-square-foot apartment in New York City?"

"It's worth a body cast, is it?"

Shivering, Karen ran ahead to open the door.

Four flights later, Ian and Robert stumbled through the apartment door. They dropped the dresser to the floor with a thud and leaned against it, panting.

Ian looked up to find Emily in form-fitting jeans, a bright

pink cashmere sweater, and UGG boots, smiling at them. His heart sank.

She rushed over, throwing her arms around him.

"Oh, Ian, I'm so sorry to hear it's over!" She was a tangle of arms and fuzz and he endured an obligatory embrace before disengaging himself. "I just want you to know that if I can do anything for you, all you need to do is call. And you're still coming to the charity party at the gallery, I hope. I want you to be there."

Ian caught Karen's wide-eyed look of shock.

"Emily," she said.

Emily gave his arm a squeeze. "We'll talk about it later."

Outside, Ian huddled into his jacket, sucking on a cigarette as Robert pulled the last of the boxes from the van.

"Did Lizzie come at all?" Ian asked.

"She was here when I left to pick you up."

Emily came out of the building in a white leather bomber jacket, trailing a long pink scarf. Probably cost more than six months' rent, Ian thought as she bounded down the steps and flattened herself against him. He stiffened.

"I'll hold the door open for you," she chirped, looking up into his face and then rushing back up the steps.

Shit.

Chapter 62

Robert woke early. He rolled on his side, watching Karen's rhythmic breathing as she slept. In sleep, her features were relaxed, peaceful. The way she used to be all the time, he thought. The peace was still in there; she was struggling to find it. If they could just get past the wedding, he was convinced her parents' spell would be broken and the peace would return. In the meantime, he would let her schlep him to every Buddhist master in the five boroughs if that's what it took. He kissed her cheek and she stirred, mumbled, and turned over. He crept out of bed, grabbing pants and a shirt from the chair, and slipped out of the bedroom.

Robert shivered as he stepped out of the building and onto the deserted street; a typical Sunday morning. He hustled two doors down to the deli. Inside he picked over the bagels and muffins, taking a dozen, just in case any of the cast dropped by to talk about their motivation, their lines, or to find out if their character was still living. There was no chance Ian would be stopping by; one look from Karen had sent him into exile. He didn't know what happened with Liz, but he felt it incumbent upon himself to look out for Ian, treating him as he treated the brother he had lost. Ian had many of Patrick's qualities: easygoing, a genuine streak of goodness that ran deep, matched by a penchant for recklessness, a heart ruled by emotion rather than reason. And he still blamed himself for introducing Ian to

Michele; that damned party at that flat in Paris. If he hadn't run into Michele by accident, if he hadn't taken her up on her invitation, if he hadn't encouraged Ian to come with him to the party . . . on and on it went.

He paid and then braced himself for the cold. Pushing the door open against the wind, he headed back.

Opening the door, Robert tossed the keys on the table overflowing with mail. He heard the sound of low, muffled voices. At first he thought it was the droning of the television, but Karen didn't like television; if left to herself she never turned it on. He realized it was her voice, and that of another woman.

The smell of bacon and eggs reached his nose, accompanied by the clanging of pans. He stuck his head into the kitchen to find a short, stout woman in a starched black-and-white uniform standing over the stove.

"Hello," he said. "Margaret lets you out. That's encouraging."

"In the bedroom."

He nodded and she returned to the skillet of sizzling bacon. He blew out a mouthful of air and went down the hall.

Pushing open the bedroom door, Robert found Karen in bed, Margaret next to her, a breakfast tray with toast and fruit on Karen's lap.

"I prefer my eggs sunny-side up," Robert said.

Margaret tensed, reminding him of a cat sensing an intruder. He had the uneasy sense of having violated an inner sanctum, being privy to an act of parental affinity Margaret didn't want him to see.

Sweeping out of bed, Margaret's pale pink suit was smooth and unwrinkled. "Robert," she began, "while your literary prowess is tolerable, your talent for providing the proper residential requirements is sorely lacking."

"*We* like the apartment," he said sharply.

"That is hardly the point. Now, I've come about the wedding."

Robert folded his arms across his chest. "Yes, we're having one."

Margaret's lips tightened. "Karen tells me you are arranging everything."

"That's right."

Margaret continued to stare at him, waiting.

"We're getting married at the Four Corners Inn in Southampton. There will be a small brunch afterward. We've invited fifty people, no children. That's it."

Margaret picked up her purse. "Fine, e-mail or fax me all the information and I'll review it."

"Review it?" Robert said. "What for?"

"Darling boy, this is my daughter's wedding. I intend to be involved." She glanced around the room. "If you organize the festivities as you have this apartment, you won't be able to find my daughter on the wedding day. She'll be lost under a pile of clothing."

"Mommy, we just moved in."

"Be that as it may, I'll have Armand here by eleven to take care of the laundry."

"Those clothes are clean," Robert said, pointing to an overflowing laundry basket.

Margaret's reply was a raised eyebrow.

Robert looked to Karen.

"Mommy, we're fine, really," she said between munches.

"I know, sweetheart, you're perfect. I just want to help. I'm sending you Nico. Hopefully, he can do something with the interior until we can break the lease."

Suddenly aware that his mouth was open, Robert closed it and glared at her. "We're *not* breaking the lease," he said.

Margaret hesitated. "Very well then, the makeover should be complete in time for the wedding. You'll be able to make do until then, I'm sure."

Robert laughed. "I will be able to make do? Where will Karen be, Trump Tower?"

Margaret gathered her coat. "At the penthouse, of course."

It took a moment to register. "Absolutely not!"

"Do you expect my daughter to wake up on her wedding day amid the ambience of your discarded underwear lying on the floor? There will be time for that"—she wrinkled her nose in distaste—"after."

"I do not throw my underwear on the floor," Robert said, his face red.

Margaret's gaze traveled to a pair of shorts lying on the floor at the foot of the bed.

He heaved a heavy sigh.

"Separate residences are traditional and important for the sake of appearances. If you can't at least appear proper, what's the point of doing anything?"

"What am I going to do, make an appointment to see her?"

"Call her personal assistant, Camille, of course."

Robert glared at Karen.

"It's only temporary," she said.

Robert narrowed his eyes at her response.

Margaret gave a theatrical sigh. "Announce yourself to the doorman at any time. Really, Robert, for a comedic playwright you have absolutely no sense of humor. Now I will deliver her to you on the day of the wedding—"

"The day before the wedding. We're staying at the inn the night before."

Margaret surveyed the bedroom. "This place may require extensive demolition." She turned to Robert. "Now, when am I meeting your parents?"

Robert gaped at her, too stunned to speak.

"You do still have parents?"

"They're in hiding," he snapped.

Margaret picked up her purse. "I will send you my availability."

She kissed Karen's forehead and headed for the door.

Robert stepped in front of her. "So, you're giving up. This is what you're saying."

"Young man, the happiness of my daughter is paramount."

"We *are* having this wedding."

She patted his cheek. "Absolutely," she said, slipping past him. "This temporary arrangement will only help to strengthen your bond—yet another of my daughter's excellent ideas. You have no idea how lucky you are to have her."

Robert stood speechless.

Mary appeared at the bedroom door with a plate of bacon and eggs.

"Oh there you are," Margaret said as she swept past her. "I thought you had gone to the henhouse to gather the eggs."

Mary deposited the plate on the tray and left.

"Did you get the bagels?" Karen asked Robert, offering him a piece of bacon.

Karen padded after Robert as he thundered through the apartment.

"I don't believe this. I go out for bagels and I come back to find you moving in with your mother. And that it was your idea? How is moving in with your mother a good idea?" He stubbed his toe on the leg of a chair, letting out a string of obscenities.

Karen's almond eyes, peering out from under the heavy fringe of her bangs, were wide as saucers. "We were talking and it just popped out. Daddy's visiting the penthouse; if I'm there I can confront him. Figure them out. I have to know."

Robert sank onto the chair, grasping his toe. "You think you're in control, that they're finally letting you have your way," he said with a grimace. "But you're playing right into their hands. She's in control. She needs someone under her thumb. I can't believe it, Karen . . . It isn't like you to be . . ."

"What?"

He hesitated. "Naïve."

"I'm naïve because I see the possibility of finding out the truth? You used to admire the philosophies I believe in."

"I still do, baby," he said, reaching for her. "They're part of what I love about you, but searching for one truth doesn't mean being blind to another." He wriggled his toe and got to his feet. "I doubt you thought this through, or else you would have considered something even more important: how are we going to work with this new arrangement?"

"We see each other every day at the playhouse."

Robert didn't answer, just continued to look at her with raised eyebrows.

"You're worried about the sex, aren't you?"

"Aren't you?" he said, his voice rising. "Don't you understand, we're now going to have to make appointments through Claudine so we can have clandestine sex."

"Camille."

"Camille, Claudine, Clouseau, who gives a shit?" he said through his teeth. "I'm thirty-five years old and I'm going to have to take my fiancée to the movies to make out. And where will we have sex . . . did you consider that?"

"Why can't we meet here?"

"Why? Why? I'll tell you why, because our apartment is going to become an annex of *This Old House* when Norbert, the interior decorator savant, has this place shrouded in tarp."

"Nico."

Robert threw up his hands. "Nico, Neil, Norbert, who the hell cares! It's not going to happen. Karen, we're moving in the wrong direction: further apart. I didn't want this. I didn't know . . ."

"What?" she said, and the alarm in her voice made him stop and take a breath.

He lowered his voice. "I didn't want this . . . ."

"Do you mean you didn't want my parents involved, or do you mean you don't want me?" she said, her voice quiet.

"Of course I want you—I don't want to fight with you. Didn't we say we weren't going to be one of those couples who argue all the way to the altar? And now we're going to be separated, which is what the queen wants."

"She's not a queen and she cares about me."

"But she doesn't care about us," he said, taking her by the shoulders.

"They're a part of me," Karen said, sudden tears filling her eyes. "If you don't want to marry me, just say so."

Robert felt a sensation akin to getting too close to the edge of a cliff. He drew in a long, slow breath, tightening his hold on her.

"Baby, I can't wait to marry you," he said. "You know that."

Karen wrapped her arms around him. "Buddha said that on the road to truth the mistake is not going all the way."

"If he knew your parents he would've told you to get off the road and take cover."

"I have to do this. Please try to understand."

Robert nodded. "Let's go back to bed," he said. "While we still can."

Chapter 63

The blustering wind and frigid temperatures of New York in February were banished from sight and sound in the warm oasis of the restaurant. Elizabeth and Nick lapsed into one of the many silences of the evening. She glanced at his plate—the rare steak swimming in the bloody red sauce—and looked away. *Ian would've ordered pasta, or a lobster ravioli, which I would be eating. Except we wouldn't be here.* They would've been at the French bistro in Midtown, the one with the beautiful, infuriatingly rude waitresses who looked down at you with disdain. Ian always ignored their bad manners, speaking to them in French, his accent rolling against the words, tipping them against their natural pronunciation. Then they would meet his eyes, their faces softening for the handsome Scotsman. *Stop. Enough. You are now in the present tense.*

"Did you like the flowers I sent?"

"I like the flowers you send every week."

He chuckled, taking her hand. "You look tired, Liz. How about a quick getaway, an early spring break, someplace warm? We could be having breakfast in Grand Cayman."

"As friends?" Liz asked.

He squeezed her hand. "Liz, I'm talking about more than friendship, you know that."

She did know, all too well. The commodity of romance allowed for a certain flexibility. She looked away from his dark eyes and mentally traced the barest shadow of his beard along his jawline. At least she would be on an equal footing with Nick. He wouldn't be pulling any power plays. He wouldn't be undressing her, keeping her naked and vulnerable, making love to her with his words and his body, keeping all the power for himself.

She could feel herself growing warm. "I have Emily's charity event," she said, hoping the blush would not reach her face. "I'm afraid Grand Cayman will have to wait."

"I like loyalty in a woman. I have an invitation myself. May I take you?"

"Nick, after all this time—" she began.

He smiled, kissing her hand. "Look, Liz, we're both too mature to play games, and I told you I wasn't giving up. I'm not going to insult your intelligence by telling you I know what you went through in California."

She bristled at the statement.

"I don't know why people let the past affect their present." *You wouldn't.*

"Yesterday is gone, Liz. I've known since I met you that you're special. You have great things in your future. I wish you would relax and let me be a part of it."

"You're a good man, Nick."

Nick smiled. "I know I am, kid, and I know we were made for each other."

She took a deep breath. She didn't answer him.

Chapter 64

The Soho gallery blazed, psychedelic colors bouncing off the walls, the mounted slim-line plasma-screen displays dotting the gallery. A lush woman, her lips glistening, filled the screen. She repeated nonsense composed of adjectives bereft of nouns and verbs, her sexy smile implying she was imparting the secrets of the universe in a coded language everyone should understand.

Parker worked the room as though the party were his. He sidled up to guests, a drink in one hand, his arm snaking around their shoulder.

"*Que pasa*, people?" he brayed as he bounded over to Karen, Robert, Nick and Elizabeth. Emily clung to his side, giggling as she had on their wedding day.

Give the lady an Oscar, Elizabeth thought. *How do you do it?*

Parker caught Elizabeth's eye. She saw the smile slip from his face and ignored him.

"I didn't know LBOs were still the rage," Karen said.

"What's a few billion in debt?" Parker said. "You sell off a few divisions, hump a few quarters for profit, and you're all set."

"LBOs are an effective way of acquiring companies without outlaying large amounts of cash," Nick said.

"But what about the workforce?" Karen said. "LBOs affect

people at the most basic level. One company can make or break entire geographic areas, socially, financially, and environmentally."

"Oh no, not the Woodstock, Buddhist 'we are all one with one another on Mother Earth' crap," Parker said, rolling his eyes.

Nick ignored him. "Your mother's fortune doesn't come from book sales; her family history includes oil and railroad barons. Do you really think they asked 'what about the workforce?' as they acquired other people's property so they could pave the way for progress? It's all well and good to ride the subway because you feel like it, but that doesn't mean you're on the same social strata as everyone else."

Elizabeth glanced at the floor so she wouldn't have to look Karen in the eye.

Robert put his arm around Karen. "Karen is very knowledgeable on social issues, and cares deeply about people, whether she rides the subway or not."

Parker chuckled and gave Nick a pat on the shoulder. "Forget it, pal, what do you expect from a bunch of damned Democrats?"

Jackass, Elizabeth thought. She looked around, her eyes reaching the entrance at the moment Ian walked through the door.

She stiffened. When she trusted herself to look into his face, she caught the shock and anger in the wide flicker of his eyes as they moved from her to Nick and back again. His face closed and he turned away.

She realized no one in their circle was talking. Nick put his arm around her shoulder and led her in the opposite direction.

Upstairs in a quiet alcove, Ian paced. At the sound of heavy footsteps, he turned to find Robert in the doorway.

"Well, well, Miss Lizzie," Ian said, letting out a low humorless chuckle. "Did she have Nicky on speed dial? Well . . . what did Karen say?"

Robert hesitated. "Nothing . . . we're Switzerland."

Ian gaped at him. "What the fuck does that mean?"

* * *

"**N**ick really cares about me," Elizabeth said, tossing back the last of her drink.

Karen gave her a sharp look.

"He's very confident in himself."

"He's a snob."

"He's dependable and solid. He's the fantasy of every woman who hopes to find her dream man . . . I'm sorry about his comment."

"Forget it. If you think he's good for you, that's what's important," Karen said. "Even if no one else does."

"At least he's concerned about me," she said, holding out her glass for the bartender to refill. "Not like some people when you tell them you're leaving, and they react like you said you're going out for a quart of milk."

"Not that you care," Karen said.

"Exactly."

Karen rubbed Elizabeth's shoulder. "I'm sorry, Liz."

"Forget it. I'm over him. Nick will give me the look."

"Will he?" Karen asked.

"Even if he doesn't, it's not important. It's not a kidney."

"No, Liz, it's your heart," she said quietly. "Don't you think you should get it right?"

Elizabeth took a gulp of her drink.

"Hey," Emily said as she strolled over, hips swaying under a thigh-high, black silk Gucci canvas dress with zippers and ties, her feet encased in silver slingback Manolo Blahnik sandals. "What's up?"

"Isn't it a little cold for those?" Elizabeth said, eyeing the shoes.

"I couldn't wait," Emily said, a chirp in her voice.

"Can you tell me why Ian is here?" Elizabeth asked.

"I invited him while you two were still a couple."

"You invited him in my apartment," Karen corrected.

"I *reminded* him in your apartment. I originally invited him while they were still together. If you had told me you were planning a breakup, I would have uninvited him . . . but no one mentioned that little detail to me."

Elizabeth opened her mouth, but Karen gripped her arm.

Emily pointed her foot outward. "Don't you just adore these?"

Robert watched Ian pace, feeling like he was at a tennis match.

"I'll go see her at the office; yeah, that'll work. She'll never cause a scene there. We'll talk."

"About what? I don't think that's a good idea."

"Oh you're back, are you? I thought you were busy with the hot chocolate after an afternoon on the slopes. Switzerland," he mumbled, continuing to pace, giving Robert a sideways glance. "It'll be all right. We'll have a bit of lunch, she'll eat my food, she'll cry, I'll comfort her, and we'll be exactly like we were before."

"That's always your answer, but it won't work and you know it. You said she mentioned marriage. She wants to get married. Are you ready to remarry?"

Ian stopped pacing, throwing him a black look.

"Look, I'm sure she understands why you're hesitating. Just talk to her."

Ian kept his head down. "I can't."

"Can't?"

"I didn't tell her I've been married."

"After Michele was here . . . in the restaurant?" Robert frowned. "Well, tell her now."

Ian hesitated. "I sort of made it sound like I've never been married."

Robert threw up his hands. "Sort of? What else did you or did you not tell her about yourself?"

"I told her I did private commissions, tutored privately, taught at university . . . but . . ." He shrugged. "I was really knocking about, doing quick portraits in town squares and such, for a few pounds or euros."

Robert shook his head. "I didn't know you were in such bad shape."

Ian shrugged. "I couldn't very well explain to her that I was a failure, now could I? And it's my business, isn't it? It's not important," Ian said.

Robert stared at him.

"Well, it's not," he persisted.

"How is it that you grew up surrounded by women and yet know nothing about them? You're right, she won't care that you were married. She'll care that you *told* her you weren't. Women have a frightening thought process, my friend. Cognitively, they can't move in a straight line. I don't know how they live. One thought becomes a miasma, a panacea, a burgeoning forest, an endless ocean of topics and ideas. Sometimes, it takes all of my powers of reasoning and deduction to follow Karen when she's talking to me. I wish she would leave breadcrumbs. While you're pontificating on the irrelevance of your previous activities, Elizabeth will zero in like a targeted missile on the fact that you lied, outright or by omission, giving way to that miasma, panacea, forest, and ocean of all the other possible lies you have told her, could be telling her now, or may tell her in the future."

Ian's shoulders sagged. "I'm fucked, aren't I?"

"I'm afraid so."

Ian glanced over the railing down to the floor below. He caught sight of Elizabeth, Nick's arm curled around her waist. "I have to try," he said.

Chapter 65

Ian ran his hands through his hair one last time, fiddling with his jacket and collar. He'd have to turn on the charm, assure her he no longer needed or wanted to go to Europe, and that he wouldn't go, even if he did need to. He couldn't afford another screwup. As he turned the corner to Elizabeth's office, he found Nick standing inside. *Fucking hell.*

"Desperate for a sale?" Nick asked, settling himself in Elizabeth's chair. "Or just desperate?"

Ian was at a loss for an answer. *Wanker.*

Nick smirked up at him. "You're wasting your time."

"I never found any time with Lizzie to be a waste."

"You're absolutely right," Nick said, getting up and coming around the desk. "Liz is special, very special. We've been spending a lot of time together. She's invested enough time in useless hobbies that don't give her any pleasure—or satisfaction."

Ian felt every muscle tense; it was all he could do to keep from slugging the pompous bastard.

"We'll see," Ian said.

"There's nothing to fucking *see*," Nick said, his eyes hard as flint. "Take off, Van Gogh. You're where you don't belong. Go back to the bar to drink with your loser friends who think smearing paint on a canvas is a career. You'll have to find another beautiful, intelligent, successful woman to be your next meal ticket." He leaned an inch closer. "When I take her to Paris and we're staying in our two-thousand-dollar-a-night room overlooking the Champs-Elysées, you'll be no more than a faded memory. Don't expect a postcard."

"If she wanted you to take her somewhere, you'd be talking to a travel agent and not me, wouldn't you?"

Nick gave a tiny chuckle. "You don't get the picture, do you? You're yesterday's news."

"There's always tomorrow."

Nick's color deepened; he opened his mouth to answer and then looked past Ian.

Ian turned to find Elizabeth standing in the doorway, cool and aloof.

"Hello, darling," Nick said, moving to her side and giving her a kiss.

"I just thought . . . to come round, to say hello," Ian said. He searched for any sign of warmth in her, any hint of feeling. Her expression didn't change. *Shit, this was a mistake and I'm standing here feeling a fool, begging in front of this bastard.*

"I'm very busy," she said, crossing to her desk. "I have no time for you."

No time for me? "I thought we could have a spot of lunch, whenever you're free," he said, keeping his tone light and un-concerned.

"Liz is unavailable for lunch," Nick said.

Ian continued to look at her.

"I'm booked," she said.

"Some other time."

"I don't think so."

"Perhaps a coffee."

"I'm off coffee."

"Bottle of water then," he snapped.

"I'm not partaking of any beverages at all, in the foresee-able future."

Nick gave a small chuckle.

Ian pursed his lips into a tight smile. "You shouldn't make rash decisions, Lizzie. You make mistakes that way."

"I've corrected all of my mistakes."

Debbie appeared in the doorway and Ian cursed silently.

"Is my twelve o'clock ready?" Elizabeth asked.

"He's just off the phone, but Mathers has a question."

"All right, tell him I'm going to walk down."

"Demarchalier for dinner?" Nick asked.

She nodded, offering her cheek.

Picking up a blue folder from her desk, she walked out without a glance at Ian.

"What was that about tomorrow?" Nick said with a smirk. "It looks like you've used up all your minutes . . . asshole."

Ian walked out of the office and headed for the elevator, feeling as if all the air had been sucked out of his lungs. *I screwed up. I've lost her.*

Chapter 66

Standing outside Margaret's apartment building, Ian leaned against an idling limousine, the frigid afternoon wind chilling him to the bone, a string of profanities dancing in his head. He was still stewing over the scene in Elizabeth's office from the week before. Nick with his arm around her, kissing her, talking about taking her away to Paris; her cold refusal to even look at him. He realized the muscles in his jaw were aching; he'd been clenching his teeth again.

He shook his head and lit another cigarette. He was freezing his bum off out here, waiting for Robert to come down with Karen and Margaret. He should never have let Robert talk him into this trip to the Island. ("It'll do you good to get away.") *Good to get away, my arse,* he thought. Robert didn't want to spend hours trapped in a limo as the only object of Margaret's attention. *Now I'm the designated decoy.*

The doorman snapped to attention and opened the building door, jarring Ian from his thoughts. A woman emerged, cool and sophisticated, in a white cashmere coat, a red silk scarf and white, Victorian, laced leather boots. Her auburn hair glistened in the weak winter sun, eyes hidden behind outsized designer sunglasses. She removed the sunglasses, giving Ian a perfunctory examination.

"So," Margaret said, "you're the artist."

Ian shifted off the car as she sauntered up to him.

"So, you're the mother."

"I can see why Miss Elizabeth was piqued by you. Everyone is quite upset with you, you know."

"I've heard."

"You're not what I expected."

"It pains me to disappoint."

Margaret laughed, fingering his collar. "On the contrary. You're above and beyond what I had hoped for."

"I'm so glad." He eyed the limousine; he wouldn't dare get into a car alone with this woman.

Upstairs in the penthouse, Robert whispered feverishly at Karen, following on her heels as she gathered her coat and purse.

"So Willis just happened to stop by. How often does he just stop by?"

Karen turned to him. "It was spur of the moment. He does that sometimes. Just to say hello. Mother can be very informal."

"Since when?" Robert muttered as they came down the hall.

They entered the living room to find Willis waiting. With a wide smile and an open expression, he embraced Karen and gave her a kiss.

"Hey, have a good trip out to the Island." Giving Robert an avuncular slap on the back, he grinned at him. "Good luck with the in-law meet and greet. You'll need it. I'll come by on Thursday, just to check in. Maybe we can grab lunch."

"Sure," Robert said through pursed lips.

When Margaret stepped closer, Ian caught the scent of her perfume—pleasing, sweet, and definitely expensive; no doubt meant to lull one into relaxation. *That's what all cunning hunters do to corner their prey.*

"Just between us, of course," Margaret said, "why do you think she left you?"

Ian sucked in a breath. "I'm sure I don't know, not that it's any of your business," he said, aware that he was violating the code instilled in him by his mother, of unfailing politeness toward the fairer sex; and the code of friendship and loyalty to Robert, to not make waves. "Perhaps I'm just a very bad man."

"How delightful to contemplate," Margaret said with a pleased smile. "Now, how many women have left you?"

"How many men have tried to kill you?"

"Touché," she said, moving away from him. "Yes, you'll do very well."

"Do?" he asked, all attention now. "For what?"

With a wave of her hand she motioned the driver to open the door. She glanced back at him with a wicked grin. "Come along, my angel," she said, disappearing into the limousine.

Robert and Karen emerged from the building and headed for the limousine. Ian remained rooted to the sidewalk.

"Why aren't you getting in?" Robert said, fixing him with a sharp look.

"I think I should stay."

Robert was silent for a moment. "You're my brother," he said. "You know that, right? I'm always there for you."

Ian nodded.

"Then get your ass in the limo. I'm not riding the hell train to Long Island by myself."

Ian shrugged and climbed in.

The limousine stopped a few blocks from the penthouse.

"Did you forget something?" Robert said to Margaret, straining to remain polite.

"Last minute details," Margaret said, glancing over at Ian, pressed into the corner of the limo, staring out the window. "Come along, *mes enfants*."

They slid out of the limousine.

"My mother's cooking," Robert whispered to Karen. "We can't be late." He spotted Ian edging away.

"Don't even think about it," Robert warned. "I know where you live."

He turned to Karen. "Why are we here?"

"For my godmother's weekly cocktail party. I told you about her. Lady Evelyn Livingston. Mother never misses the party."

"Then why the hell did she insist on visiting my parents today?"

Margaret turned around, narrowing her eyes at Robert. "Because I am a tireless multitasker and we are here for you and your cohort. I am making introductions for you both."

"I don't need any bloody introductions," Ian grumbled.

"I don't know that you deserve any," Karen said.

Ian opened his mouth but Robert placed a firm hand on his shoulder.

Karen and Margaret strolled into the building arm in arm.

Ian and Robert looked at each other and followed, like condemned men.

"**S**weetie!" Lady Evelyn Livingston drawled as she and Margaret came together for a kiss-kiss.

"Evie . . . darling."

Lady Livingston, dripping with diamonds and wearing a black silk evening gown, looked Ian up and down as he came in. "And who is this?" she asked.

"My new pet projet, darling. Ian MacKay, a brilliant artist," Margaret announced at the top of her lungs, eliciting murmurs from surrounding guests.

Ian glared at her.

Evelyn turned her attention to Robert. "And this is?"

"The fiancé," Robert said.

"Oh yes . . . the hearty soul."

"Robert," Margaret said, pointing clear across the room to a tall, angular man wearing a stark white suit. "Your wedding planner . . . Jacques."

"Wedding planner?" Robert said, shooting Karen a look of dismay.

Karen and Robert watched the hands of Jacques dancing like fireflies as he explained the fabulousness that was to be their wedding. In his late fifties, Jacques had platinum hair that spiked on its own without assistance from any styling products. The more excited he became, the more the strands rose heavenward of their own volition.

"Now the gazebo will have to be constructed the day before," he said.

"Gazebo . . . what gazebo?" Robert asked.

Jacques threw his arms around Karen. "To think I have known you from the beginning, from before the beginning. I was planning your christening party before you were born."

"I know, Jacques," she said, leaning into his embrace. "Every once in a while I look at the albums. My parents looked so happy."

Jacques gave her a kiss. "Yes, they were . . . their wedding was so chic." His face scrunched up. "I think maybe I should not have used so much tulle. Perhaps it created a shroud of disaster." He shook his head and sighed. "I use very little tulle now," he murmured, momentarily lost in his own thoughts.

"You . . . planned her parents' wedding?" Robert asked.

Jacques ignored the question. "The doves will be released at exactly twelve noon when you are pronounced husband and wife."

"Doves . . . what doves?" Robert looked at Karen. "You know about the doves?"

"Doves are a symbol of happiness," Jacques said.

"A load of birds shitting on our heads is a symbol of happiness?" Robert snapped. "How many did you release at her parents' wedding?"

Jacques flushed bright red. "Two dozen . . . perhaps it wasn't the tulle."

Robert and Karen navigated their way through the sea of people moving from room to room.

"Karen, we didn't agree on birds."

"I think it's a nice touch," Karen said.

"Only if Jacques is providing complimentary umbrellas."

Karen stopped and gave him a penetrating look.

"What?"

"Jacques is a very close friend of our family. He is—like family."

"I know, baby. I know."

"You don't think it's going to work out, do you? You're predicting a disaster, aren't you?"

Robert pulled her close to him. "No, I am not predicting disaster . . . it's going to be fine."

A tall, dignified man wearing a gray suit and red tie made his way toward them. "Who is he?" Robert murmured.

"My father's agent," she said. "Dennis—hi." She reached out to embrace him.

"Karen, how are you, dear?"

Dennis drew her in for a hug and then held her at arm's length. "You're positively glowing. Your father told me all about the play. How's it going?"

"Very well."

"He's so very proud of you, he—"

"Ian MacKay is a brilliant new talent." Margaret's voice rang out, making everyone fall silent. "And I feel very lucky to be his patron," she concluded, beaming at him. She hooked her arm in his, making it impossible for him to retreat.

Dennis turned back to Karen. "Your mother's new friend?" he asked.

Karen's lip curled. "Apparently."

"What happened to Marcus?" Dennis said.

"She bought him a Benz and sent him out on a permanent test drive."

"And this MacKay is his replacement?"

"No, he isn't," Robert interjected, nudging Karen in the opposite direction. "Look, nice to have met you, but we're on our way out to the Island."

"You're going out to the Island . . . MacKay too?" Dennis asked.

Karen gave him a look. "Yes. Mother is going to meet Robert's parents."

Dennis nodded. "Have you seen your father, Karen?"

"Not for a few weeks. Why?"

Dennis threw a dark look in Margaret's direction. "If you will excuse me," he said to Karen with a cursory smile, ignoring her question, "I have to make a phone call. Congratulations on the play. I'm sure it will be a hit."

"What's with him and the grilling?" Robert asked, looking at Dennis's retreating back. "Another member of your parents' lunatic fringe?"

"Don't talk about my mother's friends that way."

"He's your father's friend."

"He's a friend to them both. Daddy got to keep him in the settlement."

"I'm not even going to begin to examine that statement."

"Look, he's my friend too," Karen said in a sharp tone. "I had pneumonia when I was nine years old. Dennis sent flowers every day. He brought me all the newest children's book releases—before they were in stores. He read them to me himself."

"Did your parents rent a hospital wing and hire a private physician and nursing staff?"

Karen raised her eyebrows and Robert's face fell.

"And that was exceedingly generous of them. I know your parents love you more than their own lives," he said quietly.

"Then why are you making fun of them?"

"Baby, I'm not," he soothed. "These people are your friends and that's fine. But Ian is my friend and we have to get him out of here before your mother goes totally Mrs. Robinson on him. And we need to get on the road. My mother's been cooking—"

"—for hours, yes, I know."

"Everyone," Evelyn called out, "there's going to be a spectacular presentation in the den. Nathaniel is going to perform *Othello*—the entire play—in ten minutes, playing all the characters."

"That's our cue," Robert said, clutching her hand; catching Ian's eye, Robert motioned for him to move out.

* * *

"**W**hy are we stopping in Queens?" Robert said, his voice rising.

The limo pulled up to the curb and Ian threw open the door, scrambling out before it came to a full stop. He lit a cigarette and stood smoking, a sour look on his face.

"I abhor smoking, *mon amour*," Margaret called.

"Then this wee romance is over before it began, isn't it?" he snapped.

"It's not a romance," Karen said, getting out of the car with Robert.

Ian sucked in a deep breath. "I didn't start it, she did."

"She has a name," Karen said. "Women have names."

Ian opened his mouth, but Margaret's laugh cut him off. "All right, ducklings, follow after mother."

"Margaret," Robert said, sounding like a parent attempting to calm an irrational child, "why are we here?"

"Acupuncture," Karen said.

"Acupuncture," Robert said. "Now? Can't this wait until tomorrow?"

"Just a touch-up for the face," Margaret explained blithely. "One must always look one's best."

Ian threw up his hands and, rolling his eyes, he turned away.

"Margaret, please," Robert began. "You look wonderful. My mother is cooking . . . we have to go or we're going to hit rush-hour traffic."

"Young man, I do not intend to present myself to your venerable, if not quaint, parents, in today's Versace and yesterday's skin tone, *comprenez-vous?*" Margaret turned on her heel and, taking Karen's hand, trotted off.

Ian sidled up to Robert. "You know where it all went wrong, don't you?"

Robert nodded. "Getting into the limo," he said with a sigh.

An hour later, Ian and Robert stood on the sidewalk, leaning against the limo.

Margaret and Karen emerged from the building, their faces glowing.

"You should have come in with us," Margaret said, patting Ian's cheek. "You look a tad sallow. It's all that smoking, a loathsome habit. Dr. Yao can take care of that as well. She'll have you smoke-free before you know it. I'll make an appointment and have Anthony pick you up."

"I don't want any bloody appointment," Ian growled. "I like to smoke."

Margaret ignored him. "Your chi is unbalanced, and you have too much heart energy."

"Ha!" Karen said, her lip curling. "I don't think so."

Ian pushed off the limo. "You know what I think?"

Robert stepped between them. "*I* think we need to get back on the road, it's—" He stopped, his mouth open, as an Asian man, an apron tucked around his slim waist, carrying a large hardwood tray filled with spareribs, shrimp toast, skewered beef, and other tidbits trotted up to the limo. Flame was rising from the hibachi grill in the middle of the tray.

"What the hell . . . ?" Ian said.

"My mother has been cooking all day, and you ordered a pupu platter?" Robert said.

"Good Lord, man, is she roasting a pig in the backyard?" Margaret said. "A small snack on the way won't kill the appetite." She looked at her watch and sighed. "Besides, it's rush hour, we'll be on the road forever."

Robert clenched his teeth as Margaret disappeared into the limousine.

"Give it up, mate," Ian said. "You're a beaten man."

Margaret called out, "Where is my Scottish angel? Come and sit next to me."

Ian glared at Robert.

"Okay, okay, I owe you," Robert said.

"Let me count the ways," Ian said, as he and Karen exchanged vicious looks.

*   *   *

Margaret and Ian sat on opposite ends of the seat.

Across from them, Karen curled up against Robert. The pupu platter sat on the floor, Robert's jacket tucked around its base to keep it from shifting.

"Don't you think we should put that out now?" Robert said, nervously eyeing the rising flames.

"Carry your own extinguisher, do you?" Ian said.

Margaret leaned forward and selected a shrimp toast. "Stop acting like a child. Dig in, dears, it's all very tasty. We don't want to insult Yan by not eating his delicacies."

"Yan isn't here, Margaret," Robert snapped. "He'll never know."

Ian hunched further into his jacket.

"Now, my little scribes, what will you write about next?" Margaret said, handing a sparerib to Karen.

Robert shifted in his seat. "We haven't decided. We're not done with our present work."

The car hit a bump, lifting everyone up off the seat and back down again. The hibachi trembled but stayed upright.

"Anthony," Margaret called out, "we'd like to stay on terra firma, if it's all the same to you!"

Anthony mumbled an apology.

"Now is the time for you to decide what your next project will be. For the great writers, the mind is always turning. They begin their next work before the present one is done. Why not write about love? Love gained, lost, squandered . . ." Margaret brushed Ian's leg with the tip of her shoe. "The May-December romance is always so challenging, passionate, and invigorating."

"Stop the car," Ian said. "I want to get out."

"To go where?" Robert asked. "And how?"

"Wherever. I'll hitchhike."

"Shall I pull over, ma'am?" Anthony asked.

"Yes, damn it," Ian said, his face flushing. "I need a cigarette."

"Open a window," Margaret ordered, nibbling at a dumpling. "Keep driving, Anthony. Remember, dears, literature always has something new to contribute to the concept of relationships. The printed word illuminates and duplicates the destruction of all hope and happiness that befalls lovers of all ages and strata. *Cat on a Hot Tin Roof, Antony and Cleopatra*—"

"*Who's Afraid of Virginia Woolf?*" Karen said, leaning forward eagerly. "Do you think some couples have relationships that are carbon copies of works of literature?"

Robert massaged her shoulders, easing her back on the seat. "Nice try," he murmured.

"Darling, art imitates life. Life does not imitate art . . . it doesn't rhyme."

The car lurched again and the pupu platter rocked from side to side. Robert shot his foot out to steady the flaming hibachi.

"Anthony, one cannot digest a dumpling in a bumper car!"

Margaret fixed her gaze on Ian. "Now, you could write a story about a man incapable of commitment, fearful, so fearful he is unable to love—"

Ian looked at Robert. "I swear—"

"Blow it off, man, we're only thirty minutes out," Robert said.

"We must ask ourselves," Margaret went on, "why is he so afraid to give his heart to a woman he so obviously loves. That's a wonderful story. Don't you think?"

The car swayed to the right as Anthony changed lanes. Ian grabbed the door handle, trying to keep himself tucked into his corner.

"Why is he hiding? What is the reason for all his bravado about not caring for anyone?"

"He has a problem with intimacy," Karen snapped, looking directly at Ian.

"That's it!" Ian exploded. "It was Lizzie's decision!"

"And you did nothing to stop her!"

"All right, that's enough from both of you," Robert ordered. The limo lurched violently, springing in and out of a pothole. They all gasped as the pupu platter tipped and the tee-tering hibachi lurched and fell over. Flames shot out, licking at Robert's jacket, blazing up into a small bonfire. Ian and Robert began stomping on the jacket.

"Not again," Karen moaned.

"Fire in the hole!" Margaret bellowed. "Anthony, pull over!"

Robert held Karen's hand while talking into his cell phone. Every few minutes he looked over at Ian, pacing a few feet away, throwing sour glances in their direction.

"Yes, Mom, we're on the way. No, everyone's fine. I can always get another jacket."

Karen shivered and Robert put his arm around her, pulling her close.

"The fire is out . . . no, no one was burned . . . no, I'm sure there's no law regarding a pupu platter fire in a moving vehi-cle, so we should be getting back on the road. We should be there in thirty minutes . . . yes, everyone's hungry." He said good-bye and flipped the phone closed.

Robert broke the silence first. "You have to talk to her, babe."

"You think she's wrong about Ian. She didn't say anything that's not true. You're taking his side."

"I'm not taking anyone's side. Ian and Liz have to work this out by themselves."

"There's nothing to work out. You know what he did."

Robert took her by the shoulders. "This . . . this is why I didn't want us to get involved. I don't know what he did or what she did, and neither do you. I do know I don't want us fighting over our friends, your mother, or your mother's friends. And I know the way you're treating Ian is *not* part of the Noble Eightfold Path."

Karen looked past him, at Ian hunching against the cold. "I'll talk to her," she said, and walked away.

Everyone exchanged greetings in the crowded entry hall of Robert's two-story colonial, boyhood home.

Robert's mother, Leslie, had a soft, kind face and a vaguely melancholy air about her, as if she might cry at any moment, but never did. She wore her dark hair cropped close to her head and she was beginning to show the slight thickness in her midsection that comes to women in their middle years. She kissed Karen hello and gave the men a hug.

"Ian looks ill," she whispered to Robert. "Is he all right?"

Robert nodded his head.

His father, Alan, a tall, robust, pleasant man with an easy smile, gave Ian a fatherly pat on the back. At a sound behind them, they all moved aside, like the parting of the Red Sea; Margaret came forward.

Leslie took her hand. "Welcome. We're so pleased that you've come. We've been looking forward to it."

"It's my pleasure. Thank you for having me," Margaret said without pomp or ceremony. "And please, call me Peggy."

Robert and Karen looked at each other.

As the group moved toward the dining room, Leslie wrapped her arm around Ian's shoulder and he gave her a hug and a kiss on the cheek.

They all sat around the dinner table, now cluttered with empty plates. The low hum of conversation hung in the air. Ian got up from the table, his cigarette and lighter in hand. Leslie grabbed his hand as he passed. She gave him a motherly look of disapproval. He leaned over and gave her a kiss and a wink before slipping away.

"Dinner was wonderful," Margaret said.

"I'm so glad you liked it," Leslie said, looking pleased.

"More green bean casserole, Mother Wainwright?" Robert said with a smile.

"No thank you, Robert," Margaret said.

Karen elbowed Robert.

"We are just so thrilled with Karen," Leslie said. "We love her as if she were our own. You must be so proud of her."

"I am, and she has made a fine choice."

"We're glad you feel that way," Alan said, exchanging a

quick glance with Leslie. "We understood that you had some reservations about the marriage . . . initially."

Margaret didn't answer.

"And I . . . we want to assure you that Robert is a fine boy."

Robert grinned at Margaret.

"Amongst his other qualities," Margaret said, taking another sip of wine.

Leslie leaned forward. "We've worked very hard with him, and we've tried to be a good example, as you and your husband have been for Karen, of course."

"Ex-husband, and we prefer to think of our influence as more of a cautionary tale."

Karen swallowed hard.

"Robert is our first," Leslie said, her words catching in her throat. "An excellent example for his brother . . . he always looked out for Patrick. Always."

The table fell silent.

Margaret reached over and touched Leslie's hand. "I'm sure he did."

"Mother and father don't have any reservations, or objections," Karen said suddenly. "Isn't that right, Mother?"

Margaret raised her eyebrows.

Leslie brightened. "Is that right? Well, we're so glad to hear that."

Margaret and Karen looked at each other for a long moment. Then Margaret turned to Leslie and Alan. "Absolutely. I have every confidence in Karen's choices. We are eagerly anticipating the happy day."

Leslie and Alan leaned back in their chairs and smiled at each other.

"Thank you, Mother Wainwright," Robert said.

Margaret shot him a warning look.

Outside on the back porch swing, Ian huddled in his coat, gliding back and forth at a lazy pace. The sound of the storm door opening and closing made him glance over; Robert sat down next to him.

"How's the nutty contessa?" he asked.

"Sitting in the kitchen, *gabbing* with my mother."

"Get away with you."

Robert shook his head. "I kid you not. They are now BFFs. It's uncanny. If you didn't know her, you'd think she was normal."

They fell silent as Karen came out.

"Nice offense in there," Robert said. "Where'd you learn that trick?"

"From the masters," she said.

Robert nodded. "Is the hell train ready to pull out of the station?"

"Just about."

He turned to Ian. "It won't take us long to get back."

"Well . . ." Karen began.

At once Ian was all attention. "What?"

Karen looked sheepish. "She wants to stop in town at the bookstore." She shrugged.

Ian leaned back. "I knew it was too bloody easy."

The limo pulled into a back parking lot, the group emerging like prisoners climbing out of a paddywagon. Ian lagged behind as they made their way down the quaint main street.

Karen stopped outside the bookstore, staring at a poster of Penny Hargrave. She turned to Margaret. "No, Mother," she said with unexpected force.

"No to what, dear?" Margaret asked, all wide-eyed innocence.

Karen pointed at the poster. "Penny's reading. You *know* Daddy's in there; you've known all along he would be here. You never wanted to meet Robert's parents, did you? You just wanted to come here and make a scene."

"Darling, that is not true—"

"You promised there would be no more incidents. Mother, I forbid you to make a scene in this bookstore. Do you understand?"

Margaret hesitated a beat. "I thought you should be here, to support your father. And his new anorexic embryo, of course. Karen, I have no intention of making a scene."

"I'm pretty sure you do," Robert said drily.

Margaret ignored him. "Besides, your father knows I'm coming."

"How?"

"I'm sure Dennis called him hours ago, from Evie's."

"Mother, we are leaving right now."

Margaret opened the door to the bookstore. "Trust me. We'll all be one happy family . . . like Bruce, Demi and Ashton," she said, giving Ian a sly look before sweeping inside.

The bookstore had a comfortable, lived-in feel to it, with its sawdust-colored floorboards that creaked underfoot. Off to one side, a small stairway led to a second floor.

They could hear Penny, in the back, giving her reading.

Edward stood at the rear of the seated crowd, dapper in a dark suit, his hair slicked back.

At the sound of footsteps on the bare wood floor Edward turned, his expression lighting up when Karen appeared at his side.

Modest applause broke out and a woman announced that Penny would be moving upstairs for the book signing. Some of the crowd milled toward the stairway; others abandoned the scene to browse the shelves.

Edward caught sight of Margaret and his color deepened.

"Daddy, it was a lovely reading," Karen said, putting herself between them.

"Thank you, sweetheart," he said. Patting her hand, Edward maneuvered around her and advanced in Margaret's direction.

Karen glanced at Margaret and found her cuddling up to Ian.

Ian threw Robert a look, and with a jerk of his head Robert motioned for him to go outside. Ian nodded, attempting to break free.

Karen kept pace with her father. "Now, Daddy, don't be foolish. The Suffolk County police don't know you. It'll take hours for Albert to post bail."

Edward ignored her, plowing ahead, coming to stand toe-to-toe with Margaret.

"Why are you here?" he said, his voice low and dangerous. "And who the hell is he?"

Ian froze.

"I brought your daughter to support you and your Lolita. He is my support," Margaret purred.

"I thought we decided that there wouldn't be any more of this," Edward said, his voice low.

Karen looked at Robert with questioning eyes. Robert shrugged.

"You decided."

"Still playing games?"

"No more than you are."

"When are you going to stop this?" Edward demanded.

"You first," Margaret hissed.

With a sound of disgust, Edward turned to Ian. "So, you're the replacement?"

"Replacement?" Ian echoed, finally breaking Margaret's hold. "I don't know what the hell you're talking about, mate."

"Eddie, Eddie darling, I'm waiting for you," Penny's voice rang out. Heads turned, looking up at the second floor.

Edward scowled. "I'm not your mate," he said, not bothering to keep his voice down. "Do you think screwing my wife is going to make you famous?"

A crowd began to gather.

"I'm not doing anything with your wife, except trying to get the hell away from her."

Margaret's laugh rang out and Edward's face turned crimson.

"Shit," Robert breathed, rushing forward to grip Edward's shoulder.

Throwing Margaret a murderous look, Ian began backing away.

"No you don't," Edward snarled. Grabbing Ian's jacket, he yanked him toward him and let fly with a punch. Ian ducked but Edward's fist caught his chin, sending him reeling backward, careening into a table, and cascading to the floor amid a pile of books. He sat there, a stunned look on his face.

A collective gasp rang out from the crowd.

"Eddie, my God, what are you doing?" Penny cried, pushing through the crowd on the stairway to get to the main floor.

"My poor, injured lover!" Margaret cried out.

"She's mine, do you hear me, she's mine!" Edward snarled, flailing at Ian with one of the books.

Ian brought his arm up to ward off the blows.

"Have you lost your mind?" Robert said, snatching the book and shoving Edward aside.

Ian sat on the floor, testing his jaw. "Bastard," he muttered.

"Mother, how could you!" Karen said above the din.

Margaret gave her a wide-eyed stare. "Darling, I kept my word. *I* didn't make a scene."

Robert glanced down at the book, then shoved it behind his back.

"What?" Karen said.

Robert shook his head.

"Give it up."

Reluctantly he handed it to her.

"*Marriage: The Myth of Happily Ever After,*" she read aloud. She looked at Robert. "Oh God, our whole family's karma is in the toilet."

Karen wandered down the street and around the corner. She found Ian sitting slumped at a sidewalk table at a small café, an icepack on his jaw. When he tossed it down, she could see a purplish bruise. He fumbled in his pocket, pulling out a pack of cigarettes.

"I'm sorry," Karen said.

"For what, exactly?"

Karen stiffened. "For my mother. I don't think I need to apologize for anything else."

Ian raised his eyebrows and lit up.

"Why did you go see Liz? And don't tell me it was for lunch, coffee, or a bottle of water," she said. "Why do you keep hurting her?"

Ian got up out of the chair. "I didn't . . . that wasn't my intention. She made a rash decision."

"Based on your signals."

Ian shook his head. "Signals? What signals? There were no signals."

"You're right. Talk about leaving the continent isn't a signal. It's a blazing neon sign saying it's over."

"I was sorting a few things out."

"Women aren't toys to be played with."

"I wasn't playing with her."

"Yes, you were, so you could have control. So you could have—the upper hand!"

"The what?"

"You heard me. You wanted her to feel insecure so you could have all the power."

Ian stood, fidgeting with his cigarette.

"I encouraged her. Robert said you were a good guy."

"At least one person thinks so. That's something, isn't it?"

"I wanted Liz to finally be happy," she said.

"That makes two of us then, doesn't it?" His eyes narrowed. "What do you mean, finally?"

Karen didn't answer.

"Karen, I care about Liz, I do. I didn't mean for things to go so wrong. If I could talk to her, if she would listen . . . I want to fix this. If there's something I should know, something that would help me understand her . . ."

Karen hesitated. "Thank you for not hitting my father," she said finally.

"You're welcome."

They watched the limo pull up to the curb and idle. Robert got out, but didn't join them.

Ian threw down his cigarette, crushing it underfoot. "Robert will be back in ten minutes."

"Where are you going? Aren't we all going back together?"

"He's taking me to the train. I've had enough of the Margaret express for one night."

Karen gave a heavy sigh and nodded. She regarded Ian for a long moment. "Have you ever heard of Lillian Montgomery?"

His brow wrinkled in thought. "I've seen a piece of her work. Lizzie has a picture she did—half finished, but it was lovely. Why?"

"She was Liz's mother."

"Oh," he said softly.

"You're going to miss your train," Robert called.

Ian kissed Karen's cheek and walked away.

Chapter 67

"Daddy, what were you thinking?" Karen said, as she walked arm in arm with Edward on Central Park South. They passed the line of horse-drawn carriages waiting for customers, and turned into the park.

He squeezed her hand. "I wasn't, darling, it was an instinctive reaction."

"This situation is ridiculous," Karen said. "This can't go on. What about your meeting with Mommy at the penthouse? What was that about?"

He chuckled. "Not to worry. Everything is going to be fine. I'm not upset anymore. I've come to my senses. If your mother chooses to pollute herself in a cauldron of iniquity, that's entirely her affair."

She threw him a disapproving look. "Daddy, Mommy is not polluting herself in a cauldron of iniquity. You know full well she is not sleeping with Ian."

"Then the fool has no taste."

Karen stopped short. A lone biker sailed past them, leaving a rush of air in his wake. "I am getting married in four months. I will not have you and Mother turn my wedding into a Marx Brothers movie. Sometimes I just don't know you two at all."

Edward looked into his daughter's eyes and then bent to kiss her forehead. "Dearest, children aren't meant to know their parents. You would discover how ordinary we are, and that would never do."

"You and mother are anything but ordinary." She held his gaze. "Why did you go see Mother, alone?"

"Because I needed to give her a new scarf, of course."

"Daddy, I swear, if I didn't love you both, I wouldn't have either of you at the wedding."

Edward smiled. "Remember what I said? Love is a complicated emotion. Now you're beginning to understand."

This is hopeless, she thought. *Absolutely hopeless.*

Chapter 68

Ian had been working nonstop for three days, fueled by a marathon of coffee and cigarettes. Finally, the piece was coming together. He had been struggling, finally throwing down his brushes in disgust and going out for a walk to clear his head. He had managed to capture the essence without overpowering the focal point, the seated woman, looking out at him with curious eyes. He painted her in eighteenth-century clothing with a brush thick with paint and ablaze with color, something beautiful, classical, trapped in the modern world. The final stroke was his stringent use of materials—metals and cloth—to give added dimension to the composition and make the viewer feel that the subject could come off the canvas and step into their environment.

At first, Paul Ferand called him every three days, then every two days, then every day to check in. Ian could hear the careful, concerned tone in his voice, always asking if he could come to the studio to check on the progress. Each time, Ian said no. He had to do this alone; he had to make sure he had the discipline to get through this and succeed by himself. When he faltered he called home, the voices of his mother and sisters coming through the line soothing him, encouraging him. Every second he wasn't working he thought of getting back to work and when he did work, he couldn't wait for it to be over, to be finished. Every time he came up for air, he thought of

Elizabeth. Every time he looked at the clock he wondered where she was and what she was doing. Did she think of him, miss him, need to talk to him? What was she doing with Nick?

He glanced over at his laptop, the papers scattered on the desk. He had searched the Internet for Lillian Montgomery and he had found her. The articles were scant, but it was enough for him to understand what Lizzie had lived through, and who she had become because of it. Each day, he was working up his courage to go to see her. But first, he needed to finish; this time he must finish.

Chapter 69

Emily slipped into her powder-blue silk bathrobe. Standing in front of the full-length mirror, she frowned at the sight of her pinched lips and pale complexion. *I'm beginning to resemble my mother, with her plastic smile and cool anger festering just below the surface. It's time for a new look.*

Sitting down to breakfast, she smiled at Parker. They each reached for their preferred sections of the newspaper. She finished reading, casting the paper aside. The picture of herself and Parker, front and center, smiling and fabulous, looked back at her.

> Mr. and Mrs. Parker Davis at the Night of Hope Auction fund-raiser on March 1. The fund-raiser was underwritten by Davis Enterprises hedge fund. Mrs. Emily Davis (nee Watson) is the daughter of real estate magnate Arthur Watson. Mrs. Davis is actively engaged in several charities and coordinated the preparations for the event.

She asked about the business.
He said it was well.
He asked about the progress of the construction on the house in Connecticut.

She said it was coming along.

This was their morning ritual, along with having sex twice a week. Parker would roll on his back afterward, spent and satisfied. She reminded herself to coo loving sentiments she didn't mean.

He downed a last swallow of coffee, got up, and gave her a perfunctory kiss good-bye. He glanced at the paper.

"Fanfuckingtastic," he crowed, grabbing it off the table. Looking at the other side of the page, he laughed at the article and picture of her father's latest acquisition, the Palladio Hotel on the Upper East Side, an old hotel in the European tradition, known more for charm than snappy service, atmosphere rather than crispness of amenities. "I think your old man is creeping into senility, buying that piece of crap," he said, tossing the paper back down. "What's he going to do with it, rent it out for a Halloween fright night?"

"It has possibilities," she said.

"As a fucking pile of rubble."

She remembered to chuckle as she once did. How ridiculous she found it now, to have thought he was edgy and adorable.

"He's forgotten how to turn a profit," he was saying when she refocused on his babbling. "Too bad it's not publicly owned; I'd get a position on the board, force him into retirement, and then that dump would start making money."

"You'd save the hotel?" she asked.

"Fuck that, I'd demo it and then out-Trump Trump with a mega hotel."

Emily's response was a brief "mmm."

"I'll be late tonight; meeting."

"No problem, I'll be at a charity function," she lied.

She sat back, listening, as he made his way to the entry hall, followed by the sound of the door opening and shutting.

Emily met Charles Burton at twelve-thirty sharp in his small, spotless office. The door had a gold panel with Innovative Consulting Services printed on the opaque glass. Emily supposed it made clients feel more comfortable about confidentiality.

Mr. Burton wore a gray, three-button suit, vest, a black tie, and a pearl tie tack; he had salt-and-pepper hair. He was medium height with a distinguished air, and yet somehow entirely forgettable. He could've easily been an associate of her father's. He called her Mrs. Davis in a voice both soft and mellow.

"Mr. Burton, my husband prefers the company of other women."

"I understand, Mrs. Davis," he said. "Photographs, audio, video, hotel receipts—any or all of the above?"

Emily was impressed with the smorgasbord of choices. It was as easy as ordering off a takeout menu. Suddenly she remembered something Parker had said to her. *If you could use the equipment, you should go into porn!* She felt the pinch return to her lips. "Audiovisual."

She handed over a check.

It had taken all of twenty minutes. She reminded herself to commend Margaret on her choice of vendors.

Emily's last stop was her father's office. She was already planning a life beyond Mrs. Parker Davis. The newspaper article had given her ideas. She had a new project in mind.

Sitting down to breakfast the next morning, Emily smiled at Parker.

She asked him how his day was yesterday.

He said it was fine.

"The charity event is coming along well," she said. "I've arranged a dinner with Geoffrey and Corinne."

"Good. Leave Friday open so we can go up to Connecticut. I want to see how the construction is coming."

"Shall I call the interior designer?"

"Yeah, I want to make sure she's not dicking around with the plans and that they've got their shit together. I want those pricks to get it done before Memorial Day."

"We can still go to the Hamptons."

"Fuck the Hamptons, I want to be on the compound before June."

He got up and came around the table to give her a kiss. "You'll make the calls?"

Emily smiled up at him. "Of course I will."

Parker nodded. "I'll be late tonight. I've got another meeting."

Emily sat back to finish her coffee. She heard the door close. "I'm sure you do," she murmured.

Chapter 70

"**R**obert."

At the sound of Larry's familiar whimper, Robert turned from his discussion with Morris. After the Long Island debacle, returning to the daily circus of rehearsals should have been a joy, but this was worse than the Dante's inferno limo ride to hell.

"Just a minute, Larry," he said.

"It's not funny, Robert, it's just not funny," Morris kept repeating.

"I'm dead again," Larry wailed, feverishly flipping through pages, his eyes resembling those of a beaten basset hound. Robert knew he needed to do something quick; Larry was shrinking before his eyes and he might hyperventilate at any moment.

"What happened to the musical number?" Tina, a brunette with a sleek dancer's body, asked. "I had a nice spot in that. I don't see why my part should be getting smaller. If he's gonna die anyway . . ."

"Et tu, Tina?" Larry sniveled.

He crumpled to the stage, wrapping his arms around Robert's legs. "You've got to help me, Bobby, you've got to."

"It'll be okay, Larry," Robert soothed, trying to pry him loose.

Morris shook his head and began checking his pockets.

Searching for your mood elevator? Robert thought.

"Some people weren't paying attention," Morris said, his eyes on Karen. "This is a comedy. We're trying for humor here. If I want tragedy I'll direct *Oedipus Rex*."

"We're doing incest now?" Vicki said. "I did that last year. Are we doing O'Neill straight?"

"No!" Robert said. "Absolutely not!" He shook his head. *Great*, he thought. *We've now reached the phase of the rehearsals where everyone is blatantly irrational. I always enjoy this part.*

Larry reached for Vicki but she kept him at arm's length.

"Lar, I can't. You know that."

"But why?" he whimpered.

"I told you, I need someone more positive. Someone who feeds my soul."

"Shit," Robert mumbled under his breath. "A broken play and a broken relationship."

Alfred came up behind Larry, placing his hands on his shoulders. "Be of good cheer. Weeping endures for a night but joy cometh in the morning."

"There is no joy; there won't be a morning," Larry cried, pointing an accusatory finger at Karen. "She wants to kill me! It's right here!" Larry stabbed at the script.

Karen's shoulders hunched and Robert went to work massaging them. "I give up. I admit it. I'm subconsciously channeling my parents' violence into my work. It's been happening from the beginning."

Alfred slapped Larry on the back. "Faith can move mountains."

Vicki sidled over to Alfred, snaking her arms around his waist. "Righteous," she murmured.

Larry's eyes opened. "You left me for him?" he cried, jumping up and grabbing Alfred's shirt.

"Chill," Alfred said, trying to pry himself loose. "Remember, the meek shall inherit the earth."

"You are not Jesus Christ," Larry said through his teeth. "You only played him off-off Broadway!" He began shaking Alfred back and forth. "And Jesus was celibate . . . understand . . . celibate!"

With a snarl, he muscled Alfred down on to the stage, his hands closing around his neck.

Karen shrieked.

Rushing over, Robert and Morris, crowded by the cast, pulled Larry away.

"That's not cool, man," Alfred gurgled, massaging his neck. "What would Jesus do?"

"He wouldn't steal his cast-mate's girlfriend," Robert said through his teeth as he pulled Alfred to his feet. "Try to keep your light hidden under your bushel for the rest of the production, will you?"

Going to Karen, Robert hugged her to him, forcing her to stop wringing her hands.

"Common karma," she said. "I cause strangulation by association."

"Junie!" Morris yelled.

Junie came down from the back row, pulling the phone from her ear. She came up on stage and slipped one arm around Robert, her other hand hooked around her suspender. "Robert, baby, the actors are tired—"

"And psychotic."

"Yeah, it always gets a little rough toward the end. Let's take a break and have a little sidebar. Just you, me, and Morris. Okay, babe?"

"That's it for today," Morris said with a sigh. "Tomorrow is the climactic scene, the gathering of the existentialists to celebrate the meaningless existence reunion. Hopefully, everyone will get out alive." He glared at Karen.

Robert drew Karen into a quiet corner. "The end of the second act is great, babe. Hickey's three-minute infomercial and self-help seminar with Sartre and Kafka is great stuff. We just need to tweak. I need to have a quick meeting with Morris and Junie. I'll come by the penthouse when I'm done."

"Robert," she said. "Are we okay?"

He kissed her forehead. "We are always okay."

Robert glanced at Junie and Morris. They weren't smiling.

Chapter 71

Karen turned the key in the lock, tiptoed into the penthouse, and slumped onto a chair in the kitchen.

Margaret drifted in, dressed in a fuschia robe. It was not unusual to find her mother in her nightgown at three in the afternoon when a book deadline wasn't looming and the tours were over with. Karen noted the pink scarf around her neck.

"That's new," Karen said. "Where did you get it?"

"From your father, of course," Margaret said, settling in the chair opposite her.

Mary deposited a steaming cup on the table.

"It's about time. I thought you had flown to Columbia to pick the beans," she said with a dismissive wave of her hand. "Just leave the pot."

Mary walked out of the room.

"Did you two exchange anything else?"

Margaret sat stirring cream into her coffee. "How was your meeting with your father?"

"Why ask me? He's already told you about it."

Margaret sat back, smiling at Karen. "We raised an intelligent woman. Yes, he did tell me. What did he have to say for himself?"

"He doesn't care if you sleep with Ian."

Margaret chuckled.

"I think he cares. I think he cares very much who you sleep

with. And I think you care who he marries. If you love him, why didn't you stay together?"

Margaret narrowed her eyes. "Why are you home so early from rehearsal?"

Karen didn't meet her mother's gaze.

"Karen?"

"Robert's just finishing things; they didn't need me."

Margaret shot up, ramrod straight. "Oh, Karen, no!"

"I'm upsetting the actors. I keep killing people off!"

"Artistic license."

"One of the main characters, Mother; I killed off one of the main characters," Karen cried. "And then he freaked out and tried to strangle one of the cast."

Margaret mused on the statement. "Common karma. But I'm sure he deserved it. This is how it happened with your father, you know. All because of the work."

Karen's eyes opened. "You and Daddy broke up over a book?"

"It's always the work," Margaret said with a faraway look in her eyes. "We were toiling over *The Covenant* and our small disagreements turned into squabbles. You know, it's never just professional, it always becomes personal, and . . . there you have it."

She was silent for a moment and Karen assumed she was thinking back to those times.

"Why do you think I suggested a nice long vacation for you to climb Kilimanjaro last year? I knew about the farmer. I was hoping you would go away, get over him and spare yourself this very moment that I knew in my heart was coming. Do you think I didn't lie awake nights, consumed by the fear that you would be hurt? What do you think parents do? They spend the whole of their lives trying to protect their children from any possible pain, all the while knowing it cannot be done."

"Robert would never hurt me."

"And yet he is at the theater and you are here."

"You don't know Robert," she said, even as she began to feel uneasy.

"Perhaps you're right." Margaret put her hand under Karen's

chin. "Perhaps I should never have allowed you to go to Nepal. I should have taken you back to Paris. Shopping on the Champs-Elysées is always better preparation for real life than having a religious experience with a tree."

"Mother, tell me the truth. It was really the book that ended everything between you and Daddy?"

"I'm afraid so. It's too painful to talk about. Why don't you talk to Willis? I confided in him quite a bit."

Margaret returned to sipping her coffee.

Chapter 72

Robert sat down with Junie and Morris for the meeting. He knew what it meant: the last-ditch negotiation. They had already decided between themselves what needed to be done; this exercise was to convince the playwright. The last meeting he'd heard about, management was at the writer for a week, every afternoon, plying him with coffee while arguing over the second act. Finally, the writer gave in; no doubt valuing his bladder over his artistic integrity.

"We love the play," Junie said.

Morris hung back.

Junie elbowed him.

"It needs work," he said.

"But we can't have the plot changing every five minutes," Junie continued.

"It's not funny," Morris said.

"And the actors, it's all about protecting the actors," Junie said.

"And it's not funny, but it *could* be funny," Morris said.

Robert nodded his head. "I know we've gotten a little off course, but the basics of the story are still there: taking O'Neill's original thesis that life is meaningless and we need to give up our pipe dreams, making the characters millionaires, then having a reunion of the Existentialists where no one wants to give up their worldly possessions."

Junie leaned in. "And we love the concept. The concept isn't the problem. It's . . ." Junie and Morris looked at each other; Junie cleared her throat.

"It's Karen," Morris said.

Robert looked from one to the other.

Junie grabbed Robert's hands, her blue nail polish a sharp contrast against her pale skin. "We lo-o-o-ove Karen, we do, we love her. She's a doll, but—"

"She's not funny," Morris said.

"She should be," Robert said. "If exposure to misery makes comedy, she should be hilarious."

Junie did a ninety degree hair flip to clear her flaming red hair from her eyes. She adjusted her suspenders and gave him a steely gaze. "She's off concept, and we're about to start the previews. A month before the opening is not the time to address personal issues in your work."

"I'll talk to her. I'll get it straightened out," Robert said.

His suggestion met with dead silence as Junie and Morris continued to stare at him.

His shoulders slumped. "What do you suggest?"

"Karen needs a break," Junie said.

"She needs to step aside," Morris said.

"No, no way!" Robert exploded, jumping out of his seat. "We're a team, we come as a duo."

"I won't have my name on a production that flops because one of the writers decides to use the script as a substitute for therapy," Morris said, rising from his chair.

"All right, all right, let's stay calm," Junie said. "Robert, no one is saying Karen shouldn't be here."

"I'm saying that," Morris said, giving Robert an angry look. "That's exactly what I'm saying."

"Morris . . . please," Junie said.

Morris rolled his eyes and walked away.

Junie put her arm around Robert, walking him in the opposite direction. "Look, Robert, we need a set plot and a finished play. As a polisher, Karen is a goldmine of funny, working inside a given frame, inside the box," she said, outlining a box in the air. "This play is a brilliant concept, and you both are brilliant, but if we can't come to an agreement . . ." She let the words trail off and they stood there in silence. Junie had stopped smiling.

Robert took a deep breath and nodded. "I understand. I'll take care of it. You'll get one play with one message."

"Good, good," Junie said, patting his back. "It's going to be beautiful, right, baby?"

Robert didn't answer.

Chapter 73

Ian stood in the hallway outside of Elizabeth's door. Her voice had been clipped and cold through the call box, but in the end, she had buzzed him in.

He repeated his mantra in his head: stay calm, relax, breathe deeply, don't give anything away until you see how she reacts.

Taking one more deep breath, he froze. *Shit, what if Nick is in there?* No, he finally decided, no way. *She would have never let me in.* He heard the dead bolts sliding back and then the door opened.

His breath caught in his throat. Wearing a dark blue velvet robe, pale hair flowing over her shoulders, she looked like a medieval princess; except that her face was set in stone and her eyes were dark with anger. *Shit.*

His heart began to thump in his chest. "I . . . I promised a friend of Robert's I would loan him my book of Frost's poems, but it seems to have gone missing. You were so fond of my reading his poems to you . . . I thought perhaps I left the book here."

A small crooked smile touched her lips, but her face remained hard and closed. "I don't have anything that belongs to you."

His heart sank. "Could you possibly take a look?"

"Wait here," she said, closing the door.

He stood, his head down; he could feel perspiration break-ing on his skin. He realized the door hadn't clicked closed; he nudged it, edging it open.

He caught sight of a piece of modern art hanging above the mantel where his watercolor used to hang: a conglomeration of cubes and circles painted in harsh, jarring oranges, yellows, and greens; and was that a bird flying through a cone? He stared at it in disbelief.

She came down the hall. "You weren't invited in."

"You left the door open."

She followed his line of vision to the painting. "Oh yes, I al-most forgot. I do have one thing that belongs to you."

Ian swallowed hard. He glanced around, desperate to think of a way to buy an extra minute with her. *Another second, she'll be showing you the bloody door. Do something.*

Elizabeth pulled the Renoir copy from a storage cubby and held it out to him.

"It was a gift, Lizzie."

"No thanks."

"You might want to keep it, just a wee—little reminder—of us." He sounded weak and small in his own ears, like when he was a child and had done something naughty, trying to appease his mother and garner her sympathy.

"There is no us."

"There was, we'll always—"

"Have Paris?" she said, her voice heavy with disdain.

He flinched and drew in a long breath. "Keep the picture. You know how much it means to have someone appreciate your work. You know that from your own work, from your mother's work."

He watched her eyes widen. He had caught her off guard and he pressed his advantage. "I can't imagine how difficult it's been for you, Lizzie," he said, moving closer. "You could have told me about her, about everything. I would've understood."

"There's nothing to tell."

"Giving up your career, your painting, to care for someone else—especially in those last years when she didn't produce anything—I think there's a lot to tell. I always listened to you, Lizzie. I'm ready to listen now."

He closed the gap between them. "Lizzie, there's no reason for us to be apart. You know that. I want us to be together. I think I understand you. We understand each other."

Elizabeth held up the painting between them. "You're right. I do understand you. That's why I want you and your painting out of my apartment. Save it, and your bullshit, for the next woman you want to undress."

The heat of embarrassment filtered through him and, taking the painting, he stepped out into the hallway.

"You've got it all wrong, Lizzie."

She slammed the door in his face.

Ian kicked the loft door open, turned on the light and stood there, still reeling. In one sweeping motion he threw the canvas against the wall, watching it splinter and fall. One moment of weakness, one moment had caused all this. He'd pulled away with talk of travel and now she was the one who was gone. She wouldn't even give him a chance, wouldn't even listen. He shook his head again, the familiar anger seeping in. *She's done? It's over? Fine.*

SPRING

Chapter 74

Robert and Karen sat erect in straight-back chairs in a West Village church office, waiting for the Reverend Fuller. They stared at the wall behind the desk; a visual history of the pastor and his family in eight-by-ten glossies looked back at them. Pastor Fuller with his wide, toothy smile standing behind two solemn children and a woman wearing a morose, somber expression.

"So they don't want me?" she said. "What did you say?"

Robert began a mental scramble for something that would sound genuine. Waiting until they had been on their way here to say something was cowardly but expedient, the simplest way to avoid a prolonged discussion.

"I said that you had diversified visions of the material."

"And they said?"

"They only want one vision."

Karen shook her head. "I can't believe it. I'm being separated from my own project."

Robert turned to her. "No, you aren't, but Morris is out for blood. When actors bring offerings in order for you not to change the script, there's a problem."

"Alfred brought a dish of grilled lamb chops."

"Alfred's into symbolism."

Karen pulled out a tissue. "You don't want to be partners anymore, do you?"

"Of course I do. We are partners. It's one month until the play opens. We can pull this together. All Morris and Junie are asking is for you to work in the background, and concentrate on the polishing. I'll give you the framework."

"I don't believe this. Mother was right."

"That's statistically impossible."

Karen turned to him. "It was Morris, wasn't it? He never liked me. If I was on my guard instead of being 'at peace' with everything, I would have seen this coming. The Tao doesn't believe in hatred. And I can't believe you're going along with him. It's happening to us, just like it did to my parents. Your desire for the play is bigger than your desire for me. This will destroy us the way working together destroyed them."

"Who told you that?"

"My mother."

"All of a sudden your mother has turned on the confession cam?" Robert said, with a curl of his lip. "Karen, your mother is making this up as she goes along, so she can have things her way."

"That's not true. Willis gave me all the background."

"Willis?" he said, giving her a sharp look. "How often are you seeing Willis?"

"I am not *seeing* Willis," she protested. "We have lunch occasionally. He respects my background and understands me and my life."

"*He* understands you?" Robert ground his teeth, feeling his blood pressure surge. *No wonder Margaret backed off objecting. Willis is Plan B. She'll plant the seed, Willis will do the watering, and Karen will do the breakup on her own.* He turned to her and saw the anxiety and doubt in her eyes. *I'll never be able to convince her that Margaret is using Willis as a wedge between us.*

"He's been very helpful to me. I'm just trying to think through this."

Think through this or rethink us? I'd love to know what Margaret gave him as a payoff to get this job done. His own newspaper? He shook his head. It would be funny, if the rest of his life, his life with Karen, wasn't hanging in the balance. He glanced over at her; she was staring at the pictures, a look of misery on her face.

The door opened and a painfully thin man wearing a wide smile came in, followed by a woman Robert decided hadn't cracked a smile in decades; the eight-by-ten glossies come to life. *Another yin and yang shot to shit*, he thought.

"I'm Reverend Fuller," he said, beaming at them. "And this is my beautiful wife." He clutched the hand of his beloved. "We're so very glad to meet you."

The beautiful Mrs. Fuller mumbled an inaudible greeting, her face frozen into a frown.

The reverend sat down behind his desk and leaned forward. "So," he said, rubbing his hands together. "You want to be married."

"Reverend Fuller," Robert began, "first off, we have to be honest. You're the eighth minister we've visited."

"Ninth," Karen corrected. "Including an interfaith minister, a rabbi—reformed— and a Jesuit priest. No one will marry us."

"What's wrong with you?" Mrs. Fuller said, examining Karen through narrowed eyes.

"My parents used to object at weddings," Karen said. "I say *used to* because they say they're not going to do that at our wedding."

Reverend Fuller sat back, folding his hands and tapping his forefingers against his lips. "I can see how that would give an officiate pause."

Karen turned to Robert. "My parents are doing this for our own good, I'm beginning to see that now. Don't you see that? They know what will happen to us. Look what happened to them."

"Do your parents want counseling?" Revered Fuller said. "We can do a package deal."

"Not unless you throw in shock therapy as an added perk," Robert snapped. He turned to Karen. "Just how many lunches have you had with Willis?"

"There's another man?" the reverend asked.

"Already?" Mrs. Fuller said, looking at Karen with new interest. "You don't waste time, do you?"

"At least *he* doesn't make fun of my family."

Robert sat back, folding his arms across his chest. "Why don't you marry him then?"

"Maybe I should," Karen said.

"So you don't want to get married, is that what you're saying?"

"Is that what *you're* saying? If you don't have any respect for my parents, you can't possibly have any respect for me, or love me."

Robert stood up. "*I* don't respect you! *I* don't love you! I chased you for six months. I spent hours on the phone with you, not just listening to your voice but to what you were saying. If you're going to allow yourself to be taken in by two people, in spite of the fact that they love you—and you should be flattered because they sure as hell don't love anyone else—and let them convince you that I don't love you, then go ahead. I can't stop you." He threw up his hands. "We won't get married then. Go back to your mother's penthouse if that's where you think you belong." Robert turned to the reverend. "We're sorry we wasted your time."

Karen burst into tears.

"Nice going, Ace," Mrs. Fuller said, handing Karen a box of tissues.

Robert sat back down, wrapping his arms around Karen's heaving shoulders. "I'm sorry, I'm sorry. I didn't mean that. I love you, Karen. I'm sorry." He held her, comforting her until she stopped crying. "The problem is her parents," he said to Reverend Fuller. "They enjoy destroying each other, especially in a public forum."

Karen sniffed and reached into her purse. "I brought a small album for you to browse."

Reverend Fuller accepted the album with a shaky hand and flipped through the pages.

Mrs. Fuller leaned over her husband's shoulder. She let out a low, soft whistle as he turned the pages.

"Oh my," Reverend Fuller said, closing the book and handing it to Karen. "Perhaps we should look at some ways to incorporate them into the ceremony."

"They have that covered," Robert said drily.

Reverend Fuller chuckled. "No, no, what I meant was, make this a positive experience, perhaps ask them to participate in a candle-lighting ceremony."

Karen shifted in her seat. "My mother shouldn't be near flame . . . ever."

"How about having them read something? Do they have a favorite work?"

"*Taming of the Shrew*," Robert said.

Karen began to snivel.

Pulling her close, Robert whispered "I'm sorry" in her ear, kissing her cheek.

"Down deep, I'm sure your mother means well," Reverend Fuller said.

"She's the Antichrist," Robert said.

"Your father?" Reverend Fuller persisted.

"He tried to strangle my mother with a silk, hand-rolled scarf."

"Those things are expensive," Mrs. Fuller said, frowning her disapproval.

Reverend Fuller took his wife's hand, giving it a squeeze. "Marriage is like an intricate recipe. You mix all the different ingredients together and you're afraid you're going to wind up with a tasteless goulash, but instead you end up with a delightful confection. Isn't that right, my dear?"

"Delightful confection, yeah."

"Oh yes," he continued. "Our life has always been an adventure. Each day, something new to experience."

"I'd like to experience getting married," Robert said, and looked at Karen. "Wouldn't you?"

Sniffling, Karen nodded in agreement.

Reverend Fuller got up and came around to the front of the desk. He took their hands in his own. "You two are going to have a wonderful marriage and . . . I am going to marry you."

Reverend Fuller focused on Karen, his smile never wavering. "Would you like me to try an intervention with your parents?"

Karen looked at Robert.

"We couldn't live with ourselves if they destroyed a man of the cloth," he said.

Reverend Fuller chuckled. "Now, don't you worry. I will get you married." He stood up, smiling down at them benevolently, and turned to his wife. "Joy, why don't you walk them out."

Joy? Robert thought, exchanging a look with Karen.

"What a beautiful name," she said.

"Isn't it?" Reverend Fuller said, beaming at his wife. "And so apropos."

Robert and Karen followed Joy Fuller to the door. "Did you believe everything my husband said?" she asked.

"No," Robert said.

"Good. Take my advice, kids. Elope."

Chapter 75

Parker drummed his fingers on the table, his mouth pinched tight in annoyance. Stanley Werner, Parker's award-winning economist, had been droning on for over an hour. *Jesus Christ, I didn't lure this Ivy League prick to New York to listen to the sound of his voice. A corner office and a fat salary should've guaranteed window dressing, without having to actually sit through this.*

Stanley tugged at his tie and opened the button at his neck. "The leverage is forty to one. Forty borrowed dollars for every one dollar we have. The capital is plummeting."

"Fuck it, Stanley, what does that mean? I'll have to skip a new solid gold toothbrush this week? We're covered. Our options are in the bag. We borrowed at four percent. We're going to get the payout at seven percent. It's a positive carry. We're solid."

"You can't cover what you've borrowed. You don't have the money."

"Stanley, it's only paper," Parker said.

Stanley ran a hand through his hair. "We shouldn't be engaging in these currency bets now. It's too risky. For God's sake, Parker, dump some of the convertible bonds, it won't disturb the market."

"No."

"We need to change direction now—"

Parker bolted up, shoving his chair aside. "For Christ's

sake, Stanley, I know exactly what every fucker in the market is doing and right now they're pulling the trigger on my currency bets."

Stanley stood up. "Parker, I urge you—"

"Meeting's over," Parker said.

Stanley threw him an exasperated look and walked out of the office, leaving Parker to himself. He cursed under his breath. He didn't need Stanley to point out the obvious. The capital in the fund was sinking steadily, and the valuation of the portfolio was already covering up an additional loss of one hundred million. He could smell the fear on Stanley. *Well, I sure as hell am not going to tuck my dick between my legs and panic.* He still had his currency bets. He could still pull this out.

He turned to the window, staring down on the drones moving on the streets below. His thoughts turned from money to clients—in particular, Emily's father. The old man had called a week ago, polite yet cold, as always. It was a courtesy call, he said, he was moving his money in another direction, shuffling the portfolio, yada, yada, yada. The old man was pulling out, and who knew how many of his friends he might take with him? *The old bastards all stick together. Now I need to go whoring around to get more capital . . . shit.*

He left the office at eleven-thirty for a lunch meeting. He sat with clients and prospective clients, explaining how the fund was excelling, how they were operating at a thirty-percent profit, explaining his unmathematical theory that it's all a matter of timing and it's a gift; a gift he just happened to have.

On his way out, Parker made a point to stop at Stanton Perry's table. They shook hands but Perry but didn't ask him to sit down. The conversation was fast and furious, a seemingly good-natured grilling from Perry's compatriots.

"No fire sale yet? Be careful or you'll have to sell the compound before you move in."

"Are you kidding? I'm getting ready to add a new wing."

Chuckles all around the table.

Stanton walked Parker away from the table. "No danger of a downturn, is there?" Perry asked.

Parker laughed. "That's two tables down." He leaned in confidentially. "Investment bankers."

They laughed again. "What kind of yield are we looking at?"

Parker answered without hesitation. "Forty percent, maybe forty-five. Hey, how's your lovely wife?"

"Lovely as always."

"Give her my best."

"I'll do that," Perry said. "Make sure you're giving my money your best."

A half hour later, in an out-of-the-way hotel downtown, Parker Davis had Deirdre Perry spread-eagled against a chest of drawers, her dress bunched around her waist, her black thong panties lying on the floor. He shuddered as he came, then held still for a moment longer, staring into the vanity mirror, enjoying her submissive pose. He let out a chuckle, giving her backside a playful swat.

He came downstairs to the lobby first. Deirdre would follow later. Not that it was necessary. In this part of town, they wouldn't meet anyone they knew. He turned on his BlackBerry and checked for messages. Preoccupied, he bumped into a tall, stately-looking man with salt-and-pepper hair, wearing a gray suit, a cell phone at his ear. Parker mumbled his apologies as he walked away. For a moment, he thought he had seen the man somewhere before. The thought was gone as soon as it came, and Parker stepped out of the hotel and hailed a passing cab.

Chapter 76

Elizabeth picked up her office phone at five p.m.

"Hey, kid, dedication is an overrated trait in an employee."

Elizabeth laughed. "My team tells me that all the time, but they don't feel that should affect their bonuses."

Nick's low chuckle came over the line. "I have a car waiting for you downstairs."

Elizabeth leaned back in her chair. "And where would it be taking me?"

Her question was met with another chuckle. "It's a surprise."

Later that night, they sat at a table in a quiet corner of a little trattoria.

"Did you enjoy the opera?"

"Yes, I did," she said, examining his strong features. Age and experience had given him an authoritative air. He cut quite a figure in his tuxedo; polished, handsome.

"I'll get tickets for *La Traviata* next month."

Elizabeth shook her head. "I'll have to check my calendar."

"Oh?"

"Karen and Robert's play opens in four weeks."

He nodded his head, swirling his spoon in his coffee. "And?"

"It's important for me to be there," she said.

"Why is that?"

Elizabeth straightened and took a deep breath. "Because Karen is my best friend; she helped me a great deal when I came to New York."

"And you need to be grateful for how long?"

She stared at him in surprise. "Friendships don't have an expiration date."

Nick smiled, one of those tolerant smiles Liz glossed over, choosing to ignore; a lesson was coming.

"People pass in and out of your life all the time, kid."

Elizabeth smiled. "Unless you don't want them to."

He brought her hand to his lips for a kiss. "Of course. Does this require ripped jeans and peace beads? I want to be sure I'm appropriately dressed." The amusement in his tone didn't reach his eyes.

She concealed her surprise; she had assumed she would be going alone. She didn't relish the thought of his thinly veiled impatience and annoyance for an entire evening. "A suit and tie will do," she said.

His face remained pleasant, but the look in his eyes gave her a distinctly uncomfortable feeling. She imagined this was the expression he wore when sitting in the boardroom, getting ready to go in for the kill in a negotiation. "I can manage that."

He leaned in to take a kiss. "I want you to be happy," he murmured.

The car dropped her at her apartment. When she came in, she let out a long breath and leaned against the door in the darkness. Nick hadn't been happy with her excuse of a sudden migraine; she didn't care.

Making her way into the bedroom, she sank down on the bed. She found Nick handsome, challenging, and stimulating, as always. She pushed herself to feel close to him, but it wasn't there; and her desire for intimacy had turned lukewarm, decreasing as the weeks wore on.

Give it time. It will come back. Nick was strong, caring, and stable. *This is just a bad patch*, she thought, *breaking off with Ian, resuming a relationship with Nick*. The problems at work had unsettled her far more than she realized. She tried to turn the tide by rewriting history: Ian never really cared that much for her, had no feeling for her beyond the convenient and always available sex. But deep down she didn't believe it.

He had come to the apartment attempting to have some kind of communication with her, to try to make things right. She shut her eyes at the thought of how she turned him away. But she couldn't trust him now, she couldn't take the chance that he would leave her or that she would lose focus again. And yet she hadn't been able to stop thinking about him. *I can't make it more than what it was. He was never all-in*, she thought, forcing the memory of his anxious attempts to rekindle what they had out of her mind. *I can't live with this see-saw mentality. This isn't fair to Nick and it has to stop.*

Chapter 77

Karen sat on the bed, hunched over the laptop in front of her. She alternated between typing, stopping to think, then typing again.

"How are we going to make sure they don't sit next to each other?"

Robert paced in a small clutter-free zone, hemmed in by the detritus of clothes, shoes, and books. He read the manuscript, flipping back and forth. "I'm sure your parents will not want to sit next to each other."

"I meant Ian and Elizabeth."

"Don't worry about the seating, worry about the typing."

Karen shrugged, her forehead creasing into a frown. "Robert, I haven't read the play straight through in weeks, I haven't seen a rehearsal, I haven't even seen a preview performance. How do I even know that what I'm doing is good?"

"The previews are fantastic. Everything is coming together. Your work is amazing. I think it's the best you've ever done. You're going to love it when you see it, when you hear your words. Why did you take out the word 'voracious'?"

Karen handed him another page. "Because we write to tell a story, not give the audience a vocabulary lesson."

Robert opened his mouth to protest.

"You don't write to prove a point about language, language

is a tool to tell a universal truth." Her words were blunt, but her face was kind. "Save that for the lecture hall, please."

He took the paper from her. "Be careful with Larry; you're starting to move him in the direction of the window in the bar, and there is no ledge—I repeat, there is no ledge. He has to stay healthy for the musical number."

"What musical number?"

"Keep typing."

She gave a heavy sigh and returned her attention to the laptop.

"Since when are you concerned about where Ian sits? The last time you saw him, you wanted to throw him out of a moving limo."

"No, I mean yes, at first, but we talked a little at the café. He hasn't seen Liz by any chance, has he?"

Robert stopped pacing. "Yes, he has. Why?"

Karen continued typing. "How did it go?" she said without looking up.

"It didn't. Have you been meddling?"

She didn't answer.

"I thought we had an agreement? We're Switzerland, neutral, remember?"

Karen's fingers flew over the keyboard. "When Ian and I were talking—"

"Yes?"

Karen looked up. "I might have mentioned something about Liz—and her mother."

"Karen . . . you didn't. What about her mother? Never mind. Don't tell me."

"I know Liz misses him."

"Act one, scene four, needs tightening," he said, handing her several sheets of paper.

"I thought we needed to do something."

"You did something. And then Ian did something. He went to see her. And then she did something—she threw him out."

Her hands froze. "I need to call her."

He began to rifle through a stack of papers on the desk. "Please don't, baby. Think Heidi, think the Alps, okay?"

"She's my best friend and maid of honor and he's your best man. It's our duty to help. So he does care about her?"

Robert let out a sigh of exasperation, his hands dropping to his sides in defeat. "Yes, he cares. I'm sure he cares!"

"Then why doesn't he just ask her to marry him?"

"He's very internal. It's hard for him to open up. He keeps things inside. He's been that way . . ." Robert took a deep breath. "Since his divorce."

Karen's mouth dropped open. "Divorce?" she said finally.

"I'll talk," he said. "But only if you keep typing."

Chapter 78

Holding the phone to his ear, Robert fingered a newspaper clipping. He glanced over the *Publishing News Monthly* article announcing Tom Willis's two-book sweetheart deal with a major house.

"Yes?" came the bored voice from the other end of the line.

"Robert Harris. I'm calling to find out when I can pick up my check."

The sound of rustling papers came from the other end of the line. "I don't have your name on the list."

"The list needs updating. I just finished a meeting with Mrs. Wainwright regarding her daughter. The compensation for ending my relationship with her daughter is twenty-five thousand. When can I come in and pick up my check? I understand Mr. Willis has already been paid. I don't see why I should have to wait."

There was a beat of silence at the other end. "I'm not at liberty to discuss Mr.—any other arrangements."

No problem, you just did. "Why don't you call Mrs. Wainwright and go over the details of this conversation and check it with her?"

"I'll do that," came the response.

"Good, call her ASAP."

Robert hung up the phone and took a deep breath. He was taking a risk; if he was wrong, Margaret would use this to drive Karen away. *I sure as hell hope I'm not wrong.*

Chapter 79

The vernal equinox marks the beginning of spring, but the message never reached the bloody city of New York, Ian thought, huddling in his coat, puffing on a cigarette as the wind whirled around him. Camped out near a side entrance to the theater, he watched the clusters of people gathering at the front doors, waiting for the theater to open. They fidgeted and stamped their feet to keep their blood moving and chase the cold away.

"Hey," came Robert's voice from behind him.

Ian turned.

"I have your tickets."

"Great."

Robert peered at the crowd, now filing through the open doors.

"The play is brilliant. You're about to become famous," Ian said, tossing away his cigarette.

"You really read it?"

"You gave it to me, didn't you? It's brilliant; I loved it. What about George and Martha?"

"They called Karen to confirm this morning. They insist they will be in strict parental support mode and we will not need the NYPD."

A woman getting out of a taxi caught Robert's eye. She was

tall, her blond hair flowing over the shoulders of her leather jacket. She headed straight for them.

"Oh no, no, no," Robert said, turning his widening eyes on Ian. "You didn't, you can't . . ."

Ian's lips tightened; he didn't answer.

"Ian, this is a mistake, a big, big, mistake," Robert said. "This is not the way to go."

"Lizzie doesn't want me? That's fine. She's with someone else? Fine. So am I."

Robert allowed him to finish his tirade. "I hate to say this, but you just became an asshole."

"I know," Ian said. "I don't care."

Ian turned to the blonde, her open coat revealing skintight jeans straining over her hips and a silk top clinging to her full breasts. Reaching them, she slipped her arm through Ian's.

"Hello, Helena, love," he said.

She gave him a warm smile. "I'm so looking forward to this."

"I've changed my mind," Robert muttered. "If we make it to the intermission without the NYPD, we'll be lucky."

When Elizabeth and Nick arrived, the theater was already packed. Elizabeth struggled to keep her annoyance with Nick under control. He had arrived in a limo to collect her, knowing it was pretentious and unnecessary for an off-Broadway production.

"What time do you think it will be over?" he asked. "I told Warren and Ann we'd meet for drinks later on."

"I need to go to the after party," she said, fighting to keep her voice light.

His lips compressed.

"I'm sure we'll make both," she said. *I'm becoming quite the master of conciliation.*

Inside the theater, she caught sight of Ian out of the corner of her eye, standing with a platinum blonde wearing too much makeup and too little clothing. Her pulse skipped. She snapped her head forward, determined not to make eye contact or acknowledge them in any way. *Bastard*.

Ian put his arm around Helena's shoulder as they settled in their seats, taking a furtive look around to find Nick pulling Elizabeth in for a kiss. *Bastard*, he thought.

The lights went down and the curtain went up.

The restaurant buzzed with chatter. Crowds milled at the bar, shouting their orders at the overworked barmen.

Karen studied Robert from across the room as he accepted congratulations. She had been stunned while watching the production. All her words were there, exactly as she wrote them, but Robert had pulled the confusion out of her versions and mixed it into a cohesive whole. He had managed to extract the heart of all her ideas, and combine them with his own so that it all made sense. She had always known he was a master of plot, and now she knew that, conceptually, he was brilliant; he had made sure their vision had one voice. She found herself staring at him with wonder, and a new-found respect.

She smiled as he approached her, wrapping his arms around her and nuzzling her neck.

"Get a room," Elizabeth said, coming over with Nick in tow.

Elizabeth and Karen hugged and kissed. "It was amazing," Elizabeth said. She looked at Nick.

He offered his hand to Robert. "Yeah, congratulations," he said.

"Thanks."

"I'll get us drinks," Nick said and headed for the bar.

"How long until the reviews post?" Elizabeth asked.

"Any minute," Karen said, nodding toward everyone pulling out their BlackBerrys.

Elizabeth glanced around to see Vicki, Amanda, Alfred, Larry, Junie, and Morris all clicking away furiously.

"Here you go," Nick said, returning with two glasses of red wine.

She reached out for the glass just as she caught sight of Ian approaching with the blonde at his side.

I'll keep it civil, for Karen and Robert. But he didn't glance her way; he ignored her as if she wasn't there.

"Brilliant, absolutely brilliant," Ian said, slapping Robert on the back. "What did I tell you?"

"Thanks, man," Robert said.

"Hey, I'm mesmerizing," Larry shouted, waving his Black-Berry. "Bobby, I'm mesmerizing. I've got to call my mother."

Robert raised his glass and nodded. "I'm glad you resurrected him," he said to Karen.

Elizabeth took a moment to give the blonde the once over. *Cold and calculating. Like the other one. Must be what he likes. Fine.* Their eyes met and she gave Helena a cool smile.

"This is Liz," Karen jumped in. "Liz . . . uh . . . Helena . . . and . . . uh . . . everybody knows everybody else."

Elizabeth frowned at Karen.

Robert motioned for the bartender, making a wide circle with his hand.

The bartender nodded.

"Alcohol will not make this better," Karen whispered.

Helena took Ian's arm and looked at Elizabeth. "You two already know each other?"

"Yes, we do," Elizabeth said.

Junie stopped by, a BlackBerry in one hand and a cell phone in the other. " 'Imaginative and innovative, a dizzying collage of social and philosophical commentary wrapped in song and dance. And it worked.' This is what I like to see, kids. It was a fabulous production, one of the smoothest I've worked on. Let me know what you're working on next."

Robert and Karen stared after her as she melted into the crowd.

"Darling, we have to be going," Nick said.

"Oh, Liz, before you go," Karen jumped in. "I—uh—I have the bracelet that I borrowed. Let me just—well, why don't you come with me. It'll only be a sec."

Robert shifted uncomfortably.

"Right, the bracelet," Elizabeth said and then followed her.

"Ten minutes," Nick said, tapping his watch.

Elizabeth nodded.

Nick walked away.

Karen slid a look at Robert. He sighed and turned to Helena. "I need to have a word with Ian before you guys leave."

Helena shrugged.

Karen and Elizabeth found a vacuum of quiet away from the noise, at a table in the back of the restaurant.

"Bracelet?" Elizabeth said. "What gives?"

"Liz, I just wanted to tell you how glad I am that you came, because I know this is hard with Ian being here."

"You didn't have to drag me away to tell me this."

"It's hard for Ian, too."

"I see how hard it is for him." Elizabeth gave a tinny laugh. "Oh Karen, you are not going to defend him!"

"It is hard for him. It really is. In more ways than you realize."

"I don't want to hear this. I am not hearing this."

"Liz, he was married."

Elizabeth's mouth dropped open. She tried to speak, but nothing came out. Finally, she pursed her lips together. "He was married?" she said finally. "*Married?*"

"Yes . . . married."

Elizabeth was quiet for a long moment. "He lied to me."

"Yes, but that's not the reason I'm telling you this."

"Mister 'I have no desire to be married,' " she mimicked in a Scottish brogue. "I don't believe it. What else did he lie about?"

Karen hesitated.

"The lousy bastard . . . I was so right not to trust him."

"She left him," Karen said.

"Left him . . . why? What is there to object to except his smoking himself to death?"

"Not that you're worried about him."

"Exactly."

"She left him. Actually, she ripped his heart out and stepped on it. And then there was his mother . . . she almost died . . . cancer."

"Oh," Elizabeth said. "Why don't you just tell me the whole thing?"

Robert and Ian stood outside the restaurant.

"I thought you wanted to talk."

"I do. I wanted to say thanks for being here. I know it's tough with Liz here."

Ian shrugged. "Whatever."

"You're still coming to the wedding, right? You're still going to be my best man."

"Absolutely, mate."

Robert looked around. "Liz is going to be there. I mean, not that she wants to be . . . after being left at the altar."

Ian looked over at Robert. "Sorry . . . left at the altar?"

"Back in California."

Ian was silent. "Well, that explains a lot, doesn't it."

"Yeah, and since you weren't . . . completely honest . . ."

"She doesn't know that, does she?"

Robert avoided his gaze. "Look, you need to cut her some slack. Getting jilted isn't a trust builder, but she had a lot of other heavy stuff to deal with. Her mother . . . she committed suicide."

"I know about that."

"There is something else. Her mother had a boyfriend . . ."

"And?"

"Liz was under a lot of stress. She gets left at the altar, her mother was losing it, and this guy—you know the drill: an older man comforting a young, confused woman . . ."

Ian's eyes grew dark. "He didn't . . . that shit."

"He did . . . and then he left her after her mother died. Karen said Liz was a guilt-ridden wreck. O'Neill could've done a trilogy just on what she went through."

"Bastard," Ian muttered. "Well, she just can't relax, can

she? She's always thinking a bloke's going to do her a bad turn."

"Try not to be too hard on her, okay?"

Ian straightened and threw him a sharp look. "What do you take me for?"

Robert shrugged. "I'm not sure anymore."

"He married Michele right after his mother was diagnosed," Karen said, emptying her wineglass.

"Looking for comfort," Elizabeth said. *I know that one.*

"It was a long illness and then he went home because it looked like she wasn't going to make it, but she pulled through. He hasn't been back to visit since."

Elizabeth nodded. It was an old story. The fear that somehow your presence or absence will trigger something, cause the cosmos to shift. If you weren't there, if you were there, if you had done this instead of that, everything would be all right.

"I'm sure you understand how he feels," Karen said.

Elizabeth nodded. "I wish I could have seen the wife."

"You have."

Elizabeth looked at her.

"Do you remember the woman we met in the restaurant, at the celebration for Ian's exhibit?"

"The bitch in the bathroom?"

Karen nodded.

Elizabeth went silent for a moment. "He knew I was talking to his ex-wife?" she said at last. "Was he sleeping with her too?"

"Liz, I just told you she made him miserable. He wasn't sleeping with her."

"Then what was he doing?"

"I don't know. Robert said that Ian was extremely upset and angry that she was here. He didn't want anything to interfere between the two of you."

Elizabeth tapped her fingers on the table. "Anything else?"

"He didn't teach at any school in Europe, either."

Elizabeth's eyes narrowed. "More lies."

"He didn't want you to know that he hadn't done well."

"What was he doing?"

"Hanging out in village squares, tourist traps, doing quick portraits, making enough to exist day to day."

"And no doubt screwing every woman he could get his hands on," Elizabeth said.

"He was only manifesting his pain over her discarding him. All men act out through moronic behavior."

Elizabeth smirked. "Do you realize instead of quoting Taoist philosophy, you just channeled your mother?"

Karen sighed. "Don't tell Robert." She gazed out into the crowd. Suddenly she stiffened.

"What?" Elizabeth asked.

"My parents are here."

"Congratulation my darling," Margaret said, taking hold of Karen's hands. "You are brilliant."

"There are two of us, Mom, we're a team."

Margaret gave Robert a sideways glance. "I'm well acquainted with Robert's abilities," she snapped as Edward came up behind her.

"Greetings and salutations, my little Shakespeare," he said, giving Karen a kiss on her temple. "Marvelous, wonderful, *incroyable* as the French say. There are not enough adjectives to describe your talent, my little diamond. I am so proud of you."

Karen kissed her father's cheek. "Thank you, Daddy."

Margaret and Edward beamed on either side of Karen as Robert snapped a picture.

"You are the one thing we agree on in this life, my sweet," Margaret said. "The only one. Now you must write novels, my love. You will be wonderful, of course. A solo career is of utmost importance. As women, we must throw off the shackles of male dominance and have our own venue, moving out with courage. Never forget that men are feckless, fearful, and undependable creatures. Why God in his infinite wisdom chose to give men the balls in this life is beyond me."

"That must be why you tried to take mine," Edward muttered.

Robert slipped his arm around Karen's shoulder at the exact moment Willis entered the restaurant. Spotting Karen, Willis waved.

"Why don't you go over and say hello?" Robert suggested.

She gave him a quizzical look; Robert winked at her.

"My compliments on your little telephone stunt," Margaret said, when Karen was out of earshot.

"One book with an option for a second," Robert said. "Was that your version of half now, half later when he finally convinced her she should postpone, or better yet, cancel the wedding?"

Margaret and Edward exchanged glances. Margaret's lips tightened. "You've made your point, young man. Did you . . . mention this to Karen?"

"Mention that her mother and father were paying someone to destroy her relationship? No, Margaret, I love your daughter. I'm going to marry her, remember?"

"I told you he was smarter than the others," Edward said.

Lips compressed, Margaret continued to stare straight ahead.

"I liked it better when you were trying to annihilate each other," Robert said. He gripped Edward's shoulder. "The night is still young. Maybe you can borrow a scarf. Oh, and you will let Jacques know that he should continue with the wedding plans, won't you?"

Robert walked away.

As the party wound down, Liz and Nick approached Karen and Robert to say their good-byes. Elizabeth hugged her friend close. "Thanks, Karen. For everything."

As Liz turned toward the door, she found herself face-to-face with Ian. Their eyes met; suddenly the air between them seemed to be charged with electricity. They held each other's gaze a second too long.

"Good night," he said.

"Good night," she murmured, as Nick put his arm around her and led her away.

Robert and Karen looked around, realizing they were alone. They smiled.

"Hi," Robert said.

"Hi."

"Congratulations. I hear your play is a big hit."

"Yours too."

He bent and kissed her. When he lifted his head, he spotted Morris coming toward them, his BlackBerry in hand.

" '. . . the production has all the fingerprints of Morris Lewis's usual deft comic touch . . .' " Robert recited from memory.

"Okay, it was funny," Morris said, and moved on.

Later that night, Robert and Karen collapsed onto the bed, still in their clothes, listening to the noises of the city below their window.

Reaching out, Robert grasped Karen's hand and brought it to his lips. "That wasn't so bad. Your parents were almost human."

Karen sighed. "By the way, Willis won't be coming around anymore. He'll be too busy with his new book." She was silent for a moment, staring up at the ceiling. "I can't believe they thought I would leave you . . . for him."

Robert turned to look at her. "Actually, they just wanted you to leave, period. This isn't the first time they've tried this. It's just the first time they weren't successful."

Karen sighed. "I did notice that the serious suitors dropped off the map like they got caught in the Bermuda triangle. After the last one received a faculty position at a prestigious college and had to move out of state—in the back of my mind, I knew. But, the Tao says you have to be flexible as a baby, but strong enough to let the most important things go, and let things work out on their own; that's how you find the right path. So that's what I did. They left and it was right that they left. If they hadn't left, you wouldn't have come along."

He gave her a long, fierce kiss. "You know, every time I think they've driven you over the edge, you come back to me," he whispered.

"I'm never really very far away."

"It's still nerve-wracking," he said.

"What did they offer you?"

"There's nothing they could offer me," he murmured, stroking her hair. "Ever."

"Robert," she sighed, and drawing him close, she pressed her lips against his.

Chapter 80

Elizabeth saw it all coming: the elegant candlelight dinner, the flowers, the carriage ride in Central Park—as if she were a tourist to be impressed by Gotham for the first time. *The prelude to the proposal, everything I have ever hoped for,* she thought as Nick took her hand. *I should be ecstatic.* But the steady tattoo of the horse's hooves on the macadam echoed the pulsing inside her own head. It had been a week since she learned the truth about Ian and she hadn't stopped thinking about him. It didn't change the facts, the situation. She was with Nick and settled in. But she wanted to see Ian, talk to him, clear the air, apologize for what she said in the apartment. *Then I'll be able to get on with my life, a life without drama,* she thought, *the life I had planned.*

Nick squeezed her hand, pulling her back to the present. He was smiling at her.

"So, Miss Elizabeth Strait," he said, looking into her eyes. "Will you marry me?"

There's no turning back now.

He was looking at her expectantly, waiting.

"Yes," she heard herself say. "Yes, I will."

He slipped a marquise-cut diamond ring on her finger; she stared down at it and her breath caught in her throat. She looked up to find him smiling at her.

"I take it you approve?"

She nodded and he drew her close for a long kiss.

"Finally, everyone will believe me when I tell them I'm a man of great taste."

Elizabeth smiled.

"Shall we check your calendar?" he asked.

She took her BlackBerry from her purse. As she clicked through her calendar, she caught the entry for Ian's gallery showing. She quickly tapped on the BlackBerry to move along.

"How about June?" Nick said.

"This June? Is that enough time?" She heard the slight panic in her tone.

"I've been making inquiries," he said. "Cabo San Lucas has everything: the beach, the tranquility, the privacy . . . I made a tentative reservation at Esperanza but I wanted your input."

She saw the determination in his eyes.

"June it is," she said.

Nick drew her close. *I'll feel differently*, she thought, *now that I've made the commitment. Everything I've ever wanted is now here.*

Isn't it?

Chapter 81

Ian answered the knock at his door to find Emily smiling at him. She was wearing a hot pink dress and a seductive smile. The slits around the bottom of the dress revealed her long, sleek, perfectly tanned legs. His eyes traveled the length of her to rest on her face—the creamy skin, the rosy cheeks, the hair tumbling in loose, lazy curls around her shoulders.

"I've been thinking about you," she said, sweeping past him into the loft, leaving a subtle trail of expensive perfume behind her.

Ian closed the door. *Shit.*

Emily parked herself in the kitchen. He kept the island between them.

"So, where are the masterpieces?" she asked, toying with the spoon in his coffee cup.

"They've already been run over to the gallery."

She leaned over the counter, giving him an ample view of her full, round, and spectacular breasts. He could feel his body temperature rising.

"That's too bad," she drawled, her voice low. "I was hoping for a private showing."

I wasn't, but I'm getting one anyway. "We missed you at the play," he said, going to search the coffee table for cigarettes. He found the pack, realized it was empty, and tossed it down.

Emily shrugged. "Pressing business, you know how it is."

She opened her purse and pulled out a business card, placing it on the counter. "I'm announcing the launch of my new Web site. I've been working on it for quite some time. It's going to be the talk of New York. I guarantee it."

"Fantastic," he said, forcing a smile. *You can leave now.*

She sidled toward him, hips swaying in a fluid motion under the gauzy fabric of her dress.

Oh bloody hell.

She fingered the collar of his shirt, brushing up against him. "If I didn't know better, I would think you're blowing me off."

"Not at all, darling."

"You never come to visit anymore. I'm beginning to think all you wanted was information." She ran her finger along his jaw. "Then I thought, maybe it's the work keeping you away. I do actually have some information, new information . . . about Liz."

Ian kept a pleasant smile on his face. Was she all right? Since speaking with Robert, his mind had been racing. But this was bullshit. There was nothing Emily could tell him. Only Lizzie could fill in the blanks.

He backed away. "I thought you and Miss Lizzie are friends."

Emily's expression turned sulky. "We are, but you're not with Liz anymore, are you? You know, I don't mind being used—under the right circumstances," she murmured, sliding her hand along his arm. She ran her tongue over her lips and looked into his eyes. "Besides, I am curious. Liz had a lot to say about you—and your many skills."

He cleared his throat. "Isn't your husband expecting you at home?" he said.

Emily's expression soured. "My husband doesn't expect much of anything from me these days . . . but that doesn't mean I don't have a lot to offer."

"Emily," he said. "You need to go home now."

She brushed her lips against his. "I was so looking forward to spending some quality time with you," she murmured against his mouth. "Are you sure you don't want me to stay?" she whispered.

"Emily," he ordered. "Go home."

Her cheeks flushed and he could see the quick flash of anger behind the blue of her eyes. "Whatever you want," she said, tracing his mouth with her finger. "Oh . . . that's your line, isn't it?"

He gritted his teeth as she strolled to the door.

"I guess we won't have a chance to talk about Liz," she said with a shrug. "Don't forget the Web launch," she said, blowing him a kiss. She let the door slam shut behind her.

Ian sat down. *Shit.*

Chapter 82

People maneuvered through the crowded gallery carrying glasses of wine, scrutinizing, examining, judging. They gathered in front of Ian's canvas entitled *Requiem*, whispering as they stared at the woman he had created. The colors were vivid, yet the painting felt intimate and private. In the background, the figure of a man stood in deep shadow, mysterious, hidden; was he really there or only in the woman's imagination?

Ian watched each person as they studied his work, trying to gauge their reaction, taking care not to stand too close; he didn't want to appear to be hovering. His emotions wavered between satisfaction and regret. He had reached the point he desperately needed to get back to, that of a working artist. Yet he was standing in the gallery alone, without Lizzie. He had imagined this moment with her at his side.

Robert and Karen came up to him, Robert giving him an encouraging pat on his shoulder. "Stop worrying. The pieces are fantastic."

"I hope so," Ian said.

Paul Ferand pulled him away to introduce him to the crowd gathering around *Requiem*. They applauded, asking him questions, praising the work. Then he saw the red dot on the corner of the frame; sold. His heart thudded against his ribs and he felt a smile spreading across his face.

"Okay, *mon bon homme*," Ferand whispered in his ear. "*C'est excellent*. Good work, *bon travail, très bon travail, c'est le retour de Manet, de Bonnard. Un âge nouveau pour l'Impressionnisme, hunh?* Impressionism has returned, only better. The old is new and improved."

"*Merci*, thank you my friend, *mon ami*," Ian said, embracing the man who had become like a father to him.

"Okay, now you talk to the people. *C'est très important.*"

Ian shook hands with a man, a journalist, whose questions swirled in his head like a whirlwind.

How did you decide to mix contemporary with Impressionism? What was your inspiration for this piece? Your pallet is considerably stronger, brighter, than the traditional Impressionist pallet, was that a conscious choice? Is this indicative of a personal struggle between the art forms? Where do you see your style fitting into today's decidedly contemporary market?

Ian responded to each one with a carefully measured answer. When the journalist walked away, Ian scanned the gallery. *She's not coming.*

The crowd had thinned out. It was late, and Paul Ferand stood with a couple, speaking in quiet, hushed tones; a careful, polite negotiation. When they finished speaking, he placed a red dot on Ian's other canvas.

Ian stood alone in the vast white space; all his friends had gone. The rush of excitement and nail-biting nerves had finally ebbed away, leaving a fatigued calm and a sense of accomplishment in their place. He could feel a smile creeping across his face.

Sudden movement made him glance over at the door. His stomach flipped and he fussed with his jacket, trying to quell the excitement surging through him.

"Lizzie," he breathed.

She entered with tentative steps, scanning the canvases.

He approached her in silence, waiting, not wanting to startle her by calling her name.

He studied the graceful line of her profile as she stood gazing up at the *Requiem* canvas.

Finally sensing his presence, Elizabeth turned and she stared at him.

"I didn't think . . . you'd still be . . . here," she stammered, clasping her hands together.

"I have to stay to the end, don't I?" he said. "I'm glad you came . . . I appreciate it, I do."

She nodded.

He thought some of the tension left her face.

She turned back to study the canvas. "You've incorporated several different styles," she said carefully. "Pierre Bonnard, the Impressionists . . . the Fauves."

Ian nodded. "You're perfectly right, Lizzie," he said. "You understand the work."

Elizabeth continued to stare at the canvas. "You've used such strong colors for her. Are you suggesting all responsibility is resting on her? Whatever may have happened between them, it's her fault?" She looked at him. Her expression, which had been open and interested at first, turned cool.

"Lizzie, I'm not suggesting that anything is her fault, I assure you."

"I know a little something about art, remember? She's in the middle of the painting, she's the largest component of the piece. He's in the background, in the shadows."

"I believe I know the intention of my work. There's no statement here, Lizzie."

She turned to face him. "Why not just admit it? This is your way of saying it was my fault."

"I'm not saying anything was anyone's fault; that's not what I'm saying, no."

She returned to staring at the painting. "Obviously he's a coward, hiding in the background, afraid of stepping into the light and telling the truth."

"That's not what this is about and you know it."

She held his gaze, waiting.

"All right, Lizzie, I admit it. I am saying something with the painting."

She lifted her chin. "Go ahead. I'm listening."

"I'm saying you were alive, vibrant, productive, but because of your past, you chose to withdraw, to hide. You settled for being cold and hard and brittle."

"Spoken by a man who *thinks* he knows me."

"I know you won't admit my work reminds you of what you were—what you should've been."

She took a step back.

"*That's* what this is about. I did what you wanted to do— what you've been too afraid to do."

Elizabeth paled and immediately he regretted his words. *Shit.* "Lizzie—"

"You're wrong, Ian," she said, bringing herself under control. "I'm doing exactly what I want." She thrust out her hand, the diamond capturing the overhead light and throwing sparkles across the gallery walls. "Nick and I are engaged. I'm going to marry him."

Ian's jaw dropped.

He gripped her wrist, pulling her out of the gallery.

"Let go of me," she said, after attempts to free herself proved futile.

At the corner, under the street lamp, he stopped, turning her to face him.

"Is he what you want, modern marriage without love instead of the beauty of tradition?"

"I should ask you that. Traditional or modern?"

"If you're so damn happy with him, why did you come here?" he asked, still gripping her arm.

She squirmed. "I made a mistake—now let me go."

His grip tightened and he pulled her so close his lips could touch hers. "I think you're having doubts."

She looked him in the eye. "I'm sure you'd like that, but I don't have doubts anymore. If I did, they've just been relieved."

His eyes moved over her face and in one swift movement, he crushed her to him, forcing the breath out of her, giving her a hard kiss full of heat, frustration, and anger. When he let her go his eyes were dark, his face flushed. "Congratulations, Lizzie. I know he's exactly what you've always wanted."

Giving him one last look, she broke free and fled.

Chapter 83

Robert sat at his desk and hit the button to start his computer. He signed on to the Internet, listening to the noise of streaming video news breaking out of the speakers, and clicked to sign in to his mail.

Ian slammed his way around the miniscule gray nook that now served as a kitchen, impatient for the familiar burping sound of the coffeemaker to finish. He looked in disgust at the boxes littering the postage stamp–sized apartment. He shook his head. *They had to come back now. Bloody perfect time for the sublet to run out.*

He logged on to his e-mail. Ferand had found potential buyers overseas and he checked daily for any word. It would be ironic if he had come all the way to America only to become popular back home. *Then I truly will have to travel,* he thought, shaking his head.

He poured his coffee and sat down in front of the laptop.

Parker dropped his briefcase onto a chair just as his assistant, Tricia, came up behind him. He stopped short and she bumped into him. Turning, he leered at her, a wicked smile on his lips.

"Can't wait to get started, hunh?" he said.

She gave him a tolerant smile and when he turned away, curled her lip in disgust.

He looked at the brand-new laptop sitting on his desk, wrapped in a red ribbon with a card attached. He looked to Tricia.

"You wife had it delivered this morning."

Parker gave the card a cursory glance. " 'Sign on to your e-mail for a big surprise,' " he read.

He gave a snide chuckle and tossed the card on the desk.

Stanton Perry said good morning to his assistant, listening to her recitation of the morning e-mails and messages.

"There's an e-mail from Mrs. Parker Davis with an announcement of her new on-line enterprise, and a Web link."

"Preview the launch, give me a recap, and then send a gift of congratulations, please," he said.

"Yes, sir," the assistant said, and left the office.

Ian read the e-mail from Emily and clicked on the link; the Web site loaded. It was sleek and crisp, with plenty of white space and elegant writing in script. He filled in the fields certifying that he was an adult. Reaching for his cup, he took a swallow as the page loaded, and choked on his coffee. Sputtering and coughing, he managed to steady the cup and set it on the counter, wiping his chin with his free hand.

"Oh dear," he said, his eyes glued to the screen as sounds of heavy breathing began filling the miniscule space and reverberating against the walls.

Karen woke up to find Mary standing over her bed.

"Wake up, miss," she said. "Wake up now."

Karen rubbed the sleep from her eyes. "What is it?"

"It's Mister Robert."

"He's here?" she said through a yawn.

"No, miss, on the phone. He said there's something you *have* to see."

* * *

Stanton Perry leaned back as his assistant came up behind him in the conference room and whispered in his ear. As she spoke, his face flushed. He excused himself and left the room, striding down the hall, his assistant following a half-step behind. Taking a quick glance around, he found the staff averting their eyes.

Entering his office alone, he closed the door behind him and sat down at his desk. He opened his laptop, clicking on the link from Emily. He watched the man and woman on the screen in the throes of copulation, the woman spread-eagled against the dresser, her blond hair falling forward as the man took her from behind.

Then he recognized the man.

Perry sat up, inching closer to the screen as Parker drew the pale blond hair away from the woman's face. Deirdre's face. He cursed, fighting the urge to hurl the laptop across the room. He forced himself to sit back in his chair and slowly breathe in and out, until his temper began to cool. His face tightened, his features hardening into smooth stone. He watched as his wife threw her head back and opened her mouth, but no sound came out; the speakers were off.

At the kitchen table, Karen sat in front of her laptop, staring at the screen, holding a phone to her ear.

"So she really does know how to use all that equipment," Robert said.

"I told you, baby, Emily's an intelligent woman." She yawned and shook her head. "God, he has all the finesse of a jack rabbit."

"A gross understatement," Robert chuckled. "I'll see you in an hour."

"Okay, baby," Karen said, hitting the off button.

Margaret breezed into the kitchen, wrapped in a blue satin robe, her hair tied with a matching scarf. Catching sight of the screen, she leaned in for a closer look.

"Men," she sighed. "They're in love with those things but most of them have no idea of how to use them properly."

Karen looked up at her mother.

"Trust me," Margaret said. "You're looking at one of the most ill-used tools since the industrial revolution."

"**Y**ou need to calm down," Nick said.

"Calm down? Calm down?" Parker bellowed as he stomped around his office, his face a deep crimson. "Why the fuck do I need to calm down? My wife, that bitch, betrayed me!"

Snatching Emily's picture from his desk, he stared at it. "Bitch!" he snarled through his teeth, hurling the picture against the wall. "I can't believe she did this to me. I supported her through all that shit she calls work, and as a thank you she cuts my balls off. I'm going to sue her ass off and drain every dime of that fucking trust fund!" He kicked the fragments of the picture frame. "You'll come begging me for money, bitch."

"Parker," Nick said, his voice cool and calm, "you are not going to sue your wife."

"Then I'll divorce her," he said, raking his hand through his hair. "I can't believe she did this," he muttered. "That ungrateful bitch. She'd be nowhere without me, nowhere!"

"Listen to me," Nick began, "Emily is the least of your problems right now. Forget her. You have something much more important to focus on. You need—"

"The least of my problems?" Parker said, his breathing ragged. "That problem posted my dick for the whole fucking world to see."

"You need to listen to me," Nick said. "You need to worry about Perry."

Parker stared at Nick, his mouth open. "What, you think he'll pull his money out over this?" He chuckled. "He changes wives like he changes socks!"

Nick sat down, shaking his head.

A frantic pounding began on the door. "Fuck off!" Parker shouted.

The door flew open and Stanley rushed into the office.

"I'm in a meeting," Parker said through his teeth, enunciating as if he were speaking to someone with a learning disability.

"Never mind the meeting. We've got a problem in Japan."

"What?" Parker sneered. "Godzilla's attacking the city?"

Stanley's expression soured. "There's been an earthquake. The yen is taking a nosedive."

Parker made a sound of disgust. "Fuck," he said, slamming his fists down on the table.

Chapter 84

Emily enjoyed the sudden quiet of the apartment. The phone had been ringing nonstop for over an hour before it finally ceased. Parker, she was sure. Now, in the silence, she glanced around at the "lovely big room" as Ian would've called it, and ran her hand over the oval mahogany dining table. The lights were off and a weak setting sun was filtering in through the sheer draperies, giving the room an ethereal air.

A satisfied smile crawled across her lips.

A hulk of a man, perspiration dripping down his face, entered the dining room. "We're done," he said.

"Did you tell the building superintendent?"

"Yeah, I told 'em. He's puttin' the elevator back in service."

"Thank you. I'll see you at the apartment."

"Yes, ma'am," he said, and lumbered out.

As he left, a man of medium height in a blue uniform and hat entered.

"Please take my bags down to the car, Thomas," Emily said.

"Yes, ma'am." He took the bags and exited.

Emily drained the last of the dry white wine from her Lalique stemware and placed it on the table. She put down her key, picked up her purse and strolled out of the apartment, leaving the door open.

Chapter 85

Elizabeth arrived at the small, nondescript restaurant at seven a.m. Usually, she met Stanton Perry at Fives in the Peninsula Hotel. Not today; he wouldn't want to meet anyone they knew. She found him sitting in the back, staring out into the crowd.

He was dressed in a black suit, gray shirt, and red tie.

"Hello, young lady," he said, rising to pull out her chair.

Elizabeth had had previous meetings with him, one for each wife. But not after something so public, so humiliating. When she had seen the e-mail, she waited for the call she knew was coming.

He drank his coffee, lost in his thoughts. "I must confess," he said at last, "I've always invited you to breakfast for my own selfish purposes. I find a beautiful woman soothing; it helps me think clearly."

Elizabeth smiled, taking the comment in stride. "If you have any concerns about the portfolio, I'll schedule a review any time you like."

He waved the comment away with a flick of his hand. "The provisions in the prenup will take care of everything. The portfolio can stay as it is."

She knew that, but felt she had to ask. Six years and a parade of wives, girlfriends, and mistresses—Perry never changed. Through it all he had appeared robust, and healthy. For the first time he looked sallow; she could see the tightness around his mouth, a controlled anger behind his onyx eyes.

She remembered their first private dinner together as client and adviser, the awkward final moments of the evening; his unspoken desire for more than food, drink, and information on stock options. Elizabeth backed away graciously and Perry didn't press; it wasn't his style.

"Can I still reach you at the penthouse?" she asked.

"No, the soon-to-be former Mrs. Perry will be keeping it. I'm at the Trump Tower suite if you need me."

He sat back in his chair, giving her an assessing look. "I understand congratulations are in order for you."

"Yes . . . thank you."

"I'm proud of you. I admire a person mature enough to abandon their vices."

Elizabeth didn't answer.

"Do I sense reluctance? What's on your mind, young lady?"

Elizabeth hesitated, acutely aware that beneath Stanton's pleasant demeanor, he was first and always a client, not a friend. "You said everyone needs a vice."

"That's right."

Elizabeth shifted in her seat. "And Mrs. Perry was your vice?"

One eyebrow went up. "I should say so."

"What will you do now?"

Perry chuckled. "Go out and find another vice. There doesn't seem to be much else to do."

Elizabeth looked away. "Do you ever think you want something more . . . or . . . what you think could be more?"

"I assume this has to do with the painter. I liked him."

"Everyone likes him . . . sometimes you can be afraid of getting what you really want."

"Young lady, if that's the case, you never had a vice. You already had something more."

Elizabeth nodded her head.

He stood up, indicating the meeting was over. "I will, of

course, be moving my holdings from Davis Enterprises. You don't do any business with Parker, do you?"

Elizabeth smiled. "No, I don't."

Leaning over, he took her hand, and gave it a kiss. "I didn't think so," he said with a wink. "Take care of yourself, young lady."

"You too, Mr. Perry."

She watched him stride out of the restaurant, his thick, solid frame exuding strength and confidence. His question about Parker was a warning; if she had money tied up with Parker he was giving her a chance to get out while she could. Stanton Perry was about to initiate payback. She had just been witness to the beginning of the end of Parker Davis.

Chapter 86

"So, here's what I've been thinking," Nick said, reaching across the table and taking her hands. "A weekend getaway to Nantucket. I have a client who has a house right on the beach. He would love to lend it to us."

She gazed into his eyes. His hands holding hers felt warm and comfortable, and she remembered she had forgotten to say thank you for the roses that had arrived early this morning. Even though the flowers arrived every day like clockwork, she felt she shouldn't take them for granted.

New England. The perfect place for watercolor painting. Instead of envisioning a romantic weekend with Nick, an image of Ian flashed into her mind, standing before his easel on the sandy beach, capturing the sun and the waves, his own take on Monet's *Impression Sunrise*. The thought so startled her, she blinked quickly, trying to refocus.

"That sounds wonderful," she said, squeezing his hands in return. "Are you sure you'll be able to get away, considering yesterday's events?"

Nick smirked. "I just finished another meeting with Parker two hours ago."

"And?"

"His ego is considerably bruised. If he survives the Japan earthquake, my concern is how he'll survive the Stanton Perry quake."

He won't, Elizabeth thought. Perry's revenge will be thorough and devastating.

"How much time do you think Parker has?" Nick asked.

"For what? He can't exactly make amends." It was a bullshit evasive answer and Nick's sharp look told Elizabeth he knew it.

Nick straightened, leaning forward, his signal that a "Hey kid" and an important life lesson would be forthcoming. "Hey kid, this is how business works. You should know this already."

"I know I'm not your strategist. I'm your fiancée. I'm not reporting on my client's activities to help your client—who doesn't deserve any help."

"You have to pick your alliances and make the most of them."

"Meaning . . . what?" Elizabeth heard the aggressive edge in her voice.

Nick cocked his head to the side, a sign of over-exaggerated patience with her. "Meaning you can't sit around thinking Perry is your only golden goose. You got lucky last time. Parker was arrogant and showed his hand. Next time he may not send you empty boxes and give you blank business cards with no title on them. If you went down, Perry would've moved on and forgotten all about you. You're a player now, kid. Remember to act like one."

Elizabeth didn't answer, afraid of what she might say.

Nick shifted in his chair. "Never mind. Why don't we forget about this and move on to more pleasant subjects? Amanda is asking if you've chosen a dress. Have you seen the ladies?"

Elizabeth nodded. The ladies; wives of Nick's friends. Amanda was married to a partner and Patricia was the wife of a golfing buddy. Short pixie hair, summers in the Hamptons, and an Upper East Side classic six. "I met them for brunch on Sunday. I'm shopping for a dress this weekend."

"Wonderful. You'll include them in the planning, of course, it would be insulting not to."

"Of course," Elizabeth murmured, looking down at her plate, pushing the food around. *Shopping for a wedding dress, the shopping I should be doing with Karen.*

"I spoke to Warren. We're all set for weekends in June at their house in the Hamptons. They would like for us to have the ceremony there. I was thinking the weekend of the twenty-third."

Elizabeth could only stare at him for a moment. "What are you talking about? We have Karen and Robert's wedding on the twenty-third."

Nick pursed his lips. "You can't be serious about keeping that commitment."

"I'm very serious."

Nick gave her hand a condescending pat. "I don't want to disappoint our friends."

"I'm not disappointing my friend."

"Okay," Nick said, his tone clipped. "Let's not argue about it. We'll work it out. I don't want to upset you or *you* may post a video of me picking food from my teeth when I think no one's looking." He leaned in to give her a kiss; she didn't want him to touch her.

"Now, let's get to the important stuff. Are you on track with your teams and your revenue plans? You need to start thinking about elevating yourself to the next level. Now is the time to prepare."

She nodded her head but didn't answer. Something Nick had said clicked and fell into place. *Empty boxes and business cards with no titles. How did he know? I never told anyone except Ian.*

The truth hit her like a one-two punch. Nick knew all about Parker's plan to wipe her off the New York financial map. He'd always known; Parker had told him. She looked into Nick's eyes as they got up to leave, struggling to keep her face benign. He smiled, holding out her coat, ever the attentive fiancé.

Chapter 87

Ian opened the door, grunting a greeting at Robert.

Robert stepped gingerly around half-empty boxes, open suitcases, canvases, and painting paraphernalia cluttering the miniscule living room. The apartment resembled an oversized walk-in closet, one quarter the size of the loft, making it almost impossible to avoid contact. He tripped over his feet trying to avoid an open carton and let out an involuntary "shit" and then "sorry."

"You're early," Ian said.

"I know," Robert said. "I thought we could get the tux-fitting done and then grab some lunch."

Ian shrugged.

His mood was transparent; his face resembled a storm cloud. Robert tried a safe topic. "Any word from London?"

Ian drained his coffee cup and lit a cigarette. "A buyer wants all three pieces. Ferand suggested I go back and spend some time at home."

"Go home? When?"

Ian didn't answer.

Robert pulled back. "Ian, you can't leave now. What about the wedding?"

"You don't need me here."

"That's shit and you know it. And you need to be here, you

need to keep working, and you need to square this with Liz, one way or the other."

Ian gave a disgusted laugh, slamming the coffee cup down. "I don't need your pearls of wisdom to get my life in order and I don't want them."

"If you leave now, you may never have another chance to—"

"Shut it," Ian said, kicking one of the boxes. "There are no more chances."

"Think about staying. Just through the wedding. Okay?"

Ian nodded.

Chapter 88

Elizabeth arrived late at the bridal salon to find Karen and Emily already trying on their dresses. They didn't kiss or hug hello, but stood around like awkward teenagers going through the ritual of a fading friendship.

"So where is the wedding going to be?" Emily asked.

"Nick and I haven't decided yet."

"You are going to keep him, aren't you? You should at least keep one of them."

"You should keep the right one," Karen said.

"Hey, I introduced her to Nick," Emily protested.

"I'm capable of making my own decisions," Elizabeth said.

Karen turned to her. "Are you?"

"You should keep Nick," Emily said. "And you could be a little nicer. We're trying to help you—we always do," Emily persisted. "If it hadn't been for our help when you came to New York, you—"

"When Karen brought me to New York, when Karen gave me a place to live, when Karen—"

"When I introduced you to the clients that gave you a career—"

"Can we please finish the fitting?" Elizabeth said, straining to remain calm. "That's why we're here, so Karen can see how we look."

They fell silent.

Two hours later, Elizabeth and Karen stood outside the salon.

"Emily doesn't think sometimes," Karen said. "Her atmosphere is small."

"And self-contained."

"Liz, she was good to you."

"Only so I could shower her with gratitude." Her shoulders relaxed. "Okay, she did a lot for me . . . yes. I promise we'll get along at the wedding. And I'll be civil to Ian as well. I know you have your hands full worrying about your parents."

"Liz, I don't think Ian will be at the wedding. I'm pretty sure he's leaving."

"Leaving . . . for good?" she said, hearing the anxiety in her voice. "Why?"

Karen shrugged. "He lost the loft and his dealer is encouraging him to give the European market a try . . . I think he just wants to go."

They stood in silence for a moment.

Karen took Elizabeth's hand. "Do you remember when William tried to convince you to come home after Josh? Remember what you said? You knew it was wrong. Deep down, you knew it, and you went through with it anyway. I have to say this. This isn't right with Nick. Get out now."

Elizabeth shook her head. "Nick will never hurt me. He can't. I don't love him."

"Then why . . . ?"

Elizabeth took a deep breath. "Because I know what I'm dealing with."

"And you'll always know what you're doing on a Saturday night? But you love Ian."

"Ian and I are too much alike. We would just keep hurting each other. That's all we know how to do."

"Liz, I'm sorry," Karen said, and she pulled her close.

Elizabeth broke away first. "I'll call you," she said, heading toward the subway.

"Don't you want to know how Ian is?" Karen called after her.

Elizabeth turned around. "I already know. Same as me," she said, and turning, she kept walking.

Chapter 89

Arriving at the church, Karen experienced a rush of contentment at finding the sanctuary empty. She always enjoyed the feeling an empty church gave her, entering a world where man and God were alone with each other. That's how she had felt during her travels. Alone at an altar, everything crystallizes; or so she had thought. Now it was clear: she had run away, seizing every opportunity to avoid dealing with the reality of her parents' life.

She sat in the front pew staring at the pulpit. She heard rustling and Joy Fuller sat down beside her.

"Are you all right?" Mrs. Fuller asked. She was wearing beige slacks and a white shirt. Her tan loafers were showing telltale signs of wear.

"I was hoping to see the reverend."

"Canceling the wedding?"

Karen started. "No, of course not!"

Mrs. Fuller shrugged.

"I wanted to let Reverend Fuller know there may not be a best man, and if there is, he and the maid of honor had a bad breakup; she's marrying someone else."

Mrs. Fuller patted Karen's shoulder. "C'mon," she said, getting up. Karen followed her out a side door.

They sat in the tiny enclosed inner courtyard, the legs of the metal chairs shifting underneath them on the uneven ground.

Karen looked around at the overgrown foliage. If properly cared for, she imagined this place would provide someone with a tiny oasis of peace and tranquility.

Mrs. Fuller lit a cigarette and took a long pull, blowing out a stream of smoke, watching it hang in the languid air.

"So when is she getting married?" she asked.

"In June."

Mrs. Fuller nodded her head. "She loves him?"

"Nick or Ian?"

"The new one."

Karen thought. "Nick . . . no, she doesn't. But she and Ian can't seem to be together without hurting each other."

Nodding, Mrs. Fuller took another drag. "There's a lot of that going around."

"Why do you think people can't stop hurting each other?"

"No idea."

"What do you think that's a sign of in a relationship?"

"Couldn't tell you."

Karen stared.

"You expected an answer?"

"Actually, yes."

"Sorry. You believe in signs?"

Karen thought about it. "Yes, I do," she said, looking up at the ivy growing on the building closing them in. Or keeping everyone else out, she thought. Maybe that was the attraction for Joy Fuller.

"Also, I wanted to warn the reverend before he comes to the inn that my matron of honor publicly humiliated her husband by taping his sexual infidelity and putting it out on the Internet. And of course, my parents are still the wild cards . . . have you ever had a couple with this many problems?"

"Yes," Mrs. Fuller said.

"What did you tell them?"

Mrs. Fuller took another drag on her cigarette and blew out a smoke ring. "It's a sign."

"That's what I thought," Karen said with a heavy sigh.

SUMMER

Chapter 90

Parker stared out of the limo as it crawled through Midtown on a bright June morning. The days were growing warmer, and soon the sun's heat would be baking the Big Apple.

Parker watched the tourists walking up Thirty-third, craning their necks, staring up to check out the Empire State Building. Across the street were little fenced oases, each with a tree and small red and white plants. A city employee stood over one of the four-by-four squares, examining the plants intently, as if, by his will, they would thrive in the midst of the heat and frenzied pace of the city. Parker had never noticed it before, any of it.

He couldn't believe May had come and gone so quickly. Four short weeks of hemorrhaging cash. Even so, he'd thought he could save himself; it was still possible. Then it happened.

First the margin calls came in; the share prices were plummeting and the creditors wanted their trades covered. He couldn't get on top of the situation. Bonds he had offered as collateral on the debt were losing value with avalanche speed; there was no way to cover what was owed.

He could hear the whispers all over town about the hedge fund failing. He kept his game face on, talked easily about how Davis Enterprises was well-equipped to handle these event risks, how he was handling the "challenging market."

The limo pulled up to the curb. The driver got out and

opened the door. Parker emerged and stood for a minute, looking up at the building. He was going to the thirtieth floor, just as he did every day. But today was different.

He tried to work out the situation in his head, wrap his mind around it. When the holdings in his portfolio were first being liquidated, he chalked it up to risk. Competitors always knew a little about what you had going on in the portfolio. They would try to drive the price down, just to make the other guy's life more difficult, force him to move. But this was different. It was as if someone had stolen the keys to his kingdom, studied his portfolio, and then, one by one, made each stock disappear. The stocks lose value, everyone panics. *The fucking flight to liquidity. Everybody going apeshit all at once, and selling to get cash fast.* He shook his head. It wasn't risk, a market downturn, or the Easter Bunny that had driven him under.

He got out of the elevator and walked into his offices. The receptionist said good morning, but he didn't answer. He handed off his jacket to his assistant and went straight to the conference room. He had spent most of his time there over the last month, consumed with strategy sessions, meetings, and the looming prospect of auditors coming through the door.

As of Memorial Day, two billion in portfolio value had vanished. As Parker entered the conference room, Nick and his team stood up to greet him. Parker felt like he'd been sucker punched. Davis Enterprises was coming to an end as quietly as it began.

Hours later, Nick and his team closed their briefcases. He shook hands with them, one by one. As the clock struck six p.m. Parker stood in the conference room alone, the only one left in the office. He gazed out of the window while a flatscreen television behind him broadcasted the day's financial news. He kept looking out the window, listening.

"In a stunning act of hubris, Davis Enterprises, a rogue hedge fund helmed by the flamboyant man-about-town, Parker Davis, closed its doors today. The company released a brief statement that the portfolio's remaining value would be liquidated in a timely manner in order for customers to recoup their investments as soon as pos-

*sible. Mr. Davis was recently at the center of a sex scandal. A video-
tape of Mr. Davis's tryst with Deirdre Perry, wife of financial giant
Stanton Perry, was broadcast on the Internet, sending shock waves
through the financial community. Mr. Perry has been in the south of
France with his new companion, the former Miss Florida, twenty-
two-year-old Alicia Wentworth, and could not be reached for comment.*"

Parker turned, staring at the picture of Stanton Perry on
the screen. He turned away, taking a last look at his opulent
conference room, the mahogany table gleaming under the
myriad lights of the cut-glass chandelier. He had chosen the
wood himself and had it made to his specifications, a far cry
from the scratched and worn formica square he and his sib-
lings had crowded around every evening all of their young
lives. For a moment he experienced déjà vu, feeling the same
way he had when he stood on the banks of Jersey, staring
across the river from inside a black hole. Empty.

Across town a kickoff party was in full swing at the Palladio
Hotel. Emily beamed as she announced the new joint venture
of her company, EW Consultants, in partnership with Arthur
Watson. She grasped the ceremonial scissors and cut the rib-
bon. The seventy-five million dollar renovation had begun.
They poured the champagne and toasted the first of their
many successes. Emily gazed over the room and drank deep.
I'm back, she thought, *and better than ever.*

Chapter 91

Elizabeth moved around Nick's kitchen, clearing away the dishes in silence. He had pressed her to come to dinner; their conversation had been halting and stilted.

The apartment was sleek and shiny. Nick was a minimalist, not fond of the warm, cozy look. He seldom cooked, but his kitchen was outfitted with the newest high-tech stainless steel appliances.

"Leave the rest," he said from the living room. He set down two glasses on the coffee table and opened a bottle of wine.

She passed by his desk, fingering the pile of paper.

Nick chuckled as she settled onto the couch. He handed her a glass and took one for himself before settling down next to her.

"That's Parker's post mortem. I should have gone into wills and trusts."

Elizabeth nodded, not knowing what to say. She never liked Parker but it went against the grain to be cavalier about his personal and professional implosion, even if he was a little shit.

"Will he come out with anything?"

Nick draped his arm around her and she leaned back without settling into his embrace. He shrugged. "Between the investigations and the dissolution of the company, and of course the legal fees, he won't have much spending cash." He chuckled again. "Who knows? He's so ballsy, he might actually have the nerve to come back and set up shop again, if he can. If not, I don't really know where he could go now."

Elizabeth winced at the thought. Parker deserved everything he got, but there was something about the destruction of a seemingly indestructible life that always gave one pause.

"And soon he won't have a lawyer, but he doesn't have any assets anyway."

Elizabeth lifted up her head to stare at him. He caught her look.

"C'mon, kid, what did I tell you? People pass in and out of your life all the time."

Elizabeth didn't hide her distaste at the remark, turning away from him.

Nick laughed. "You're going to miss Parker? We can all meet up at the diner once a month for a Danish and coffee and catch up. We'll have to pay, of course."

"You can just send flowers."

Nick's face clouded. "What the hell does that mean? You want to have a pity party for Parker Davis?"

She got up off the couch. "No. Everything has a value, and everyone, right?"

"That's right, kid. Now you're learning."

"And now the value of your relationship with Parker is zero."

Nick gave a short, bitter laugh. "I think you've had too much wine, kid. Why don't you drop this thing and forget about it." He looked at her. "What's this really about? It's not about Parker. You don't give a shit about Parker. So what is it? Your hippie friends? We'll go to that damn wedding if that's what you want."

"I was going under, and you didn't show your face until I came out of it," she said. "You knew all along what Parker was doing to me. No one jumps onto a sinking ship, right, Nick? But now that I'm making my budget, my teams are producing, and my revenue growth plan is on track, everything's okay now? I'm a good bet?"

He slammed the glass down. "Cut the crap. What did you

expect me to do? Bail you out? How could I know you wouldn't collapse anyway, and go back to painting and drinking and fucking around like your mother?"

Her mouth dropped open; she stood there, feeling like she'd been slapped. She stared at him, not seeing him for the first time but seeing what she always knew he was.

How stupid to have kept convincing herself she could go through with this, as if it was a business transaction; to become one of the fixtures, like a table, a chair, a painting. She imagined entertaining in the spacious living room, chatting with guests, her handsome husband with his brilliant legal mind next to her; an empty farce. He would take her anywhere she wanted to go, send her flowers, buy her gifts, and evaluate people and things, including her, for their net worth. She had decided to ignore the fact that she didn't love him and keep herself safe. In the end, she would have made the very mistake she sought so hard to avoid. *What I said to Karen was wrong. Nick would hurt me, leaving me hollow and empty inside, as Parker almost did to Emily.*

"Liz—"

"I'm sure you have someone to take my place," she said, picking up her purse. "An intelligent man always has a Plan B."

Nick took her by the shoulders. "Liz, don't. I didn't mean that. You're special. You know that. I picked you out."

"Yes. I had value."

Gathering her overnight bag, she let herself out, closing the door behind her.

Chapter 92

Suitcases lay open on Karen and Robert's bed. The wedding dress, shrouded in plastic, hung on a hook on the back of the closet door.

"Did you assign the bedrooms?" Karen asked, stuffing clothing into a suitcase.

"We're assigning bedrooms?" he said, watching the destruction of the clothes with interest. "Are you planning on wearing those?"

"Is Ian coming?"

"Yes, Ian is coming."

"We need to keep him and Liz at opposite ends of the hallway. My parents need to be far away from each other too, just in case. Emily is coming, alone, thank goodness, or we'd have to pitch a tent for Parker on the lawn."

Robert took her by the hands. "Step away from the suitcase," he said, pulling her down next to him on the bed. "Karen, strangely enough, this is the happiest time of our lives. It doesn't feel that way, and yet it is."

"No one in our wedding party likes each other."

"I like you." He kissed her forehead, enveloping her in an embrace. "Listen to me. Nothing is going to go wrong. Jacques is having a simple gazebo constructed for the ceremony. We'll take pictures by the pond. We'll eat a nice lunch of chicken or fish with our guests, at tables covered with white tablecloths and under blinking lights strung across the tent, and when the sun goes down, we'll dance under the stars. And then we'll have the rest of our lives together."

Karen looked into his eyes. "Do you really think it's going to be that easy?"

"I do."

She leaned her head on his chest. "Remember those words. You'll need them tomorrow."

Chapter 93

By four o'clock, Karen, Robert, and Elizabeth had packed up the car and were on their way. Robert was behind the wheel, the women staring out of their respective windows, watching Manhattan fade behind them as they crossed under the mammoth steel spikes of the Fifty-ninth Street Bridge. Elizabeth and Karen chatted easily over the dress and wedding details; Elizabeth was careful to stay upbeat. Every once in a while, the conversation would die out and they would lapse into silence. Then she thought about Ian being at the inn and her heart would skip.

Three hours and one traffic delay due to an accident on the LIE later, they drove past a plain wooden mailbox, tires crunching on the graveled driveway leading to the bed and breakfast. At the end of the winding lane they found a rambling, cornflower blue, two-story house with white shutters, nestled in pine and birch. It had a wraparound porch with several white painted rockers and a swing; a riot of colorful flowers bordered the front porch and the path leading to the inn.

Robert cut the engine, popped the trunk, and they got out.

Hearing noises not associated with peaceful relaxation, they walked over to the side of the inn to find a team of men working in a hive of activity, constructing some type of edifice, complete with columns.

Elizabeth looked at her. "That's not a gazebo."

"No, it isn't," Karen said, and looked at Robert.

Robert cursed under his breath.

They turned at the sound of cars coming up the driveway. Two limousines and a taxi came to a halt.

Edward emerged from one limo, Margaret from the other. Ian got out of the taxi.

Elizabeth's heart began to beat faster as she watched him take his bag from the trunk of the cab, slamming it closed.

He turned; their eyes met. They stood still, looking at each other, until Jacques came rushing over, his hair stretching skyward. He exchanged multiple kisses with Karen. "It is going to be beautiful, just gorgeous. My best work."

"Jacques, what's with the barn raising?" Robert asked.

"It is a Greek tetra-style portico, for the taking of the vows," Margaret said from behind him.

Robert turned to glare at her. "Of course it is. And why are they putting up all those poles?"

"For the tents," Jacques said.

"For the reception luncheon," Margaret said.

"We need only one tent, Jacques," Robert said. "This isn't Cirque du Soleil."

"We're only having fifty guests," Karen said.

"I added a few friends," Margaret said.

"Do you have any of those?" Edward said.

"Let's go inside," Robert said, taking Karen's hand.

They found Mrs. Hendricks, the proprietress of the bed and breakfast—a short, heavyset woman with a stern face—standing on the porch with her arms folded.

"All that's going to cost extra," she said to Robert and Karen as they came up the steps.

"Send her the bill," Robert said, pointing to Margaret.

As Elizabeth came up the walk, she found Ian pacing on the lawn, smoking.

They stood there for a moment, the weight of everything unspoken hanging between them. Then Liz turned away and walked inside.

Chapter 94

Jacques flitted through the sitting room. "Since we're not ready outside, we can just have the rehearsal in here. It will work just as well."

Margaret and Edward relaxed in two overstuffed chairs.

Elizabeth and Ian stood on opposite sides of the room. She glanced over to find him staring out the window, lost in thought.

She turned away, pretending to study the porcelain knick-knacks on the display shelf. *Fine, he's ignoring me. I can deal with this.* She fidgeted, wanting to run out the door.

"That's fine with us," Robert said, giving Ian and Elizabeth a worried glance. "Let's get this going. Where's Reverend Fuller?"

At that moment, Mrs. Hendricks came out of the kitchen and crooked her finger at Karen and Robert.

Robert and Karen followed her through the kitchen door and stopped in their tracks.

They looked at each other and then at Reverend Fuller, who sat slumped at the table.

Oh God, please don't let him be loaded, Karen thought, rushing over and hovering over his crumpled figure. He lifted his head, revealing red eyes and wet cheeks.

"She left me," he cried. "My Joy is gone."

"There's a lot of that going around," Robert muttered.

"Out of the blue," Reverend Fuller whimpered. "Twenty wonderful years. And she flies the coop."

"Well . . ." Robert began.

Karen began to pat Reverend Fuller's shoulder. "I'm sure this is only temporary," she soothed.

"Do you think so?" he said, his voice hopeful. "Maybe she just needs some alone time."

"Right," Robert said carefully. "Look, we are both so sorry about this, but just think, marrying us is a sign of faith and affirmation and it will be an encouragement to you."

Reverend Fuller gave him a wide-eyed look. "You're not really going through with this, are you?"

Karen gave Robert a pleading look.

"We'll give you an extra three hundred," Robert said.

"Cash?"

Robert nodded.

Reverend Fuller sniffled. "It's your funeral."

Liz gave Karen a questioning look as she came back into the sitting room with Robert and a sniveling Reverend Fuller in tow.

"Don't ask," Karen whispered.

"All right, let's get this over with," Fuller bellowed, red eyes blazing in his pale face.

"Good Lord, man, what is wrong with you?" Margaret demanded as everyone stared.

"Nothing, nothing is wrong with him," Robert said.

"My wife usually counsels the bride before the wedding," Fuller said to Karen. "But since she's bailed . . . flown the coop . . . hit the road—"

"I'll wing it," Karen snapped. She turned narrowed eyes on her parents.

"What, darling?" Margaret said. "We think it's terrible. We had nothing to do with it."

"Ironic, isn't it?" Elizabeth whispered to Karen.

Jacques began directing everyone to their places, but Reverend Fuller held up his hand.

"Put it in park, cupid, I got this," he said. "Bride and groom in front of me." He looked at Ian. "Dumpee, next to the groom." He turned to Elizabeth. "Dumper, next to the bride."

Ian and Elizabeth stood across from each other, eyes averted. After a few minutes she couldn't bear it and she looked over at him. His face looked tired and strained.

As if sensing her scrutiny, he looked up; she averted her eyes.

"Why didn't you just elope?" Fuller was saying to Karen.

Karen turned to glare at Margaret and Edward.

"Darling, we haven't paid him a cent," Margaret said.

Edward nodded. "We are not interfering."

"Since when?" Karen asked.

"Are we almost bloody done?" Ian asked.

Robert grasped his shoulder. "Soon. Reverend, let's get on with this, okay?"

"We're missing people," Reverend Fuller said, looking around. "Where are your parents?"

"They're not combat ready," Robert said, looking over at Margaret and Edward. "They'll be here tomorrow."

"And where's the matron of honor—out filming other sinners with the porn cam?"

"Emily will be late," Karen said. "She might make the dinner."

"Maybe my wife was having an affair," Fuller said under his breath.

"There's a lot of that going around," Robert said.

"Okay, let's get moving. The bride's parents—the strangler and the victim—stand off to the left."

"Not too close!" Karen warned.

Margaret laughed. "Oh darling, don't be silly."

Karen's mouth dropped open.

The Reverend Fuller cleared his throat, as if ready to begin, and then his face crumpled and he fell back into a chair. "I miss her. I miss my pumpkin," he moaned.

The group stared at him in stunned silence.

Ian threw up his hands. "Son of a bitch," he muttered.

"You could show a little sympathy," Elizabeth said.

"He'll live."

"Like you did? You seem just fine now."

"Aren't you?"

"You're damn right I am."

"Guys, please," Robert pleaded. "This isn't helping."

Ian and Elizabeth lapsed into a strained silence.

Jacques began to pace. "Okay, okay, the reverend is down, no problem. Let's move on and stay positive. You know the drill. You say I do, you light the candles—"

"No!" Karen protested. "We said no flame."

"Right, right, okay," Jacques said. "Let's forget the rehearsal for now and have a nice dinner."

Jacques took Karen by the hand and gave her a hug. "Karen, my love—"

"It's a disaster, isn't it?" she asked.

"Don't worry, honey, your mother's picking up the tab. Try to make the best of it."

Chapter 95

They entered the dining room. The table was elegantly arranged with a white linen cloth and candles dotting the length of the table. Mrs. Hendricks moved about, pouring wine, bringing the salads, her eyes dark with disapproval.

Suddenly, Emily appeared in the doorway and rushed in, breathless, a cell phone glued to her ear. She waved at everyone and then plunked down in the chair next to Karen. "Love the columns outside," she whispered to Karen. "Whose idea was that?"

"Not ours," Karen said.

As Ian walked to the end of the table, Margaret and Edward exchanged a glance, then quickly slid into the end seats, leaving only one chair open, directly across from Elizabeth. He paused, giving them a filthy look, then took his seat.

The main course was served and they ate in silence.

Karen watched Margaret and Edward talking softly to each other, heads together. "What are you two discussing down there?"

Margaret smiled. "Nothing of importance, darling, nothing at all."

Reverend Fuller took out a handkerchief and blew his nose, honking loudly.

"So Ian," Margaret said. "When are you leaving?"

"I'm not." He continued to chew, staring at his plate.

"Oh, I must have been mistaken," Margaret said.

He looked up and found Elizabeth watching him.

"I thought you said you were leaving," she said.

"No, I told you to forget all about that, but you weren't listening," he grumbled.

"I read between the lines," she said.

"And Miss Elizabeth," Margaret asked, "where is Nicholas?"

Ian leaned back, arms folded, waiting for Elizabeth's answer.

"He's not here."

"Yes, dear, that's obvious. When is he coming?"

"Are you taking a census?" Robert asked.

"He's not," Elizabeth said quietly.

Ian looked at her and she thought she saw a hint of a smile. She cast a cold eye on him and looked away.

"No, I want Anton to handle the décor in the dining room," Emily chattered into her phone, "and Trevor will handle the décor in the main foyer, is that understood?"

"We're having dinner," Robert said.

Emily pulled the phone from her ear. "And it has all the ambiance of a viewing at a funeral home. The rehearsal dinner isn't supposed to be like this—you know that, right?"

Karen gave a heavy sigh.

"Can I stay here tonight?" Reverend Fuller begged, grasping Mrs. Hendricks's hand as she passed by with a basket of rolls. "I can't go back to that empty motel room."

She looked at Robert. "This is gonna cost extra," she said.

The door flew open and all heads turned. Parker burst in, wild-eyed, with two days' growth of beard, his clothes disheveled and hanging loosely on his frame.

"Who the hell is he?" Fuller asked.

"The adulterer," everyone answered.

"Emily!" Parker roared. "We have issues to discuss!"

Emily pulled the phone away from her ear. "Take your issues and shove them up your ass," she said, returning to her call.

Edward chuckled. "Well, I guess dinner is a wrap."

"Well then," Margaret said. "Shall we all go to bed?"

Chapter 96

After a post-dinner discussion with a perturbed Mrs. Hendricks about the extra costs he was incurring, Robert climbed the stairs to find everyone lingering in the hallway. "Okay, there are six rooms," he said, looking around, "and this is how it's going to go. Reverend Fuller solo, Karen and myself, Margaret, Edward—separate rooms—"

"I don't trust them," Karen whispered. "They're quiet—they're too quiet. We should each stay with one of them."

"Yeah, that's not gonna happen. Ian and Parker—"

"No, no way, mate," Ian began.

Robert silenced him by holding up a hand.

"Elizabeth and Emily," Robert finished.

"Robert, it's not happening," Ian said.

"Alone again, always alone," Reverend Fuller moaned. "Pumpkin, pumpkin, where are you?"

Robert gestured toward Fuller. "You have a choice."

Ian shuddered. "I'll take Parker."

Sitting on the edge of the bed, Ian cursed under his breath as Parker paced the room, tugging at his clothes, swigging freely from a bottle of scotch.

"I loved her, man, you know, loved her." He stopped, opened the door, shouting into the hallway. "I loved you, bitch! You destroyed me!"

"Shut the bloody door," Ian said. "If you continue to shout for Stella, you're staying with the vicar, understand?"

, Parker collapsed next to Ian. "She was everything to me. She completed me, you know? And then she kicks me in the balls."

Getting up, he unbuttoned his pants, letting them hang around his hips. He pointed to his shorts. "Right in the balls," he slurred. "And does she care? Hell, no. She's got a brand-new business, and I'm broke, bound for fucking Hoboken, the armpit of New Jersey."

"I'm sure there's a song in there somewhere," Ian said.

As Parker resumed his pacing, his pants fell to his ankles. "Right in the balls," he snarled, letting out a string of obscenities as his feet tangled in his pants. Reeling unsteadily, he hit the floor with a thud.

"Stupid git," Ian muttered, reaching for a cigarette.

"She's in her room," Parker continued from the floor, still struggling to get out of his pants. "Negotiating. Doing business because of me. Because of me!" he finished, finally kicking them off. He hopped up and was out the door and into the hallway before Ian could stop him.

"Robert," Ian shouted, close on his heels.

Emily had taken over the entire room, her suitcases open and papers strewn across the bed. She talked a mile a minute, stopping intermittently to mouth something to Elizabeth such as "sorry" as she commandeered all but one dresser drawer, or "do you mind?" as she filled the sink top with a mound of cosmetics.

Elizabeth stood in the middle of the room, feeling the heat rising in her face. The sudden thudding on the door sent her over the edge.

"She's on the phone!" she shouted.

Heavy footsteps followed, then scuffling, thumping noises, and muffled cursing.

Emily strutted to the door, swinging it open to find a wild-eyed Parker being restrained by Robert and Ian. "Do you mind?" she said sweetly, swinging it closed again.

Parker managed to shove his foot in the door before it shut, kicking it open as Ian and Robert struggled to pull him away.

"You're a success because of me, bitch! If I hadn't paid for all of your failures, you'd never be where you are today," he shouted, twisting and turning to break free.

"Hold on, Peta," Emily said into the phone in a calm, even tone and turning to Parker. "Up yours."

Ian and Robert managed to drag Parker away as Karen and Elizabeth stood in the hallway, frowning at the scene.

"She owes me," Parker grumbled.

"Give it up, mate," Ian said.

"I should sue her for damages—I should sue you!" Parker yelled.

"Actually, I'm suing you," Emily said, "for adultery."

Parker opened his mouth.

"Let it go," Robert said. "No man wins an argument standing in his underwear."

"What the hell is going on up here?" The group turned to see Mrs. Hendricks, her hair in jumbo rollers, swathed in a long, green robe covered with giant sunflowers.

"Un—believable," Ian murmured. "Van Gogh is spinning in his grave."

Throwing him a warning look, Robert approached the great blooming bundle. "Nothing, nothing at all, Mrs. Hendricks. Everything is fine. We're all going to sleep now." He turned, giving everyone a pointed stare. "Aren't we?"

"Yes," came the chorus.

He ushered her back toward the staircase.

"Any more noise and I'll be back with my taser, understand? This is it," she mumbled to herself. "No more weddings."

Robert waited until she waddled back down the stairs, then stepped into the middle of the group. "Okay, one more time," he said through clenched teeth. "Karen and I are getting married tomorrow, no matter how many people have to be restrained, restricted, or medicated. So everyone—get the hell back into your rooms and get ready for the happiest day of our lives."

Looking properly chastised, everyone stood in respectful silence. Muted whimpering filtered out through Reverend Fuller's door.

"Bloody hell," Ian muttered.

"Emily, you are still my wife and we have issues to discuss," Parker said.

"I'll call you back, Peta," Emily said, snapping the phone shut. "You want to have this out?" she said to Parker. "I'm right here." She walked into her room.

Parker stumbled after her, slamming the door shut.

Ian, Elizabeth, Robert, and Karen stood staring at the door. It opened and Emily set Elizabeth's suitcase down in the hall, mouthing the word "sorry" and shut the door.

They all stood around for a moment, the only sound the occasional whimper from Reverend Fuller's room. Ian picked up Elizabeth's suitcase. He stepped aside to allow her to enter his room. He followed and closed the door.

Karen and Robert moved around their room, unpacking. She went to the door and peeked out at the closed doors on either side and then shut the door.

She unpacked a few more things and then went to the door again, this time creeping farther into the hallway to listen. When she returned, Robert was standing there watching her.

"Something's going on with them," Karen said.

"Do we care?"

"My parents are not civilized. They're feral and uncontrollable."

Karen started for the door again but Robert caught her gently by the wrist, pulling her close.

"I would love to spend the night before our wedding obsessing over Crouching Margaret, Hidden Edward, but I have other things planned for us."

Karen laughed, relaxing against him. "Such as?"

Robert trailed a string of kisses down her forehead, her nose, until he reached her lips. "A nice, quiet, private walk on the grounds, just us, the man in the moon, and our lucky star," he said against her mouth.

"Oh."

"And then I plan to take advantage of you."

"That's okay," Karen said softly. "You're about to make an honest woman of me."

Robert gave a low chuckle.

Parker stalked Emily around the room.

"You'd be nothing without me. I inspired you to greatness. I taught you everything I know! I made you who you are!"

"What I was, was a person buying into your crap. But as you see, I don't need your crap."

"You can't make it without me."

"I already have."

Parker ran his eyes over her and licked his lips. "My God, you are so hot."

She smirked. "Don't I know it."

"I love you, babe. I always have. Deirdre meant nothing to me. We belong together. We're a team."

She looked at him through narrowed eyes. "All right," she said. "I'll give you one chance. Let's see what you've got; and if you're any good, I'll have my father help you open a new fund."

"You asked for it, babe," Parker said, tossing her on the bed.

Emily giggled.

Ian and Elizabeth tiptoed around each other as if the floors were hot coals, their heads down, eyes averted, careful to keep a safe distance between them.

When there was nothing left to brush, wash, or scrub, they each took to their side of the bed, careful to stay near the edge.

Ian turned away from her, then turned back to lie face up, then turned on his side again.

"Is there a problem?" Elizabeth asked.

"This isn't my side."

Elizabeth sighed, throwing off the covers. They both got up and stalked around, switching sides.

They lay there, the only light the soft glow of the moon filtering through the curtains.

"When did you break up with Nick?"

Elizabeth turned away, tugging at the covers. "It doesn't matter. It doesn't change anything."

He sat up and switched on the lamp. "Why the hell not?"

"Me not being with Nick doesn't mean I'm going to be with you. I don't want to play any more of your games, or anyone's games."

"I wasn't playing games," he said, throwing off the covers and bolting out of bed. "I was the one standing there when you walked out!"

"Only because I knew you were getting ready to make a run for it," she said, getting out of bed to stand toe-to-toe with him.

"Lizzie, you—"

Sounds of moaning drifted through the door followed by Parker's gasping, "Oh baby, oh yeah!"

Ian threw up his hands. "Unfuckingbelievable."

Edward walked noiselessly into Margaret's room and came up behind her, watching her in the mirror as she smoothed cream onto her neck, slowly massaging it into her skin.

"It's been almost a month," he said.

"Has it?" she asked, glancing into the mirror and catching Edward's slow smile. "Where's Penny?"

"Are you going to drop the lawsuits?" he murmured.

"Are you going to stop taking partners?"

"Are you?" he said.

"We'll see," she said.

He ran his hands over her shoulders, brushed back her robe, and bent his head low, kissing her shoulders, her collarbone, her neck.

* * *

Ian and Elizabeth stood on either side of the bed, looking at each other.

"I was talking to your ex-wife. You lied to me about who she was," she said. "How will I ever know if you're telling the truth!"

Ian began pulling on his clothing. "You want the truth? Okay, here's the truth: I know about Josh, about William, and I know about your mother, and it doesn't change how I feel about you. You're no different in my eyes, Lizzie."

She closed her eyes and caught her breath. "You always make it sound so simple, like everything is okay."

He came around to her side of the bed. "Because it is okay, Lizzie. I'm not him. Did you think I wouldn't understand what you went through—giving up your work to take care of your mother?"

"I didn't give up my work . . . I finished it. And then I finished her work, and she destroyed it all. All of it . . . everything I created . . ."

He searched for something to say. "Jesus Christ, I didn't know," he said finally. "I never would've said those things to you in the gallery, about you being jealous, if I knew. I'm sorry."

They were silent.

"How many pieces were there?"

"Twenty, maybe thirty. She left me to find them, with her . . . after she . . ." A tear slid down her face. She didn't bother hiding it.

"You should've told me everything."

"And what would you have done?"

"I would've helped you. I was trying to help you."

Elizabeth shrugged. "I don't need any more artists helping me."

"Damn it, Lizzie, you're doing it again. I'm not him."

"He left. You were going to—"

Ian threw up his hands and began to pace. "I never wanted to go."

"Don't lie. You were looking for a way to get out."

"I never wanted out, Lizzie!" he exploded, bringing his fist down on the dresser. The lamp teetered, then righted itself.

They stood in the weighted silence that told them the whole house was awake, listening to them.

Ian ran his hands through his hair. "I know how it feels when someone leaves. I thought—I was afraid you wanted to go." He let out a long breath. "Lizzie, what do you want from me?"

"Everything!" Elizabeth said. "I want all of you, not just the broken pieces she left behind. I want all of your heart . . . and I want you to trust me not to break it. I want to know I can count on you . . . that I have a husband I can trust."

"And you think getting married, being married, will give that to you? You think marriage is a guarantee? There is no guarantee. Marriage doesn't matter, Lizzie. Trust me. It doesn't."

"I need it. I need you to be in all the way. It matters to me."

Ian took a breath. "I can't fail again, Lizzie. Do you understand? Not this time. Not with you. Let's just go back to the city together, leave it the way it was. It was all right. It'll be all right."

She looked at him for a long moment. "No."

Ian pressed his lips tight and held his tongue, then he left the room.

Elizabeth sank onto the bed and began to cry.

Karen and Robert wandered the grounds, their arms wrapped around each other, sharing kisses and caresses as they walked.

They stopped under a large pine tree to share a deep kiss.

"You know," Karen said when they parted. "You should be warned. Statistically, ninety-eight percent of women become their mothers."

"You made that up."

Karen ran her fingers over his cheeks, his lips. "This is your last chance. Are you really sure?"

Robert smiled. "I'm sure. Trust me, something will happen one day, and you'll see the light about your parents. You will."

Robert was about to steal another kiss when a low groaning interrupted them.

"What was that?" Karen asked, looking around.

"Maybe Jacques installed a petting zoo to amuse the guests. Don't worry about it," Robert said, pulling her close.

Another moan, deeper and louder, sounded in the distance.

"That's human," Karen said and broke away from him. "It's coming from the backyard."

She followed the sounds to the bride and groom's tent. She hesitated only a moment before throwing the flap aside. She gasped.

Racing up behind her and nearly knocking her over, Robert peered over her shoulder. "*Holy shit.*"

On top of the bride and groom's table, Margaret sat mounted on Edward, riding him like a horse.

Karen made a gurgling noise. Whirling blindly, she ran back to the inn.

Robert turned to follow as Mrs. Hendricks, resembling a mobile flower cart in her robe, rollers bobbing, rushed up and peered in the tent, waving her taser. "What the hell do you think this is, an al fresco whorehouse?"

"Do you know those things are illegal in New York State?" Robert said, turning around and trotting toward the inn.

Ian was sitting on the front steps smoking, when Karen raced past him and into the house.

Seconds later, Ian stood up as Robert hustled up the walk. "What the—?"

"You don't want to know," Robert said, rushing inside.

Ian sat back down.

A minute later, Margaret came trotting up the walkway, re-arranging her clothes. "Karen, darling, let me explain . . ."

At the sight of Ian, she stopped.

He stood up and held the door open. "Mrs. Robinson," he said.

She sniffed, and lifting her chin, threw her scarf around her neck and sauntered inside.

Ian let the door close and sat back down.

A moment later, Edward followed, hobbling around the side of the building, holding up his pants with one hand, and carrying his shirt, shoes and jacket with the other. "Margaret . . . I'm coming, wait for me."

Ian stared after him, shaking his head.

Back in Karen and Robert's room, Margaret and Edward both babbled at Karen simultaneously.

"Darling, let me explain," Margaret said. "It certainly was *not* what it looked like."

"I'm sure it was," Robert said, closing the door.

Karen raised her hand. Suddenly, the Zen that she had sought so desperately in the months leading up to the wedding filled her mind. "Am I to understand that throughout your marriage, your divorce, and father's subsequent marriages and divorces, you have continued to know each other . . . in the biblical sense?"

"We didn't want to confuse you."

"And can I assume the reason father's divorce agreements have a nondisclosure clause is that the biblical relationship is the reason for said divorces?"

"Remember what I told you, Karen," Edward said. "Love is a complicated emotion."

"Of course. The ceremony begins at noon tomorrow. Father, please be ready at ten minutes to. I expect you both to be mute during the ceremony and for our entire married life. Thank you. Have a restful evening, wherever that may be."

Karen went to the bedroom door, opened it, and stared expectantly at her parents.

Margaret and Edward exchanged looks and left the room without another word.

After they left, Karen sank onto the bed. Robert sat down next to her.

"Desire is the root of all suffering," she said.

"Not always," Robert said, brushing a strand of hair away from her face.

"The Buddhist master was right, you know. My 'me' was in the way. All this time, I thought this was about me, about this wedding. It was never about me. It was always about them and their desire for each other."

"Sometimes that happens."

Karen turned to him. "We're not them."

"No, baby, we're not," he said.

Karen leaned in, giving him a lingering kiss. "I love you," she said.

"I love you too, babe."

Ian sat on the porch steps for a long time. When he went back into the house, it was quiet; the dawn still hadn't broken. He lay down on the sofa in the den and closed his eyes. Before the day was over, there was one final thing he knew he had to do.

Chapter 97

In the morning, the bed and breakfast was filled with hustle and bustle. Jacques raced around in command mode, ordering his minions with authority and efficiency. The members of the wedding party were smiling politely, talking congenially, pretending the previous night was a dream they'd forgotten upon waking.

Liz sat and watched the organized chaos from the breakfast room, oversized sunglasses hiding her puffy eyes. Emily and Parker cooed and doted on each other. Margaret and Edward sat drinking their coffee in the companionable silence that only comes after spending many years together.

What a night, she thought, remembering, in glaring Technicolor, everything that had gone on. Whatever she'd had with Ian was now officially over. She willed herself not to look up as he walked in, but couldn't help it. She watched him pour a coffee and walk out. She waited for him to steal a glance before leaving; he didn't. She pushed down a sudden urge to cry and forced a smile as Karen came in.

It was almost noon. Ian and Robert waited in the kitchen until it was time to go out and take their places, both lost in their own thoughts. Ian showed Robert the ring.

"No worries, I have it," he said.

Robert nodded.

"Are you nervous?"

Robert shook his head. "What do I have to be nervous about?"

Ian smiled. "Nothing. She's a lovely girl, your Karen." He offered his hand but Robert pulled him into a brother's embrace.

Elizabeth stood across from Ian, desperately trying to concentrate on the Reverend Fuller, who had somehow managed to pull himself together for the ceremony.

Before he began, he leaned toward Robert and Karen. "Are you sure?" he whispered.

"We are," Robert said.

Reverend Fuller began. "Dearly beloved . . ." and continued until "If there is anyone who can show just cause why they may not lawfully be joined together, let him speak now, or forever hold his peace."

Everyone turned to stare at Margaret and Edward.

They smiled, blew Karen a kiss and then folded their hands in their laps. A relieved sigh went up from the guests.

Karen and Robert turned to each other. Ian gave Robert the ring, and a pat on the back.

Elizabeth wiped away tears as Reverend Fuller declared Robert and Karen husband and wife, wishing it were possible with Ian. But it wasn't. It was impossible.

Balloons were released. The guests applauded.

The tents easily held the two hundred guests. Everyone was there; from the upper-crust salons of Park Avenue to The Americans from the Village. Robert's parents, beaming with joy, took turns crushing Robert and Karen in embraces and kisses. They released the newlyweds when the orchestra began to play and the maestro called all couples to the floor.

Robert pulled Karen in to dance cheek to cheek. "Beautiful dress," he said, fingering the delicate lace. "Beautiful girl." He kissed her cheek.

"You were right," Karen said, gazing into his eyes. "It's a beautiful wedding."

Parker and Emily were twirling on the floor when he stopped short. "What do you mean, we're not getting back together? What about how good we are together? What about our partnership? What about the new hedge fund? What about last night?"

"Do you remember what you said about screwing Deirdre? That it didn't mean anything to you?" Emily purred.

"Yeah—so?"

"Well, that's how I feel."

With that she swished off the floor, Parker trailing after her. "Aw, Emily, c'mon."

Ian sat alone at a table, a drink in front of him, his eyes on Elizabeth. She had never been out of his sight throughout the reception, though they'd both managed to keep their distance. He watched her moving across the floor, lithe and graceful in cool blue satin, her hair flowing like silk over her bare shoulders. A surge of desire rolled over him. He remembered how she looked the first time he saw her—her slip of a dress clinging to her, her hair in a twist. In that instant, he had known: she was the one.

Elizabeth interrupted Robert and Karen on the floor, taking Karen off to the side.

"Stay a little longer, please," Karen said.

"I can't," Elizabeth said, her voice tight. "I have to go." She crushed Karen to her. "When you get back from the Caymans, bacon, eggs, and coffee at the café around the corner from my apartment."

"Deal," Karen said, her eyes misting. "Liz, I really am so sorry."

Elizabeth, feeling her throat close, just nodded and walked off the dance floor and out of the tent.

Suddenly, a warm hand gripped her arm. She turned to find Ian, his expression solemn. "I can't give you a guarantee," he said.

The music, the conversation, all faded to a vague white noise around her. There was only Ian. He wrapped his arms around her, holding her close. She didn't struggle against his embrace.

"But I can give you a vow."

Her breath caught in her throat.

"I, Ian, do promise you, Elizabeth, to always give you my food and the covers, and to paint in the kitchen, and to love you more each day, for as long as we both shall live."

She didn't answer and she saw a flutter of apprehension behind his eyes.

"If you'll have me, all of me, I won't hold anything back, I promise. Marry me, Lizzie?"

Then she saw it, what she'd been waiting for: his eyes wide with fear and wonder, defenseless.

She touched his cheek and he caught her hand, pressing it against his mouth.

"Lizzie?" he said, his voice wavering.

"I will," she said. "I will have you."

Then she heard the sound of her own laughter as she wrapped her arms around his neck. Crushing her to him, he held her fast.

"To have and to hold, dear Lizzie, from this day forward," he whispered.